William J. Linton

Lyrics of the XIVth Century

William J. Linton

Lyrics of the XIVth Century

ISBN/EAN: 9783744783200

Printed in Europe, USA, Canada, Australia, Japan

Cover: Foto ©Andreas Hilbeck / pixelio.de

More available books at **www.hansebooks.com**

English Verse

EDITED BY

W. J. LINTON AND R. H. STODDARD

LYRICS

OF THE

XIXTH CENTURY

NEW YORK

CHARLES SCRIBNER'S SONS

1883

INTRODUCTION.

The history of English Verse in the nineteenth century implies more than appears in the Verse itself, for granting that it is understood by contemporary students—a supposition which is contradicted by literary history in general—its origins are still to be sought and discovered. Bibliography enables us to trace its progress from year to year, and, if it be carefully studied, enables us to trace its intellectual direction likewise. Biography is also of service, conducting us through its special province like a guide who is familiar with the ground that he traverses ; and history is of the greatest service, provided it be largely written and intelligently read, for so written and read, it authenticates and justifies all that it embraces—the violence of passion as well as the repose of power, Thersites and Ajax as well as Achilles and Nestor. If we place ourselves in thought on the threshold of the nineteenth century, and look back with critical eyes upon the poetical literature of the eighteenth century—or upon the small portion of it which continued to be read at its close—the prospect is not an enlivening one. To say that it was in any large sense a poetical period would not be true. It was not a creative period like the age of Elizabeth, for though its most famous hands cultivated the art of writing tragedies, and produced their Catos, Jane Shores, Distrest Mothers, Mariamnes, Sophonisbas, Irenes, and what not besides, they added nothing to the English Drama. The creative energy of the eighteenth century exhausted itself in The Rape of the Lock and The Dunciad. Pope carried the satire of manners and of character as far as it could go: he was a wit, but not a poet. Thomson tried to open the eyes of his contemporaries to Nature, and succeeded in a measure, though not nearly so well as Collins in his unrhymed Ode to Evening, or Gray in the opening stanzas of his immortal Elegy. The Elegy is more read to-day than any poem of its time, partly because it is the most perfect specimen of its poetic art, and partly because the train of thought which runs through it can never be dismissed from the human mind. It will live as long as men live and die. It was surpassed, perhaps, by certain poetic qualities in the Odes of Collins, which fell dead from the press about four years before it was published, but it was not surpassed or equalled by anything else. Looking back upon it now we can see what Gray's contemporaries could not see—that it was a great landmark in the monotonous waste of their verse. The dead level of prose to which Pope had reduced all metrical writing surrounded it like a desert. While he lived the springs of his genius watered the roots of stately palms, but when he died only stunted reeds remained to show where the watercourses had been. Ethics had dwindled into didacticism, and the heroic measure into jingling couplets which school-boys wrote for pastime.   If we had lived in the first half of the eighteenth century, and had shared the poetic taste of our contemporaries, what would we have had to read? We would have had to read The Splendid Shilling and the Cyder of Philips, the Pastorals of Pope and his Essay on Criticism, Gay's Rural Sports and Shepherd's Week, Glover's Leonidas, and Shenstone's Pastoral Ballad. A little later we would have had to read Young's Night Thoughts, Armstrong's Art of Preserving Health, Akenside's Pleasures of Imagination, Dyer's Fleece, and Grainger's Sugar Cane. If the saccharine production of good Dr. Grainger had not been to our liking, and it is possible that we might have found its sweetness a little cloying, we could have taken the prescription of another physician—an uncouth, pock-marked Irishman, who had studied at Edinburgh and Leyden, and, after travelling about the Continent on foot, occasionally playing upon the flute for his victuals when his funds ran low, had settled down in London as a bookseller's hack.

We could have read Dr. Goldsmith's Traveller, or a Prospect of Society, and if we had done so we could not but have felt the spell of his frank and manly genius. We might have been prompted to make his acquaintance, if we had chanced to be in London at the time, and perhaps the acquaintance of his bullying friend and patron, the great Dr. Johnson, who, if he had taken a fancy to us, after a good dinner at the Mitre Tavern, might have asked us to visit him at his lodgings in Bolt Court, where we would have seen his strange menagerie of pensioners—Robert Levett, practitioner of physic, poor, stuttering Miss Jane Williams, the blind poetess, Miss Carmichael, Mrs. Dumoulin, the widow of a writing-master, the negro, Francis Barber, and that pert young coxcomb (cowed there), Mr. James Boswell, advocate, of Auchinleck, Scotland. Goldsmith would no doubt have told us of Johnson's kindness to him, particularly in selling the manuscript of his Vicar of Wakefield, and releasing him from the clutches of his landlady, who insisted upon his marrying her or settling his score, and have asked us to subscribe to Johnson's Shakespeare, which we would have done gladly, having already upon our shelves the editions of Rowe, Pope, Theobald, Hanmer, and Warburton, to say nothing of the Folios, which we had inherited with the old manor-house in Surrey. Six years later we would have had another poem from the pen of the ingenious Dr. Goldsmith, The Deserted Village, and the public journals would have informed us of the death of Dr. Akenside. They might also have informed us of the death of one Thomas Chatterton, a Bristol boy of eighteen, who was supposed to have poisoned himself; but the paragraph, if we had seen it, would have had no significance to us, for little was talked about then in the coffee-houses except the letters of Junius in the Public Advertiser. The dearth of good contemporary poetry in the seventh decade of the eighteenth century drove us back to the earlier poets, of whom we could not well help knowing something by that time, since the Reverend Dr. Thomas Percy, a Northumberland vicar, whom we remember to have met one day in the chambers of Dr. Goldsmith (the very day, by the way, in which the little daughter of a fellow-lodger borrowed the coals in her eccentric scuttle), had published in the year after The Traveller three solid volumes of Reliques of Ancient English Poetry, the materials for which he obtained from an old manuscript collection, and which, of course, he polished and modernized lest they should offend the polite taste of his contemporaries. We differed with Johnson in our estimate of this work, for he ridiculed it as a useless resurrection of obsolete rubbish, while we thought it a rude but interesting monument of poetic antiquity. There were many things which Johnson could not comprehend—which the coarseness of his mind would not allow him to apprehend—and one of these things was poetry. If the tenor of his writings had not indicated this fact, if it was not apparent in his edition of Shakespeare, it would have been forced upon us—it would have been driven into us—by his Lives of the Poets. They could not have been written in any period that had not forfeited every claim to poetic criticism as well as poetic creation. No poet would have consented to begin a collection of English Poets with Cowley, or would have admitted into a collection of English Poets such dreary versifiers as Roscommon, and Sheffield, and Congreve, and Sprat, and Walsh, and no critic could have stultified himself as Johnson did when he penned his animadversions upon the sonnets of Milton. Criticism and poetry were fallen on evil days and evil tongues in the last quarter of the eighteenth century. Poetry indeed—at any rate poetry of a high order— was no longer written. Nor was there any reason why it ever should be again. There was nothing that appealed to it—nothing heroic that demanded it—no movement in the life of the time that did not find the fullest expression in prose—no seed of light in the darkness, no prophecy and promise of Morning, however remote, that might smite the silent lips of Memnon into Song.

But the darkest hour is just before day. It is so in nature, we are told, and it is sometimes so in art and letters. It was certainly so in poetry, for while Johnson was writing the last of his Lives of the Poets a new poet was writing the first of his grave and thoughtful strains. The son of a chaplain of George the Second, a Westminster scholar, and a solicitor of the Middle Temple, he had been crossed in love, had attempted his own life, and had been placed in the mad-house of a brother poet. Released from durance before he was quite sane (if he ever was quite sane), he retired to lodgings in the country, and became the inmate of a clergyman's family, first at Huntingdon, and afterward at Olney, where he had the misfortune to fall into the spiritual hands of a curate who had once been master of a slave-vessel, and who pressed him into religion and the writing of lugubrious hymns. Another attack of lunacy led to another attempt upon his life. He recovered, however, and, watched over by the clergyman's widow, was induced to divert his mind with gardening and the gambols of tame hares. To these rational amusements he was at last persuaded to add the composition of verse, and having up to this time learned nothing that was of value to himself, he naturally proceeded to instruct mankind. Such was William Cowper, when, at the age of forty-eight, he began to sing of Truth and the Progress of Error, of Hope and Charity, of Conversation and Retirement. His themes and his method of handling them were not poetical, but they were not averse from the good sense with which he illustrated them, and which made readers for him among the serious classes of his countrymen. His didacticism was accepted for all it was worth. The writing of these poems confirmed Cowper in the literary habit, and revealed to him the natural direction of his talents. He cast them in the heroic couplet, which still maintained its ascendency in English Verse, though its most polished master had been dead nearly forty years, but with a force and freedom that would have startled the delicate sensibilities of Pope. He wrote all like a man, as Ben Jonson said of his poetic son Cartwright, but not like the man he was to prove himself in his next work. The Task, which was published in the year after the death of Dr. Johnson, placed him at once at the head of living English poets. A greater than he was singing, but his first volume was not published until a year later than The Task, when it stole into English Verse at Kilmarnock. The long and dreary reign of Pope and his followers, the reign of prose in the singing robes of poetry, was over when Cowper and Burns began to celebrate what they felt and what they saw—one pursuing a suggestion of Lady Austin, which led him from a sofa into the sober world of English thought and the charming world of English rural scenery, the other pursuing the inspiration of his own genius, which, while he followed the plough along the mountain side, led him into the canny world of Scottish wisdom and the stormy world of Scottish passion and indulgence. Long hidden from the priests who had thronged her sanctuary and offered her their empty lip service, the Muse revealed herself to Cowper and Burns, and the face which smiled upon them as she lifted her veil was the face of the Sovereign Mother. Lesser poetic voices in the last two decades of the eighteenth century were Erasmus Darwin, who mistook a Botanic Garden for Tempe and the vales of Arcady: Charlotte Smith and William Lisle Bowles, who prolonged their personal disappointments in indifferent sonnets: William Hayley, who placated the Triumphs of Temper: Samuel Rogers, who, walking in the steps of Akenside, sang The Pleasures of Memory; Thomas Campbell, who, walking in the steps of Rogers, sang The Pleasures of Hope; and Robert Bloomfield, who, trying to walk in the steps of Cowper and Thomson, sang The Farmer's Boy.

Looking back along the literature of the eighteenth century we see that English Verse was largely cultivated therein, but we do not see that the harvest was ever abundant. Looking upon it as we look upon the nineteenth century, or so much of the nineteenth century as lies behind us, and comparing the one with the other—the sterility of the reigns of Queen Anne and the first two Georges with the fertility of the reigns of the fourth George and Victoria—we are disposed to pity our ancestors and to congratulate ourselves. From whatever point of view we compare ourselves with them we are struck with our own superiority. Waiving our knowledge of the natural sciences, the most advanced branches of which were the merest empiricism in their day, and our proficiency in philology, the nature and extent of which were scarcely suspected then ; and waiving, also, the perfection of our civilization, of which railways and steamships, the electric telegraph and the telephone, are the material manifestations ; waiving, in short, everything except literature, which depends less than any other intellectual pursuit upon the social condition of the people among whom it is cultivated—what relation, we ask, does the literature of the eighteenth century bear to the literature of the nineteenth century? Let us take one department thereof in which both centuries have produced acknowledged masters ; a department which is least liable to change in that it concerns itself with what is least changeable in man—his passions—what did the eighteenth century offer its readers in the shape of prose fiction? Tracing back the succession of English novelists we pass the names of Sophia and Harriet Lee, Matthew Gregory Lewis, Charlotte Smith, Ann Radcliff, Frances Burney, and Henry Mackenzie. When we come to the name of Goldsmith we stop, and yawning over our early recollections of The Man of Feeling, Evelina, and The Mysteries of Udolpho, we take up The Vicar of Wakefield for the twentieth time, and find it as delightful as at the first reading. If we have a strong sense of humor, and are willing to follow it whithersoever it may lead, we can still be amused by Humphrey Clinker and Roderick Random, although they become rather tedious before we finish them. We enjoy portions of Tristram Shandy, but it is with a sort of protest, for we feel that we are being fooled with, and we resent the foolery. We try to read Richardson, but the more we try the less we read ; for granting that all the fine things which have been said of him are true, they count for nothing with us, he is such a tiresome old prig. We forgive him, however, as we forgive Southey for writing his Vision of Judgment, for without that we should not have had Byron's Vision of Judgment, as without Pamela we should not have had Joseph Andrews. Fielding is the only eighteenth century novelist whom it is possible to read with pleasure and profit now—with the pleasure that we always receive from masterly delineations of character, and the profit that we always receive from contemporary delineations of manners. We feel that we can trust him as we trust Shakespeare, for though we may never have met them or their kind before, the moment his personages appear they authenticate themselves. Byron summed up the world's verdict upon Fielding when he called him the Prose Homer of human nature. Thirty years before Fielding wrote Tom Jones, a much-writing Englishman, a Dissenter, who had been a hosier in Cornhill, a traitor with Monmouth, a trader in Spain and Portugal, a financial projector, and a political pamphleteer, and who had stood in the Pillory, as Pope took care to inform his polite readers — this restless, adventurous spirit, weary at last of persecutions and arrests, sat down in retirement, at the age of fifty-eight, with a wife and six children, and penned The Life and Surprising Adventures of Robinson Crusoe, of York, Mariner. Like nothing that had ever been written before, it was read with avidity by the common English people, who had not the least suspicion that they were reading fiction. It was so simple and natural indeed, so circumstantial in its enumeration of details, and so thorough in its narration of incidents that it could not have been invented. There was the same air of verisimilitude in The Life and Piracies of Captain Singleton, Moll Flanders, and the Life and Adventures of Colonel Jack, which followed at intervals of a year each, and in The Memoirs of a Cavalier, Roxana, and The Life of Captain Carleton. The literary art of De Foe was so perfect that it deceived Dr. Johnson, who believed the last of these fictions to be a genuine contribution to history. Such, in brief, was English fiction in the eighteenth century, and, think as kindly of it as we may, we must confess that it was not worthy of the genius of the English people. There was something in the condition of that people during the greater portion of that century, which was not favorable to the exercise and development of their nobler qualities, which obstructed the operations of the mind, checked the excursions of the imagination, and suspended if it did not destroy the creative energy. They proved their patriotism by winning victories for Churchill in the Low Countries, and for Walpole in the House of Commons. They set up an idol they called Loyalty—an insular Janus of Church and State, which high and low alike worshipped. The Church upheld the State, and the State upheld the Church, and between the two the subject went to the wall. Authority demanded submission, and if it were refused enforced it. But it was not often refused, for the Englishman of the eighteenth century knew his place. He was Master, or he was man. If he was statesman, he kept himself in power by obeying the commands of His Majesty : if he was churchman, he kissed benefices out of the hands of His

Majesty's Mistresses : if he was soldier—but perhaps there is no truth in the stories that they tell about Marlborough. It was not a high-minded century, but it was a successful one, for its master-spirits, wiser in their generation than the children of light, contrived to prosper in their double worship of God and Mammon.

That the literature of the nineteenth century should have grown out of the literature of the eighteenth century seems at the first sight impossible, so different are their forms and the spirit by which they are animated. But when we study them attentively we discover their relation to each other, and to the literature of the preceding centuries, for whether we see it or not, the whole Literature of England is distinguished by the same intellectual characteristics,—the qualities and energies which constitute the English Mind, and which run through it like the family likeness in a gallery of ancestral portraits. The chief defect which nineteenth century criticism finds in eighteenth century Verse is that it is prose in a metrical form. The quality which we feel in Chaucer, and Spenser, and Shakespeare, and Milton, among the older poets, and in Burns, and Byron, and Shelley, and Keats, among the poets of our own time, is not in it. Precisely what this quality is criticism has not determined, its manifestations are so multiform, and so colored by the personality of its possessors. It was a certain simplicity and freshness in Chaucer, who had a childlike delight in telling stories ; a sense of spiritual purity and loveliness in Spenser, who was at once the most melodious and most picturesque of poets ; an intuitive comprehension of mankind in Shakespeare, from whom nature had no secrets ; a reverence for austerity of conduct and sublimity of aspiration in Milton ; a hunger and thirst of passion in Burns and Byron ; a blind devotion to impossible ideals in Shelley, and in Keats the perpetual worship of the Beautiful. The faculty of selecting poetical actions,—actions, that is, which are poetical because they are heroic, or pathetic, and the rarer faculty of creating them when they are lacking in human annals,—neither was vouchsafed to the eighteenth century poets. They were not large enough, nor simple enough, to care for man as he came from the hand of nature,—the creature of impulse, or circumstance, a law unto himself : what interested them, so far as they could be interested, were men in their sophisticated condition, the entangling congeries of artificiality which they called the Town. Now and then they were on the eve of writing poetry, and in almost any other period than the prosaic one in which it was their misfortune to live, they would have written poetry, for among their number there were several men of genius. The penniless young Scotchman who went up to London in his twenty-fifth year, and had faith enough in himself, and in what he had observed of nature in his native land, to write a poem about it, in his own way, was a man of genius. And he was recognized as such by his contemporaries, against whose favorite poets and their methods of poetizing his simple, honest work was a protest, in that it dealt with nature, and not with society, with the pomps and shows of the Seasons, and not with powdered beaux and patched and painted belles. Nor was he alone, for another Scotchman who was fifteen years his elder, who had worked in a lead mine in his childhood, and in his manhood at a barber's chair in Edinburgh,—instructed by the Muse, had gathered from the neglected gardens of Henryson, Dunbar, Lyndsay, and other of his country's early poets, a handful of wilding flowers, which were still in sturdy bloom, and which he fitly named The Evergreen. Following the departure which he had thus taken from the highway of popular poetry, he explored the lanes and by-ways of old balladry and song, and plucking in his haste the flowers and weeds that were alike abundant there, he modishly called his armfuls of both a Tea Table Miscellany. A year later he won the laurel which so many English poets had long and assiduously sought,—which Spenser hoped to obtain by his Shepherd's Calendar, and Browne by his Britannia's Pastorals,—which Pope snatched at, but missed, when he wrote his Pastorals, and which Gay also missed, although he did not snatch at it,—good, easy man !—the laurel of pastoral poetry, which he was the first British poet to be crowned with, and worthily crowned, not only by the Muse who inspired him to sing, but by the plain, simple country folk whom he sang, and who certainly knew whether he sang them truly or not. If ever poet reached the people, it was Allan Ramsay in The Gentle Shepherd. Whether Ramsay and Thomson were aware of the radical difference between their poetry and the poetry of the period, and were also aware of its significance as an intellectual movement, may fairly be questioned. That they had a circle of readers, and perhaps a large one, proves that they succeeded in awakening poetical curiosity, but nothing more. If their verse violated the existing canons of taste, it was from no deep-seated design on their part to overthrow those canons, but simply because their natural bent in writing happened to lie outside of them. If it had happened to lie within them, they would have followed it,—at any rate the lettered Thomson would have followed it,—as closely as Pope followed the artificial manner that he inherited from Dryden. Still they were not without influence upon English Verse, for tracing its main stream as it meanders along lazily through the eighteenth century we detect from time to time the pulsation of fresh currents therein. We are conscious of them in Somerville's Chace (1735), Shenstone's Schoolmistress (1742), Thomson's Castle of Indolence (1748), and Gray's Elegy (1751). Whether the contemporary readers of these poems compared them with other poems of the time, and accepted them, or rejected them, as they happened to like or dislike them, we have no positive means of knowing, for with the exception of the Elegy, which at once established itself in popular favor, they excited no critical comment. We find them in a poetic literature to which they are dissimilar, and we conclude that a change has come over this literature which accounts for their dissimilarity, and that they represent this change, whether they originated it or not. One need but glance at the history of English Verse to see that it was not the same in the seventeenth century as in the eighteenth, and that it was not quite the same in the second quarter of the latter as in the first. The decadence of the spirit of false classicism began with Thomson's Winter, and closed with Cowper's Task. What the English poets learned in the intervening half century was to discard the practice of Pope and Boileau, who compounded poetry as apothecaries compounded medicines, after authoritative recipes, and trust to nature. They learned to shut their books, and look into themselves.

There was one book, however, of which they did not think much, but which was read with pleasure and profit by their children, and that was Percy's Reliques. Scott always remembered the spot where he read the volumes for the first time. It was beneath a huge plantanus-tree, in the ruins of what had been intended for an old-fashioned arbor in the garden of his Aunt Janet at Kelso. "The summer day sped onward so fast that, notwithstanding the sharp appetite of thirteen, I forgot the hour of dinner, was sought for with anxiety, and was still found entranced in my intellectual banquet. To read and to remember was in this instance the same thing, and henceforth I overwhelmed my school-fellows, and all who would hearken to me, with tragical recitations from the ballads of Bishop Percy. The first time, too, I could scrape a few shillings together, which were not common occurrences with me, I bought unto myself a copy of these beloved volumes; nor do I believe I ever read a book half so frequently, or with half the enthusiasm." Another English poet, whose family was settled in the reign of Edward the Third at Peniston, near Doncaster, the scene of the combat described in The Dragon of Wantley, and one of whose ancestors was stated in the Notes to have been a cousin of the Dragon (Sir Francis

Wortley), Wordsworth maintained that the Reliques were next in importance in English Verse to Thomson's Seasons, and pointed out in one of his Prefaces that while Dr. Johnson and the little senate to which he gave laws succeeded in making them an object of contempt, Bürger and other able writers of Germany were translating, or imitating them, and composing, with the aid of the inspiration thence derived, ballads which were the delight of the German nation. They were read with avidity by Bürger in his young manhood, as well as by the Göttingen circle of poets with whom he was affiliated, and their influence was manifest in his ballads, notably in Ellenore, which was published only nine years later than the Reliques, and at once became popular. If the old ballads in Percy inspired Bürger to write this ballad, a translation of this ballad, which was read in manuscript by Mrs. Barbauld at a party in Edinburgh, and of which Scott learned through the imperfect recollection of a friend who had heard it, inspired him to obtain the original, and to spend a night in translating it himself, and by awakening his early love of poetry, and with it the ambition to excel therein, made him a poet. He crossed the invisible threshold between the world of Prose and the world of Verse in his twenty-sixth year (1796), bearing in his hands a thin quarto containing his translation of two of Bürger's ballads, Ellenore, which he Englished into Lenore, and The Wild Huntsman. That there was poetic vitality in the prosaic eighteenth century was proved by the Reliques, which were followed in England by twenty-eight similar collections before the century closed, and by the profound impression they made in Germany, where they helped to create a school of balladists. What they were to Scott in his boyhood he has told us. What they were to him in his early manhood, when they were recalled to his memory by the ballads of Bürger, his translations from Bürger show us. What they were to him at a later period we see by turning to his poetical writings, and noting the order in which they were written. After the Bürger ballads he wrote, within the next three years, the ballads of Glenfinlas, The Eve of St. John, The Grey Brothers, and translated The Fire King. Then came the Minstrelsy of the Scottish Border, The Lay of the Last Minstrel, Marmion, The Lady of the Lake, Rokeby, The Lord of the Isles, and, latest of all, Harold the Dauntless. The literary inspiration of these writings was the old ballads collected by Bishop Percy and his successors, and the old metrical romances of which some of these ballads were undoubtedly reminiscences, while others may have been the original germs. We have in Scott the last of the race of English and Scottish balladists, the last of the kings of song and story,—lords paramount of the enchanted world of Romance. He is the Laureate of Chivalry.

Another English poet, of whom we have already spoken, and whom we usually associate with the immortals of the nineteenth century, appeared, like Scott, in the last decade of the eighteenth century, but, unlike Scott, in the livery which the lackeys of Pope had worn threadbare. Wordsworth's first poetical ventures, which were published three years before Scott's translations from Bürger, were An Evening

Walk—an attempt to paint a series of landscape views in his own country, and Descriptive Sketches, an attempt to paint the scenery of the Alps, among which he had lately made a pedestrian tour with a college friend. The most that can be said of these productions is that they are fairly well written, and that there are touches of natural description in them which could only have been the result of actual observation. A copy of the Descriptive Sketches fell into the hands of a young man in Cambridge, who was charmed with them, and who declared years afterward that seldom, if ever, was the emergence of an original poetic genius above the literary horizon more evidently announced than in these same Sketches. This young man was a poet himself, and about this time was writing Songs to the Pixies, verses on Roses, and Kisses, an Address to a Young Ass, and other little pieces. Being in love, or debt, or both, he suddenly left college, and went up to London, where he was soon reduced to want. To alleviate this prosaic misfortune, he enlisted as a private in the 15th Light Dragoons, which were then stationed at Reading, and during his four months' continuance in the awkward squad it is hard to say which was the most to be pitied,—he, or his horse. A chance recognition in the street made his whereabouts known to his family, who procured his release. Two or three months later he went to Oxford, where he made the acquaintance of another poet, whom he met again at Bristol, and by whom he was introduced to a third poet, who had recently taken to himself a wife, which wife had two pretty unmarried sisters, of one of whom he became at once enamored, his friend being

enamored of the other.   This trio of poets was Robert
Southey, Robert Lovell, and Samuel Taylor Coleridge.
Southey made love to his Edith, and Coleridge to his
Sarah, and in the intervals of that delightful employ-
ment both made love to the Muse, joining their forces,
such as they were then, in the composition of a contemporary drama, The Fall of Robespierre, which got
into print in 1794.   In the same year Southey published
a volume of Poems, in conjunction with his friend
Lovell, and in the following year the first of his epics,
Joan of Arc, which he believed to be the most important addition to English Verse since Glover's Leonidas,
which was given to the world about sixty years before.
Stimulated by an offer of thirty guineas from Cottle,
another poet, Coleridge collected his Address to a
Young Ass, his verses on Roses, and Kisses, and other
juvenilia, and published them as Poems in 1796.   A
second edition, which was reached in the next year,
contained additions by two of his tuneful friends,
Charles Lamb and Charles Lloyd.   Four years had
elapsed since Wordsworth published his Descriptive
Sketches, and he had not been idle during that time,
though he had printed nothing.   He had written
several poems, among them Guilt and Sorrow, and a
tragedy called The Borderers.   In the summer of 1797
he was visited at Racedown by Coleridge, who repeated
to him and his sister Dorothy, after tea, two acts and
a half of a tragedy he had in hand, and to whom the
next morning he read the whole five acts of his own
tragedy.   A visit with his sister to Coleridge, at Nether-
Stowey, in the autumn, led to a little tour in the
neighborhood, and as their united funds were very

small, the two poets agreed to defray the expense of
the tour by writing a poem. They set off along the
Quantock Hills, and in the course of their walk the
poem was planned, Coleridge supplying the story
which was to be narrated, and Wordsworth suggest-
ing the crime upon which it should hinge, and which
was to be punished in the spiritual suffering of the
hero. They began it the same evening, but did not
proceed far before they discovered that their respec-
tive manners could not be successfully combined, and
Wordsworth withdrew from the undertaking. They
continued their tour, the poem growing in the mean-
time until it became too important for their first object, which was limited to their expectation of five
pounds, so they began to think of writing a volume,
which was to consist of poems chiefly on supernatural
subjects, taken from common life, and looked at, as
much as might be, through an imaginative medium.
The poem thus conceived was The Ancient Mariner,
and the volume thus projected was the Lyrical
Ballads. Looking back upon the eighteenth century
now we can distinguish therein four great years, four
years that are memorable in the history of English
Verse, years in which old elements were discarded and
new elements introduced, in which the old order
yielded, giving place to new—the years in which
Thomson published his Winter (1726), Gray the Elegy
(1751), Cowper The Task (1785), and Wordsworth and
Coleridge the Lyrical Ballads (1798). The year that
witnessed the publication, in the same volume, of The
Ancient Mariner, and Lines written a few miles above
Tintern Abbey, was the *annus mirabilis*.

The prospects of English Verse were prosperous when the nineteenth century opened. Dispirited and benumbed during the greater part of the eighteenth century, it had shaken off the fetters which had been imposed upon it, and rousing as its energies were awakened had revolted and declared its freedom. It was attended by four torch-bearers, Southey, who was in his twenty-sixth year, Coleridge, who was in his twenty-eighth year, Scott, who was in his twenty-ninth year, and Wordsworth, who was in his thirtieth year. To these should be added three link-boys, who were younger, Campbell being twenty-seven, Landor twenty-five, and Moore twenty-one. Behind these, unconscious of their future renown, the imagination sees three bright, eager-eyed lads, George Gordon Byron, who was twelve, Percy Bysshe Shelley, the son of a country baronet, who was eight, and John Keats, the son of the head servant of a livery-stable keeper, who was five. Tracing the current of English Verse hitherward from the beginning of the century, we find the four torch-bearers following the paths upon which they had already entered,—Southey, the path of the epic in Thalaba (1801), Madoc (1805), Curse of Kehema (1810), Roderick, the Last of the Goths (1814); Scott, the path of balladry, which soon broadened into the shining high-way of the metrical romance, in The Minstrelsy of the Scottish Border (1802–3), The Lay of the Last Minstrel (1805), Marmion (1808), The Lady of the Lake (1810), Vision of Don Roderick (1811), Rokeby (1812), The Bridal of Triermain (1813), The Lord of the Isles (1815), Harold the Dauntless (1817); Wordsworth, the path of philosophic meditation and nature-worship in The Excursion (1814), The White Doe of Rylstone (1815), Peter Bell (1819), The Waggoner (1819); and Coleridge, the path of dramatic fantasy, in Christabel (1806), Remorse (1813), Sibylline Leaves (1816), and Zapolya (1816). Of the four, the one who made poetry the business of his life was the least popular. Subversive of the conventional standard of taste, there were puerilities in his poetry which provoked derision, and an originality which was offensive. Such readers as he had, and they were not many, he made, and made slowly. What Coleridge might have become if, like Wordsworth, he could have devoted himself wholly to poetry, we can only conjecture; that he had a richer nature and a more creative imagination can scarcely be doubted. As it was, however, he frittered away his time in dreaming and travelling, in preaching and lecturing, in writing for newspapers and projecting periodicals, but chiefly in opium-eating. He had married his Sarah, who had borne him children, as his friend Southey had married his Edith, who had borne him children, and it was Southey's roof that sheltered the young Coleridges and their mother. With fewer poetic gifts than Coleridge, Southey contrived to thrive better, for while he composed his epics, which had no sale to speak of, he devised letters of travel, edited poets, translated romances of chivalry, wrote a Life of Nelson, a History of Brazil, a Book of the Church, and numberless articles in the Quarterly Review. Reputation, which had been refused to Coleridge and Wordsworth, though a share of it had fallen to the lot of Southey, and the reward which follows reputation, often in the guise of its evil genius,—these things had been lavished upon Scott as upon few English poets before. The greatest poet of the time in general estimation, he was the most in demand among the Trade, for he had the rare art of coining money for them as well as for himself. Scott's reign as the monarch of English Verse in the nineteenth century was brilliant but brief, for in its seventh year his power was shaken by a young lord of twenty-four, whose claim to the sovereignty was a poem called Childe Harold. He abdicated gracefully, carrying the sceptre with which he had ruled over the world of metrical romance into the greater world of historical prose romance, which he discovered, and in which his genius still reigns supreme. Nowhere in the history of letters do we find a career like that of Byron, nowhere so powerful a personality as his. He was what Marlowe might have been but for that fatal tavern brawl—the possessor of all poetic gifts, except that instinctive knowledge of mankind which was Shakespeare's, and that reverence for moral greatness which was Milton's,—a swift and glorious Spirit, an elemental Force in English Verse. Belonging to the same race of high intelligences, but of a different order, was Shelley, who was of too ethereal a mould for the material England of the Georges. He had the heart of a woman, or a child,—the heart which suffering first moves to pity, then to anger, and then stings to the unreason which clamors against the Maker of a world in which such suffering exists. He confounded religion with priestcraft, and kingcraft with the human imperfection of the laws it administered, and would have abolished both, and put man back once more in a state of nature, which, poet-like, he peopled with all the civic virtues. A chartered libertine in his beliefs, the soul of goodness shone through his life and his work, than which there is none more imaginative in English Verse. More purely poetical than either was Keats, who, without learning, revived the spirit of the Greek pastoral in Endymion, and the spirit of the Greek tragedy in Hyperion, and summoned back as with the wand of an enchanter the light and loveliness of the Middle Ages in The Eve of St. Agnes. His masters were Chaucer, Spenser, and the Shakespeare of the Sonnets, and their pupil was worthy of them. One's first thought, when he remembers that he died in his twenty-seventh year, is, that he died young ; but when one remembers what his life was, with what scorn his poetry was received, and how he was tortured by a hopeless passion, one cannot but change his mind, and say, with old Bosola in the Duchess of Malfy,

> " I think not so ; his infelicity
> Seemed to have years too many."

Of the later nineteenth century poets, successors of Keats, Shelley, and Byron, born in their lifetime, but not singing until the grave had closed over them,— the perfect poet who has restored to us the gracious Arthur from his long slumber in the island valley of Avilion ; the subtle dramatist who has poured his own heart's blood into Sebald and Ottima, Colombe and Valence, and a score of other live men and women ; the tender and pensive singer, who has created an Earthly Paradise for the immortal stories that he loves so well, and that we love, too ; the fiery, impassioned improvisator, dramatist at once and lyrist, who has plucked out the heart of Mary Stuart's secret, and snatched the light and sound of the sea ; of these, and others, all that a contemporary should say,—and he cannot say less,—was said by Keats in the first line of the second sonnet that he addressed to Haydon:

"Great spirits now on earth are sojourning."

R. H. STODDARD.

THE CENTURY,
    NEW YORK, September 20, 1883.

*** The Editors and Publishers of ENGLISH VERSE cordially acknowledge the kindness which has allowed them to print in it many poems, which could be so included only by authority of the owners of the American copyrights. The permission has been willingly granted in every case ; and it is through this kind co-operation that it has been possible to make thoroughly comprehensive a Collection which must otherwise have been unduly limited in the field of American poetry. Besides their indebtedness to the living American authors whose names appear in these volumes, they desire to express their thanks to MESSRS. HOUGHTON, MIFFLIN & CO. for their consent to the use of many poems from the long list of poets of whose works they are the publishers ; to MESSRS. D. APPLETON & CO. for the use of poems by Bryant ; to MESSRS. ROBERTS BROTHERS and JAMES R. OSGOOD & CO. ; to MESSRS. J. B. LIPPINCOTT & CO. ; and to MESSRS A. C. ARMSTRONG & SON.

CONTENTS.

CONTENTS.

CONTENTS. xxxix

CONTENTS. xli

LYRICS

OF THE

XIXTH CENTURY

Song should breathe of scents and flowers;
  Song should like a river flow;
Song should bring back scenes and hours
  That we loved—ah! long ago.

Song from baser thoughts should win us;
  Song should charm us out of woe;
Song should stir the heart within us,
  Like a patriot's friendly blow.

Pains and pleasures, all man doeth,
  War and peace, and right and wrong,
All things that the soul subdueth
  Should be vanquish'd too by Song.

Song should spur the mind to duty,
  Nerve the weak, and stir the strong;
Every deed of truth and beauty
  Should be crown'd by starry Song.

Barry Cornwall.

Lyrics of the XIXth Century.

WILLIAM WORDSWORTH.

1770—1850.

INVOCATION.

TO THE POWER OF SOUND.

Thy functions are ethereal,
As if within thee dwelt a glancing mind,
Organ of Vision! And a Spirit aèrial
Informs the cell of Hearing, dark and blind:
Intricate labyrinth, more dread for thought
To enter than oracular cave :
Strict passage, through which sighs are brought,
And whispers for the heart, their slave ;
And shrieks that revel in abuse
Of shivering flesh ; and warbled air,
Whose piercing sweetness can unloose
The chains of frenzy or entice a smile
Into the ambush of despair ;
Hozannas pealing down the long-drawn aisle ;
And requiems answer'd by the pulse that beats
Devoutly in life's last retreats.

The headlong streams and fountains
Serve thee ! Invisible Spirit ! with untired powers :
Cheering the wakeful tent on Syrian mountains,
They lull perchance ten thousand thousand flowers.
That roar, the prowling lion's " Here I am ! "

II.—1

How fearful to the desert wide!
That bleat, how tender! of the dam
Calling a straggler to her side.
Shout, cuckoo! let the vernal soul
Go with thee to the frozen zone ;
Toll from thy loftiest perch, lone bell-bird! toll,
At the still hour to Mercy dear :
Mercy from her twilight throne
Listening to nun's faint throb of holy fear,
To sailor's prayer breathed from a darkening sea,
Or widow's cottage-lullaby.

Ye Voices! and ye Shadows
And Images of Voice, to hound and horn
From rocky steep and rock-bestudded meadows
Flung back and in the sky's blue caves reborn !
On with your pastime, till the church-tower bells
A greeting give of measured glee ;
And milder Echoes from their cells
Repeat the bridal symphony.
Then, or far earlier, let us rove
Where mists are breaking up or gone,
And from aloft look down into a cove
Besprinkled with a careless quire :
Happy milkmaids, one by one
Scattering a ditty each to her desire,—
A liquid concert matchless by nice art,
A stream as if from one full heart.

Bless'd be the song that brightens
The blind man's gloom, exalts the veteran's mirth!
Unscorn'd the peasant's whistling breath that lightens
His duteous toil of furrowing the green earth !
For the tired slave Song lifts the languid oar,
And bids it aptly fall, with chime
That beautifies the fairest shore
And mitigates the harshest clime.
Yon pilgrims see !—in lagging file

They move ; but soon the appointed way
A choral " Avè, Marie ! " shall beguile,
And to their hope the distant shrine
Glisten with a livelier ray.
Nor friendless he, the prisoner of the mine,
Who from the well-spring of his own clear breast
Can draw, and sing his griefs to rest.

When civic renovation
Dawns on a kingdom, and for needful haste
Best eloquence avails not, Inspiration
Mounts with a tune that travels like a blast,
Piping through cave and battlemented tower :
Then starts the sluggard, pleased to meet
That voice of Freedom in its power
Of promises, shrill, wild and sweet.
Who from a martial pageant spreads
Incitements of a battle-day,
Thrilling the unweapon'd crowd with plumeless heads ?
Even She whose Lydian airs inspire
Peaceful striving, gentle play
Of timid hope and innocent desire
Shot from the dancing Graces as they move
Fann'd by the plausive wings of Love.

How oft along thy mazes,
Regent of Sound ! have dangerous passions trod.
O thou ! through whom the temple rings with praises,
And blackening clouds in thunder speak of God,
Betray not by the cozenage of sense
Thy votaries, wooingly resign'd
To a voluptuous influence
That taints the purer, better mind ;
But lead sick Fancy to a harp
That hath in noble tasks been tried !
And, if the virtuous feel a pang too sharp,
Soothe it into patience !—stay
The uplifted arm of Suicide ;

And let some mood of thine in firm array
Knit every thought the impending issue needs,
Ere martyr burns or patriot bleeds !

As Conscience to the centre
Of Being smites with irresistible pain,
So shall a solemn cadence, if it enter
The mouldy vaults of the dull idiot's brain,
Transmute him to a wretch from quiet hurl'd,
Convulsed as by a jarring din ;
And then aghast, as at the world
Of reason partially let in
By concords winding with a sway
Terrible for sense and soul :
Or awed he weeps, struggling to quell dismay.
Point not these mysteries to an art,
Lodged above the starry pole ?
Pure modulations flowing from the heart
Of Divine Love, where Wisdom, Beauty, Truth,
With Order, dwell in endless youth.

Oblivion may not cover
All treasures hoarded by the miser Time.
Orphean Insight !   Truth's undaunted lover,
To the first leagues of tutor'd passion climb,
When Music deign'd within this grosser sphere
Her subtle essence to enfold,
And voice and shell drew forth a tear
Softer than Nature's self could mould.
Yet strenuous was the infant age :
Art, daring because souls could feel,
Stirr'd nowhere but an urgent equipage
Of rapt imagination sped her march
Through the realms of woe and weal :
Hell to the lyre bow'd low ; the upper arch
Rejoiced that clamorous spell and magic verse
Her wan disasters could disperse.

WILLIAM WORDSWORTH.

The Gift to King Amphion,
That wall'd a city with its melody,
Was for belief no dream.   Thy skill, Arion !
Could humanize the creatures of the sea,
Where men were monsters : a last grace he craves,
Leave for one chant ; the dulcet sound
Steals from the deck o'er willing waves,
And listening dolphins gather round ;
Self-cast, as with a desperate course
'Mid that strange audience, he bestrides
A proud One docile as a managed horse,
And singing, while the accordant hand
Sweeps his harp, the Master rides ;
So shall he touch at length a friendly strand,
And he with his preserver shine star-bright
In memory, through silent night.

The pipe of Pan to shepherds
Couch'd in the shadow of Mænalian pines
Was passing sweet ; the eyeballs of the leopards
That in high triumph drew the Lord of Vines,
How did they sparkle to the cymbals' clang !
While Fauns and Satyrs beat the ground
In cadence, and Silenus swang
This way and that, with wild-flowers crown'd.
To life, to life give back thine ear !
Ye, who are longing to be rid
Of fable though to truth subservient ! hear
The little sprinkling of cold earth that fell
Echoed from the coffin-lid ;
The convict's summons in the steeple's knell ;
The vain distress-gun, from a leeward shore
Repeated, heard,—and heard no more.

For terror, joy, or pity,
Vast is the compass and the swell of notes :
From the babe's first cry to voice of regal city

Rolling a solemn sea-like bass, that floats
Far as the woodlands, with the trill to blend
Of that shy songstress whose love-tale
Might tempt an angel to descend
While hovering o'er the moonlight vale.
Ye wandering Utterances! has earth no scheme,
No scale of moral music, to unite
Powers that survive but in the faintest dream
Of memory?   O that ye might stoop to bear
Chains, such precious chains of sight
As labour'd minstrelsies through ages wear!
O for a balance fit the truth to tell
Of the Unsubstantial, ponder'd well!

By one pervading spirit
Of tones and numbers all things are controul'd :
As sages taught, where faith was found to merit
Initiation in that mystery old.
The heavens, whose aspect makes our minds as still
As they themselves appear to be,
Innumerable voices fill
With everlasting harmony;
The towering headlands, crown'd with mist,
Their feet among the billows, know
That Ocean is a mighty harmonist;
Thy pinions, universal Air!
Ever waving to and fro,
Are delegates of harmony, and bear
Strains that support the Seasons in their round :
Stern Winter loves a dirge-like sound.

Break forth into thanksgiving,
Ye banded instruments of wind and chords!
Unite, to magnify the Ever-living,
Your inarticulate notes with the voice of words!
Nor hush'd be service from the lowing mead;
Nor mute the forest hum of noon!

Thou too be heard, lone eagle ! freed
From snowy peak and cloud, attune
Thy hungry barkings to the hymn
Of joy that from her utmost walls
The Six-days' Work by flaming Seraphim
Transmits to Heaven.   As Deep to Deep
Shouting through one valley calls,
All worlds, all natures mood and measure keep
For praise and ceaseless gratulation, pour'd
Into the ear of God, their Lord.

A Voice to light gave being,
To Time, and Man, his earth-born chronicler ;
A Voice shall finish doubt and dim foreseeing,
And sweep away life's visionary stir :
The trumpet (we intoxicate with pride
Arm at its blast for deadly wars),
To archangelic lips applied,
The grave shall open, quench the stars.
O Silence ! are Man's noisy years
No more than moments of thy life ?
Is Harmony, bless'd queen of smiles and tears,
With her smooth tones and discords just
Temper'd into rapturous strife,
Thy destined bond-slave ?   No ! though earth be dust
And vanish, though the heavens dissolve, her stay
Is in The Word, that shall not pass away.

ODE TO DUTY.

Stern daughter of the Voice of God :
    O Duty ! if that name thou love
    Who art a light to guide, a rod
    To check the erring, and reprove !
    Thou who art victory and law
    When empty terrors overawe ;

From vain temptations dost set free,
And calm'st the weary strife of frail Humanity !

There are who ask not if thine eye
Be on them : who in love and truth,
Where no misgiving is, rely
Upon the genial sense of youth.
Glad Hearts ! without reproach or blot,
Who do thy work and know it not :
Long may the kindly impulse last !
But thou, if they should totter, teach them to stand fast !

Serene will be our days and bright,
And happy will our nature be,
When love is an unerring light,
And joy its own security :
And they a blissful course may hold
Even now, who, not unwisely bold,
Live in the spirit of this creed,
Yet find that other strength, according to their need.

I, loving freedom, and untried,
No sport of every random gust,
Yet being to myself a guide,
Too blindly have reposed my trust ;
And oft, when in my heart was heard
Thy timely mandate, I deferr'd
The task, in smoother walks to stray :
But thee I now would serve more strictly, if I may.

Through no disturbance of my soul
Or strong compunction in me wrought
I supplicate for thy controul,
But in the quietness of thought :
Me this uncharter'd freedom tries,
I feel the weight of chance desires,
My hopes no more must change their name ;
I long for a repose that ever is the same.

Stern Law-giver! Yet thou dost wear
The Godhead's most benignant grace;
Nor know we anything so fair
As is the smile upon thy face:
Flowers laugh before thee on their beds,
And fragrance in thy footing treads;
Thou dost preserve the stars from wrong;
And the most ancient heavens through Thee are fresh
    and strong.

To humble functions, awful Power!
I call thee: I myself commend
Unto thy guidance from this hour.
O, let my weakness have an end!
Give unto me, made lowly wise,
The spirit of self-sacrifice;
The confidence of reason give;
And in the light of Truth thy Bondman let me live!

NATURE'S DARLING.

Three years she grew in sun and shower:
Then Nature said—A lovelier flower
    On earth was never sown:
This Child I to myself will take;
She shall be mine, and I will make
    A Lady of my own.

Myself will to my darling be
Both law and impulse; and with me
    The Girl, in rock and plain,
In earth and heaven, in glade and bower,
Shall feel an overseeing power,
    To kindle or restrain.

She shall be sportive as the fawn
That wild with glee across the lawn
    Or up the mountain springs;

And hers shall be the breathing balm,
And hers the silence and the calm
    Of mute insensate things.

The floating clouds their state shall lend
To her ; for her the willow bend ;
    Nor shall she fail to see
Even in the motions of the storm
Grace that shall mould the Maiden's form
    By silent sympathy.

The stars of midnight shall be dear
To her ; and she shall lean her ear
    In many a secret place
 Where rivulets dance their wayward round,
And beauty born of murmuring sound
    Shall pass into her face.

And vital feelings of delight
Shall rear her form to stately height,
    Her virgin bosom swell :
Such thoughts to Lucy I will give
While she and I together live
    Here in this happy dell.—

Thus Nature spake : the work was done.
How soon my Lucy's race was run !
    She died : and left to me
This health, this calm, and quiet scene,
The memory of what has been,
    And never more will be.

THE TRIAD.

Show me the noblest Youth of present time
Whose trembling fancy would to love give birth ;
Some God, or Hero from the Olympian clime
Return'd to seek a Consort upon earth !
Or, in no doubtful prospect, let me see

The brightest Star of ages yet to be !
And I will mate and match him blissfully.

I will not fetch a Naiad from a flood
Pure as herself (Song lacks not mightier power),
Nor leaf-crown'd Dryad from a pathless wood,
Nor Sea-Nymph glistening from her coral bower :
Mere Mortals, bodied forth in vision, still
Shall with Mount Ida's triple lustre fill
The chaster coverts of a British hill.

Appear ! obey my lyre's command !
Come, like the Graces, hand in hand !
For ye, though not by birth allied,
Are Sisters in the bond of love ;
Nor shall the tongue of envious pride
Presume those interweavings to reprove
In you, which that fair progeny of Jove
Learn'd from the tuneful spheres that glide
In endless union earth and sea above.
—I sing in vain :—the pines have hush'd their waving :
A peerless Youth expectant at my side,
Breathless as they, with unabated craving
Looks to the earth and to the vacant air
And, with a wandering eye that seems to chide,
Asks of the clouds what occupants they hide.
But why solicit more than sight could bear
By casting on a moment all we dare ?
Invoke we those bright Beings, one by one !
And what was boldly promised truly shall be done.

Fear not a constraining measure !
—Yielding to this gentle spell,
Lucida ! from domes of pleasure,
Or from cottage-sprinkled dell,
Come to regions solitary
Where the eagle builds her aery
Above the hermit's long-forsaken cell !

      She comes !   Behold
That Figure, like a ship with snow-white sail !
Nearer she draws ; a breeze uplifts her veil ;
Upon her coming wait
As pure a sunshine and as soft a gale
As e'er on herbage covering earthly mould
Tempted the bird of Juno to unfold
His richest splendour, when his veering gait
And every motion of his starry train
Seem governed by a strain
Of music, audible to him alone.

O Lady ! worthy of earth's proudest throne,
Nor less, by excellence of nature, fit
Beside an unambitious hearth to sit,
Domestic queen, where grandeur is unknown :
What living man could fear
The worst of Fortune's malice wert Thou near,
Humbling that lily-stem, thy sceptre meek,
That its fair flowers may from his cheek
Brush the too happy tear ?
Queen and handmaid lowly !
Whose skill can speed the day with lively cares,
And banish melancholy
By all that mind invents or hand prepares :
O Thou ! against whose lip, without its smile,
And in its silence even, no heart is proof ;
Whose goodness, sinking deep, would reconcile
The softest nursling of a gorgeous palace
To the bare life beneath the hawthorn roof
Of Sherwood's Archer, or in caves of Wallace :
Who that hath seen thy beauty could content
His soul with but a glimpse of heavenly day ?
Who that hath loved thee but would lay
His strong hand on the Wind if it were bent
To take thee in thy majesty away ?
—Pass onward !   Even the glancing deer

Till we depart intrude not here :
That mossy slope, o'er which the woodbine throws
A canopy, is smoothed for thy repose.

Glad moment is it when the throng
Of warblers in full concert strong
Strive, and not vainly strive to rout
The lagging shower, and force coy Phœbus out,—
Met by the rainbow's form divine,
Issuing from her cloudy shrine :
So may the thrillings of the lyre
Prevail to further our desire,
While to these shades a sister Nymph I call.

Come, if the notes thine ear may pierce,
Come, Youngest of the Lovely Three !
Submissive to the might of Verse
And the dear voice of Harmony,
By none more deeply felt than thee.
—I sang ; and lo ! from pastimes virginal
She hastens to the tents
Of Nature and the lonely elements.
Air sparkles round her with a dazzling sheen ;
But mark her glowing cheek, her vesture green !
And, as if wishful to disarm
Or to repay the potent Charm,
She bears the stringed lute of old Romance,
That cheer'd the trellis'd arbour's privacy,
And soothed war-wearied knights in rafter'd hall.
How vivid, yet how delicate her glee !
So tripp'd the Muse, inventress of the dance :
So, truant in waste woods, the blithe Euphrosyne.

But the ringlets of that head,
Why are they ungarlanded ?
Why bedeck her temples less
Than the simplest shepherdess ?

Is it not a brow inviting
Choicest flowers that ever breathed,
Which the myrtle would delight in,
With Idalian rose enwreathed ?
But her humility is well content
With one wild floweret (call it not forlorn !)—
Flower-of-the-winds, beneath her bosom worn,
But more for love than ornament.

Open, ye thickets ! let her fly,
Swift as a Thracian Nymph o'er field and height :
For she, to all but those who love her shy,
Would gladly vanish from a stranger's sight ;
Though where she is beloved and loves
Light as the wheeling butterfly she moves :
Her happy spirit as a bird is free
That rifles blossoms on a tree,
Turning them inside out with arch audacity.
Alas ! how little can a moment show
Of an eye where feeling plays
In ten thousand dewy rays ;
A face o'er which a thousand shadows go !
She stops,—is fasten'd to that rivulet's side ;
And there (while with sedater mien
O'er timid waters that have scarcely left
Their birth-place in the rocky cleft
She bends) at leisure may be seen
Features, to old ideal grace allied,
Amid their smiles and dimples dignified :
Fit countenance for the soul of primal truth,
The bland composure of eternal youth !

What more changeful than the sea ?
But over his great tides
Fidelity presides :
And this light-hearted Maiden constant is as he.
High is her aim as heaven above,

And wide as ether her good-will ;
And, like the lowly reed, her love
Can drink its nurture from the scantiest rill ;
Insight as keen as frosty star
Is to her charity no bar,
Nor interrupts her frolic graces
When she is, far from these wild places,
Encircled by familiar faces.

O the charm that manners draw,
Nature ! from thy genuine law :
If from what her hand would do,
Her voice would utter, aught ensue
Untoward or unfit,
She in benign affections pure,
In self-forgetfulness secure,
Sheds round the transient harm or vague mischance
A light unknown to tutor'd elegance :
Hers is not a cheek shame-stricken ;
But her blushes are joy-flushes,
And the fault, if fault it be,
Only ministers to quicken
Laughter-loving gaiety,
And kindle sportive wit,—
Leaving this Daughter of the Mountains free
As if she knew that Oberon, King of Faery,
Had cross'd her purpose with some vague vagary,
And heard his viewless bands
Over their mirthful triumph clapping hands.

—Last of the Three, though eldest born !
Reveal thyself, like pensive Morn
Touch'd by the skylark's earliest note,
Ere humbler gladness be afloat.
But whether in the semblance dress'd
Of Dawn, or Eve (fair Vision of the West),
Come with each anxious hope subdued

By woman's gentle fortitude,
Each grief through meekness settling into rest !
Or I would hail thee when some high-wrought page
Of a closed volume lingering in thy hand
Has raised thy spirit to a peaceful stand
Among the glories of a happier age.

Her brow hath open'd on me : see it there
Brightening the umbrage of her hair !
So gleams the crescent moon, that loves
To be descried through shady groves.
Tenderest bloom is on her cheek :
Wish not for a richer streak,
Nor dread the depth of meditative eye !
But let thy love, upon that azure field
Of thoughtfulness and beauty, yield
Its homage, offer'd up in purity !
What wouldst thou more ?   In sunny glade,
Or under leaves of thickest shade,
Was such a stillness e'er diffused
Since earth grew calm while angels mused ?
Softly she treads, as if her foot were loath
To crush the mountain dew-drops, soon to melt
On the flower's breast,—as if she felt
That flowers themselves, whate'er their hue,
With all their fragrance, all their glistening,
Call to the heart for inward listening ;
And though for bridal wreaths and tokens true
Welcomed wisely, though a growth
Which the careless shepherd sleeps on,
As fitly spring from turf the mourner weeps on,
And without wrong are cropp'd the marble tomb to strew.

The Charm is over ! the mute Phantoms gone,
Nor will return !   But droop not, favour'd Youth !
The apparition that before thee shone
Obey'd a summons covetous of truth.

From these wild rocks thy footsteps I will guide
To bowers in which thy fortune may be tried,
And one of the Bright Three become thy happy Bride.

NATURAL PIETY.

My heart leaps up when I behold
    A rainbow in the sky :
So was it when my life began,
So is it now I am a man,
So be it when I shall grow old,
    Or let me die !
The Child is father of the Man :
And I could wish my days to be
Bound each to each by natural piety.

SONNETS.

It is a beauteous evening, calm and free !
The holy time is quiet as a Nun
Breathless with adoration ; the broad sun
Is sinking down in its tranquillity ;
The gentleness of heaven broods o'er the sea :
Listen ! the mighty Being is awake,
And doth with his eternal motion make
A sound like thunder—everlastingly.
Dear Child ! dear Girl ! that walkest with me here,
If thou appear untouch'd by solemn thought,
Thy nature is not therefore less divine :
Thou liest in Abraham's bosom all the year,
And worship'st at the Temple's inner shrine,
God being with thee when we know it not.

———

This world is too much with us : late and soon,
Getting and spending, we lay waste our powers ;
Little we see of Nature that is ours ;
We have given our hearts away,—a sordid boon !
    II.—2

This sea that bares her bosom to the moon,—
The winds, that will be howling at all hours,
And are upgather'd now like sleeping flowers,—
For this, for every thing, we are out of tune;
It moves us not.   Great God! I'd rather be
A Pagan, suckled in a creed outworn:
So might I, standing on this pleasant lea,
Have glimpses that would make me less forlorn;
Have sight of Proteus rising from the sea,
Or hear old Triton blow his wreathèd horn.

O'er the wide earth, on mountain and on plain,
Dwells in the affections and the soul of man
A Godhead, like the universal Pan,
But more exalted, with a brighter train:
And shall his bounty be dispensed in vain,
Shower'd equally on city and on field,
And neither hope nor steadfast promise yield
In these usurping times of fear and pain?
Such doom awaits us.   Nay! forbid it, Heaven!
We know the arduous strife, the eternal laws
To which the triumph of all good is given,—
High sacrifice and labour without pause
Even to the death: else wherefore should the eye
Of man converse with immortality?

There is a bondage worse, far worse, to bear
Than his who breathes, by roof and flower and wall
Pent in, a tyrant's solitary Thrall.
'Tis his who walks about in the open air
One of a Nation who henceforth must wear
Their fetters in their souls: for who could be,
Who, even the best, in such condition free
From self-reproach, reproach that he must share
With human nature?   Never be it ours

To see the sun how brightly it will shine,
And know that noble feelings, manly powers,
Instead of gathering strength, must droop and pine;
And earth, with all her pleasant fruits and flowers,
Fade and participate in man's decline !

———

Methought I saw the footsteps of a throne
Which mists and vapours from mine eyes did shroud,
Nor view of who might sit thereon allow'd;
But all the steps and ground about were strown
With sights the ruefullest that flesh and bone
Ever put on,—a miserable crowd,
Sick, hale, old, young, who cried before that cloud—
" Thou art our king, O Death ! to thee we groan."
Those steps I clomb, the mists before me gave
Smooth way; and I beheld the face of One
Sleeping alone within a mossy cave,
With her face up to heaven, that seem'd to have
Pleasing remembrance of a thought foregone :
A lovely Beauty in a summer grave !

SAMUEL TAYLOR COLERIDGE.
1772—1834.

———

GENEVIEVE.

All thoughts, all passions, all delights,
Whatever stirs this mortal frame,
All are but ministers of Love,
    And feed his sacred flame.

Oft in my waking dreams do I
Live o'er again that happy hour
When midway on the mount I lay
    Beside the ruin'd tower.

The moonshine, stealing o'er the scene,
Had blended with the lights of eve,

And she was there, my hope, my joy,
   My own dear Genevieve.

She lean'd against the armed man,
The statue of the armed knight;
She stood and listen'd to my lay
   Amid the lingering light.

Few sorrows hath she of her own,
My hope, my joy, my Genevieve :
She loves me best whene'er I sing
   The songs that make her grieve.

I play'd a soft and doleful air,
I sang an old and moving story,
An old rude song that suited well
   The ruin wild and hoary.

She listen'd, with a flitting blush,
With downcast eyes, and modest grace,
For well she knew I could not choose
   But gaze upon her face.

I told her of the knight that bore
Upon his shield a burning brand ;
And how for ten long years he woo'd
   The Lady of the Land :

I told her how he pined ; and ah !
The deep, the low, the pleading tone
With which I sang another's love
   Interpreted my own.

She listen'd, with a flitting blush,
With downcast eyes, and modest grace ;
And she forgave me that I gazed
   Too fondly on her face.

But when I told the cruel scorn
That crazed this bold and lovely knight,

And how he roam'd the mountain woods,
    Nor rested, day or night;

And how he cross'd the woodman's paths,
Through briars and swampy mosses beat;
How boughs rebounding scourged his limbs,
    And low stubs gored his feet;

That sometimes from the savage den,
And sometimes from the darksome shade,
And sometimes starting up at once
    In green and sunny glade,

There came, and look'd him in the face,
An Angel beautiful and bright,
And that he knew it was a Fiend,
    This miserable Knight;

And how, unknowing what he did,
He leap'd amid a murderous band
And saved from outrage worse than death
    The Lady of the Land;

And how she wept, and clasp'd his knees;
And how she tended him in vain,
And ever strove to expiate
    The scorn that crazed his brain;

And how she nursed him in a cave;
And that his madness went away
When on the yellow forest-leaves
    A dying man he lay;

His dying words;—But when I reach'd
That tenderest strain of all the ditty
My faltering voice and pausing harp
    Disturb'd her soul with pity.

All impulses of soul and sense
Had thrill'd my guileless Genevieve:

The music and the doleful tale,
    The rich and balmy eve ;

And hopes, and fears that kindle hope,
An undistinguishable throng,
And gentle wishes long subdued,
    Subdued and cherish'd long.

She wept, with pity and delight ;
She blush'd, with love and virgin shame ;
And, like the murmur of a dream,
    I heard her breathe my name.

Her bosom heaved,—she stepp'd aside,
As conscious of my look she stepp'd ;
Then suddenly, with timorous eye,
    She fled to me, and wept.

She half-enclosed me in her arms ;
She press'd me with a meek embrace ;
And, bending back her head, look'd up
    And gazed upon my face.

'Twas partly love, and partly fear,
And partly 'twas a bashful art
That I might rather feel than see
    The swelling of her heart.

I calm'd her fears, and she was calm,
And told her love with virgin pride :
And so I won my Genevieve,
    My bright and beauteous Bride.

NAMES.

I ask'd my Fair, one happy day,
What I should call her in my lay,—
By what sweet name from Rome or Greece :
    Lalagè, Neæra, Chloris,

Sappho, Lesbia, or Doris,
Arethusa, or Lucrece.

Ah! replied my gentle Fair :
Belovèd ! what are names but air ?
Choose thou whatever suits the line !
    Call me Sappho, call me Chloris,
    Call me Lalagè, or Doris,—
    Only, only call me Thine !

TO A YOUNG ASS.

Its mother being tethered near it.

Poor little Foal of an oppressed race !
I love the languid patience of thy face ;
And oft with gentle hand I give thee bread,
And clap thy ragged coat, and pat thy head.
But what thy dulled spirits hath dismay'd,
That never thou dost sport along the glade ;
And, most unlike the nature of things young,
That earthward still thy moveless head is hung ?
Do thy prophetic fears anticipate,
Meek Child of Misery ! thy future fate :
The starving meal, and all the thousand aches
That patient Merit of the Unworthy takes ?
Or is thy sad heart thrill'd with filial pain
To see thy wretched mother's shorten'd chain ?
And truly, very piteous is her lot,
Chain'd to a log within a narrow spot
Where the close-eaten grass is scarcely seen,
While sweet around her waves the tempting green.

Poor Ass ! thy master should have learn'd to show
Pity, best taught by fellowship of woe :
For much I fear me that he lives like thee,
Half famish'd in a land of luxury.
How askingly its footsteps hither bend !
It seems to say—And have I then one friend ?

Innocent Foal! thou poor despised Forlorn!
I hail thee Brother, spite of the fool's scorn;
And fain would take thee with me, in the dell
Of Peace and mild Equality to dwell,
Where Toil shall call the charmer Health his bride,
And Laughter tickle Plenty's ribless side.
How thou wouldst toss thy heels in gamesome play,
And frisk about, as lamb or kitten gay!
Yea! and more musically sweet to me
Thy dissonant harsh bray of joy would be
Than warbled melodies that soothe to rest
The aching of pale Fashion's vacant breast.

LOVE AND HOPE AND PATIENCE IN EDUCATION.

O'er wayward childhood wouldst thou hold firm rule
And sun thee in the light of happy faces,
Love, Hope, and Patience,—these must be thy Graces;
And in thine own heart let them first keep school!
For, as old Atlas on his broad neck places
Heaven's starry globe and there sustains it, so
Do these upbear the little world below
Of Education,—Patience, Love, and Hope.
Methinks I see them group'd in seemly show,
The straiten'd arms upraised, the palms aslope,
And robes that, touching as adown they flow
Distinctly, blend like snow emboss'd in snow.
O part them never! If Hope prostrate lie,
　　　Love too will sink and die.
But love is subtle, and doth proof derive
From her own life that Hope is yet alive;
And bending o'er, with soul-transfusing eyes,
And the soft murmurs of the mother dove,
Woos back the fleeting spirit, and half supplies:
Thus Love repays to Hope what Hope first gave to Love.
Yet haply there will come a weary day
　　　When, overtask'd at length,

Both Love and Hope beneath the load give way.
Then with a statue's smile, a statue's strength,
Stands the mute sister, Patience, nothing loath,
And, both supporting, does the work of both.

YOUTH AND AGE.

Verse, a breeze 'mid blossoms straying,
Where Hope clung feeding like a bee :
Both were mine ; Life went a-maying
With Nature, Hope, and Poesy,
　　　　　　When I was young.
When I was young ?　Ah, woeful when !
Ah, for the change 'twixt now and then !
This breathing house not built with hands,
This body that does me grievous wrong,
O'er airy cliffs and glittering sands
How lightly then it flash'd along !
Like those trim skiffs, unknown of yore,
On winding lakes and rivers wide,
That ask no aid of sail or oar,
That fear no spite of wind or tide,
Nought cared this body for wind or weather
When Youth and I lived in it together.

Flowers are lovely, Love is flower-like ;
Friendship is a sheltering tree :
O the joys that came down shower-like
Of Friendship, Love, and Liberty,
　　　　　　Ere I was old !
Ere I was old ?　Ah, woeful ere !
Which tells me Youth's no longer here.
O youth ! for years so many and sweet
'Tis known that thou and I were one,
I'll think it but a fond conceit
(It can not be) that thou art gone.
Thy vesper-bell hath not yet toll'd,

And thou wert aye a masquer bold :
What strange disguise hast now put on
To make believe that thou art gone ?
I see these locks in silvery slips,
This drooping gait, this alter'd size ;
But Spring-tide blossoms on thy lips,
And tears take sunshine from thine eyes !
Life is but thought : so think I will
That Youth and I are house-mates still.

Dew-drops are the gems of Morning,
But the tears of mournful Eve ;
Where no hope is, life's a warning
That only serves to make us grieve
                        When we are old :
That only serves to make us grieve
With oft and tedious taking leave :
Like some poor nigh-related guest,
That may not rudely be dismiss'd,
Yet hath outstay'd his welcome-while
And tells the jest without the smile.

ROBERT SOUTHEY.

1774—1843.

THE HOLLY TREE.

O Reader ! hast thou ever stood to see
                The Holly Tree ?
The eye that contemplates it well perceives
                Its glossy leaves
Order'd by an intelligence so wise
As might confound the Atheist's sophistries.

Below, a circling fence, its leaves are seen
                Wrinkled and keen :

No grazing cattle through their prickly round
        Can reach to wound ;
But as they grow where nothing is to fear
Smooth and unarm'd the pointless leaves appear.

I love to view these things with curious eyes,
        And moralize ;
And in this wisdom of the Holly Tree
        Can emblems see
Wherewith, perchance, to make a pleasant rhyme,
One which may profit in the after-time.

Thus, though abroad perchance I might appear
        Harsh and austere,
To those who on my leisure would intrude
        Reserved and rude,—
Gentle at home amid my friends I'd be,
Like the high leaves upon the Holly Tree.

And should my youth, as youth is apt I know,
        Some harshness show,
All vain asperities I day by day
        Would wear away,
Till the smooth temper of my age should be
Like the high leaves upon the Holly Tree.

And as, when all the summer trees are seen
        So bright and green,
The Holly leaves their fadeless hues display
        Less bright than they,
But when the bare and wintry woods we see
What then so cheerful as the Holly Tree,—

So, serious should my youth appear among
        The thoughtless throng,
So would I seem, amid the young and gay
        More grave than they,
That in my age as cheerful I might be
As the green winter of the Holly Tree.

THE SCHOLAR.

My days among the Dead are pass'd
  Around me I behold,
Where'er these casual eyes are cast,
  The mighty Minds of Old :
My never-failing friends are they,
With whom I converse day by day.

With them I take delight in weal,
  And seek relief in woe ;
And while I understand and feel
  How much to them I owe
My cheeks have often been bedew'd
With tears of thoughtful gratitude.

My thoughts are with the Dead : with them
  I live in long-past years ;
Their virtues love, their faults condemn,
  Partake their hopes and fears ;
And from their lessons seek and find
Instruction with an humble mind.

My hopes are with the Dead; anon
  My place with them will be ;
And I with them shall travel on
  Through all futurity :
Yet leaving here a name, I trust,
That will not perish in the dust.

ROBERT TANNAHILL.

1774—1810.

LOVE'S FEAR.

O sair I rue the witless wish
  That gart me gang wi' you at e'en !
And sair I rue the birken bush
  That screen'd us with its leaves sae green !

And though you vow'd you would be mine,
  The tear of grief aye dims my ee,
For O I'm fear'd that I may tine
  The love that ye hae promised me

While others seek their evening sports,
  I wander dowie, a' my lane :
For when I join their glad resorts
  Their daffin' gie's me mickle pain.
Alas ! it was na sae short syne,
  When a' my nights were spent wi' glee :
But O I'm fear'd that I may tine
  The love that ye hae promised me.

Dear Lassie ! keep thy heart aboon,
  For I hae wair'd my winter's fee :
I've coft a bonnie silken gown
  To be a bridal gift for thee.
And sooner shall the hills fa' down,
  And mountain high shall stand the sea,
Ere I'd accept a gowden crown
  To change that love I bear for thee.

MINE AIN DEAR SOMEBODY.

When gloaming treads the heels of day,
And birds sit cowering on the spray,
Alang the flowery hedge I stray
    To meet mine ain dear Somebody.

The scented briar, the fragrant bean,
The clover bloom, the dewy green,
A' charm me as I rove at e'en
    To meet mine ain dear Somebody.

Let warriors prize the hero's name !
Let mad Ambition tower for fame !
I'm happier in my lowly hame,
    Obscurely bless'd wi' Somebody.

SIR WALTER SCOTT.
1771—1832.

THE CLAN-GATHERING.

Pibroch of Donuil Dhu !
  Pibroch of Donuil !
Wake thy wild voice anew !
  Summon Clan-Conuil !
Come away ! come away !
  Hark to the summons !
Come in your war array,
  Gentles and Commons !

Come from deep glen, and
  From mountain so rocky !
The war-pipe and pennon
  Are at Inverlochy.
Come, every hill-plaid and
  True heart that wears one !
Come, every steel blade and
  Strong hand that bears one !

Leave untended the herd,
  The flock without shelter !
Leave the corpse uninterr'd,
  The bride at the altar !
Leave the deer ! leave the steer !
  Leave nets and barges !
Come with your fighting gear,
  Broadswords and targes !

Come, as the winds come when
  Forests are rended !
Come, as the waves come when
  Navies are stranded !
Faster come ! faster come !

> Faster and faster——
> Chief, vassal, page, and groom,
>   Tenant, and master!
>
> Fast they come, fast they come :
>   See how they gather!
> Wide waves the eagle plume
>   Blended with heather.
> Cast your plaids ! draw your blades !
>   Forward each man set !
> Pibroch of Donuil Dhu !
>   Knell for the onset !

JOCK O' HAZELDEAN.

" Why weep ye by the tide ? Lady !
  Why weep ye by the tide ?
I'll wed ye to my youngest son,
  And ye shall be his bride :
And ye shall be his bride, Lady !
  Sae comely to be seen."
But aye she loot the tears downfa'
  For Jock o' Hazeldean.

" Now let this wilfu' grief be done,
  And dry that cheek so pale !
Young Frank is chief of Errington,
  And lord of Langley-dale ;
His step is first in peaceful ha',
  His sword in battle keen."
But aye she loot the tears downfa'
  For Jock o' Hazeldean.

" A chain of gold ye shall not lack,
  Nor braid to bind your hair,
Nor mettled hound, nor managed hawk,
  Nor palfrey fresh and fair ;

And you the foremost of them a'
  Shall ride, our forest queen."
But aye she loot the tears downfa'
  For Jock o' Hazeldean.

The kirk was deck'd at morning-tide,
  The tapers glimmer'd fair ;
The priest and bridegroom wait the bride,
  But ne'er a bride was there.
They sought her baith by bower and ha' ;
  The lady was not seen :
She's o'er the Border, and awa'
  Wi' Jock o' Hazeldean.

LIGHT LOVE.

A weary lot is thine, fair Maid !
  A weary lot is thine :
To pull the thorn thy brow to braid,
  And press the rue for wine.
A lightsome eye, a soldier's mien,
  A feather of the blue,
A doublet of the Lincoln green,—
  No more of me you knew,
          My Love !
No more of me you knew.

This morn is merry June, I trow
  The rose is budding fain ;
But she shall bloom in winter snow
  Ere we two meet again.
He turned his charger as he spake,
  Upon the river shore ;
He gave his bridle rein a shake,—
  Said Adieu forevermore,
          My Love !
And Adieu forevermore !

DEATH-CHANT.

Wasted, weary, wherefore stay,
Wrestling thus with earth and clay?
From the body pass away!
   Hark! the mass is singing.

From thee doff thy mortal weed!
Mary Mother be thy speed!
Saints to help thee at thy need!
   Hark! the knell is ringing.

Fear not snow-drift driving fast,
Sleet, or hail, or levin blast!
Soon the shroud shall lap thee fast,
And the sleep be on thee cast
   That shall ne'er know waking.

Haste thee, haste thee to be gone!
Earth flits fast, and time draws on:
Gasp thy gasp, and groan thy groan!
   Day is near the breaking.

PROUD MAISIE.

Proud Maisie is in the wood,
   Walking so early;
Sweet Robin sits on the bush,
   Singing so rarely.

" Tell me, thou bonny bird!
   When shall I marry me?"
" When six braw gentlemen
   Kirkward shall carry thee."

" Who makes the bridal bed?
   Birdie! say truly."
" The grey-headed sexton
   That delves the grave duly.

II.—3

" The glowworm o'er grave and stone
Shall light thee steady ;
The owl from the steeple sing
Welcome, proud Lady ! "

JAMES MONTGOMERY.
1771—1854.

THE BLACKBIRD.

MORNING :

Golden Bill ! Golden Bill !
Lo, the peep of day :
All the air is cool and still :
From the elm-tree on the hill
Chant away !
While the moon drops down the West,
Like thy mate upon her nest,
And the stars before the sun
Melt like snowflakes, one by one,
Let thy loud and welcome lay
Pour along
Few notes, but strong !

EVENING :

Jet-bright Wing ! Jet-bright Wing !
Flit across the sunset glade :
Lying there in wait to sing,
Listen with thy head awry,
Keeping time with twinkling eye,
While from all the woodland shade
Birds of every plume and note
Strain the throat,
Till both hill and valley ring,
And the warbled minstrelsy,
Ebbing, flowing, like the sea,
Claims brief interludes from thee !

Then with simple swell and fall,
Breaking beautiful through all,
Let thy Pan-like pipe repeat
Few notes, but sweet!

WINTER LIGHTNING.

The flash at midnight,—'twas a light
That gave the blind a moment's sight,
　　Then sunk in tenfold gloom ;
Loud, deep, and long, the thunder broke,
The deaf ear instantly awoke,
　　Then closed as in the tomb :
An angel might have pass'd my bed,
Sounded the trump of God, and fled.

So Life appears : a sudden birth,
A glance revealing heaven and earth ;
　　It is, and it is not!
So Fame the poet's hope deceives,
Who sings for after-time, and leaves
　　A name—to be forgot.
Life is a lightning-flash of breath ;
Fame but a thunder-clap at death.

JAMES HOGG.

1772—1835.

TO THE LARK.

Bird of the wilderness !
Blithesome and cumberless,—
Sweet be thy matin, o'er moorland and lea !
　　Emblem of happiness !
　　Bless'd is thy dwelling-place :
O to abide in the desert with thee !

Wild is thy lay, and loud,
Far in the downy cloud :

Love gives it energy, love gave it birth.
　　Where on thy dewy wing,
　　Where art thou journeying ?
Thy lay is in heaven, thy love is on earth.

　　O'er fell, and fountain sheen,
　　O'er moor and mountain green,
O'er the red streamer that heralds the Day,
　　Over the cloudlet dim,
　　Over the rainbow's rim,
Musical Cherub ! soar singing away !

　　Then, when the gloaming comes,
　　Low in the heather blooms
Sweet will thy welcome and bed of love be :
　　Emblem of happiness !
　　Bless'd is thy dwelling-place :
O to abide in the desert with thee !

MAGGIE AWAY.

　　O, what will a' the lads do
　　　　When Maggie gangs away ?
　　O what will a' the lads do
　　　　When Maggie gangs away ?
　　There's no a heart in a' the glen
　　　　That doesna dread the day :
　　O, what will a' the lads do
　　　　When Maggie gangs away ?

　　Young Jock has ta'en the hill for't,—
　　　　A waefu' wight is he ;
　　Poor Harry's ta'en the bed for't,
　　　　And laid him down to dee ;
　　And Sandy's gane unto the kirk,
　　　　And learnin' fast to pray :
　　And O, what will the lads do
　　　　When Maggie gangs away ?

The young laird o' the Lang-Shaw
  Has drunk her health in wine ;
The priest has said (in confidence)
  The lassie was divine :
And that is mair in maiden's praise
  Than any priest should say :
But O ! what will the lads do
  When Maggie gangs away ?

The wailing in our green glen
  That day will quaver high ;
'Twill draw the red-breast frae the wood,
  The laverock frae the sky ;
The fairies frae their beds o' dew
  Will rise and join the lay :
And hey ! what a day will be
  When Maggie gangs away !

CHARLES LAMB.

1775—1834.

HESTER.

When maidens such as Hester die,
Their place ye may not well supply,
Though ye among a thousand try,
  With vain endeavour.

A month or more hath she been dead,
Yet can I not by force be led
To think upon the wormy bed
  And her together.

A springy motion in her gait,
A rising step, did indicate
Of pride and joy no common rate
  That flush'd her spirit :

I know not by what name beside
I shall it call,—if 'twas not pride,
It was a joy to that allied
    She did inherit.

Her parents held the Quaker rule,
Which doth the human feeling cool ;
But she was train'd in Nature's school,—
    Nature had bless'd her.

A waking eye, a prying mind,
A heart that stirs, is hard to bind :
A hawk's keen sight ye can not blind,—
    Ye could not Hester.

My sprightly Neighbor ! gone before
To that unknown and silent shore :
Shall we not meet, as heretofore
    Some summer morning ?

When from thy cheerful eyes a ray
Hath struck a bliss upon the day,
A bliss that would not go away,
    A sweet forewarning.

THE OLD FAMILIAR FACES.

I have had playmates, I have had companions,
In my days of childhood, in my joyful school-days :
All, all are gone, the old familiar faces !

I have been laughing, I have been carousing,
Drinking late, sitting late, with my bosom cronies :
All, all are gone, the old familiar faces !

I loved a Love once, fairest among women ;
Closed are her doors on me, I must not see her ;
All, all are gone, the old familiar faces !

I have a friend, a kinder friend has no man :
Like an ingrate, I left my friend abruptly ;
Left him, to muse on the old familiar faces.

Ghost-like I paced round the haunts of my childhood :
Earth seem'd a desert I was bound to traverse,
Seeking to find the old familiar faces.

Friend of my bosom ! thou more than a brother !
Why wert thou not born in my father's dwelling ?
So might we talk of the old familiar faces :

How some they have died, and some they have left me,
And some are taken from me,—all are departed.
All, all are gone, the old familiar faces !

THE GYPSY'S MALISON.

" Suck, baby ! suck ! mother's love grows by giving :
Drain the sweet founts that only thrive by wasting !
Black manhood comes, when riotous guilty living
Hands thee the cup that shall be death in tasting.

" Kiss, baby ! kiss ! mother's lips shine by kisses :
Choke the warm breath that else would fall in blessings !
Black manhood comes, when turbulent guilty blisses
Tend thee the kiss that poisons 'mid caressings.

" Hang, baby ! hang ! mother's love loves such forces :
Strain the fond neck that bends still to thy clinging !
Black manhood comes, when violent lawless courses
Leave thee a spectacle in rude air swinging."

So sang a wither'd beldam energetical ;
And bann'd the ungiving door with lips prophetical.

WALTER SAVAGE LANDOR.

1775—1864.

TO HESPERUS.

Hesperus! hail! thy winking light
  Best befriends the lover,
Whom the sadder Moon for spite
  Gladly would discover.

Thou art fairer far than she,
  Fairer far, and chaster:
She may guess who smiled on me,
  I know who embraced her.

Pan of Arcady,—'twas Pan,
  In the tamarisk-bushes:
Bid her tell thee, if she can,
  Where were then her blushes!

And, were I inclined to tattle,
  I could name a second
Whom, asleep with sleeping cattle,
  To her cave she beckon'd.

Hesperus! hail! thy friendly ray
  Watches o'er the lover,
Lest the nodding beams betray,
  Lest the Moon discover.

Phrynè heard my kisses given
  Actè's rival bosom:
'Twas the buds (I swore by heaven)
  Bursting into blossom.

What she heard, and half espied
  By the gleam, she doubted;
And with arms uplifted cried—
  " How they must have sprouted!"

Hesperus ! hail again ! thy light
  Best befriends the lover,
Whom the sadder Moon for spite
  Gladly would discover.

RUBIES.

Often have I heard it said
That her lips are ruby-red :
Little heed I what they say,—
I have seen as red as they.
Ere she smiled on other men,
Real rubies were they then.

When she kiss'd me once in play,
Rubies were less bright than they ;
And less bright were those which shone
In the palace of the Sun.
Will they be as bright agen ?
Not if kiss'd by other men.

THE NEREID.

Beloved the last ! beloved the most !
  With willing arms and brow benign
Receive a bosom tempest-toss'd,
  And bid it ever beat to thine !

The Nereid Maids, in days of yore,
  Saw the lost pilot loose the helm,
Saw the wreck blacken all the shore,
  And every wave some head o'erwhelm.

Afar, the youngest of the train
  Beheld (but fear'd and aided not)
A minstrel from the billowy main
  Borne breathless near her coral grot.

Then terror fled, and pity rose :
  "Ah me !" she cried, "I come too late !
Rather than not have soothed his woes
  I would, but may not, share his fate."

She raised his hand : "What hand like this
  Could reach the heart, athwart the lyre !
What lips like these return my kiss,
  Or breathe, incessant, soft desire !"

From eve to morn, from morn to eve,
  She gazed his features o'er and o'er :
And those who love and who believe
  May hear her sigh along the shore.

THE MAID'S LAMENT.

I loved him not ; and yet, now he is gone,
  I feel I am alone.
I check'd him while he spoke ; yet could he speak,
  Alas ! I would not check.
For reasons not to love him once I sought,
  And wearied all my thought
To vex myself and him ; I now would give
  My love, could he but live
Who lately lived for me and, when he found
  'Twas vain, in holy ground
He hid his face amid the shades of death.
  I waste for him my breath
Who wasted his for me ; but mine returns
  And this lorn bosom burns
With stifling heat, heaving it up in sleep,
  And waking me to weep
Tears that had melted his soft heart : for years
  Wept he as bitter tears.
"Merciful God !"—such was his latest prayer :
  "These may she never share !"

Quieter is his breath, his breast more cold
    Than daisies in the mould,
Where children spell athwart the churchyard-gate
    His name and life's brief date.
Pray for him, gentle souls! whoe'er you be ;
    And O, pray too for me!

MARGARET.

Mother! I cannot mind my wheel ;
My fingers ache, my lips are dry.
O, if you felt that pain I feel——
But O, who ever felt as I ?
No longer could I doubt him true :
All other men may use deceit,—
He always said my eyes were blue,
And often swore my lips were sweet.

TO YOUTH.

Where art thou gone ? light-ankled Youth !
    With wing at either shoulder,
And smile that never left thy mouth
    Until the hours grew colder.

Then somewhat seem'd to whisper near
    That thou and I must part :
I doubted it,—I felt no fear,
    No weight upon the heart.

If aught befell it, Love was by
    And roll'd it off again :
So, if there ever was a sigh,
    'Twas not a sigh of pain.

I may not call thee back ; but thou
    Returnest when the hand
Of gentle Sleep waves o'er my brow
    His poppy-crested wand.

Then smiling eyes bend over mine ;
  Then lips, once press'd, invite :
But Sleep hath given a silent sign,
  And both, alas ! take flight.

ERINNA TO LOVE.

Who breathes to thee the holiest prayer,
  O Love ! is ever least thy care.
Alas ! I may not ask thee why 'tis so :
  Because a fiery scroll I see
  Hung at the throne of Destiny,—
" Reason with Love and register with Woe ! "

Few question thee, for thou art strong,
  And, laughing loud at Right and Wrong,
Seizest and dashest down the rich, the poor ;
  Thy sceptre's iron studs alike
  The meaner and the prouder strike,
And wise and simple fear thee and adore.

THOMAS CAMPBELL.

1777—1844.

THE BATTLE OF THE BALTIC.

Of Nelson and the North
Sing the glorious day's renown !
When to battle fierce came forth
All the might of Denmark's Crown,
And her arms along the deep proudly shone :
By each gun the lighted brand
In a bold determined hand,
And the Prince of all the land
                    Led them on.

Like leviathans afloat
Lay their bulwarks on the brine

While the sign of battle flew
On the lofty British line :
It was ten of April morn by the chime.
As they drifted on their path
There was silence deep as death,
And the boldest held his breath
              For a time.

But the might of England flush'd
To anticipate the scene ;
And her van the fleeter rush'd
O'er the deadly space between :
" Hearts of oak ! " our captains cried : when each gun
From its adamantine lips
Spread a death-shade round the ships,
Like the hurricane eclipse
              Of the sun.

Again ! again ! again !
And the havoc did not slack
Till a feeble cheer the Dane
To our cheering sent us back ;
Their shots along the deep slowly boom ;—
Then ceased ;—and all is wail,
As they strike the shatter'd sail,
Or in conflagration pale
              Light the gloom.

Out spoke the Victor then,
As he hail'd them o'er the wave :
" Ye are brothers ! ye are men !
And we conquer but to save,—
So peace instead of death let us bring !
But yield, proud foe ! thy fleet,
With the crews, at England's feet,
And make submission meet
              To our king ! "

Then Denmark bless'd our chief,
That he gave her wounds repose :
And the sounds of joy and grief
From her people wildly rose,
As Death withdrew his shades from the day ;
While the sun look'd smiling bright
O'er a wide and woeful sight
Where the fires of funeral light
              Died away.

Now joy, Old England ! raise
For the tidings of thy might,
By the festal cities' blaze
Whilst the wine-cup shines in light !
And yet, amidst that joy and uproar,
Let us think of them that sleep,
Full many a fathom deep,
By thy wild and stormy steep,
              Elsinore !

Brave hearts ! to Britain's pride,
Once so faithful and so true,
On the deck of Fame that died
With the gallant good Riou :
Soft sigh the winds of heaven o'er their grave !
While the billow mournful rolls,
And the mermaid's song condoles,
Singing Glory to the souls
              Of the Brave !

THE MARINERS OF ENGLAND.

Ye Mariners of England !
That guard our native seas,—
Whose flag has braved a thousand years
The battle and the breeze,—
Your glorious standard launch again,

To match another foe ;
And sweep through the deep
While the stormy winds do blow,—
While the battle rages loud and long
And the stormy winds do blow !

The spirits of your fathers
Shall start from every wave :
For the deck it was their field of fame,
And ocean was their grave.
Where Blake and mighty Nelson fell
Your manly hearts shall glow,
As ye sweep through the deep
While the stormy winds do blow,—
While the battle rages loud and long
And the stormy winds do blow.

Britannia needs no bulwarks,
No towers along the steep :
Her march is o'er the mountain wave,
Her home is on the deep.
With thunders from her native oak
She quells the floods below,
As they roar on the shore
When the stormy winds do blow,—
When the battle rages loud and long
And the stormy winds do blow.

The meteor flag of England
Shall yet terrific burn
Till danger's troubled night depart
And the star of peace return.
Then, then, ye Ocean-Warriors !
Our song and feast shall flow
To the fame of your name,
When the storm has ceased to blow,—
When the fiery fight is heard no more,
And the storm has ceased to blow.

HALLOWED GROUND.

What's hallow'd ground ?   Has earth a clod
Its Maker mean'd not should be trod
By Man, the image of his God,
          Erect and free,
Unscourged by Superstition's rod
          To bow the knee ?

That's hallow'd ground where, mourn'd and miss'd,
The lips repose our love has kiss'd :
But where's their memory's mansion ?   Is't
          Yon churchyard's bowers ?
No ! in ourselves their souls exist,
          A part of ours.

A kiss can consecrate the ground
Where mated hearts are mutual bound :
The spot where love's first links were wound,
          That ne'er are riven,
Is hallow'd down to earth's profound
          And up to heaven.

For time makes all but true love old :
The burning thoughts that then were told
Run molten still in memory's mould,
          And will not cool,
Until the heart itself be cold
          In Lethè's pool.

What hallows ground where heroes sleep ?
'Tis not the sculptured piles you heap :
In dews that heavens far distant weep
          Their turf may bloom,
Or genii twine beneath the deep
          Their coral tomb.

But strew his ashes to the wind
Whose sword or voice has served mankind !

And is he dead, whose glorious mind
          Lifts thine on high?
To live in hearts we leave behind
          Is not to die.

Is't death to fall for Freedom's right?
He's dead alone that lacks her light;
And Murder sullies in Heaven's sight
          The sword he draws:
What can alone ennoble fight?
          A noble cause.

Give that, and welcome War to brace
Her drums and rend heaven's reeking space!
The colours planted face to face,
          The charging cheer,
Though Death's Pale Horse lead on the chase,
          Shall still be dear.

And place our trophies where men kneel
To Heaven!——but Heaven rebukes my zeal:
The cause of Truth and human weal,
          O God above!
Transfer it from the sword's appeal
          To Peace and Love!

Peace! Love! the cherubim that join
Their spread wings o'er Devotion's shrine:
Prayers sound in vain, and temples shine,
          Where they are not;
The heart alone can make divine
          Religion's spot.

To incantations dost thou trust,
And pompous rites in domes august?
See mouldering stones and metal's rust
          Belie the vaunt
     II.—4

That men can bless one pile of dust
          With chime or chant !

The ticking wood-worm mocks thee, Man !
Thy temples——creeds themselves grow wan :
But there's a dome of nobler span,
          A temple given
Thy faith, that bigots dare not ban,—
          Its space is heaven :

Its roof star-pictured Nature's ceiling,
Where, trancing the rapt spirit's feeling
And God himself to Man revealing,
          The harmonious spheres
Make music, though unheard their pealing
          By mortal ears.

Fair Stars ! are not your beings pure ?
Can sin, can death your worlds obscure ?
Else why so swell the thoughts at your
          Aspect above ?
Ye must be Heavens that make us sure
          Of heavenly love.

And in your harmony sublime
I read the doom of distant time :
That Man's regenerate soul from crime
          Shall yet be drawn,
And Reason on his mortal clime,
          Immortal dawn.

What's hallow'd ground ?   'Tis what gives birth
To sacred thoughts in souls of worth :
Peace ! Independence ! Truth ! go forth
          Earth's compass round !
And your high priesthood shall make earth
          All hallow'd ground.

THOMAS MOORE.
1779—1852.

THEN FARE THEE WELL!

Then fare thee well, my own dear Love!
   This world has now for us
No greater grief, no pain above
    The pain of parting thus,
       Dear Love!
   The pain of parting thus.

Had we but known, since first we met,
   Some few short hours of bliss,
We might in numbering them forget
    The deep deep pain of this,
       Dear Love!
   The deep deep pain of this.

But no, alas! we've never seen
   One glimpse of pleasure's ray
But still there came a cloud between
    And chased it all away,
       Dear Love!
   And chased it all away.

Yet even could those sad moments last,
   Far dearer to my heart
Were hours of grief together pass'd
    Than years of mirth apart,
       Dear Love!
   Than years of mirth apart.

Farewell! our hope was born in fears
   And nursed 'mid vain regrets :
Like winter suns, it rose in tears,
    Like them in tears it sets,
       Dear Love!
   Like them in tears it sets.

PEACE BE AROUND THEE!

Peace be around thee wherever thou rovest!
  May life be for thee one summer's day,
And all that thou wishest, and all that thou lovest,
  Come smiling around thy sunny way!
If sorrow e'er this calm should break,
  May even thy tears pass off so lightly,
Like Spring showers they'll only make
  The smiles that follow shine more brightly!

May Time, who sheds his blight o'er all,
  And daily dooms some joy to death,
On thee let years so gently fall
  They shall not crush one flower beneath!
As half in shade and half in sun
  This world along its path advances,
May that side the sun's upon
  Be all that e'er shall meet thy glances!

BRING THE BRIGHT GARLANDS!

Bring the bright garlands hither,
  Ere yet a leaf is dying!
If so soon they must wither,
  Ours be their last sweet sighing!
Hark! that low dismal chime:
'Tis the dreary voice of Time.
O, bring beauty, bring roses,
  Bring all that yet is ours!
Let life's day as it closes
  Shine to the last through flowers!

Haste ere the bowl's declining!
  Drink of it now, or never!
Now, while Beauty is shining,
  Love! or she's lost for ever.

Hark ! again that dull chime :
'Tis the dreary voice of Time.
O, if life be a torrent
  Down to oblivion going,
Like this cup be its current,
  Bright to the last drop flowing !

BATTLE SONG.

O the sight entrancing
When morning's beam is glancing
    O'er files array'd,
    With helm and blade,
And plumes in the gay wind dancing !
When hearts are all high beating,
And the trumpet's voice repeating
    That song whose breath
    May lead to death
But never to retreating.
Then should some cloud pass over
The brow of sire or lover,
    Think 'tis the shade
    By Victory made,
Whose wings right o'er us hover !
O the sight entrancing,
When morning's beam is glancing
    O'er files array'd,
    With helm and blade,
And plumes in the gay wind dancing.

Yet 'tis not helm or feather :
For ask yon despot whether
    His plumèd bands
    Could bring such hands
And hearts as ours together !
Leave pomps to those who need 'em !

Give man but heart and freedom,
   And proud he braves
   The gaudiest slaves
That crawl where monarchs lead 'em.
The sword may pierce the beaver,
Stone walls in time may sever;
   'Tis mind alone,
   Worth steel and stone,
That keeps men free for ever.
O that sight entrancing,
When morning's beam is glancing
   O'er files array'd,
   With helm and blade,
And in Freedom's cause advancing !

AFTER DEFEAT.

Night closed around the conqueror's way,
  And lightnings show'd the distant hill
Where those who lost that dreadful day
  Stood, few and faint, but fearless still :
The soldier's hope, the patriot's zeal,
  For ever dimm'd, for ever cross'd,—
O ! who shall say what heroes feel
  When all but life and honour's lost ?

The last sad hours of Freedom's dream
  And Valour's task moved slowly by,
While mute they watch'd, till morning's beam
  Should rise and give them light to die.
There's yet a world where souls are free,
  Where Tyrants taint not Nature's bliss :
If death that world's bright opening be,
  O ! who would live a slave in this ?

HORACE SMITH.

1779—1849.

HYMN OF THE FLOWERS.

Day Stars ! that ope your frownless eyes to twinkle
.From rainbow galaxies of Earth's creation,
And dew-drops on her lonely altars sprinkle
　　　As a libation :

Ye Matin Worshipers ! who, bending lowly
Before the uprisen Sun, God's lidless eye,
Throw from your chalices a sweet and holy
　　　Incense on high :

Ye bright Mosaics ! that with storied beauty
The floor of Nature's temple tesselate :
What numerous emblems of instructive duty
　　　Your forms create !

'Neath cloistered boughs each floral bell that swingeth
And tolls its perfume on the passing air
Makes Sabbath in the fields, and ever ringeth
　　　A call to prayer :

Not to the domes where crumbling arch and column
Attest the feebleness of mortal hand,
But to that fane most catholic and solemn
　　　Which God hath plann'd,—

To that cathedral, boundless as our wonder,
Whose quenchless lamps the sun and moon supply,
Its choir the winds and waves, its organ thunder,
　　　Its dome the sky.

There, as in solitude and shade I wander
Through the green aisles or stretch'd upon the sod,
Awed by the silence, reverently ponder
　　　The ways of God,

Your voiceless lips, O Flowers ! are living preachers,
Each cup a pulpit and each leaf a book,
Supplying to my fancy numerous teachers
       From loneliest nook.

Floral Apostles ! that in dewy splendour
" Weep without woe and blush without a crime : "
O may I deeply learn, and ne'er surrender
       Your lore sublime !

" Thou wast not, Solomon ! in all thy glory
Array'd," the lilies cry, " in robes like ours :
How vain your grandeur ! ah, how transitory
       Are human flowers ! "

In the sweet-scented pictures, Heavenly Artist !
With which thou paintest Nature's wide-spread hall,
What a delightful lesson thou impartest
       Of love to all !

Not useless are ye, Flowers ! though made for pleasure ;
Blooming o'er field and wave, by day and night,
From every source your sanction bids me treasure
       Harmless delight.

Ephemeral Sages ! what instructors hoary
For such a world of thought could furnish scope ?
Each fading calyx a *memento mori*,
       Yet fount of hope !

Posthumous Glories ! angel-like collection,
Upraised from seed or bulb interr'd in earth :
Ye are to me a type of resurrection
       And second birth.

Were I in church-less solitudes remaining,
Far from all voice of teachers or divines,
My soul would find in flowers, of God's ordaining,
       Priests, sermons, shrines.

EBENEZER ELLIOTT.
1781—1849.

FLOWERS FOR THE HEART.

Flowers ! winter flowers ! The child is dead,
  The mother can not speak.
O, softly couch his little head !
  Or Mary's heart will break.
Amid those curls of flaxen hair
  This pale pink ribbon twine ;
And on the little bosom there
  Place this wan lock of mine !
How like a form in cold white stone
  The coffin'd infant lies !
Look, Mother ! on thy little one :
  And tears will fill thine eyes.
She can not weep ; more faint she grows,
  More deadly pale and still :—
Flowers ! O, a flower ! a winter rose,
  That tiny hand to fill.
Go, search the fields ! the lichen wet
  Bends o'er the unfailing well ;
Beneath the furrow lingers yet
  The scarlet pimpernel.
Peeps not a snowdrop in the bower
  Where never froze the spring ?
A daisy ? Ah, bring childhood's flower !
  The half-blown daisy bring !
Yes ! lay the daisy's little head
  Beside the little cheek ;
O haste ! The last of five is dead :
  The childless can not speak.

THE BRAMBLE-FLOWER.

Thy fruit full well the schoolboy knows,
   Wild bramble of the brake !
So put thou forth thy small white rose !
   I love it for his sake.
Though woodbines flaunt and roses glow
   O'er all the fragrant bowers,
Thou need'st not be ashamed to show
   Thy satin-threaded flowers :
For dull the eye, the heart is dull,
   That can not feel how fair,
Amid all beauty beautiful,
   Thy tender blossoms are ;
How delicate thy gauzy frill,
   How rich thy branchy stem,
How soft thy voice when woods are still
   And thou sing'st hymns to them,
While silent showers are falling slow
   And, 'mid the general hush,
A sweet air lifts the little bough,
   Lone whispering through the bush !
The primrose to the grave is gone ;
   The hawthorn flower is dead ;
The violet by the moss'd grey stone
   Hath laid her weary head :
But thou, wild bramble ! back dost bring,
   In all their beauteous power,
The fresh green days of life's fair Spring
   And boyhood's blossomy hour.
Scorn'd bramble of the brake ! once more
   Thou bidd'st me be a boy,
To gad with thee, the woodlands o'er,
   In freedom and in joy.

ELEGY ON WILLIAM COBBETT.

O bear him where the rain can fall,
  And where the winds can blow;
And let the sun weep o'er his pall
  As to the grave ye go!

And in some little lone churchyard,
  Beside the growing corn,
Lay gentle Nature's stern prose bard,
  Her mightiest peasant-born!

Yes! let the wild-flower wed his grave,
  That bees may murmur near,
When o'er his last home bend the brave,
  And say—" A man lies here! "

For Britons honour Cobbett's name,
  Though rashly oft he spoke;
And none can scorn, and few will blame,
  The low-laid heart of oak.

See, o'er his prostrate branches, see!
  E'en factious hate consents
To reverence, in the fallen tree,
  His British lineaments.

Though gnarl'd the storm-tost boughs that braved
  The thunder's gather'd scowl,
Not always through his darkness raved
  The storm-winds of the soul.

O, no! in hours of golden calm
  Morn met his forehead bold;
And breezy evening sang her psalm
  Beneath his dew-dropp'd gold.

The wren its crest of fibred fire
  With his rich bronze compared;

While many a youngling's songful sire
His acorn'd twiglets shared.

The lark, above, sweet tribute paid,
Where clouds with light were riven ;
And true love sought his blue-bell'd shade,
" To bless the hour of heaven."

E'en when his stormy voice was loud,
And guilt quaked at the sound,
Beneath the frown that shook the proud
The poor a shelter found.

Dead Oak ! thou livest.   Thy smitten hands,
The thunder of thy brow,
Speak, with strange tongues, in many lands,
And tyrants hear thee, now !

Beneath the shadow of thy name,
Inspired by thy renown,
Shall future patriots rise to fame,
And many a sun go down.

HANNAH RATCLIFFE.

If e'er she knew an evil thought,
She spoke no evil word :
Peace to the gentle !   She hath sought
The bosom of her Lord.

She lived to love, and loved to bless
Whatever He hath made ;
But early on her gentleness
His chastening hand he laid.

Like a maim'd linnet nursed with care,
She graced a home of bliss ;
And dwelt in thankful quiet there,
To show what goodness is.

Her presence was a noiseless power,
   That soothed us day by day,—
A modest, meek, secluded flower,
   That smiled, and pass'd away.

So meek she was that, when she died,
   We miss'd the lonely one
As when we feel, on Loxley's side,
   The silent sunshine gone.

But memory brings to sunless bowers
   The light they knew before :
And Hannah's quiet smile is ours,
   Though Hannah is no more.

Her pale face visits yet my heart,
   And oft my guest will be :
O White Rose ! thou shalt not depart,
   But wither here with me.

JAMES HENRY LEIGH HUNT.
1784—1859.

ABOU BEN ADHEM.

Abou Ben Adhem (may his tribe increase !)
Awoke one night from a deep dream of peace,
And saw within the moonlight in his room,
Making it rich and like a lily in bloom,
An Angel writing in a book of gold.
Exceeding peace had made Ben Adhem bold ;
And to the Presence in the room he said—
" What writest thou ? " The Vision raised its head ;
And, with a look made of all sweet accord,
Answer'd—" The names of those who love the Lord."
" And is mine one ? " said Abou. " Nay ! not so ! "
Replied the Angel. Abou spoke more low,
But cheerly still, and said—" I pray thee then,
Write me as One that loves his fellow men ! "

The Angel wrote, and vanish'd.   The next night
It came again, with a great wakening light,
And show'd their names whom love of God had bless'd :
And lo! Ben Adhem's name led all the rest.

SONG OF PEACE.

O Thou that art our Queen again,
And may in the sun be seen again,
    Come, Ceres! come!
    For the war's gone home,
And the fields are quiet and green again.

The air, dear Goddess! sighs for thee ;
The light-heart brooks arise for thee ;
    And the poppies red
    On their wistful bed
Turn up their dark blue eyes for thee.

Laugh out, in the loose green jerkin
That's fit for a Goddess to work in!
    With shoulders brown,
    And the wheaten crown
About thy temples perking.

And with thee come Stout-Heart in ;
And Toil, that sleeps his cart in ;
    And Exercise,
    The ruddy and wise,
His bathèd forelocks parting !

And Dancing too, that's lither
Than willow or birch, drop hither !
    To thread the place
    With a finishing grace
And carry our smooth eyes with her.

A NUN.

If you become a Nun, Dear!
  A Friar I will be :
In any cell you run, Dear!
  Pray look behind for me!
The roses all turn pale too ;
The doves all take the veil too ;
  The blind will see the show :
What! you become a Nun? my Dear!
  I'll not believe it. No!

If you become a Nun, Dear!
  The bishop Love will be ;
The Cupids, every one, Dear!
  Will chant—" We trust in thee ! "
The incense will go sighing ;
The candles fall a-dying ;
  The water turn to wine :
What! You go take the vows? my Dear!
  You may,—but they'll be mine.

GRASSHOPPER AND CRICKET.

Green little vaulter in the sunny grass,
Catching your heart up at the feel of June,—
Sole voice that's heard amidst the lazy noon,
When even the bees lag at the summoning brass !
And you, warm little housekeeper ! who class
With those who think the candles come too soon,
Loving the fire, and with your tricksome tune
Nick the glad silent moments as they pass :
O sweet and tiny cousins ! that belong,
One to the fields, the other to the hearth :
Both have your sunshine ; both, though small, are strong
At your clear hearts ; and both were sent on earth
To sing in thoughtful ears this natural song,
In-doors and out, summer and winter, Mirth.

TO HIS WIFE,

While she was modeling the Poet's bust.

Ah, Marian mine! the face you look on now
Is not exactly like my wedding-day's :
Sunk is its cheek, deeper-retired its gaze,
Less white and smooth its temple-flatten'd brow.
Sorrow has been there with his silent plough
And strait stern hand.   No matter! if it raise
Aught that affection fancies it may praise,
Or make me worthier of Apollo's bough.
Loss after all, such loss especially,
Is transfer, change, but not extinction.   No!
Part in our children's apple-cheeks I see;
And for the rest,—while you look at me so,
Take care you do not smile it back to me,
And miss the copied furrows as you go!

TO HIS PIANO-FORTE.

O Friend! whom glad or grave we seek,
    Heaven-holding shrine!
I ope thee, touch thee, hear thee speak,
    And peace is mine.
No fairy casket full of bliss
    Outvalues thee :
Love only, waken'd with a kiss,
    More sweet may be.

To thee, when our full hearts o'erflow
    In griefs or joys,
Unspeakable emotions owe
    A fitting voice :
Mirth flies to thee, and Love's unrest,
    And Memory dear ;
And Sorrow, with his tighten'd breast,
    Comes for a tear.

O, since few joys of human mould
    Thus wait us still,
Thrice bless'd be thine, thou gentle fold
    Of peace at will !
No change, no sullenness, no cheat,
    In thee we find :
Thy saddest voice is ever sweet,
    Thine answer kind.

ALLAN CUNNINGHAM.

1784—1842.

THE SUN IN FRANCE.

The sun rises bright in France,
  And fair sets he :
But he has tint the blithe blink he had
  In my ain countree.

O, it's nae my ain ruin
  That saddens aye my ee,
But the dear Marie I left behin'
  Wi' sweet bairnies three.

My lanely hearth burn'd bonnie,
  And smiled my ain Marie :
I've left a' my heart behin'
  In my ain countree.

The bud comes back to summer,
  And the blossom to the bee ;
But I'll win back——O, never !
  To my ain countree.

O I am leal to high Heaven,
  Where soon I hope to be :
And there I'll meet ye a'
  Frae my ain countree.

II.—5

GEORGE DARLEY.
1785—1849.

WAKING SONG.

Awake thee, my Lady-Love !
 Wake thee, and rise !
The sun through the bower peeps
 Into thine eyes.

Behold how the early lark
 Springs from the corn !
Hark, hark how the flower-bird
 Winds her wee horn !

The swallow's glad shriek is heard
 All through the air ;
The stock-dove is murmuring
 Loud as she dare.

Apollo's wing'd bugleman
 Can not contain,
But peals his loud trumpet-call
 Once and again.

Then wake thee, my Lady-Love !
 Bird of my bower !
The sweetest and sleepiest
 Bird at this hour.

SYLVIA'S SONG.

The streams that wind amid the hills
 And lost in pleasure slowly roam,
While their deep joy the valley fills,—
 Even these will leave their mountain home ;
  So may it, Love ! with others be,
  But I will never wend from thee.

The leaf forsakes the parent spray,
  The blossom quits the stem as fast ;
The rose-enamour'd bird will stray
  And leave his eglantine at last :
      So may it, Love ! with others be,
      But I will never wend from thee.

DIRGE.

Wail ! wail ye o'er the Dead !
    Wail, wail ye o'er her !
Youth's ta'en and Beauty's fled :
    O then deplore her !

Strew ! strew, ye Maidens ! strew
    Sweet flowers and fairest :
Pale rose, and pansy blue,
    Lily the rarest !
            Wail !——

Lay, lay her gently down
    On her moss pillow,
While we our foreheads crown
    With the sad willow !
            Wail !——

Raise, raise the song of woe,
    Youths ! to her honour ;
Fresh leaves and blossoms throw,
    Virgins ! upon her.
            Wail !——

Round, round the cypress bier
    Where she lies sleeping,
On every turf a tear,
    Let us go, weeping !
            Wail !——

THOMAS LOVE PEACOCK.
1785—1866.

CASTLES IN THE AIR.

My thoughts by night are often fill'd
  With visions false as fair :
For in the Past alone I build
  My castles in the air.

I dwell not now on what may be ;
  Night shadows o'er the scene :
But still my fancy wanders free
  Through that which might have been.

DAYS OF OLD.

In the days of old
Lovers felt true passion,
Deeming years of sorrow
By a smile repaid :
Now the charms of gold,
Spells of pride and fashion,
Bid them say Good-morrow
To the best-loved Maid.

Through the forests wild,
O'er the mountains lonely,
They were never weary
Honour to pursue :
If the Damsel smiled
Once in seven years only,
All their wanderings dreary
Ample guerdon knew.

Now one day's caprice
Weighs down years of smiling,
Youthful hearts are rovers,

Love is bought and sold.
Fortune's gifts may cease,
Love is less beguiling :
Wiser were the lovers
In the days of old.

MARGARET LOVE PEACOCK.

Three years old.

Long night succeeds thy little day :
    O, blighted blossom ! can it be
That this grey stone and grassy clay
    Have closed our anxious care of thee ?

The half-form'd speech of artless thought,
    That spoke a mind beyond thy years,
The song, the dance by Nature taught,
    The sunny smiles, the transient tears,

The symmetry of face and form,
    The eye with light and life replete,
The little heart so fondly warm,
    The voice so musically sweet,—

These, lost to hope, in memory yet
    Around the hearts that loved thee cling,
Shadowing with long and vain regret
    The too fair promise of thy Spring.

BRYAN WALLER PROCTER.

("BARRY CORNWALL.")

1787—1874.

___

THE STORMY PETREL.

A thousand miles from land are we,
Tossing about on the roaring sea,—
From billow to bounding billow cast,

Like fleecy snow on the stormy blast :
The sails are scatter'd abroad like weeds ;
The strong masts shake like quivering reeds ;
The mighty cables and iron chains,
The hull, which all earthly strength disdains,—
They strain and they crack : and hearts like stone
Their natural hard proud strength disown.

Up and down ! up and down !
From the base of the wave to the billow's crown :
And amidst the flashing and feathery foam
The Stormy Petrel finds a home :
A home, if such a place may be
For her who lives on the wide, wide sea,
On the craggy ice, in the frozen air,
And only seeketh her rocky lair
To warm her young and to teach them spring
At once o'er the waves on their stormy wing.

O'er the deep ! o'er the deep !
Where the whale and the shark and the sword-fish sleep,—
Outflying the blast and the driving rain,
The Petrel telleth her tale—in vain :
For the mariner curseth the warning bird
Who bringeth him news of the storms unheard.
Ah, thus does the prophet of good or ill
Meet hate from the creatures he serveth still !
Yet he ne'er falters.   So, Petrel ! spring
Once more o'er the waves on thy stormy wing !

TO OUR NEIGHBOUR'S HEALTH.

Send the red wine round to-night !
  For the blast is bitter cold :
Let us sing a song that's light !
  Merry rhymes are good as gold.

Here's unto Our Neighbour's health !
  O he plays the better part,—
Doing good, but not by stealth :
  Is he not a noble heart?

Should you bid me tell his name,
  Show wherein his virtues dwell :
'Faith (I speak it to my shame),
  I should scarce know what to tell.

" Is he—? " Sir ! he is a thing
  Cast in common human clay,—
'Tween a beggar and a king,—
  Fit to order or obey.

" He is then a soldier brave ? "
  No ! he doth not kill his kin,
Pampering the luxurious Grave
  With the blood and bones of Sin.

" Or a judge ? " He doth not sit,
  Making hucksters' bargains plain ;
Piercing cobwebs with his wit,
  Cutting tangled knots in twain.

" He's an Abbot then at least ? "
  No ! he is not proud and blithe,
Leaving prayer to humble priest,
  Whilst he champs the golden tithe.

He is brave, but he is meek,—
  Not as judge or soldier seems,
Not like Abbot proud and sleek :
  Yet his dreams are starry dreams,—

Such as lit the World of old
  Through the darkness of her way ;

Such as might, if clearly told,
  Guide blind Future into day.

Never hath he sought to rise
  On a friend's or neighbour's fall ;
Never slurr'd a foe with lies ;
  Never shrunk from Hunger's call :

But from morning until eve,
  And through Autumn into Spring,
He hath kept his course (believe !),
  Courting neither slave nor king.

He, whatever be his name
  (For I know it not aright),
He deserves a wider fame.
  Come ! here's to his health to-night.

BACCHANALIAN.

Sing !—Who sings
To her who weareth a hundred rings ?
  Ah, who is this lady fine ?
  The Vine, boys ! the Vine !
  The mother of mighty Wine.
    A roamer is she
    O'er wall and tree,
And sometimes very good company.

Drink !—Who drinks
To her who blusheth and never thinks ?
  Ah, who is this maid of thine ?
  The Grape, boys ! the Grape !
  O never let her escape
  Until she be turn'd to Wine !
    For better is she
    Than Vine can be,
And very very good company.

Dream !—Who dreams
Of the God who governs a thousand streams ?
    Ah, who is this Spirit fine ?
    'Tis Wine, boys ! 'tis Wine !
    God Bacchus, a friend of mine.
        O, better is he
        Than Grape or Tree,
And the best of all good company.

SONG.

Let us sing and sigh !
    Let us sigh and sing !
Sunny haunts have no such pleasures
    As the shadows bring.

Who would seek the crowd,
    Who would seek the noon,
That could woo the pale maid Silence
    Underneath the moon ?

Smiles are things for youth,
    Things for a merry rhyme :
But the voice of Pity suiteth
    Any mood or time.

I LOVE HIM.

I love him, I dream of him,
    I sing of him by day,
And all the night I hear him talk,—
    And yet, he's far away.

There's beauty in the morning ;
    There's sweetness in the May ;
There's music in the running stream :
    And yet, he's far away.

I love him, I trust in him ;
    He trusteth me alway :
And so the time flies hopefully,
    Although he's far away.

IGNORANCE IS BLISS.

Rains fall, suns shine, winds flee,
    Brooks run ; yet few know how :
Do not thou too deeply search
    Why thou lovest me now !

Perhaps, by some command
    Sent earthward from above,
Thy heart was doom'd to lean on mine,
    Mine to enjoy thy love.

Why ask when joy doth smile,
    From what bright heaven it fell ?
Men mar the beauty of their dreams,
    Tracing their source too well.

SHE WAS NOT FAIR.

She was not fair, nor full of grace,
    Nor crown'd with thought or aught beside,
No wealth had she of mind or face,
    To win our love or raise our pride ;
No lover's thought her cheek did touch,
    No poet's dream was round her thrown :
And yet we miss her,—ah ! too much,
    Now she hath flown.

We miss her when the morning calls,
    As one that mingled in our mirth ;
We miss her when the evening falls,—
    A trifle wanted on the earth :

Some fancy small or subtle thought
  Is check'd ere to its blossom grown,
Some chain is broken that we wrought,—
  Now she hath flown.

No solid good nor hope defined
  Is marr'd now she hath sunk in night;
And yet the strong immortal Mind
  Is stopp'd in its triumphant flight.
Stern friend! what power is in a tear,
  What strength in one poor thought alone,
When all we know is—She was here
  And She hath flown!

THE POET TO HIS WIFE.

How many summers, Love!
  Have I been thine?
How many days, thou Dove!
  Hast thou been mine?
Time, like the winged wind
  When it bends the flowers,
Hath left no mark behind
  To count the hours.

Some weight of thought, though loath,
  On thee he leaves;
Some lines of care round both
  Perhaps he weaves;
Some fears, a soft regret
  For joys scarce known;
Sweet looks we half forget:
  All else is flown.

Ah! with what thankless heart
  I mourn and sing!
Look, where our children start
  Like sudden Spring!

  With tongues all sweet and low,
   Like a pleasant rhyme,
  They tell how much I owe
   To Thee and Thine.

RICHARD HENRY DANA.

1787—1879.

THE LITTLE BEACHBIRD.

Thou little bird! thou dweller by the sea!
Why takèst thou its melancholy voice,
  And with that boding cry
  O'er the waves dost thou fly?
O rather, bird! with me
Through the fair land rejoice!

Thy flitting form comes ghostly dim and pale,
As driven by the beating storm at sea;
  Thy cry is weak and scared,
  As if thy mates had shared
The doom of us; thy wail—
What does it bring to me?

Thou call'st along the sand and haunt'st the surge,
Restless and sad, as if, in strange accord
  With the motion and the roar
  Of waves that drive to shore,
One spirit did ye urge,—
The Mystery—the Word.

Of thousands thou both sepulchre and pall,
Old Ocean! art. A requiem o'er the dead
  From out thy gloomy cells
  A tale of mourning tells:
Tells of man's woe and fall,
His sinless glory fled.

Then turn thee, little bird ! and take thy flight
Where the complaining sea shall sadness bring
   Thy spirit never more !
   Come, quit with me the shore
For gladness and the light
Where birds of summer sing !

GEORGE GORDON BYRON (LORD BYRON).
1788—1824.

THE ISLES OF GREECE.

The Isles of Greece ! the Isles of Greece !
   Where burning Sappho loved and sung,—
Where grew the arts of war and peace,
   Where Delos rose, and Phœbus sprung !
Eternal summer gilds them yet :
But all except their sun is set.

The Scian and the Teian muse,
   The hero's harp, the lover's lute,
Have found the fame your shores refuse ;
   Their place of birth alone is mute
To sounds which echo further West
Than your sires' " Islands of the Bless'd."

The mountains look on Marathon,
   And Marathon looks on the sea ;
And musing there an hour alone
   I dream'd that Greece might still be free :
For standing on the Persians' grave
I could not deem myself a slave.

A King sate on the rocky brow
   Which looks o'er sea-born Salamis,
And ships by thousands lay below,
   And men in nations,—all were his ;
He counted them at break of day ;
But when the sun set where were they ?

And where are they ?   And where art thou ?
  My Country !   On thy voiceless shore
The heroic lay is tuneless now,
  The heroic bosom beats no more.
And must thy lyre, so long divine,
Degenerate into hands like mine ?

'Tis something in the dearth of fame,
  Though link'd among a fetter'd race,
To feel at least a patriot's shame,
  Even as I sing, suffuse my face :
For what is left the poet here ?
For Greeks a blush—for Greece a tear.

Must we but weep o'er days more bless'd ?
  Must we but blush ?   Our fathers bled.
Earth ! render back from out thy breast
  A remnant of our Spartan dead !
Of the Three Hundred grant but three,
To make a new Thermopylæ !

What ! silent still ? and silent all ?
  Ah, no ! the voices of the Dead
Sound like a distant torrent's fall,
  And answer—" Let one living head,
But one arise,—we come, we come ! "
'Tis but the living who are dumb.

In vain ! in vain !—Strike other chords !
  Fill high the cup with Samian wine !
Leave battles to the Turkish hordes,
  And shed the blood of Scio's vine !
Hark ! rising to the ignoble call,
How answers each bold Bacchanal !

You have the Pyrrhic dance as yet :
  Where is the Pyrrhic phalanx gone ?
Of two such lessons, why forget

The nobler and the manlier one ?
You have the letters Cadmus gave :
Think ye he mean'd them for a slave ?

Fill high the bowl with Samian wine !
    We will not think of themes like these.
It made Anacreon's song divine ;
    He served——but served Polycrates :
A tyrant,—but our masters then
Were still at least our countrymen.

The tyrant of the Chersonese
    Was Freedom's best and bravest friend :
That tyrant was Miltiades :
    O that the present hour would lend
Another despot of the kind !
Such chains as his were sure to bind.

Fill high the bowl with Samian wine !
    On Suli's rock, and Parga's shore,
Exists the remnant of a line
    Such as the Doric mothers bore ;
And there perhaps some seed is sown
The Heracleidan blood might own.

Trust not for freedom to the Franks !
    They have a king who buys and sells :
In native swords and native ranks
    The only hope of courage dwells ;
But Turkish force and Latin fraud
Would break your shield however broad.

Fill high the bowl with Samian wine !
    Our virgins dance beneath the shade :
I see their glorious black eyes shine ;
    But, gazing on each glowing maid,
My own the burning tear-drop laves,
To think such breasts must suckle slaves.

Place me on Sunium's marbled steep,
  Where nothing save the waves and I
May hear our mutual murmurs sweep!
  There, swan-like, let me sing and die!
A Land of Slaves shall ne'er be mine:
Dash down yon cup of Samian wine!

TO THYRZA.

And thou art dead! as young and fair
  As aught of mortal birth:
And form so soft, and charms so rare,
  Too soon return'd to Earth.
Though Earth received them in her bed,
And o'er the spot the crowd may tread
  In carelessness of mirth,
There is an eye which could not brook
A moment on that grave to look.

I will not ask where thou liest low,
  Nor gaze upon the spot:
There flowers or weeds at will may grow,
  So I behold them not.
It is enough for me to prove
That what I loved, and long must love,
  Like common earth can rot.
To me there needs no stone to tell
'Tis Nothing that I loved so well.

Yet did I love thee to the last,
  As fervently as thou
Who didst not change through all the past,
  And canst not alter now.
The love where Death has set his seal
Nor age can chill, nor rival steal,
  Nor falsehood disavow;
And, what were worse, thou canst not see
Or wrong or change or fault in me.

The better days of life were ours,
  The worst can be but mine ;
The sun that cheers, the storm that lours,
  Shall never more be thine :
The silence of that dreamless sleep
I envy now too much to weep ;
  Nor need I to repine
That all those charms have pass'd away
I might have watch'd through long decay.

The flower in ripen'd bloom unmatch'd
  Must fall the earliest prey ;
Though by no hand untimely snatch'd,
  The leaves must drop away :
And yet it were a greater grief
To watch it withering, leaf by leaf,
  Than see it plucked to-day,—
Since earthly eye but ill can bear
To trace the change to foul from fair.

I know not if I could have borne
  To see thy beauties fade :
The night that follow'd such a morn
  Had worn a deeper shade.
Thy day without a cloud hath pass'd,
And thou wert lovely to the last,
  Extinguish'd, not decay'd :
As stars that shoot along the sky
Shine brightest as they fall from high.

As once I wept—if I could weep,
  My tears might well be shed
To think I was not near to keep
  One vigil o'er thy bed ;
To gaze, how fondly ! on thy face,
To fold thee in a faint embrace,
  Uphold thy drooping head,
  II.—6

And show that love, however vain,
Nor thou nor I can feel again.

Yet how much less it were to gain
  (Though thou hast left me free)
The loveliest things that still remain,
  Than thus remember thee:
The all of thine that can not die
Through dark and dread eternity
  Returns again to me;
And more thy buried love endears
Than aught, except its living years.

SONG OF SAUL.

BEFORE HIS LAST BATTLE.

Warriors and chiefs! should the shaft or the sword
Pierce me in leading the host of the Lord,
Heed not the corse, though a king's, in your path!
Bury your steel in the bosoms of Gath!

Thou who art bearing my buckler and bow!
Should the soldiers of Saul look away from the foe,
Stretch me that moment in blood at thy feet!
Mine be the doom which they dared not to meet!

Farewell to others! but never we part,
Heir to my royalty, son of my heart!
Bright is the diadem, boundless the sway,—
Or kingly the death which awaits us to-day.

THE PATRIOT.

Thy days are done, thy fame begun;
  Thy country's strains record
The triumphs of her chosen son,
  The slaughters of his sword:
The deeds he did, the fields he won,
  The freedom he restored.

Though thou art fallen, while we are free
  Thou shalt not taste of death :
The generous blood that flow'd from thee
  Disdain'd to sink beneath ;
Within our veins its currents be,
  Thy spirit in our breath.

Thy name, our charging hosts along,
  Shall be the battle-word ;
Thy fall the theme of choral song
  From virgin voices pour'd :
To weep would do thy glory wrong,—
  Thou shalt not be deplored !

SHE WALKS IN BEAUTY.

She walks in beauty, like the night
Of cloudless climes and starry skies,
And all that's best of dark and bright
Meets in her aspect and her eyes :
Thus mellow'd to that tender light
Which heaven to gaudy day denies.

One shade the more, one ray the less,
Had half impair'd the nameless grace
Which waves in every raven tress
Or softly lightens o'er her face,
Where thoughts serenely sweet express
How pure, how dear their dwelling-place.

And on that cheek, and o'er that brow,
So soft, so calm, yet eloquent,
The smiles that win, the tints that glow,
But tell of days in goodness spent,—
A mind at peace with all below,
A heart whose love is innocent.

BYRON'S LAST VERSE.

"On this day I complete my thirty-sixth year."

'Tis time this heart should be unmoved,
  Since others it hath ceased to move:
Yet, though I can not be beloved,
      Still let me love!

My days are in the yellow leaf;
  The flowers and fruits of love are gone:
The worm, the canker, and the grief,
      Are mine alone.

The fire that on my bosom preys
  Is lone as some volcanic isle:
No torch is kindled at its blaze,—
      A funeral pile.

The hope, the fear, the jealous care,
  The exalted portion of the pain
And power of love, I can not share,
      But wear the chain.

But 'tis not thus, and 'tis not here,
  Such thoughts should shake my soul, nor now,—
Where glory decks the hero's bier
      Or binds his brow.

The sword, the banner, and the field,—
  Glory and Greece, around me see!
The Spartan borne upon his shield
      Was not more free.

Awake——not Greece! she is awake:
  Awake, my Spirit!   Think through whom
Thy life-blood tracks its parent lake,
      And then strike home!

Tread those reviving passions down,
  Unworthy manhood!   Unto thee

Indifferent should the smile or frown
     Of Beauty be.

If thou regret'st thy youth, why live?
   The land of honourable death
Is here. Up, to the field, and give
     Away thy breath!

Seek out (less often sought than found)
  A soldier's grave, for thee the best!
Then look around, and choose thy ground,
     And take thy rest!

PERCY BYSSHE SHELLEY.

1792—1822.

TO A SKYLARK.

Hail to thee, blithe Spirit!
  Bird thou never wert,
That from heaven, or near it,
  Pourest thy full heart
In profuse strains of unpremeditated art.

Higher still and higher
  From the earth thou springest;
Like a cloud of fire,
  The blue deep thou wingest;
And singing still dost soar, and soaring ever singest.

In the golden lightning
  Of the sunken sun,
O'er which clouds are brightening,
  Thou dost float and run,
Like an unbodied Joy whose race is just begun.

The pale purple even
  Melts around thy flight:

Like a star of heaven
  In the broad daylight,
Thou art unseen, but yet I hear thy shrill delight:

Keen as are the arrows
  Of that silver sphere
Whose intense lamp narrows
  In the white dawn clear
Until we hardly see, we feel that it is there.

All the earth and air
  With thy voice is loud,
As, when night is bare,
  From one lonely cloud
The moon rains out her beams, and heaven is overflow'd.

What thou art we know not:
  What is most like thee?
From rainbow clouds there flow not
  Drops so bright to see
As from thy presence showers a rain of melody.

Like a poet hidden
  In the light of thought,
Singing hymns unbidden,
  Till the world is wrought
To sympathy with hopes and fears it heeded not.

Like a high-born maiden
  In a palace tower,
Soothing her love-laden
  Soul in secret hour
With music sweet as love, which overflows her bower.

Like a glow-worm golden
  In a dell of dew,
Scattering unbeholden
  Its aërial hue
Among the flowers and grass which screen it from the view.

Like a rose embower'd
    In its own green leaves,
By warm winds deflower'd,
    Till the scent it gives
Makes faint with too much sweet these heavy-winged thieves.

Sound of vernal showers
    On the twinkling grass,
Rain-awaken'd flowers,
    All that ever was
Joyous and clear and fresh, thy music doth surpass.

Teach us, sprite or bird !
    What sweet thoughts are thine :
I have never heard
    Praise of love or wine
That panted forth a flood of rapture so divine.

Chorus hymeneal,
    Or triumphal chant,
Match'd with thine would be all
    But an empty vaunt,
A thing wherein we feel there is some hidden want.

What objects are the fountains
    Of thy happy strain ?
What fields, or waves, or mountains ?
    What shapes of sky or plain ?
What love of thine own kind ? what ignorance of pain ?

With thy clear keen joyance
    Languor can not be ;
Shadow of annoyance
    Never came near thee ;
Thou lovèst, but ne'er knew love's sad satiety.

Waking or asleep,
    Thou of death must deem
Things more true and deep

Than we mortals dream,
Or how could thy notes flow in such a crystal stream ?

We look before and after,
And pine for what is not ;
Our sincerest laughter
With some pain is fraught ;
Our sweetest songs are those that tell of saddest thought.

Yet, if we could scorn
Hate and pride and fear,
If we were things born
Not to shed a tear,
I know not how thy joy we ever should come near.

Better than all measures
Of delightful sound,
Better than all treasures
That in books are found,
Thy skill to poet were, thou scorner of the ground !

Teach me half the gladness
That thy brain must know,
Such harmonious madness
From my lips would flow,
The world should listen then as I am listening now.

LINES TO AN INDIAN AIR.

I arise from dreams of Thee,
In the first sweet sleep of night,
When the winds are breathing low,
And the stars are shining bright :
I arise from dreams of Thee,
And a spirit in my feet
Has led me (who knows how ?)
To thy chamber window, Sweet !

The wandering airs, they faint
On the dark and silent stream,

The champak odours pine
Like sweet thoughts in a dream ;
The nightingale's complaint,
It dies upon her heart,—
As I must die on thine,
Belovèd as thou art !

O, lift me from the grass !
I die ! I faint ! I fail !
Let thy love in kisses rain
On my lips and eyelids pale !
My cheek is cold and white, alas !
My heart beats loud and fast :
O, press it close to thine again,
Where it will break at last.

TO NIGHT.

Swiftly walk over the Western wave,
　　Spirit of Night !
Out of the misty Eastern cave,
Where all the long and lone daylight
Thou wovèst dreams of joy and fear,
Which make thee terrible and dear :
　　Swift be thy flight !

Wrap thy form in a mantle grey,
　　Star-inwrought !
Blind with thine hair the eyes of Day !
Kiss him until he be wearied out !
Then wander o'er city and sea and land,
Touching all with thine opiate wand !
　　Come, long-sought !

When I arose and saw the dawn,
　　I sigh'd for thee :
When light rode high, and the dew was gone,
And noon lay heavy on flower and tree ;
And the weary Day turn'd to his rest,

Lingering like an unloved guest,
    I sigh'd for thee.

Thy brother Death came, and cried—
    " Wouldst thou me ? "
Thy sweet child, Sleep the filmy-eyed,
Murmur'd like a noontide bee—
" Shall I nestle by thy side ?
Wouldst thou me ? " And I replied—
    No ! not thee.

Death will come when thou art dead,
    Soon, too soon !
Sleep will come when thou art fled :
Of neither would I ask the boon
I ask of thee, belovèd Night !
Swift be thine approaching flight !
    Come soon, soon !

A BRIDAL SONG.

The golden gates of sleep unbar
    Where Strength and Beauty, met together,
Kindle their image like a star
    In a sea of glassy weather !
Night ! with all thy stars look down ;
    Darkness ! weep thy holiest dew :
Never smiled the inconstant Moon
    On a pair so true.
Let eyes not see their own delight !
Haste, swift Hour ! and thy flight
        Oft renew !

Fairies ! sprites ! and angels ! keep her ;
    Holy stars ! permit no wrong ;
And return to wake the sleeper,
    Dawn ! ere it be long.
O joy ! O fear ! what will be done
In the absence of the sun ?
        Come along !

SONG.

False Friend ! wilt thou smile or weep
When my life is laid asleep ?
Little cares for a smile or a tear
The clay-cold corpse upon the bier.
   Farewell ! heigh ho !
   What is this whispers low ?
There is a snake in thy smile, my Dear !
And bitter poison within thy tear.

Sweet Sleep ! were Death like to thee,
Or if thou couldst mortal be,
I would close these eyes of pain :
When to wake ?   Never again.
   O World ! farewell !
   Listen to the passing bell !
It says thou and I must part,
With a light and a heavy heart.

POLITICAL GREATNESS.

Nor happiness, nor majesty, nor fame,
Nor peace, nor strength, nor skill in arms or arts,
Shepherd those herds whom Tyranny makes tame :
Verse echoes not one beating of their hearts ;
History is but the shadow of their shame ;
Art veils her glass, or from the pageant starts,
As to Oblivion their millions fleet
Staining that heaven with obscene imagery
Of their own likeness.   What are numbers knit
By force or custom ?   Man, who man would be,
Must rule the empire of himself ; in it
Must be supreme, establishing his throne
On vanquish'd will, quelling the anarchy
Of hopes and fears,—being Himself alone.

A WAIL.

Rough Wind ! that moanest loud
  Grief too sad for song,—
Wild Wind, when sullen cloud
  Knells all the night long !
Sad Storm, whose tears are vain !
Bare Woods, whose branches strain !
Deep Caves ! and dreary Main !
  Wail for the world's wrong !

JOHN KEATS.

1795—1821.

HYMN TO PAN.

O Thou ! whose mighty palace-roof doth hang
From jagged trunks, and overshadoweth
Eternal whispers, glooms, the birth, life, death,
Of unseen flowers in heavy peacefulness,—
Who lovest to see the Hamadryads dress
Their ruffled locks where meeting hazels darken,—
And through whole solemn hours dost sit and hearken
The dreary melody of bedded reeds,
In desolate places where dank moisture breeds
The pipy hemlock to strange overgrowth,
Bethinking thee how melancholy loath
Thou wast to lose fair Syrinx,—do thou now,
By thy Love's milky brow,
By all the trembling mazes that she ran,
      Hear us, great Pan !

O Thou ! for whose soul-soothing quiet turtles
Passion their voices cooingly 'mong myrtles,
What time thou wanderest at eventide
Through sunny meadows that outskirt the side
Of thine enmossed realms,—O Thou ! to whom

Broad-leafed fig-trees even now foredoom
Their ripen'd fruitage, yellow-girted bees
Their golden honeycombs, our village leas
Their fairest-blossom'd beans and poppied corn,
The chuckling linnet its five young unborn
(To sing for thee), low-creeping strawberries
Their summer coolness, pent up butterflies
Their freckled wings,—yea! the fresh-budding year
All its completions,—be quickly near!
By every wind that nods the mountain pine,
       O forester divine!

Thou! to whom every faun and satyr flies
For willing service, whether to surprise
The squatted hare while in half-sleeping fit,
Or upward ragged precipices flit
To save poor lambkins from the eagle's maw,
Or by mysterious enticement draw
Bewilder'd shepherds to their path again,
Or to tread breathless round the frothy main
And gather up all fancifullest shells
For thee to tumble into Naiads' cells
And (being hidden) laugh at their out-peeping,—
Or to delight thee with fantastic leaping
The while they pelt each other on the crown
With silvery oak-apples and fir-cones brown,—
By all the echoes that about thee ring,
       Hear us, O Satyr King!

O hearkener to the loud-clapping shears!
While ever and anon to his shorn peers
A ram goes bleating,—winder of the horn!
When snouted wild boars, routing tender corn,
Anger our huntsmen,—breather round our farms!
To keep off mildews and all weather harms,—
Strange ministrant of undescribed sounds
That come a-swooning over hollow grounds
And wither drearily on barren moors!

Dread opener of the mysterious doors
Leading to universal knowledge ! see
Great Son of Dryopè !
The many that are come to pay their vows,
        With leaves about their brows.

Be still the unimaginable lodge
For solitary thinkings, such as dodge
Conception to the very bourne of heaven,
Then leave the naked brain ! be still the leaven
That, spreading in this dull and clodded earth,
Gives it a touch ethereal, a new birth !
Be still a symbol of immensity,
A firmament reflected in a sea,
An element filling the space between !
An unknown——But, no more !   We humbly screen
With uplift hands our foreheads, lowly bending,
And, giving out a shout most heaven-rending,
Conjure thee to receive our humble pæan
        Upon thy Mount Lycean !

ROUNDELAY.

        O, Sorrow !
        Why dost borrow
The natural hue of health from vermeil lips ?—
        To give maiden blushes
        To the white rose bushes ?
Or is it thy dewy hand the daisy tips ?

        O, Sorrow !
        Why dost borrow
The lustrous passion from a falcon eye ?—
        To give the glow-worm light ?
        Or on a moonless night
To tinge, on syren shores, the salt sea-spry ?

        O, Sorrow !
        Why dost borrow

The mellow ditties from a mourning tongue ?—
        To give at evening pale
        Unto the nightingale,
That thou mayst listen the cold dews among ?

        O, Sorrow !
        Why dost borrow
Heart's lightness from the merriment of May ?—
        A lover would not tread
        A cowslip on the head,
Though he should dance from eve till peep of day,—
        Nor any drooping flower
        Held sacred for thy bower,
Wherever he may sport himself and play.

        To Sorrow
        I bade Good-morrow !
And thought to leave her far away behind :
        But, cheerly ! cheerly !
        She loves me dearly,—
She is so constant to me and so kind :
        I would deceive her,
        And so leave her,
But, ah ! she is so constant and so kind.

Beneath my palm-trees, by the river side,
I sat a-weeping : in the whole world wide
There was no one to ask me why I wept ;
        And so I kept
Brimming the water-lily cups with tears
        Cold as my fears.

Beneath my palm-trees, by the river side,
I sat a-weeping : what enamour'd bride,
Cheated by shadowy wooer from the clouds,
        But hides and shrouds
Beneath dark palm-trees by a river side ?

And, as I sat, over the light blue hills
There came a noise of revellers; the rills
Into the wide stream came of purple hue :—
          'Twas Bacchus and his crew!
The earnest trumpet spake, and silver thrills
From kissing cymbals made a merry din :
          'Twas Bacchus and his kin!
Like to a moving vintage down they came,
Crown'd with green leaves, and faces all on flame;
All madly dancing through the pleasant valley,
          To scare thee, Melancholy!
O then, O then, thou wast a simple name,
And I forgot thee, as the berried holly
By shepherds is forgotten when in June
Tall chestnuts keep away the sun and moon :—
          I rush'd into the folly.

Within his car aloft young Bacchus stood,
Trifling his ivy dart, in dancing mood,
          With sidelong laughing ;
And little rills of crimson wine imbrued
His plump white arms, and shoulders enough white
          For Venus' pearly bite ;
And near him rode Silenus on his ass,
Pelted with flowers as he on did pass
          Tipsily quaffing.

Whence came ye? merry Damsels! whence came ye,
So many, and so many, and such glee ?
Why have ye left your bowers desolate,
          Your lutes, and gentler fate ?—
" We follow Bacchus, Bacchus on the wing,
          A-conquering.
Bacchus! young Bacchus! good or ill betide,
We dance before him thorough kingdoms wide :
Come hither, Lady fair! and joined be
          To our wild minstrelsy ! "

Whence came ye? jolly Satyrs! whence came ye,
So many, and so many, and such glee?
Why have ye left your forest haunts, why left
    Your nuts in oak-tree cleft?—
" For wine, for wine we left our kernel tree;
For wine we left our heath and yellow brooms
    And cold mushrooms;
For wine we follow Bacchus through the earth,—
Great God of breathless cups and chirping mirth!
Come hither, Lady fair! and joined be
    To our mad minstrelsy!"

Over wide streams and mountains great we went,
And, save when Bacchus kept his ivy tent,
Onward the tiger and the leopard pants,
    With Asian elephants;
Onward these myriads, with song and dance:
With zebras striped, and sleek Arabians' prance,
Web-footed alligators, crocodiles
Bearing upon their scaly backs, in files,
Plump infant laughers mimicking the coil
Of seamen and stout galley-rowers' toil:
With toying oars and silken sails they glide,
    Nor care for wind and tide.
Mounted on panthers' furs and lions' manes,
From rear to van they scour about the plains,
A three days' journey in a moment done;
And always, at the rising of the sun,
About the wilds they hunt with spear and horn,
    On spleenful unicorn.

I saw Osirian Egypt kneel adown
    Before the vine-wreath crown;
I saw parch'd Abyssinia rouse and sing
    To the silver cymbals ring;
I saw the whelming vintage hotly pierce
    Old Tartary the fierce;
  II.—7

The kings of Ind their jewel-sceptres vail,
And from their treasures scatter pearled hail;
Great Brahma from his mystic heaven groans,
        And all his priesthood moans,
Before young Bacchus' eye-wink turning pale.
Into these regions came I, following him,
Sick-hearted, weary: so I took a whim
To stray away into these forests drear,
        Alone, without a peer:
And I have told thee all thou mayest hear.

        Young Stranger!
        I've been a ranger
In search of pleasure throughout every clime:
        Alas! 'tis not for me;
        Bewitch'd I sure must be
To lose in grieving all my maiden prime.

        Come then, Sorrow!
        Sweetest Sorrow!
Like an own babe I nurse thee on my breast:
        I thought to leave thee,
        And deceive thee,
But now of all the world I love thee best.

        There is not one,
        No! no! not one
But thee to comfort a poor lonely maid:
        Thou art her mother,
        And her brother,
Her playmate, and her wooer in the shade.

ODE ON A GRECIAN URN.

Thou still unravish'd bride of quietness!
Thou foster-child of Silence and slow Time!
Sylvan historian! who canst thus express

A flowery tale more sweetly than our rhyme:
What leaf-fringed legend haunts about thy shape
Of deities or mortals, or of both,
In Tempè or the dales of Arcady?
What men, or Gods, are these! what maidens loath!
What mad pursuit! what struggle to escape!
What pipes and timbrels! what wild ecstacy!

Heard melodies are sweet, but those unheard
Are sweeter: therefore, ye soft pipes! play on,—
Not to the sensual ear, but, more endear'd,
Pipe to the spirit ditties of no tone!
Fair youth beneath the trees! thou canst not leave
Thy song, nor ever can those trees be bare.
Bold lover! never, never canst thou kiss,
Though winning near the goal; yet do not grieve!
She can not fade, though thou hast not thy bliss:
For ever wilt thou love and she be fair.

Ah, happy, happy boughs! that can not shed
Your leaves nor ever bid the Spring adieu;
And happy melodist! unwearied,
For ever piping songs for ever new;
More happy love! more happy happy love!
For ever warm, and still to be enjoy'd,
For ever panting and for ever young,—
All breathing human passion far above,
That leaves a heart high sorrowful and cloy'd,
A burning forehead and a parching tongue.

Who are these coming to the sacrifice?
To what green altar, O mysterious priest!
Lead'st thou that heifer lowing at the skies,
And all her silken flanks with garlands dress'd?
What little town, by river or sea-shore,
Or mountain-built with peaceful citadel,
Is emptied of its folk this pious morn?

And, little town ! thy streets for evermore
Will silent be ; and not a soul, to tell
Why thou art desolate, can e'er return.

O Attic shape ! fair attitude ! with brede
Of marble men and maidens overwrought,
With forest branches and the trodden weed.
Thou, silent form ! dost tease us out of thought,
As doth Eternity.   Cold Pastoral !
When old age shall this generation waste,
Thou shalt remain, in midst of other woe
Than ours, a friend to Man, to whom thou say'st—
Beauty is Truth, Truth Beauty : that is all
Ye know on earth, and all ye need to know.

TO AUTUMN.

Season of mists and mellow fruitfulness !
Close bosom-friend of the maturing Sun !
Conspiring with him how to load and bless
With fruit the vines that round the thatch-eaves run ;
To bend with apples the moss'd cottage-trees,
And fill all fruit with ripeness to the core ;
To swell the gourd, and plump the hazel shells
With a sweet kernel ; to set budding more,
And still more, later flowers for the bees,
Until they think warm days will never cease,
For Summer has o'erbrimm'd their clammy cells.

Who hath not seen Thee oft amid thy store ?
Sometimes whoever seeks abroad may find
Thee sitting careless on a granary floor,
Thy hair soft-lifted by the winnowing wind ;
Or on a half-reap'd furrow sound asleep,
Drowsed with the fume of poppies, while thy hook
Spares the next swath and all its twinèd flowers ;

And sometimes like a gleaner thou dost keep
Steady thy laden head across a brook ;
Or by a cider-press, with patient look,
Thou watchest the last oozings, hours by hours.

Where are the songs of Spring ?   Ay ! where are they ?
Think not of them ! thou hast thy music too,
While barred clouds bloom the soft-dying day,
And touch the stubble-plains with rosy hue :
Then in a wailful choir the small gnats mourn
Among the river sallows, borne aloft
Or sinking as the light wind lives or dies ;
And full-grown lambs loud bleat from hilly bourn ;
Hedge-crickets sing ; and now with treble soft
The redbreast whistles from a garden-croft,
And gathering swallows twitter in the skies.

GRASSHOPPER AND CRICKET.

The poetry of earth is never dead !
When all the birds are faint with the hot sun,
And hide in cooling trees, a voice will run
From hedge to hedge about the new-mown mead :
That is the Grasshopper's, he takes the lead
In summer luxury ; he has never done
With his delights, for when tired out with fun
He rests at ease beneath some pleasant weed.
The poetry of earth is ceasing never :
On a lone winter evening, when the frost
Has wrought a silence, from the stove there shrills
The Cricket's song, in warmth increasing ever ;
And seems to One in drowsiness half lost
The Grasshopper's among some grassy hills,

CHARLES WOLFE.
1791—1823.

THE BURIAL OF SIR JOHN MOORE,
On the ramparts of Corunna.

Not a drum was heard, not a funeral note,
   As his corse to the ramparts we hurried ;
Not a soldier discharged his farewell shot
   O'er the grave where our hero we buried.

We buried him darkly at dead of night,
   The sods with our bayonets turning,
By the struggling moonbeam's misty light
   And the lantern dimly burning.

No useless coffin enclosed his breast,
   Nor in sheet or in shroud we wound him ;
But he lay like a warrior taking his rest
   With his martial cloak around him.

Few and short were the prayers we said,
   And we spoke not a word of sorrow ;
But we steadfastly gazed on the face that was dead,
   And we bitterly thought of the morrow.

We thought, as we hollow'd his narrow bed
   And smooth'd down his lonely pillow,
That the foe and the stranger would tread o'er his head,
   And we far away on the billow.

Lightly they'll talk of the spirit that's gone,
   And o'er his cold ashes upbraid him ;
But little he'll reck if they let him sleep on
   In the grave where a Briton has laid him.

But half of our heavy task was done,
   When the clock struck the hour for retiring,
And we heard the distant and random gun
   Of the enemy suddenly firing.

Slowly and sadly we laid him down,
From the field of his fame fresh and gory :
We carved not a line, and we raised not a stone,
But we left him alone in his glory.

FELICIA DOROTHEA HEMANS.
1793—1835.

HER GRAVE.

Where shall we make her grave ?
O, where the wild flowers wave
        In the free air :
When shower and singing bird
'Midst the young leaves are heard,
        There—lay her there !

Harsh was the world to her :
Now may sleep minister
        Balm for each ill !
Low on sweet Nature's breast
Let the meek heart find rest,
        Deep, deep and still !

Murmur, glad waters ! by ;
Faint gales ! with happy sigh
        Come wandering o'er
That green and mossy bed,
Where on a gentle head
        Storms beat no more.

What though for her in vain
Falls now the bright Spring rain,
        Plays the soft wind,
Yet still from where she lies
Should blessed breathings rise,
        Gracious and kind.

Therefore let song and dew
Thence in the heart renew

> Life's vernal glow;
> And o'er that holy earth
> Scents of the violets' birth
> Still come and go!
>
> O then, where wild flowers wave
> Make ye her mossy grave
> In the free air,
> Where shower and singing bird
> 'Midst the young leaves are heard!
> There, lay her there!

WILLIAM CULLEN BRYANT.

1794—1878.

TO A WATER-FOWL.

Whither, midst falling dew,
While glow the heavens with the last steps of day,
Far through their rosy depths dost thou pursue
Thy solitary way?

Vainly the fowler's eye
Might mark thy distant flight to do thee wrong,
As, darkly painted on the crimson sky,
Thy figure floats along.

Seek'st thou the plashy brink
Of weedy lake, or marge of river wide,
Or where the rocking billows rise and sink
On the chafed ocean-side?

There is a Power whose care
Teaches thy way along that pathless coast,—
The desert and illimitable air
Lone wandering, but not lost.

All day thy wings have fann'd
At that far height the cold thin atmosphere,

Yet stoop not weary to the welcome land,
   Though the dark night is near.

And soon that toil shall end :
Soon shalt thou find a summer home, and rest,
And scream among thy fellows ; reeds shall bend,
   Soon, o'er thy shelter'd nest.

Thou art gone, the abyss of heaven
Hath swallow'd up thy form ; yet on my heart
Deeply hath sunk the lesson thou hast given,
   And shall not soon depart.

He, who from zone to zone
Guides through the boundless sky thy certain flight,
In the long way that I must tread alone
   Will lead my steps aright.

TO THE FRINGED GENTIAN.

Thou blossom ! bright with autumn dew,
And colour'd with the heaven's own blue,
That openest when the quiet light
Succeeds the keen and frosty night :

Thou comèst not when violets lean
O'er wandering brooks and springs unseen,
Or columbines, in purple dress'd,
Nod o'er the ground-bird's hidden nest ;

Thou waitest late, and comest alone,
When woods are bare and birds are flown,
And frosts and shortening days portend
The agèd year is near his end.

Then doth thy sweet and quiet eye
Look through its fringes to the sky :
Blue, blue as if that sky let fall
A flower from its cerulean wall.

I would that thus, when I shall see
The hour of death draw near to me,
Hope, blossoming within my heart,
May look to heaven as I depart.

HYMN OF THE CITY.

Not in the solitude
Alone may man commune with Heaven, or see
Only in savage wood
And sunny vale the present Deity,
Or only hear His voice
Where the winds whisper and the waves rejoice.

Even here do I behold
Thy steps, Almighty !—here, amidst the crowd,
Through the great City roll'd
With everlasting murmur deep and loud,
Choking the ways that wind
'Mongst the proud piles, the work of human kind.

Thy golden sunshine comes
From the round heaven, and on their dwellings lies,
And lights their inner homes ;
For them Thou fill'st with air the unbounded skies,
And givèst them the stores
Of ocean, and the harvests of its shores.

Thy Spirit is around,
Quickening the restless mass that sweeps along ;
And this eternal sound,
(Voices and footfalls of the numberless throng)
Like the resounding sea
Or like the rainy tempest, speaks of Thee.

And when the hours of rest
Come, like a calm upon the mid-sea brine
Hushing its billowy breast,

> The quiet of that moment too is Thine :
> It breathes of Him who keeps
> The vast and helpless City while it sleeps.

TO THE NORTH STAR.

The sad and solemn Night
Hath yet her multitude of cheerful fires :
    The glorious host of light
Walk the dark hemisphere till she retires ;
All through her silent watches, gliding slow,
Her constellations come, and climb the heavens, and go.

Day too hath many a star
To grace his gorgeous reign, as bright as they :
    Through the blue fields afar,
Unseen, they follow in his flaming way :
Many a bright lingerer, as the eve grows dim,
Tells what a radiant troop arose and set with him.

And thou dost see them rise,
Star of the Pole ! and thou dost see them set.
    Alone, in thy cold skies,
Thou keep'st thy old unmoving station yet ;
Nor join'st the dances of that glittering train,
Nor dipp'st thy virgin orb in the blue western main.

There, at morn's rosy birth,
Thou lookest meekly through the kindling air ;
    And eve, that round the earth
Chases the day, beholds thee watching there ;
There noontide finds thee, and the hour that calls
The shapes of polar flame to scale heaven's azure walls.

Alike beneath thine eye
The deeds of darkness and of light are done :
    High tow'rds the star-lit sky
Towns blaze ; the smoke of battle blots the sun ;

The night-storm on a thousand hills is loud;
And the strong wind of day doth mingle sea and cloud.

On thine unaltering blaze
The half-wreck'd mariner, his compass lost,
    Fixes his steady gaze,
And steers undoubting to the friendly coast;
And they who stray in perilous wastes by night
Are glad when thou dost shine to guide their footsteps right.

And therefore bards of old,
Sages, and hermits of the solemn wood,
    Did in thy beams behold
A beauteous type of that Unchanging Good,
That bright eternal beacon, by whose ray
The voyager of Time should shape his heedful way.

THE THIRD OF NOVEMBER.

1861.

Softly breathes the West wind beside the ruddy forest,
Taking leaf by leaf from the branches where he flies;
Sweetly streams the sunshine this third day of November,
Through the golden haze of the quiet autumn skies.

Tenderly the season has spared the grassy meadows,
Spared the petted flowers that the old world gave the new:
Spared the autumn rose and the garden's group of pansies,
Late-blown dandelions and periwinkles blue.

On my cornice linger the ripe black grapes ungather'd;
Children fill the groves with the echoes of their glee,
Gathering tawny chestnuts, and shouting when beside them
Drops the heavy fruit of the tall black-walnut tree.

Glorious are the woods in their latest gold and crimson,
Yet our full-leaved willows are in their freshest green:
Such a kindly autumn, so mercifully dealing
With the growths of summer, I never yet have seen.

Like this kindly season may life's decline come o'er me !
Pass'd is manhood's summer, the frosty months are here :
Yet be genial airs and a pleasant sunshine left me,
Leaf and fruit and blossom, to mark the closing year !

Dreary is the time when the flowers of earth are wither'd ;
Dreary is the time when the woodland leaves are cast,
When upon the hillside, all harden'd into iron,
Howling like a wolf flies the famish'd Northern blast.

Dreary are the years when the eye can look no longer
With delight on Nature or hope on human kind :
O, may those that whiten my temples, as they pass me,
Leave the heart unfrozen and spare the cheerful mind.

THOMAS CARLYLE.

1795—1881.

ADIEU!

Let Time and Chance combine, combine !
Let Time and Chance combine !
The fairest love from heaven above,
    That love of yours, was mine,
            My Dear !
That love of yours was mine.

The Past is fled and gone, and gone :
The Past is fled and gone :
If nought but pain to me remain,
    I'll fare in memory on,
            My dear !
I'll fare in memory on.

The saddest tears must fall, must fall :
The saddest tears must fall :
In weal or woe, in this world below,
    I love you ever and all,
            My Dear !
I love you ever and all.

A long road full of pain, of pain :
A long road full of pain :
One soul, one heart, sworn ne'er to part,—
　　We ne'er can meet again,
　　　　　　　　My Dear !
　　We ne'er can meet again.

Hard fate will not allow, allow;
Hard fate will not allow :
We blessed were as the angels are :—
　　Adieu for ever now,
　　　　　　　　My Dear !
　　Adieu for ever now !

JOHN HAMILTON REYNOLDS.

1794—1852.

HOUR AFTER HOUR.

Hour after hour departs,
　Recklessly flying ;
The golden time of our hearts
　Is fast a-dying :
O, how soon it will have faded !
Joy droops, with forehead shaded ;
　And Memory starts.

When I am gone, O wear
　Sweet smiles ! thy dwelling
Choose where flowers feed the air,
　And the sea is swelling !
And near where some rivulet lingers
In the grass, like an infant's fingers
　In its mother's hair.

Thy spirit should steep its wing
　In the dews of Nature ;
And the living airs of Spring

Should give each feature
Of thy face a rich lustrous smiling,—
Thy thoughts from that gloom beguiling
  Which cold hours bring.

Farewell to our delights !
  Love ! we are parted.
Come with thy silvery nights,
  Autumn, gold-hearted !
Let our two hearts be wreathing
Their hopes when the eve is breathing
  Through leaf-starr'd lights !

SONG.

Go where the water glideth gently ever,
    Glideth by meadows that the greenest be ;
Go, listen to our own belovèd river :
    And think of me !

Wander in forests where the small flower layeth
    Its fairy gem beside the giant tree ;
Listen the dim brook pining while it playeth :
    And think of me !

Watch when the sky is silver pale at even,
    And the wind grieveth in the lonely tree ;
Go out beneath the solitary heaven :
    And think of me !

And when the moon riseth as she were dreaming,
    And treadeth with white feet the lulled sea,
Go, silent as a star beneath her beaming,
    And think of me !

SHERWOOD FOREST.

The trees in Sherwood Forest are old and good,
The grass beneath them now is dimly green :
Are they deserted all ? Is no young mien,

With loose-slung bugle, met within the wood ?
No arrow found, foil'd of its antler'd food,
Stuck in the oak's rude side ?   Is there nought seen
To mark the revelries which there have been,
In the sweet days of merry Robin Hood ?
Go there, with summer and with evening, go
In the soft shadows, like some wandering man !
And thou shalt far amid the forest know
The archer men in green, with belt and bow,
Feasting on pheasant, river-fowl and swan,
With Robin at their head, and Marian.

HARTLEY COLERIDGE.
1796—1849.

SONG.

She is not fair to outward view
   As many maidens be ;
Her loveliness I never knew
   Until she smiled on me :
O then I saw her eye was bright,
A well of love, a spring of light.

But now her looks are coy and cold,
   To mine they ne'er reply ;
And yet I cease not to behold
   The love-light in her eye :
Her very frowns are fairer far
Than smiles of other maidens are.

WHITHER?

Whither is gone the wisdom and the power
That ancient sages scatter'd with the notes
Of thought-suggesting lyres ?   The music floats
In the void air; even at this breathing hour,
In every cell and every blooming bower

The sweetness of old lays is hovering still :
But the strong soul, the self-sustaining will,
The rugged root that bare the winsome flower,
Is weak and wither'd.   Were we like the Fays
That sweetly nestle in the fox-glove bells,
Or lurk and murmur in the rose-lipp'd shells
Which Neptune to the earth for quit-rent pays,
Then might our pretty modern Philomels
Sustain our spirits with their roundelays.

WILLIAM MOTHERWELL.
1798—1835.

JEANIE MORRISON.

I've wander'd East, I've wander'd West,
  Through mony a weary way,
But never, never can forget
  The luve of life's young day :
The fire that's blawn on Beltane e'en
  May weel be black gin Yule ;
But blacker fa' awaits the heart
  Where first fond luve grows cool.

O dear dear Jeanie Morrison !
  The thoughts o' bygane years
Still fling their shadows o'er my path,
  And blind my een wi' tears :
They blind my een wi' salt salt tears,
  And sair and sick I pine,
As memory idly summons up
  The blithe blinks o' langsyne.

'Twas then we luvit ilk ither weel ;
  'Twas then we twa did part :
Sweet time ! sad time ! twa bairns at scule,
  Twa bairns and but ae heart.
  II.—8

'Twas then we sat on ae laigh bink,
  To leir ilk ither lear ;
And tones and looks and smiles were shed,
  Remember'd evermair.

I wonder, Jeanie ! aften yet,
  When sitting on that bink,
Cheek touchin' cheek, loof lock'd in loof,
  What our wee heads could think :
When baith bent down o'er ae braid page,
  Wi' ae buik on our knee,
Thy lips were on thy lesson, but
  My lesson was in thee.

O, mind ye how we hung our heads,
  How cheeks brent red wi' shame,
Whene'er the scule-weans laughin' said
  We cleek'd thegither hame ?
And mind ye o' the Saturdays
  (The scule then skailt at noon)
When we ran aff to speel the braes,
  The broomy braes o' June ?

My head rins round and round about,
  My heart flows like a sea,
As ane by ane the thoughts rush back
  O scule-time and o' thee :
O mornin' life ! O mornin' luve !
  O lightsome days and lang,
When hinnied hopes around our hearts
  Like simmer blossoms sprang !

O mind ye, Luve ! how aft we left
  The deavin' dinsome toun,
To wander by the green burnside,
  And hear its waters croon ?
The simmer leaves hung o'er our heads,
  The flowers burst round our feet,

And in the gloamin' o' the wood
   The throssil whusslit sweet.

The throssil whusslit in the wood,
   The burn sang to the trees,
And we, with Nature's heart in tune,
   Concerted harmonies ;
And on the knowe, abune the burn,
   For hours thegither sat,
In the silentness o' joy, till baith
   Wi' very gladness grat.

Ay ! ay ! dear Jeanie Morrison !
   Tears trickled down your cheek,
Like dewbeads on a rose, yet nane
   Had ony power to speak.
That was a time, a blessed time,
   When hearts were fresh and young,
When freely gush'd all feelings forth,
   Unsyllabled, unsung.

I marvel, Jeanie Morrison !
   Gin I hae been to thee
As closely twined wi' earliest thoughts
   As ye hae been to me.
O tell me gin their music fills
   Thine ear as it does mine !
O say gin e'er your heart grows grit
   Wi' dreamings o' lang syne !

I've wander'd East, I've wander'd West,
   I've borne a weary lot :
But in my wanderings, far or near,
   Ye never were forgot.
The fount that first burst frae this heart
   Still travels on its way,
And channels deeper, as it rins,
   The luve o' life's young day.

O dear dear Jeanie Morrison!
  Since we were sinder'd young
I've never seen your face nor heard
  The music o' your tongue :
But I could hug all wretchedness,
  And happy could I dee,
Did I but ken your heart still dream'd
  O' bygane days and me.

THOMAS HOOD.
1799—1845.

THE BRIDGE OF SIGHS.

One more Unfortunate
Weary of breath,
Rashly importunate,
Gone to her death !

Take her up tenderly !
Lift her with care !
Fashion'd so slenderly,
Young, and so fair !

Look at her garments
Clinging like cerements,
Whilst the wave constantly
Drips from her clothing !
Take her up instantly !
Loving, not loathing.

Touch her not scornfully !
Think of her mournfully,
Gently, and humanly !
Not of the stains of her !
All that remains of her
Now is pure womanly.

Make no deep scrutiny
Into her mutiny
Rash and undutiful !
Past all dishonour,
Death has left on her
Only the Beautiful.

Still, for all slips of hers,
One of Eve's family,—
Wipe those poor lips of hers
Oozing so clammily !

Loop up her tresses,
Escaped from the comb !
Her fair auburn tresses :
Whilst wonderment guesses—
Where was her home ?

Who was her father ?
Who was her mother ?
Had she a sister ?
Had she a brother ?
Or was there a dearer One
Still, and a nearer One
Yet than all other ?

Alas for the rarity
Of Christian charity
Under the sun !
O, it was pitiful !
Near a whole city full
Home she had none.

Sisterly, brotherly,
Fatherly, motherly,
Feelings had changed ;
Love by harsh evidence
Thrown from its eminence ;

Even God's providence
Seeming estranged.

Where the lamps quiver
So far in the river,
With many a light
From window and casement,
From garret to basement,
She stood, with amazement,
Houseless by night.

The bleak wind of March
Made her tremble and shiver;
But not the dark arch
Or the black flowing river:
Mad from life's history,
Glad to death's mystery
Swift to be hurl'd,—
Any where, any where
Out of the world!

In she plunged boldly,
No matter how coldly
The rough river ran.—
Over the brink of it,
Picture it, think of it,
Dissolute Man!
Lave in it, drink of it,
Then, if you can!

Take her up tenderly,
Lift her with care!
Fashion'd so slenderly,
Young, and so fair!

Ere her limbs frigidly
Stiffen too rigidly,
Decently, kindly,
Smooth and compose them!

And her eyes, close them
Staring so blindly !

Dreadfully staring
Through muddy impurity,
As when with the daring
Last look of despairing
Fix'd on futurity.

Perishing gloomily,—
Spurr'd by contumely,
Cold inhumanity,
Burning insanity,
Into her rest.
—Cross her hands humbly !
As if praying dumbly,
Over her breast,—

Owning her weakness,
Her evil behaviour :
And leaving, with meekness,
Her sins to her Saviour.

ODE TO AUTUMN.

I saw old Autumn in the misty morn
Stand shadowless, like Silence listening
To silence (for no lonely bird would sing
Into his hollow ear from woods forlorn,
Nor lowly hedge nor solitary thorn),
Shaking his languid locks all dewy bright
With tangled gossamer that fell by night,
Pearling his coronet of golden corn.

Where are the songs of Summer ?   With the Sun,
Oping the dusky eyelids of the South,
Till shade and silence waken up as one,
And Morning sings with a warm odorous mouth.

Where are the merry birds ?   Away, away
On panting wings through the inclement skies,
        Lest owls should prey
        Undazzled at noon-day,
And tear with horny beak their lustrous eyes.

Where are the blooms of Summer ?   In the West,
Blushing their last to the last sunny hours,
When the mild Eve by sudden Night is press'd,
Like tearful Proserpine snatch'd from her flowers,
        To a most gloomy breast.
Where is the pride of Summer, the green prime,
The many many leaves all twinkling ?   Three
On the moss'd elm, three on the naked lime
Trembling, and one upon the old oak tree.
Where is the Dryads' immortality ?
Gone into mournful cypress and dark yew,
Or wearing the long gloomy winter through
In the smooth holly's green eternity.

The squirrel gloats on his accomplish'd hoard ;
The ants have brimm'd their garners with ripe grain ;
        And honey-bees have stored
The sweets of summer in their luscious cells ;
The swallows all have wing'd across the main ;
But here the autumn Melancholy dwells,
        And sighs her tearful spells
Amongst the sunless shadows of the plain.
        Alone, alone,
        Upon a mossy stone
She sits and reckons up the Dead and Gone,
With the last leaves for a love-rosary :
Whilst all the wither'd world looks drearily,
Like a dim picture of the drowned Past
In the hush'd mind's mysterious far-away,
Doubtful what ghostly thing will steal the last
Into that distance, grey upon the grey.

O, go and sit with her, and be o'ershaded
Under the languid downfall of her hair !
She wears a coronal of flowers faded
Upon her forehead, and a face of care ;—
There is enough of wither'd everywhere
To make her bower, and enough of gloom ;
There is enough of sadness to invite,
If only for the rose that died, whose doom
Is Beauty's,—she that with the living bloom
Of conscious cheeks most beautifies the light ;—
There is enough of sorrowing, and quite
Enough of bitter fruits the earth doth bear,
Enough of chilly droppings from her bowl ;
Enough of fear and shadowy despair
To frame her cloudy prison for the soul.

TO A COLD BEAUTY.

Lady ! wouldst thou heiress be
   To Winter's cold and cruel part ?
When he sets the rivers free,
   Thou dost still lock up thy heart :
Thou that shouldst outlast the snow
But in the whiteness of thy brow.

Scorn and cold neglect are made
   For winter gloom and winter wind ;
But thou wilt wrong the summer air
   Breathing it to words unkind,—
Breath which only should belong
To love, to sunlight, and to song.

When the little buds unclose,
   Red, and white, and pied, and blue,
And that virgin flower, the rose,
   Opes her heart to hold the dew,
Wilt thou lock thy bosom up
With no jewel in its cup ?

Let not cold December sit
  Thus in Love's peculiar throne !
Brooklets are not prison'd now,
  But crystal frosts are all agone ;
And that which hangs upon the spray,
It is no snow, but flower of May.

LOVE'S CONSTANCY.

Still glides the gentle streamlet on,
  With shifting current new and strange ;
The water that was here is gone :
  But those green shadows do not change.

Serene, or ruffled by the storm,
  On present waves, as on the past,
The mirror'd grove retains its form,
  The self-same trees their semblance cast.

The hue each fleeting globule wears,
  That drop bequeaths it to the next :
One picture still the surface bears
  To illustrate the murmur'd text.

So, Love ! however time may flow,
  Fresh hours pursuing those that flee,
One constant image still shall show
  My tide of life is true to thee.

RUTH.

She stood breast high amid the corn,
Clasp'd by the golden light of morn,
Like the sweetheart of the Sun,
Who many a glowing kiss had won.

On her cheek an autumn flush
Deeply ripen'd : such a blush

In the midst of brown was born,
Like red poppies grown with corn.

Round her eyes her tresses fell,—
Which were blackest none could tell:
But long lashes veil'd a light
That had else been all too bright.

And her hat with shady brim
Made her tressy forehead dim:
Thus she stood amid the stooks,
Praising God with sweetest looks.

Sure, I said, heaven did not mean
Where I reap thou shouldst but glean:
Lay thy sheaf adown, and come!
Share my harvest and my home!

THE TIME OF ROSES.

It was not in the winter
  Our loving lot was cast:
It was the Time of Roses,—
  We pluck'd them as we pass'd.

That churlish season never frown'd
  On early lovers yet:
O no! the world was newly crown'd
  With flowers when first we met.

'Twas twilight, and I bade you go;
  But still you held me fast:
It was the Time of Roses,—
  We pluck'd them as we pass'd.

What else could peer thy glowing cheek,
  That tears began to stud?
And when I ask'd the like of Love,
  You snatch'd a damask bud,

And oped it to the dainty core,
　Still glowing to the last.
It was the Time of Roses :
　We pluck'd them as we pass'd.

CHARLES WELLS.

1800—1879.

SONG.

Kiss no more the Vintages,
　Thou hot-lipp'd Sun !
Flow no more the merry wine
　From the dark tun !

Above my bed hang dull nightshade,
　And o'er my brows the willow !
With maiden flowers from dewy bowers
　Cover my last pillow !

Away ! away to the green sward !
　My young heart breaks :
Break the earth, and lay me deep !
　Love my breath takes.

Angels ! pity, and hear this ditty
　Breathed from a poor girl's lips :
O'er her lover ever hover,
　Scattering earthly bliss !

Come, thou iron-crowned Death !
　Into my stretched arms,
Bridegroom to my maiden breast ;
　End my sad alarms !

Lead on, lead on, thou Love of Bone !
　Over the heath wild ;
And 'neath the grass secure fast
　Thy melancholy child !

SIR HENRY TAYLOR.

1800—

SONG.

The morning broke, and Spring was there,
  And lusty Summer near her birth ;
The birds awoke and waked the air,
  The flowers awoke and waked the earth.

" Up ! " quoth he : " what joy for me,
  On dewy plain, in budding brake !
A sweet bird sings on every tree,
  And flowers are sweeter, for my sake."

Lightly o'er the plain he stepp'd,
  Lightly brush'd he through the wood,
And snared a little bird that slept
  And had not waken'd when she should.

Lightly through the wood he brush'd
  Lightly stepp'd he o'er the plain :
And yet—a little flower was crush'd
  That never raised its head again.

WILLIAM BARNES.

1801—

NOT FAR TO GO.

As upland fields were sun-burn'd brown,
  And heat-dried brooks were running small,
  And sheep were gather'd, panting all,
Below the hawthorn on the down,—
The while my mare, with dipping head,
  Pull'd on my cart, above the bridge,—
  I saw come on, beside the ridge,
A maiden white in skin and thread,
And walking, with an elbow load,
The way I drove along my road.

As there with comely steps up-hill
　　She rose, by elm trees all in ranks,
　　From shade to shade, by flowery banks
Where flew the bird with whistling bill,—
I kindly said—" Now won't you ride,
　　This burning weather, up the knap ?
　　I have a seat that fits the trap,
And now is swung from side to side."
" O no ! " she cried,—" I thank you, no !
I've little further now to go."

Then, up the timber'd slope, I found
　　The prettiest house a good day's ride
　　Would bring you by, with porch and side
By rose and jessamine well bound ;
And near at hand a spring and pool,
With lawn well-sunn'd and bower cool :
　　And, while the wicket fell behind
　　Her steps, I thought—If I would find
A wife I need not blush to show
I've little further now to go.

MY FORE-ELDERS.

When from the child, that still is led
　　By hand, a father's hand is gone,—
Or when a few-year'd mother dead
　　Has left her children growing on,—
When men have left their children staid,
And they again have boy and maid,—
O, can they know, as years may roll,
Their children's children, soul by soul ?
If this with souls in heaven can be,
Do my fore-elders know of me ?

My elders' elders, man and wife,
　　Were borne full early to the tomb,

With children still in childhood life
  To play with butterfly or bloom.
And did they see the seasons mould
Their faces on, from young to old,
As years might bring them, turn by turn,
A time to laugh or time to mourn ?
If this with souls in heaven can be,
Do my fore-elders know of me ?

How fain I now would walk the floor
  Within their mossy porch's bow,
Or linger by their church's door,
  Or road that bore them to and fro,
Or nook where once they built their mow,
Or gateway open to their plough
(Though now indeed no gate is swung
That their live hands had ever hung),—
If I could know that they would see
Their child's late child, and know of me.

JOHN HENRY NEWMAN.
1801—

THE ELEMENTS.
(*A tragic chorus.*)

Man is permitted much
  To scan and learn
  In Nature's frame :
Till he well-nigh can tame
Brute mischiefs, and can touch
Invisible things, and turn
All warring ills to purposes of good.
  Thus, as a God below,
  He can controul
And harmonize what seems amiss to flow
  As sever'd from the whole
  And dimly understood.

But o'er the elements
        One Hand alone,
        One Hand has sway.
What influence day by day
In straiter belt prevents
The impious Ocean, thrown
Alternate o'er the ever-sounding shore ?
        Or who has eye to trace
        How the Plague came ?
Forerun the doublings of the Tempest's race ?
        Or the Air's weight and flame
        On a set scale explore !

Thus God has will'd :
That man, when fully skill'd,
Still gropes in twilight dim ;
Encompass'd all his hours
By fearfullest powers
        Inflexible to him :
That so he may discern
        His feebleness,
And even for earth's success
To Him in wisdom turn
Who holds for us the keys of either home—
        Earth and the world-to-come.

A VOICE FROM AFAR.

        Weep not for me !
Be blithe as wont, nor tinge with gloom
The stream of love that circles home,
        Light hearts and free !
Joy in the gifts Heaven's bounty lends ;
Nor miss my face, dear friends!

        I still am near :
Watching the smiles I prized on earth,
Your converse mild, your blameless mirth ;

Now too I hear
Of whisper'd sounds the tale complete,
Low prayers, and musings sweet.

A sea before
The Throne is spread : its pure still glass
Pictures all earth-scenes as they pass ;
We on its shore
Share, in the bosom of our rest,
God's knowledge, and are bless'd.

HARRIET MARTINEAU.

1802—1876.

BENEATH THE ARCH.

Beneath this starry arch
  Nought resteth or is still ;
But all things hold their march
  As if by one great Will :
Moves one, move all : hark to the foot-fall !
               On, on, forever !

Yon sheaves were once but seed ;
Will ripens into deed ;
As cave-drops swell the streams,
Day-thoughts feed nightly dreams ;
And sorrow tracketh wrong,
As echo follows song :
               On, on, forever !

By night, like stars on high,
  The Hours reveal their train ;
They whisper, and go by :
  I never watch in vain.
Moves one, move all : hark to the foot-fall !
               On, on, forever !

They pass the cradle-head,
And there a promise shed ;
They pass the moist new grave,
And bid rank verdure wave ;
They bear through every clime
The harvests of all time
              On, on, forever!

THOMAS LOVELL BEDDOES.
1803—1849.

SONG OF THE STYGIAN NAIADS.

Prosperine may pull her flowers,
  Wet with dew or wet with tears,
  Red with anger, pale with fears :
Is it any fault of ours
If Pluto be an amorous king,
  And comes home nightly laden,
Underneath his broad bat-wing,
  With a gentle mortal maiden ?
    Is it so?   Wind ! is it so ?
    All that you and I do know
    Is that we saw fly and fix
'Mongst the reeds and flowers of Styx,
          Yesterday,
Where the Furies made their hay
For a bed of tiger-cubs,
A great fly of Beelzebub's,—
The bee of hearts, which mortals name
Cupid, Love, and Fie-for-shame.

Proserpine may weep in rage,
  But, ere I and you have done
  Kissing, bathing in the sun,
What I have in yonder cage,
Bird or serpent, wild or tame,
She shall guess and ask in vain :

But if Pluto does it again,
It shall sing out loud his shame.
What hast caught then ? what hast caught ?
Nothing but a poet's thought
   Which so light did fall and fix
'Mongst the reeds and flowers of Styx
         Yesterday,
Where the Furies made their hay
For a bed of tiger-cubs,
A great fly of Beelzebub's,—
The bee of hearts, which mortals name
Cupid, Love, and Fie-for-shame.

HOW MANY TIMES?

How many times do I love thee ? Dear !
Tell me how many thoughts there be
      In the atmosphere
      Of a new-fallen year,
Whose white and sable hours appear
The latest flake of Eternity :—
So many times do I love thee, Dear !

How many times do I love, again ?
Tell me how many beads there are
      In a silver chain
      Of evening rain
Unraveled from the trembling main
And threading the eye of a yellow star :—
So many times do I love again.

SEA SONG.

To sea ! to sea ! The calm is o'er :
   The wanton water leaps in sport,
And rattles down the pebbly shore ;
   The dolphin wheels, the sea-cows snort,
And unseen mermaids' pearly song
Comes bubbling up the weeds among.

Fling broad the sail ! dip deep the oar !
To sea ! to sea ! the calm is o'er.

To sea ! to sea ! our wide-wing'd bark
   Shall billowy cleave its sunny way,
And with its shadow, fleet and dark,
   Break the caved Tritons' azure day :
Like mighty eagles soaring light
O'er antelopes on Alpine height.
The anchor heaves, the ship swings free,
The sail swells full : to sea ! to sea !

RICHARD HENGIST HORNE.

1803—

GENIUS.

Far out at sea,—the sun was high,
While veer'd the wind and flapp'd the sail,
We saw a snow-white butterfly
Dancing before the fitful gale,
          Far out at sea.

The little wanderer, who had lost
His way, of danger nothing knew ;
Settled awhile upon the mast,—
Then flutter'd o'er the waters blue,
          Far out at sea.

Above, there gleam'd the boundless sky ;
Beneath, the boundless ocean sheen ;
Between them danced the butterfly,
The spirit-life of this vast scene,—
          Far out at sea,

The tiny soul then soar'd away,
Seeking the clouds on fragile wings,
Lured by the brighter, purer ray
Which hope's ecstatic morning brings,—
          Far out at sea.

Away he sped with shimmering glee,
Scarce seen, now lost, yet onward borne !
Night comes, with wind and rain, and he
No more will dance before the Morn,
                    Far out at sea.

He dies, unlike his mates, I ween,
Perhaps not sooner or worse cross'd ;
And he hath felt, thought, known, and seen
A larger life and hope—though lost
                    Far out at sea.

THE LAUREL-SEED.

Marmora findit.

I.

A despot gazed on sun-set clouds,
    Then sank to sleep amidst the gleam ;—
Forthwith, a myriad starving slaves
    Must realize his lofty dream.

Year upon year, all night and day,
    They toil'd, they died—and were replaced ;
At length a marble fabric rose,
    With cloud-like domes and turrets graced.

No anguish of those herds of slaves
    E'er shook one dome or wall asunder,
Nor wars of other mighty Kings,
    Nor lustrous javelins of the thunder.

II.

One sunny morn a lonely bird
    Pass'd o'er, and dropt a laurel-seed ;
The plant sprang up amidst the walls
    Whose chinks were full of moss and weed.

The laurel tree grew large and strong,
    Its roots went searching deeply down ;

It split the marble walls of Wrong,
   And blossom'd o'er the Despot's crown.

And in its boughs a nightingale
   Sings to those world-forgotten graves ;
And o'er its head a skylark's voice
   Consoles the spirits of the slaves.

SOLITUDE AND THE LILY.

THE LILY.

I bend above the moving stream,
And see myself in my own dream,—
   Heaven passing, while I do not pass.
Something divine pertains to me,
     Or I to it : reality
Escapes me on this liquid glass.

SOLITUDE.

The changeful clouds that float or poise on high
   Emblem earth's night and day of history :
   Renew'd for ever, evermore to die.
   Thy life-dream is thy fleeting loveliness ;
   But mine is concentrated consciousness,
   A life apart from pleasure or distress.
     The grandeur of the Whole
     Absorbs my soul,
While my caves sigh o'er human littleness.

THE LILY.

     Ah, Solitude !
   Of marble Silence fit abode,—
I do prefer my fading face,
My loss of loveliness and grace,
   With cloud-dreams ever in my view;
Also the hope that other eyes
May share my rapture in the skies
     And, if illusion, feel it true.

THE PLOUGH.

Above yon sombre swell of land
  Thou seest the dawn's grave orange hue,
With one pale streak like yellow sand,
  And over that a vein of blue.

The air is cold above the woods ;
  All silent is the earth and sky,
Except with his own lonely moods
  The blackbird holds a colloquy.

Over the broad hill creeps a beam,
  Like hope that gilds a good man's brow ;
And now ascends the nostril-steam
  Of stalwart horses come to plough.

Ye rigid Ploughmen ! bear in mind
  Your labor is for future hours.
Advance ! spare not ! nor look behind !
  Plough deep and straight with all your powers !

DIRGE.

On me, on me
Time and Change can heap no more !
The painful past with blighting grief
Hath left my heart a wither'd leaf :
  Time and Change can do no more.

Earth's barbed woes
Poised on the breath of Fate's dull roar !
Ye move me not, nor breed one fear ;
I wait your coming, and can bear :
  Time and Change can do no more.

NEWTON.

The Earth was but a platform for thy power,
Whereon to watch and work, by day and night;
The Moon to thee was but heaven's evening flower;
The Sun a loftier argument of light;
Each Planet was thy fellow traveler bright,
In vision,—and, in thought, still nearer home :
Throughout the Universe thy soul took flight,
And touch'd at suns whose rays may never come.
Though star-tranced Tycho and the thought sublime
Of Kepler fathom'd Heaven's infinity,
To thee 'twas left to prove the laws that chime
Through spheres and atoms,—being, and to be :
Profound alike in thy humility,—
" A child that gather'd shells, kneeling beside the sea."

RALPH WALDO EMERSON.
1803—1882.

THE PROBLEM.

I like a church, I like a cowl,
I love a prophet of the soul;
And on my heart monastic aisles
Fall like sweet strains or pensive smiles :
Yet not for all his faith can see
Would I that cowled churchman be.

Why should the vest on him allure
Which I could not on me endure?

Not from a vain or shallow thought
His awful Jove young Phidias brought;
Never from lips of cunning fell
The thrilling Delphic oracle;
Out from the heart of Nature roll'd
The burdens of the Bible old;

The litanies of nations came,
Like the volcano's tongue of flame,
Up from the burning core below,—
The canticles of love and woe;
The hand that rounded Peter's dome
And groin'd the aisles of Christian Rome
Wrought in a sad sincerity:
Himself from God he could not free;
He builded better than he knew:
The conscious stone to beauty grew.

Know'st thou what wove yon woodbird's nest
Of leaves and feathers from her breast?
Or how the fish outbuilt her shell,
Painting with morn each annual cell?
Or how the sacred pine-tree adds
To her old leaves new myriads?
Such and so grew these holy piles,
Whilst love and terror laid the tiles.
Earth proudly wears the Parthenon,
As the best gem upon her zone;
And Morning opes with haste her lids,
To gaze upon the Pyramids;
O'er England's Abbeys bends the sky,
As on its friends, with kindred eye:
For out of Thought's interior sphere
These wonders rose to upper air;
And Nature gladly gave them place,
Adopted them into her race,
And granted them an equal date
With Andes and with Ararat.

These temples grew, as grows the grass:
Art might obey, but not surpass.
The passive Master lent his hand
To the vast Soul that o'er him plann'd;
And the same Power that rear'd the shrine

Bestrode the tribes that knelt within.
Ever the fiery Pentecost
Girds with one flame the countless host,
Trances the heart through chanting choirs,
And through the priest the mind inspires.

The Word unto the prophet spoken
Was writ on tablets yet unbroken;
The Word by seers or sybils told,
In groves of oak or fanes of gold,
Still floats upon the morning wind,
Still whispers to the willing mind.
One accent of the Holy Ghost
The heedless world hath never lost.
I know what say the Fathers wise:
The Book itself before me lies,
Old Chrysostom, best Augustine,
And he who blent both in his line,
The younger Golden-Lips (or Mines)—
Taylor, the Shakespeare of Divines.
His words are music in my ear;
I see his cowled portrait dear:
And yet, for all his faith could see,
I would not the good bishop be.

TO THE HUMBLE-BEE.

Burly, dozing Humble-Bee!
Where thou art is clime for me.
Let them sail for Porto Rique,
Far off heats through seas to seek!
I will follow thee alone,
Thou animated Torrid Zone!
Zigzag steerer! desert cheerer!
Let me chase thy waving lines;
Keep me nearer, me thy hearer,
Singing over shrubs and vines!

Insect lover of the sun !
Joy of thy dominion !
Sailor of the atmosphere !
Swimmer through the waves of air !
Voyager of light and noon !
Epicurean of June !
Wait, I prithee, till I come
Within earshot of thy hum !
All without is martyrdom.

When the South wind, in May days,
With a net of shining haze
Silvers the horizon wall,
And, with softness touching all,
Tints the human countenance
With a colour of romance,—
And, infusing subtle heats,
Turns the sod to violets,—
Thou in sunny solitudes,
Rover of the underwoods !
The green silence dost displace
With thy mellow breezy bass.

Hot Midsummer's petted crone !
Sweet to me thy drowsy tone,
Tells of countless sunny hours,
Long days, and solid banks of flowers ;
Of gulfs of sweetness without bound
In Indian wildernesses found ;
Of Syrian peace, immortal leisure,
Firmest cheer, and bird-like pleasure.

Aught unsavory or unclean
Hath my Insect never seen ;
But violets and bilberry bells,
Maple sap, and daffodels,
Grass with green flag half-mast high,

Succory to match the sky,
Columbine with horn of honey,
Scented fern, and agrimony,
Clover, catch-fly, adder's tongue,
And briar roses dwelt among.
All beside was unknown waste :
All was picture as he pass'd.

Wiser far than human seer,
Yellow-breech'd philosopher !
Seeing only what is fair,
Sipping only what is sweet,
Thou dost mock at Fate and Care,
Leave the chaff and take the wheat.
When the fierce North-Western blast
Cools sea and land so far and fast,
Thou already slumberest deep.
Woe and want thou canst outsleep ;
Want and woe, which torture us,
Thy sleep makes ridiculous.

TO EVA.

O fair and stately Maid ! whose eyes
Were kindled in the upper skies
At the same torch that lighted mine,—
For so I must interpret still
Thy sweet dominion o'er my will,
A sympathy divine :

Ah ! let me blameless gaze upon
Features that seem in heart my own ;
Nor fear those watchful sentinels
Which charm the more their glance forbids,—
Chaste-glowing underneath their lids
With fire that draws while it repels.

THE APOLOGY.

Think me not unkind and rude
   That I walk alone in grove and glen!
I go to the God of the Wood,
   To fetch his word to men.

Tax not my sloth that I
   Fold my arms beside the brook!
Each cloud that floateth in the sky
   Writes a letter in my book.

Chide me not, laborious band!
   For the idle flowers I brought :
Every aster in my hand
   Goes home loaded with a thought.

There was never mystery
   But 'tis figured in the flowers;
Was never secret history
   But birds tell it in the bowers.

One harvest from thy field
   Homeward brought the oxen strong :
A second crop thine acres yield,
   Which I gather in a song.

GERALD GRIFFIN.

1803—1840.

IN THY MEMORY.

A place in thy memory, Dearest!
   Is all that I claim :
To pause and look back when thou hearest
   The sound of my name.
Another may woo thee, nearer;

Another may win and wear :
I care not though he be dearer,
  If I am remember'd there.

Remember me, not as a lover
  Whose hope was cross'd,
Whose bosom can never recover
  The light it hath lost !
As the young bride remembers the mother
  She loves, though she never may see,
As a sister remembers a brother,
  O Dearest ! remember me !

Could I be thy true lover, Dearest !
  Couldst thou smile on me,
I would be the fondest and nearest
  That ever loved thee :
But a cloud on my pathway is glooming
  That never must burst upon thine ;
And heaven, that made thee all blooming,
  Ne'er made thee to wither on mine.

Remember me then ! O remember
  My calm light love !
Though bleak as the blasts of November
  My life may prove.
That life will, though lonely, be sweet
  If its brightest enjoyment should be
A smile and kind word when we meet
  And a place in thy memory.

MAIDEN EYES.

You never bade me hope, 'tis true ;
  I ask'd you not to swear :
But I look'd in those eyes of blue,
  And read a promise there.

The vow should bind, with maiden sighs
  That maiden lips have spoken :
But that which looks from maiden eyes
  Should last of all be broken.

JAMES CLARENCE MANGAN.
1803—1849.

SOUL AND COUNTRY.

Arise, my slumbering soul ! arise !
And learn what yet remains for thee
    To dree or do :
The signs are flaming in the skies ;
A struggling world would yet be free,
    And live anew.
The earthquake hath not yet been born
That soon shall rock the lands around,
    Beneath their base ;
Immortal Freedom's thunder horn
As yet yields but a doleful sound
    To Europe's race.

Look round, my soul ! and see, and say
If those about thee understand
    Their mission here :
The will to smite, the power to slay,
Abound in every heart and hand
    Afar, anear ;
But, God ! must yet the conqueror's sword
Pierce mind, as heart, in this proud year ?
    O, dream it not !
It sounds a false, blaspheming word,
Begot and born of moral fear,
    And ill-begot.

To leave the world a name is nought :
To leave a name for glorious deeds

And works of love,
A name to waken lightning thought
And fire the soul of him who reads,
This tells above.
Napoleon sinks to-day before
The ungilded shrine, the single soul
Of Washington :
Truth's name alone shall man adore
Long as the waves of Time shall roll
Henceforward on !

My countrymen ! my words are weak :
My health is gone, my soul is dark,
My heart is chill ;
Yet would I fain and fondly seek
To see you borne in freedom's bark
O'er ocean still.
Beseech your God ! and bide your hour !
He can not, will not long be dumb :
Even now his tread
Is heard o'er earth with coming power ;
And coming (trust me !) it will come,—
Else were He dead.

SAMUEL LAMAN BLANCHARD.
1803—1845.

- - - - - - -

NELL GWYNNE'S LOOKING-GLASS.

Glass antique ! 'twixt thee and Nell
Draw we here a parallel !
She like thee was forced to bear
All reflections, foul or fair.
Thou art deep and bright within,—
Depths as bright belong'd to Gwynne ;
Thou art very frail as well,
Frail as flesh is,—so was Nell.

Thou, her glass, art silver-lined,—
She too had a silver mind;
Thine is fresh to this far day,—
Hers till death ne'er wore away :
    Thou dost to thy surface win
    Wandering glances,—so did Gwynne;
    Eyes on thee long love to dwell,—
    So men's eyes would do on Nell.

Life-like forms in thee are sought,—
Such the forms the Actress wrought;
Truth unfailing rests in you,—
Nell, whate'er she was, was true :
    Clear as virtue, dull as sin,
    Thou art oft,—as oft was Gwynne;
    Breathe on thee, and drops will swell,—
    Bright tears dimm'd the eyes of Nell.

Thine's a frame to charm the sight,—
Framed was she to give delight;
Waxen forms here, truly, show
Charles above and Nell below
    (But between them, chin with chin,
    Stuart stands as low as Gwynne),
    Pair'd yet parted,—mean'd to tell
    Charles was opposite to Nell.

Round the glass, wherein her face
Smiled so oft, her Arms we trace :
Thou, her mirror, hast the pair—
Lion here and leopard there.
    She had part in these : akin
    To the lion-heart was Gwynne;
    And the leopard's beauty fell,
    With its spots, to bounding Nell.

Oft inspected, ne'er seen through,
Thou art firm, if brittle too :
    II.—10

So her will, on good intent,
Might be broken, never bent.
    What the glass was when therein
    Beam'd the face of glad Nell Gwynne
    Was that face by beauty's spell
    To the honest soul of Nell.

ROBERT STEPHEN HAWKER.
1804—1875.

ISHA CHERIOTH.

They say his sin was dark and deep,
    Men shudder at his name;
They spurn at me because I weep,
    They call my sorrow shame.

I know not!   I remember well
    Our city's native street,
The path, the olive trees, the dell
    Where Cherioth's daughters meet:

And there, where clustering vineyards rest
    And palms look forth above,
He kindled in my maiden breast
    The glory of his love.

He left me,—but with holier thought,
    Bound for a mightier scene:
In proud Capernaum's path he sought
    The noble Nazarene.

They tell of treachery, bought and sold
    (Perchance their words be truth):
I only see the scenes of old;
    I hear his voice in youth.

And I will sit, as Rizpah sate,
    Where life and hope are fled:

I sought him not in happier state,—
I will not leave my Dead.

No ! I must weep, though all around
Be hatred and despair :
One sigh shall soothe this fatal ground,—
A Cherioth maiden's prayer.

THE WAIL OF THE CORNISH MOTHER.

They say 'tis a sin to sorrow,
That what God doth is best :
But 'tis only a month to-morrow
I buried it from my breast.

I know it should be a pleasure
Your child to God to send :
But mine was a precious treasure
To me and to my poor friend.

I thought it would call me Mother,
The very first words it said :
O, I never can love another
Like the blessed babe that's dead.

Well ! God is its own dear Father ;
It was carried to church, and bless'd ;
And our Saviour's arms will gather
Such children to their rest.

I will make my best endeavour
That my sins may be forgiven ;
I will serve God more than ever :
To meet my child in heaven.

I will check this foolish sorrow,
For what God doth is best—
But O, 'tis a month to-morrow
I buried it from my breast !

SARAH FLOWER ADAMS.

1805—1849.

THE OLIVE BOUGHS.

They bear the hero from the fight, dying;
  But the foe is flying:
They lay him down beneath the shade
By the olive branches made:
    The olive boughs are sighing.

He hears the wind among the leaves, dying;
  But the foe is flying:
He hears the voice that used to be
When he sat beneath the tree:
    The olive boughs are sighing.

Comes the mist around his brow, dying;
  But the foe is flying:
Comes that form of peace so fair,—
Stretch his hands unto the air:
    The olive boughs are sighing.

Fadeth life as fadeth day, dying;
  But the foe is flying:
There's an urn beneath the shade
By the olive branches made:
    The olive boughs are sighing.

SIR WILLIAM ROWAN HAMILTON.

1805—1865.

A PRAYER.

O brooding Spirit of Wisdom and of Love!
Whose mighty wings even now o'ershadow me,—
Absorb me in thine own immensity,
And raise me far my finite self above!
Purge vanity away, and the weak care

That name or fame of me may widely spread ;
And the deep wish keep burning in their stead
Thy blissful influence afar to bear,
Or see it borne !　Let no desire of ease,
No lack of courage, faith, or love, delay
Mine own steps on that high thought-paven way
In which my soul her clear commission sees :
Yet with an equal joy let me behold
Thy chariot o'er that way by others roll'd !

THOMAS WADE.
1805—1876.

THE NET-BRAIDERS.

Within a low-thatch'd hut, built in a lane
　　Whose narrow pathway tends toward the ocean,
A solitude which, save of some rude swain
　　Or fisherman, doth scarce know human motion,—
Or of some silent poet to the main
　　Straying, to offer infinite devotion
To God in the free universe,—there dwelt
Two women old, to whom small store was dealt

Of the world's mis-named good, mother and child,
　　Both aged and mateless.　These two life sustain'd
By braiding fishing-nets ; and so beguil'd
　　Time and their cares, and little e'er complain'd
Of Fate or Providence : resign'd and mild,
　　Whilst day by day, for years, their hour-glass rain'd
Its trickling sand, to track the wing of Time,
They toil'd in peace : and much there was sublime

In their obscure contentment : of mankind
　　They little knew, or reck'd ; but for their being
They bless'd their Maker, with a simple mind ;
　　And in the constant gaze of his all-seeing

Eye, to his poorest creatures never blind,
  Deeming they dwelt, they bore their sorrows fleeing,
Glad still to live, but not afraid to die,
In calm expectance of Eternity.

And since I first did greet those braiders poor,
  If ever I behold fair women's cheeks
Sin-pale in stately mansions, where the door
  Is shut to all but Pride, my cleft heart seeks
For refuge in my thoughts,—which then explore
  That pathway lone near which the wild sea breaks :
And to Imagination's humble eyes
That hut, with all its want, is Paradise.

NYMPHS.

Beautiful Things of Old ! why are ye gone for ever
      Out of the earth ?   O, why ?
    Dryad and Oread, and ye, Nereids blue !
    Whose presence woods and hills and sea-rocks knew.
      Ye have pass'd from Faith's dim eye,
And save by poet's lip your names are honour'd never.

The sun on the calm sea sheddeth a golden glory,
      The rippling waves break whitely,
    The sands are level and the shingle bright,
    The green cliffs wear the pomp of heaven's light,
      And sea-weeds idle lightly
Over the rocks ; but ye appear not, Dreams of Story !

Nymphs of the Sea !   Faith's heart hath fled from ye—hath
      fled ;
      Ye are her boasted scorn ;
    Save to the poet's soul, the sculptor's thought,
    The painter's fancy, ye are now as nought :
      Mute is old Triton's horn,
And with it half the voice of the Old World is dead.

Our creeds are not less vain ; our sleeping life still dreams ;
    The present, like the past,
  Passes in joy and sorrow, love and shame ;
  Truth dwells as deep ; wisdom is yet a name ;
    Life still to death flies fast ;
And the same shrouded light from the dark future gleams.

Spirits of vale and hill, of river and of ocean,—
    Ye thousand deities !
  Over the earth be president again ;
  And dance upon the mountain and the main
    In view of mortal eyes :
Love us, and be beloved, with the Old Time's devotion !

JOHN STERLING.

1806—1844.

DÆDALUS.

Wail for Dædalus, all that is fairest !
  All that is tuneful in air or wave !
Shapes whose beauty is truest and rarest,
  Haunt with your lamps and spells his grave !

Statues ! bend your heads in sorrow :
  Ye that glance amid ruins old,
That know not a past nor expect a morrow,
  On many a moonlight Grecian wold.

By sculptured cave and speaking river,
  Thee, Dædalus ! oft the Nymphs recall ;
The leaves with a sound of winter quiver,
  Murmur thy name, and withering fall.

Yet are thy visions in soul the grandest
  Of all that crowd on the tear-dimm'd eye,
Though, Dædalus ! thou no more commandest
  New stars to that ever widening sky.

Ever thy phantoms arise before us,
  Our loftier brothers, but one in blood;
By bed and table they lord it o'er us,
  With looks of beauty and words of good.

Calmly they show us mankind victorious
  O'er all that is aimless, blind, and base;
Their presence has made our nature glorious,
  Unveiling our night's illumined face.

Thy toil has won them a god-like quiet;
  Thou hast wrought their path to a lovely sphere;
Their eyes to peace rebuke our riot
  And shape us a home of refuge here.

For Dædalus breathed in them his spirit;
  In them their sire his beauty sees:
We too, a younger brood, inherit
  The gifts and blessings bestow'd on these.

But ah! their wise and graceful seeming
  Recalls the more that the Sage is gone:
Weeping we wake from deceitful dreaming
  And find our voiceless chamber lone.

Dædalus! thou from the twilight fleèst
  Which thou with visions hast made so bright;
And when no more those shapes thou seèst,
  Wanting thine eye they lose their light.

Even in the noblest of Man's creations,
  Those fresh worlds round this old of ours,
When the Seer is gone, the orphan'd nations
  See but the tombs of perish'd powers.

Wail for Dædalus, Earth and Ocean!
  Stars and Sun! lament for him;
Ages! quake in strange commotion;
  All ye realms of Life! be dim!

Wail for Dædalus ! awful Voices
  From earth's deep centre mankind appal.
Seldom ye sound, and then Death rejoices :
  For he knows that then the Mightiest fall.

WILLIAM GILMORE SIMMS.

1806—1870.

THE LOST PLEIAD.

Not in the sky,
Where it was seen,
Nor on the white tops of the glistening wave,
Nor in the mansions of the hidden deep
(Though green
And beautiful its caves of mystery)
Shall the bright watcher have
A place, and as of old high station keep.

Gone ! gone !
O, never more to cheer
The mariner who holds his course alone
On the Atlantic, through the weary night
When the stars turn to watchers and do sleep,
Shall it appear,
With the sweet fixedness of certain light
Down-shining on the shut eyes of the deep.

Vain ! vain !
Hopeful most idly then shall he look forth,
That mariner from his bark.
Howe'er the North
Doth raise his certain lamp when tempests lower,
He sees no more that perish'd light again ;
And gloomier grows the hour
Which may not, through the thick and crowding dark,
Restore that lost and loved One to her tower.

He looks,—the shepherd on Chaldea's hills
Tending his flocks,—
And wonders the rich beacon doth not blaze,
Gladdening his gaze,
And from his dreary watch along the rocks
Guiding him safely home through perilous ways.
How stands he in amaze,
Still wondering as the drowsy silence fills
The sorrowful scene and every hour distils
Its leaden dews ! how chafes he at the night,
Still slow to bring the expected and sweet light
So natural to his sight !

And lone,
Where its first splendours shone,
Shall be that pleasant company of stars :
How should they know that death
Such perfect beauty mars ?
And, like the earth, its common bloom and breath,
Fallen from on high,
Their lights grow blasted by its touch, and die,—
All their concerted springs of harmony
Snapp'd rudely, and the generous music gone.

A strain, a mellow strain
Of wailing sweetness, fill'd the earth and sky :
The stars lamenting in unborrow'd pain
That one of the Selected Ones must die,
Must vanish, when most lovely, from the rest !
Alas ! 'tis evermore the destiny :
The hope heart-cherish'd is the soonest lost ;
The flower first budded soonest feels the frost :
Are not the shortest-lived still loveliest ?
And, like the pale star shooting down the sky,
Look they not ever brightest when they fly
The desolate home they bless'd ?

NATHANIEL PARKER WILLIS.
1807—1867.

TWO WOMEN.

The shadows lay along Broadway,
  'Twas near the twilight-tide,
And slowly there a Lady fair
  Was walking in her pride :
Alone walk'd she ; but viewlessly
  Walk'd spirits at her side.

Peace charm'd the street beneath her feet,
  And Honour charm'd the air;
And all astir look'd kind on her,
  And call'd her good as fair :
For all God ever gave to her
  She kept with chary care.

She kept with care her beauties rare
  From lovers warm and true,
For her heart was cold to all but gold,
  And the rich came not to woo :
But honour'd well are charms to sell,
  If priests the selling do.

Now walking there was One more fair,
  A slight Girl, lily pale ;
And she had unseen company
  To make the spirit quail :
'Twixt Want and Scorn she walk'd forlorn
  And nothing could avail.

No mercy now can clear her brow
  For this world's peace to pray :
For as love's wild prayer dissolved in air,
  Her woman's heart gave way :
But the sin forgiven by Christ in Heaven
  By man is cursed alway.

HENRY WADSWORTH LONGFELLOW.

1807—1882.

THE ARROW AND THE SONG.

I shot an arrow into the air ;
It fell to earth, I knew not where :
For, so swiftly it flew, the sight
Could not follow it in its flight.

I breathed a song into the air ;
It fell to earth, I knew not where :
For who has sight so keen and strong,
That it can follow the flight of song ?

Long, long afterward, in an oak
I found the arrow, still unbroke ;
And the song, from beginning to end,
I found again in the heart of a friend.

THE LIGHT OF STARS.

The night is come, but not too soon ;
　And sinking silently,
All silently, the little moon
　Drops down behind the sky.

There is no light in earth or heaven
　But the cold light of stars ;
And the first watch of night is given
　To the red planet Mars.

Is it the tender star of love,
　The star of love and dreams ?
O no ! from that blue tent above
　A hero's armour gleams.

And earnest thoughts within me rise
　When I behold afar,

Suspended in the evening skies,
  The shield of that red star.

O star of strength! I see thee stand
  And smile upon my pain;
Thou beckonest with thy mailed hand,
  And I am strong again.

Within my breast there is no light
  But the cold light of stars:
I give the first watch of the night
  To the red planet Mars.

The star of the unconquer'd will:
  He rises in my breast,
Serene, and resolute, and still,
  And calm, and self-possess'd.

And thou too, whosoe'er thou art,
  That readest this brief psalm!
As one by one thy hopes depart,
  Be resolute and calm!

O, fear not in a world like this!
  And thou shalt know ere long,
Know how sublime a thing it is
  To suffer and be strong.

THE CUMBERLAND.

At anchor in Hampton Roads we lay,
On board of the Cumberland, sloop of war;
And at times from the fortress across the bay
The alarum of drums swept past,
      Or a bugle blast
      From the camp on the shore.

Then far away to the South uprose
A little feather of snow-white smoke;

And we knew that the iron ship of our foes
Was steadily steering its course
        To try the force
        Of our ribs of oak.

Down upon us heavily runs,
Silent and sullen, the floating fort ;
Then comes a puff of smoke from her guns,
And leaps the terrible death
        With fiery breath
        From each open port.

We are not idle, but send her straight
Defiance back in a full broadside :
As hail rebounds from a roof of slate,
Rebounds our heavier hail
        From each iron scale
        Of the monster's hide.

" Strike your flag ! " the rebel cries,
In his arrogant old plantation strain ;
" Never ! " our gallant Morris replies,—
" It is better to sink than to yield."
        And the whole air peal'd
        With the cheers of our men.

Then, like a kraken huge and black,
She crush'd our ribs in her iron grasp :
Down went the Cumberland, all a wrack,
With a sudden shudder of death
        And the cannon's breath
        For her dying gasp.

Next morn, as the sun rose over the bay,
Still floated our flag at the mainmast-head.
Lord ! how beautiful was thy day :
Every waft of the air
        Was a whisper of prayer,
        Or a dirge for the Dead.

Ho! brave hearts that went down in the seas!
Ye are at peace in the troubled stream;
Ho! brave land! with hearts like these
Thy flag, that is rent in twain,
   Shall be one again,
   And without a seam!

EXCELSIOR.

The shades of night were falling fast
As through an Alpine village pass'd
A youth who bore, 'mid snow and ice,
A banner with the strange device—
   Excelsior!

His brow was sad, his eye beneath
Flash'd like a falchion from its sheath;
And like a silver clarion rung
The accents of that unknown tongue—
   Excelsior!

In happy homes he saw the light
Of household fires gleam warm and bright;
Above, the spectral glaciers shone:
And from his lips escaped a groan—
   Excelsior!

" Try not the Pass!" the old man said;
" Dark lowers the tempest over-head,
 The roaring torrent is deep and wide!"
 And loud that clarion voice replied—
   Excelsior!

" O stay!" the maiden said, " and rest
 Thy weary head upon this breast!"
 A tear stood in his bright blue eye;
 But still he answer'd, with a sigh,
   Excelsior!

" Beware the pine-tree's wither'd branch !
Beware the awful avalanche ! "
This was the peasant's last Good-night :
A voice replied, far up the height,
Excelsior !

At break of day, as heavenward
The pious monks of St. Bernard
Utter'd the oft-repeated prayer,
A voice cried through the startled air --
Excelsior !

A traveler, by the faithful hound,
Half-buried in the snow was found,
Still grasping in his hand of ice
That banner with the strange device—
Excelsior !

There, in the twilight cold and grey,
Lifeless, but beautiful, he lay ;
And from the sky, serene and far,
A voice fell like a falling star—
Excelsior !

THE RAINY DAY.

The day is cold and dark and dreary ;
It rains, and the wind is never weary ;
The vine still clings to the mouldering wall,
But at every gust the dead leaves fall :
And the day is dark and dreary.

My life is cold, and dark, and dreary ;
It rains, and the wind is never weary ;
My thoughts still cling to the mouldering past,
But the hopes of youth fall thick in the blast,
And the days are dark and dreary.

Be still, sad heart ! and cease repining :
Behind the clouds is the sun still shining ;
Thy fate is the common fate of all :
Into each life some rain must fall,
   Some days must be dark and dreary.

CHILDREN.

Come to me, O ye children !
   For I hear you at your play :
And the questions that perplex'd me
   Have vanish'd quite away.

Ye open the Eastern windows
   That look toward the sun,
Where thoughts are singing swallows
   And the brooks of morning run.

In your hearts are the birds and the sunshine,
   In your thoughts the brooklets flow :
But in mine is the wind of Autumn
   And the first fall of the snow.

Ah ! what would the world be to us,
   If the children were no more ?
We should dread the desert behind us
   Worse than the dark before.

What the leaves are to the forest,
   With light and air for food,
Ere their sweet and tender juices
   Have been harden'd into wood,—

That to the world are children :
   Through them it feels the glow
Of a brighter and sunnier climate
   Than reaches the trunks below.

Come to me, O ye children !
   And whisper in my ear
   II.—11

What the birds and the winds are singing
  In your sunny atmosphere.

For what are all our contrivings,
  And the wisdom of our books,
When compared with your caresses
  And the gladness of your looks?

Ye are better than all the ballads
  That ever were sung or said:
For ye are living poems,
  And all the rest are dead.

JOHN GREENLEAF WHITTIER.
1807—

IN SCHOOL-DAYS.

Still sits the school-house by the road,
  A ragged beggar, sunning:
Around it still the sumachs grow,
  And blackberry vines are running.

Within the master's desk is seen,
  Deep-scarr'd by raps official;
The warping floor, the batter'd seats,
  The jack-knife's carved initial;

The charcoal frescoes on its wall;
  Its door's worn sill, betraying
The feet that, creeping slow to school,
  Went storming out to playing.

Long years ago a winter sun
  Shone over it at setting;
Lit up its Western window panes
  And low eaves icy fretting.

It touch'd the tangled golden curls,
  And brown eyes full of grieving,

Of One who still her steps delay'd
  When all the school were leaving.

For near her stood the little boy
  Her childish favour singled,
His cap pull'd low upon a face
  Where pride and shame were mingled.

Pushing with restless feet the snow
  To right and left, he linger'd,
As restlessly her tiny hands
  The blue-check'd apron finger'd.

He saw her lift her eyes ; he felt
  The soft hand's light caressing ;
And heard the tremble of her voice,
  As if a fault confessing :

" I'm sorry that I spell'd the word ;
  I hate to go above you,
Because " (the brown eyes lower fell),
  " Because, you see, I love you."

Still memory to a grey-hair'd man
  That sweet child-face is showing :
Dear girl ! the grasses on her grave
  Have forty years been growing.

He lives to learn, in life's hard school,
  How few who pass above him
Lament their triumph and his loss,
  Like her,—because they love him.

TELLING THE BEES.

Here is the place : right over the hill
  Runs the path I took ;
You can see the gap in the old wall still,
  And the stepping-stones in the shallow brook.

There is the house, with the gate red-barr'd,
  And the poplars tall,
And the barn's brown length, and the cattle yard,
  And the white horns tossing above the wall.

There are the bee-hives ranged in the sun;
  And down by the brink
Of the brook are her poor flowers, weed o'er-run,
  Pansy and daffodil, rose and pink.

A year has gone, as the tortoise goes,
  Heavy and slow;
And the same rose blows, and the same sun glows,
  And the same brook sings, of a year ago.

There's the same sweet clover-smell in the breeze;
  And the June sun warm
Tangles his wings of fire in the trees,
  Setting, as then, over Fernside Farm.

I mind me how, with a lover's care,
  From my Sunday coat
I brush'd off the burrs, and smoothed my hair,
  And cool'd at the brookside my brow and throat.

Since we parted a month had pass'd,—
  To love a year;
Down through the beeches I look'd at last
  On the little red gate and the well-sweep near.

I can see it all now,—the slant-wise rain
  Of light through the leaves,
The sun-down's blaze on her window-pane,
  The bloom of her roses under the eaves.

Just the same as a month before,
  The house and the trees,
The barn's brown gable, the vine by the door,—
  Nothing changed but the hives of bees.

Before them, under the garden wall,
  Forward and back,
Went drearily singing the chore-girl small,
  Draping each hive with a shred of black.

Trembling I listen'd : the summer sun
  Had the chill of snow ;
For I knew she was telling the bees of One
  Gone on the journey we all must go.

Then I said to myself—My Mary weeps
  For the Dead to-day :
Haply her blind old grandsire sleeps
  The fret and the pain of his age away.

But her dog whined low ; on the doorway sill,
  With his cane to his chin,
The old man sat ; and the chore-girl still
  Sang to the bees stealing out and in.

And the song she was singing ever since
  In my ear sounds on :
" Stay at home, pretty bees ! fly not hence !
  Mistress Mary is dead and gone ! "

ICHABOD.

So fallen ! so lost ! the light withdrawn
      Which once he wore !
The glory from his grey hairs gone
      For evermore !

Revile him not ! the Tempter hath
      A snare for all ;
And pitying tears, not scorn and wrath,
      Befit his fall.

O ! dumb be passion's stormy rage,
      When he who might
Have lighted up and led his age
      Falls back in night !

Scorn ?   Would the angels laugh to mark
        A bright soul driven,
Fiend-goaded, down the endless dark
        From hope and heaven ?

Let not the land once proud of him
        Insult him now;
Nor brand with deeper shame his dim
        Dishonour'd brow !

But let its humbled sons, instead,
        From sea to lake
A long lament as for the Dead
        In sadness make !

Of all we loved and honour'd nought
        Save power remains,—
A fallen angel's pride of thought,
        Still strong in chains.

All else is gone; from those great eyes
        The soul hath fled :
When faith is lost, when honour dies,
        The Man is dead.

Then pay the reverence of old days
        To his dead fame :
Walk backward, with averted gaze,
        And hide the shame !

THE RIVER-PATH.

No bird-song floated down the hill,
The tangled bank below was still;
No rustle from the birchen stem,
No ripple from the water's hem :
The dusk of twilight round us grew,
We felt the falling of the dew,

For from us ere the day was done
The wooded hills shut out the sun.
But on the river's farther side
We saw the hill-tops glorified :
A tender glow, exceeding fair,
A dream of day without its glare :
With us the damp, the chill, the gloom ;
With them the sunset's rosy bloom :
While dark, through willowy vistas seen,
The river roll'd in shade between.
From out the darkness where we trod
We gazed upon those hills of God,
Whose light seem'd not of moon or sun.
We spake not, but our thought was one.
We paused, as if from that bright shore
Beckon'd our Dear Ones gone before ;
And still'd our beating hearts to hear
The voices lost to mortal ear.
Sudden our pathway turn'd from night :
The hills swung open to the light ;
Through their green gates the sunshine show'd,
A long slant splendour downward flow'd :
Down glade and glen and bank it roll'd ;
It bridged the shaded stream with gold ;
And, borne on piers of mist, allied
The shadowy with the sunlit side.

So (pray'd we), when our feet draw near
The river dark with mortal fear,
And the night cometh chill with dew,
O Father ! let thy light break through !
So let the hills of doubt divide !
So bridge with faith the sunless tide !
So let the eyes that fail on earth
On thy eternal hills look forth,
And in thy beckoning Angels know
The Dear Ones whom we loved below !

RICHARD CHENEVIX TRENCH.
1807—

THE LENT JEWELS.

In schools of wisdom all the day was spent :
His steps at eve the Rabbi homeward bent,
With homeward thoughts which dwelt upon the wife
And two fair children who consoled his life.
She, meeting at the threshold, led him in,
And, with these words preventing, did begin :—
" Ever rejoicing at your wish'd return,
Yet am I most so now : for since this morn
I have been much perplex'd and sorely tried
Upon one point which you shall now decide.
Some years ago, a friend into my care
Some jewels gave,—rich precious gems they were ;
But having given them in my charge, this friend
Did afterward nor come for them, nor send,
But left them in my keeping for so long
That now it almost seems to me a wrong
That he should suddenly arrive to-day,
To take those jewels which he left away.
What think you ? Shall I freely yield them back,
And with no murmuring ?—so henceforth to lack
Those gems myself, which I had learn'd to see
Almost as mine for ever, mine in fee."

" What question can be here ? Your own true heart
Must needs advise you of the only part :
That may be claim'd again which was but lent,
And should be yielded with no discontent ;
Nor surely can we find herein a wrong,
That it was left us to enjoy so long."

" Good is the word ! " she answer'd : " may we now
And evermore that it is good allow ! "
And, rising, to an inner chamber led ;

And there she show'd him, stretch'd upon one bed,
Two children pale.   And he the jewels knew
Which God had lent him and resumed anew.

EDGAR ALLAN POE.

1809—1849.

THE BELLS.

Hear the sledges with the bells,
    Silver bells!
What a world of merriment their melody foretells!
    How they tinkle, tinkle, tinkle,
        In the icy air of night!
    While the stars that oversprinkle
    All the heavens seem to twinkle
        With a crystalline delight:
    Keeping time, time, time,
    In a sort of Runic rhyme,
To the tintinnabulation that so musically wells
    From the bells, bells, bells, bells,
            Bells, bells, bells,—
From the jingling and the tinkling of the bells.

    Hear the mellow wedding bells,
        Golden bells!
What a world of happiness their harmony fortells!
    Through the balmy air of night
    How they ring out their delight!
    From the molten-golden notes,
        And all in tune,
    What a liquid ditty floats
To the turtle-dove that listens, while she gloats
        On the moon!
    O, from out the sounding cells
What a gush of euphony voluminously wells!
        How it swells!
        How it dwells

On the future! how it tells
Of the rapture that impels
To the swinging and the ringing
    Of the bells, bells, bells,
Of the bells, bells, bells, bells,
        Bells, bells, bells,—
To the rhyming and the chiming of the bells!

Hear the loud alarum bells,
        Brazen bells!
What a tale of terror now their turbulency tells!
    In the startled ear of night
    How they scream out their affright!
    Too much horrified to speak,
    They can only shriek, shriek
        Out of tune,
In the clamorous appealing to the mercy of the fire,
In a mad expostulation with the deaf and frantic fire
    Leaping higher, higher, higher,
    With a desperate desire,
    And a resolute endeavour,
    Now, now to sit or never
By the side of the pale-faced moon.
    O the bells, bells, bells,
    What a tale their terror tells
        Of despair!
    How they clang, and clash, and roar!
    What a horror they outpour
On the bosom of the palpitating air!
    Yet the ear it fully knows,
        By the twanging,
        And the clanging,
    How the danger ebbs and flows ;
    Yet the ear distinctly tells,
        In the jangling,
        And the wrangling,

How the danger sinks and swells,
By the sinking or the swelling in the anger of the
            bells,—
            Of the bells,
Of the bells, bells, bells, bells,
        Bells, bells, bells,—
In the clamor and the clangor of the bells!

    Hear the tolling of the bells,
            Iron bells !
What a world of solemn thought their monody compels !
    In the silence of the night
    How we shiver with affright
At the melancholy menace of their tone !
    For every sound that floats
    From the rust within their throats
            Is a groan.
And the people (ah ! the people,
They that dwell up in the steeple,
            All alone,
And who tolling, tolling, tolling,
    In that muffled monotone,
Feel a glory in so rolling
    On the human heart a stone),
They are neither man nor woman,
They are neither brute nor human,
            They are Ghouls :
And their king it is who tolls ;
And he rolls, rolls, rolls,
            Rolls,
    A pæan from the bells !
And his merry bosom swells
    With the pæan of the bells ;
And he dances, and he yells,
Keeping time, time, time,
In a sort of Runic rhyme

To the pæan of the bells,
        Of the bells !
Keeping time, time, time,
In a sort of Runic rhyme,
To the throbbing of the bells,
    Of the bells, bells, bells,
To the sobbing of the bells,—
Keeping time, time, time,
As he knells, knells, knells,
In a happy Runic rhyme,
To the rolling of the bells,
    Of the bells, bells, bells,
To the tolling of the bells,
Of the bells, bells, bells, bells,
        Bells, bells, bells,—
To the moaning and the groaning of the bells.

TO HELEN.

Helen ! thy beauty is to me
    Like those Nicean barks of yore
That gently o'er a perfumed sea
The weary way-worn wanderer bore
    To his own native shore.

On desperate seas long wont to roam,
    Thy hyacinth hair, thy classic face,
Thy Naiad airs, have brought me home
To the glory that was Greece
    And the grandeur that was Rome.

Lo ! in your brilliant window-niche
    How statue-like I see thee stand,
The agate lamp within thy hand !
Ah, Psychè ! from the regions which
    Are holy land.

OLIVER WENDELL HOLMES.

1809—

THE CHAMBERED NAUTILUS.

This is the Ship of Pearl which (poets feign)
     Sails the unshadow'd main,
     The venturous bark that flings
On the sweet summer wind its purpled wings
In gulfs enchanted, where the Siren sings,
     And coral reefs lie bare,
Where the cold Sea-Maids rise to sun their streaming hair.

Its webs of living gauze no more unfurl :
     Wreck'd is the Ship of Pearl ;
     And every chamber'd cell,
Where its dim dreaming life was wont to dwell
As the frail tenant shaped his growing shell,
     Before thee lies reveal'd :
Its iris'd ceiling rent, its sunless crypt unseal'd.

Year after year beheld the silent toil
     That spread his lustrous coil ;
     Still as the spiral grew
He left the past year's dwelling for the new,
Stole with soft step its shining archway through,
     Built up its idle door,
Stretch'd in his last-found home, and knew the old no more.

Thanks for the heavenly message brought by thee,
     Child of the wandering Sea,
     Cast from her lap, forlorn !
From thy dead lips a clearer note is borne
Than ever Triton blew from wreathèd horn !
     While on mine ear it rings,
Through the deep caves of thought I hear a voice that sings :

Build thee more stately mansions, O my soul !
        As the swift seasons roll :
        Leave thy low-vaulted past !
Let each new temple, nobler than the last,
Shut thee from heaven with a dome more vast,
        Till thou at length art free,
Leaving thine outgrown shell by life's unresting sea !

ALFRED TENNYSON.

1809—

TITHONUS.

The woods decay, the woods decay and fall,
The vapours weep their burthen to the ground,
Man comes and tills the field and lies beneath,
And after many a summer dies the swan.
Me only cruel immortality
Consumes : I wither slowly in thine arms,
Here at the quiet limit of the world,
A white-hair'd shadow roaming like a dream
The ever-silent spaces of the East,
Far-folded mists, and gleaming halls of Morn.

Alas for this grey shadow, once a man,
So glorious in his beauty and thy choice,
Who madèst him thy chosen, that he seem'd
To his great heart none other than a God !
I ask'd thee—" Give me immortality ! "
Then didst thou grant mine asking with a smile,
Like wealthy men who care not how they give.
But thy strong Hours, indignant, work'd their wills,
And beat me down, and marr'd and wasted me ;
And, though they could not end me, left me maim'd
To dwell in presence of immortal youth,
Immortal Age beside immortal Youth,
And all I was in ashes.   Can thy love,

Thy beauty, make amends? though even now
Close over us the silver star, thy guide,
Shines in those tremulous eyes that fill with tears
To hear me. Let me go! Take back thy gift!
Why should a man desire in any way
To vary from the kindly race of men,
Or pass beyond the goal of ordinance
Where all should pause, as is most meet for all?

A soft air fans the cloud apart; there comes
A glimpse of that dark world where I was born.
Once more the old mysterious glimmer steals
From thy pure brows, and from thy shoulders pure,
And bosom beating with a heart renew'd.
Thy cheek begins to redden through the gloom;
Thy sweet eyes brighten slowly close to mine
Ere yet they blind the stars, and the wild team
Which love thee, yearning for thy yoke, arise
And shake the darkness from their loosen'd manes
And beat the twilight into flakes of fire.

Lo! ever thus thou growest beautiful
In silence; then, before thine answer given,
Departest, and thy tears are on my cheek.

Why wilt thou ever scare me with thy tears,
And make me tremble lest a saying learn'd
In days far off, on that dark earth, be true?
" The Gods themselves can not recall their gifts."

Ay me! ay me! with what another heart,
In days far off, and with what other eyes
I used to watch (if I be he that watch'd)
The lucid outline forming round thee; saw
The dim curls kindle into sunny rings;
Changed with thy mystic change, and felt my blood
Glow with the glow that slowly crimson'd all
Thy presence and thy portals,—while I lay,

Mouth, forehead, eyelids, growing dewy-warm
With kisses balmier than half-opening buds
Of April, and could hear the lips that kiss'd,
Whispering I knew not what of wild and sweet:
Like that strange song I heard Apollo sing,
While Ilion like a mist rose into towers.

Yet hold me not for ever in thine East!
How can my nature longer mix with thine?
Coldly thy rosy shadows bathe me, cold
Are all my lights, and cold my wrinkled feet
Upon thy glimmering thresholds, when the steam
Floats up from those dim fields about the homes
Of happy men that have the power to die,
And grassy barrows of the happier dead.
Release me and restore me to the ground!
Thou seèst all things, thou wilt see my grave:
Thou wilt renew thy beauty morn by morn;
I, earth in earth, forget these empty courts
And thee returning on thy silver wheels.

MARIANA

"IN THE MOATED GRANGE."

With blackest moss the flower plots
Were thickly crusted, one and all;
The rusted nails fell from the knots
That held the peach to the garden wall.
The broken sheds look'd sad and strange,
Unlifted was the clinking latch,
Weeded and worn the ancient thatch
Upon the lonely moated grange.
  She only said—" My life is dreary,
   He cometh not:" she said.
  She said—" I am aweary, aweary,—
   I would that I were dead!"

Her tears fell with the dews at even,
Her tears fell ere the dews were dried ;
She could not look on the sweet heaven
Either at morn or eventide.
After the flitting of the bats,
When thickest dark did trance the sky,
She drew her casement curtain by,
And glanced athwart the glooming flats.
          She only said—" The night is dreary,
              He cometh not : " she said.
          She said—" I am aweary, aweary,—
              I would that I were dead ! "

Upon the middle of the night,
Waking, she heard the night fowl crow ;
The cock sung out an hour ere light ;
From the dark fen the oxen's low
Came to her : without hope of change,
In sleep she seem'd to walk forlorn,
Till colds winds woke the grey-eyed morn
About the lonely moated grange.
          She only said—" The day is dreary,
              He cometh not : " she said.
          She said—" I am aweary, aweary,—
              I would that I were dead ! "

About a stone-cast from the wall,
A sluice with blacken'd waters slept,
And o'er it many, round and small,
The cluster'd marish-mosses crept.
Hard by a poplar shook alway,
All silver green with gnarled bark :
For leagues no other tree did dark
The level waste, the rounding grey.
          She only said—" My life is dreary,
              He cometh not : " she said.
          She said—" I am aweary, aweary,—
              I would that I were dead ! "

II.—12

And ever when the moon was low,
And the shrill winds were up and away,
In the white curtain, to and fro,
She saw the gusty shadow sway.
But when the moon was very low,
And wild winds bound within their cell,
The shadow of the poplar fell
Upon her bed, across her brow.
    She only said—" The night is dreary,
      He cometh not : " she said.
    She said—" I am aweary, aweary,—
      I would that I were dead ! "

All day within the dreamy house
The doors upon their hinges creak'd ;
The blue fly sang i' the pane ; the mouse
Behind the mouldering wainscot shriek'd,
Or from the crevice peer'd about.
Old faces glimmer'd through the doors,
Old footsteps trod the upper floors,
Old voices called her from without.
    She only said—" My life is dreary,
      He cometh not : " she said.
    She said—" I am aweary, aweary,—
      I would that I were dead ! "

The sparrow's chirrup on the roof,
The slow clock ticking, and the sound
Which to the wooing wind aloof
The poplar made, did all confound
Her sense ; but most she loathed the hour
When the thick-moted sunbeam lay
Athwart the chambers, and the day
Was sloping toward his western bower.
    Then said she—" I am very dreary,
      He will not come : " she said.
    She wept,—" I am aweary, aweary,—
      O God, that I were dead ! "

THE POET'S SONG.

The rain had fallen; the Poet arose,
  He pass'd by the town and out of the street:
A light wind blew from the gates of the sun,
  And waves of shadow went over the wheat:
And he sat him down in a lonely place,
  And chanted a melody loud and sweet,
That made the wild swan pause in her cloud
  And the lark drop down at his feet.

The swallow stopp'd as he hunted the bee,
  The snake slipp'd under a spray,
The wild hawk stood with the down on his beak
  And stared, with his foot on the prey;
And the nightingale thought—" I have sung many songs,
  But never a one so gay,—
For he sings of what the world will be
  When the years have died away."

THE DAYS THAT ARE NO MORE.

Tears, idle tears, I know not what they mean:
Tears from the depth of some divine despair
Rise in the heart and gather to the eyes
In looking on the happy autumn fields
And thinking of the days that are no more.

Fresh as the first beam glittering on a sail
That brings our friends up from the under world,
Sad as the last which reddens over one
That sinks with all we love below the verge,—
So sad, so fresh, the days that are no more!

Ah! sad and strange as in dark summer dawns
The earliest pipe of half-awaken'd birds
To dying ears, when unto dying eyes

The casement slowly grows a glimmering square,—
So sad, so strange, the days that are no more !

Dear as remember'd kisses after death,
And sweet as those by hopeless fancy feign'd
On lips that are for others ; deep as love,
Deep as first love, and wild with all regret,
O death in life ! the days that are no more.

RICHARD MONCKTON MILNES.
(LORD HOUGHTON.)
1809—

THE BROOK-SIDE.

I wander'd by the brook-side,
  I wander'd by the mill,—
I could not hear the brook flow,
  The noisy wheel was still ;
There was no burr of grasshopper,
  No chirp of any bird :
But the beating of my own heart
  Was all the sound I heard.

I sat beneath the elm-tree ;
  I watch'd the long long shade,
And as it grew still longer
  I did not feel afraid :
For I listen'd for a footfall,
  I listen'd for a word,—
But the beating of my own heart
  Was all the sound I heard.

He came not,—no ! he came not ;
  The night came on alone,
The little stars sat one by one
  Each on his golden throne ;
The evening wind pass'd by my cheek,
  The leaves above were stirr'd,—

But the beating of my own heart
  Was all the sound I heard.

Fast silent tears were flowing,
  When something stood behind;
A hand was on my shoulder,—
  I knew its touch was kind;
It drew me nearer, nearer;
  We did not speak one word,—
For the beating of our own hearts
  Was all the sound we heard.

THE TREASURE SHIP.

My heart is freighted full of love,
As full as any argosy,
With gems below and gems above,—
And ready for the open sea,
For the wind is blowing summerly:

Full strings of Nature's beaded pearl,
Sweet tears, composed in amorous ties
And turkis-lockets, that no churl
Hath fashion'd out mechanic-wise,
But all made up of thy blue eyes;

And girdles wove of subtle sound,
And thoughts not trusted to the air,
Of antique mould, the same as bound
In Paradise the primal pair
Before Love's arts and niceness were;

And carcanets of living sighs,
Gums that have dropp'd from Love's own stem;
And one small jewel most I prize,
The darling gaud of all of them:
I wot, so rare and fine a gem
Ne'er glow'd on Eastern anadem.

I've cased the rubies of thy smiles
In rich and triply-plated gold ;
But this no other wealth defiles :
Itself—itself can only hold—
The stealthy kiss on Maple-Wold.

WILLIAM MAKEPEACE THACKERAY.

1811—1863.

AT THE CHURCH GATE.

Although I enter not,
Yet round about the spot
    Ofttimes I hover ;
And near the sacred gate,
With longing eyes I wait,
    Expectant of her.

The Minster bell tolls out
Above the city's rout
    And noise and humming ;
They've hush'd the Minster bell ;
The organ 'gins to swell :
    She's coming ! she's coming !

My Lady comes at last,
Timid and stepping fast
    And hastening hither,
With modest eyes down-cast :
She comes—she's here—she's pass'd.
    May heaven go with her !

Kneel undisturb'd, fair Saint !
Pour out your praise or plaint
    Meekly and duly !
I will not enter there
To sully your pure prayer
    With thoughts unruly.

But suffer me to pace
Round the forbidden place,
　Lingering a minute!
Like outcast spirits who wait
And see through heaven's gate
　Angels within it.

THE AGE OF WISDOM.

Ho, pretty Page with the dimpled chin
　That never has known the barber's shear!
All your wish is woman to win :
This is the way that boys begin :
　Wait till you come to Forty Year!

Curly gold locks cover foolish brains;
　Billing and cooing is all your cheer,
Sighing, and singing of midnight strains
Under Bonnybell's window panes :
　Wait till you come to Forty Year!

Forty times over let Michaelmas pass,
　Grizzling hair the brain doth clear :
Then you know a boy is an ass,
Then you know the worth of a lass,
　Once you have come to Forty Year.

Pledge me round!　I bid ye declare,
　All good fellows whose beards are grey!
Did not the fairest of the fair
Common grow and wearisome ere
　Ever a month was pass'd away?

The reddest lips that ever were kiss'd,
　The brightest eyes that ever have shone,
May pray and whisper, and we not list,
Or look away ; and never be miss'd
　Ere yet ever a month is gone.

Gillian's dead : God rest her bier !
 How I loved her twenty years syne !
Marian's married : but I sit here,
Alone and merry at Forty Year,
 Dipping my nose in the Gascon wine.

SIR FRANCIS HASTINGS DOYLE.
1810—1883.

THE PRIVATE OF THE BUFFS.

Last night, among his fellow roughs,
 He jested, quaff'd, and swore,—
A drunken Private of the Buffs,
 Who never look'd before :
To-day, beneath the foeman's frown,
 He stands in Elgin's place,
Ambassador from Britain's crown,
 And type of all her race.

Poor, reckless, rude, low-born, untaught,
 Bewilder'd, and alone,
A heart with English instinct fraught
 He yet can call his own.
Ay ! tear his body limb from limb !
 Bring cord, or axe, or flame !
He only knows that not through him
 Shall England come to shame.

Far Kentish hop-fields round him seem'd
 Like dreams to come and go ;
Bright leagues of cherry-blossom gleam'd,
 One sheet of living snow ;
The smoke above his father's door
 In grey soft eddyings hung,—
Must he then watch it rise no more,
 Doom'd by himself, so young?

Yes ! honour calls : with strength like steel
    He put the vision by.
Let dusky Indians whine and kneel !
    An English lad must die.
And thus, with eyes that would not shrink,
    With knee to man unbent,
Unfaltering on its dreadful brink,
    To his red grave he went.

Vain mightiest fleets of iron framed,
    Vain those all-shattering guns,
Unless proud England keep untamed
    The strong heart of her sons !
So let his name through Europe ring !
    A man of mean estate
Who died as firm as Sparta's king,
    Because his soul was great.

ALFRED DOMETT.

1811—

WHAT MATTER ?

I

What matter, what matter, O friend ! though the sea
In lines of silvery fire may slide
O'er the sands so tawny and tender and wide,
    Murmuring soft as a bee ?—
No matter ! no matter ! in sooth, said he :
But the sunlit sands and the silvery play
Are a truthful smile long pass'd away :
    No more to me.

II

What matter, what matter, dear friend ! can it be
If a long blue stripe, dim-swelling and dark
Beneath the lighter blue headland, may mark
    All of the town we can see ?

No matter ! no matter ! in truth, said he :
But the streak, that fades and fades as we part,
Is a broken voice and a breaking heart :
    No more to me.

ELIZABETH BARRETT BROWNING.

1809—1861.

A MUSICAL INSTRUMENT.

What was he doing, the great God Pan,
    Down in the reeds by the river?
Spreading ruin and scattering ban,
Splashing and paddling with hoofs of a goat,
And breaking the golden lilies afloat
    With the dragon-fly on the river.

He tore out a reed, the great God Pan,
    From the deep cool bed of the river :
The limpid water turbidly ran,
And the broken lilies a-dying lay,
And the dragon-fly had fled away,
    Ere he brought it out of the river.

High on the shore sat the great God Pan,
    While turbidly flow'd the river ;
And hack'd and hew'd, as a great God can,
With his hard bleak steel at the patient reed,
Till there was not a sign of a leaf indeed
    To prove it fresh from the river.

He cut it short, did the great God Pan,
    (How tall it stood in the river !)
Then drew the pith, like the heart of a man,
Steadily from the outside ring,
And notch'd the poor dry empty thing
    In holes, as he sat by the river.

" This is the way," laugh'd the great God Pan,
       Laugh'd while he sat by the river,—
" The only way, since Gods began
   To make sweet music, they could succeed."
   Then, dropping his mouth to a hole in the reed,
       He blew in power, by the river.

Sweet, sweet, sweet, O Pan !
       Piercing sweet by the river !
Blinding sweet, O great God Pan !
The sun on the hill forgot to die,
And the lilies revived, and the dragon-fly
       Came back to dream on the river.

Yet half a beast is the great God Pan,
       To laugh as he sits by the river,
Making a poet out of a man !
The true Gods sigh for the cost and pain,—
For the reed which grows nevermore again
       As a reed with the reeds in the river.

A FALSE STEP.

Sweet ! thou hast trod on a heart :
   Pass ! there's a world full of men ;
And women as fair as thou art
   Must do such things now and then.

Thou only hast stepp'd unaware,
   (Malice not one can impute) ;
And why should a heart have been there
   In the way of a fair woman's foot ?

It was not a stone that could trip,
   Nor was it a thorn that could rend :
Put up thy proud under-lip !
   'Twas merely the heart of a friend.

And yet, peradventure, one day
　Thou sitting alone at the glass,
Remarking the bloom gone away,
　Where the smile in its dimplement was,

And seeking around thee in vain,
　From hundreds who flatter'd before,
Such a word as " O, not in the main
　Do I hold thee less precious, but more : "

Thou wilt sigh, very like, on thy part—
　" Of all I have known or can know
I wish I had only that Heart
　I trod upon ages ago ! "

THE SEA-MEW.

How joyously the young Sea-Mew
Lay dreaming on the waters blue,
Whereon our little bark had thrown
A forward shade, the only one :
But shadows aye will man pursue.

Familiar with the waves, and free
As if their own white foam were he,
His heart upon the heart of ocean
Lay, learning all its mystic motion
And throbbing to the throbbing sea.

And such a brightness in his eye,
As if the ocean and the sky
Within him had lit up and nursed
A soul God gave him not at first,
To comprehend their majesty.

We were not cruel, yet did sunder
His white wing from the blue waves under,
And bound it,—while his fearless eyes
Shone up to ours in calm surprise,
As deeming us some ocean wonder.

We bore our ocean bird unto
A grassy place where he might view
The flowers that curtsey to the bees,
The waving of the tall green trees,
The falling of the silver dew.

But flowers of earth were pale to him
Who had seen the rainbow fishes swim ;
And when earth's dew around him lay
He thought of ocean's winged spray :
And his eye waxed sad and dim.

The green trees round him only made
A prison with their darksome shade ;
And droop'd his wing, and mourned he
For his own boundless glittering sea,—
Albeit he knew not they could fade.

Then One her gladsome face did bring,
Her gentle voice's murmuring,
In ocean's stead his heart to move
And teach him what was human love :
He thought it a strange mournful thing.

He lay down in his grief to die
(First looking to the sea-like sky
That hath no waves) : because, alas !
Our human touch did on him pass,
And with our touch our agony.

SONNETS.

Unlike are we, unlike, O Princely Heart !
Unlike our uses and our destinies.
Our ministering two angels look surprise
On one another as they strike athwart
Their wings in passing.   Thou (bethink thee !) art
A guest for queens to social pageantries,

With gages, from a hundred brighter eyes
Than tears even can make mine, to ply thy part
Of chief musician.　What hast Thou to do
With looking from the lattice-lights at me,
A poor tired wandering singer, singing through
The dark, and leaning up a cypress tree?
The chrism is on thine head, on mine the dew :
And Death must dig the level where these agree.

Go from me!　Yet I feel that I shall stand
Henceforward in thy shadow.　Nevermore,
Alone upon the threshold of my door
Of individual life, I shall command
The uses of my soul, nor lift my hand
Serenely in the sunshine as before,
Without the sense of that which I forebore—
Thy touch upon the palm.　The widest land
Doom takes to part us leaves thy heart in mine
With pulses that beat double.　What I do
And what I dream include Thee, as the wine
Must taste of its own grapes.　And when I sue
God for myself, he hears that name of thine,
And sees within my eyes the tears of two.

Say over again, and yet once over again,
That thou dost love me!　Though the word repeated
Should seem "a cuckoo song," as thou dost treat it,
Remember never to the hill or plain,
Valley and wood, without her cuckoo strain
Comes the fresh Spring in all her green completed!
Belovèd!　I, amid the darkness greeted
By a doubtful spirit's voice, in that doubt's pain
Cry—Speak once more, thou lovèst!　Who can fear
Too many stars, though each in heaven shall roll;
Too many flowers, though each shall crown the year?

Say thou dost love me, love me, love me ! toll
The silver iterance !—only minding, Dear !
To love me also in silence, with thy soul.

First time he kiss'd me, he but only kiss'd
The fingers of this hand wherewith I write ;
And ever since it grew more clean and white,
Slow to world-greetings, quick with its "O list !"
When the angels speak.   A ring of amethyst
I could not wear here plainer to my sight
Than that first kiss.   The second pass'd in height
The first, and sought the forehead and half-miss'd,
Half-falling on the hair.   O, beyond meed,
That was the chrism of Love, which Love's own crown,
With sanctifying sweetness, did precede.
The third upon my lips was folded down
In perfect purple state.   Since when indeed
I have been proud, and said—My Love ! my own !

ROBERT BROWNING.

1812—

THE LOST LEADER.

Just for a handful of silver he left us,
Just for a ribbon to stick in his coat ;
Found the one gift of which Fortune bereft us,
Lost all the others she lets us devote.
They with the gold to give doled him out silver,
So much was theirs who so little allow'd :
How all our copper had gone for his service !
Rags—were they purple, his heart had been proud.
We that had loved him so, follow'd him, honour'd him,
Lived in his mild and magnificent eye,
Learn'd his great language, caught his clear accents,
Made him our pattern to live and to die !
Shakespeare was of us, Milton was for us,

Burns, Shelley, were with us,—they watch from their graves!
He alone breaks from the van and the freemen;
He alone sinks to the rear and the slaves.

We shall march prospering, not through his presence;
Songs may inspirit us, not from his lyre;
Deeds will be done, while he boasts his quiescence,
Still bidding crouch whom the rest bade aspire.
Blot out his name then! record one lost soul more,
One task more declined, one more foot-path untrod,
One more devils'-triumph and sorrow for angels,
One wrong more for man, one more insult to God!
Life's night begins: let him never come back to us!
There would be doubt, hesitation, and pain,
Forced praise on our part, the glimmer of twilight,
Never glad confident morning again.
Best fight on, well, for we taught him; strike gallantly,
Menace our heart ere we master his own!
Then let him receive the new knowledge, and wait us,
Pardon'd, in heaven, the first by the Throne!

THE MOTH'S KISS.

The moth's kiss first!
    Kiss me as if you made believe
    You were not sure, this eve,
How my face, your flower, had pursed
    Its petals up: so here and there
    You brush it, till I grow aware
Who wants me, and wide ope I burst!

The bee's kiss now!
    Kiss me as if you enter'd gay
    My heart, at some noon-day,
A bud that dares not disallow
    The claim, so all is render'd up,
    And passively its shatter'd cup
Over your head to sleep I bow!

EVELYN HOPE.

Beautiful Evelyn Hope is dead !
  Sit and watch by her side an hour.
That is her book-shelf, this her bed ;
  She pluck'd that piece of geranium-flower,
Beginning to die too, in the glass.
  Little has yet been changed, I think,—
The shutters are shut, no light may pass
  Save two long rays through the hinge's chink.

Sixteen years old when she died !
  Perhaps she had scarcely heard my name :
It was not her time to love ; beside,
  Her life had many a hope and aim,
Duties enough, and little cares ;
  And now was quiet, now astir,
Till God's hand beckon'd unawares,
  And the sweet white brow is all of her.

Is it too late then ? Evelyn Hope !
  What ! your soul was pure and true,
The good stars met in your horoscope,
  Made you of spirit, fire and dew,—
And just because I was thrice as old,
  And our paths in the world diverged so wide,
Each was nought to each—must I be told ?
  We were fellow-mortals—nought beside ?

No, indeed ! for God above
  Is great to grant as mighty to make,
And creates the love to reward the love :
  I claim you still, for my own love's sake !
Delay'd it may be, for more lives yet,
  Through worlds I shall traverse, not a few :
Much is to learn and much to forget
  Ere the time be come for taking you.
    II.—13

But the time will come—at last it will—
  When, Evelyn Hope! what mean'd, I shall say,
In the lower earth, in the years long still,
  That body and soul so pure and gay?
Why your hair was amber I shall divine,
  And your mouth of your own geranium's red :
And what you would do with me, in fine,
  In the new life come in the old one's stead.

I have lived (I shall say) so much since then ;
  Given up myself so many times,
Gain'd me the gains of various men,
  Ransack'd the ages, spoil'd the climes :
Yet one thing, one, in my soul's full scope,
  Either I miss'd or itself miss'd me,—
And I want and find you, Evelyn Hope !
  What is the issue ?   Let us see !

I loved you, Evelyn ! all the while
  My heart seem'd full as it would hold :
There was place and to spare for the frank young smile
  And the red young mouth and the hair's young gold.
So, hush ! I will give you this leaf to keep ;
  See ! I shut it inside the sweet cold hand.
There ! that is our secret : go to sleep !
  You will wake and remember, and understand.

NIGHT AND MORNING.

I.

The grey sea and the long black land,
And the yellow half-moon large and low,
And the startled little waves that leap
In fiery ringlets from their sleep
As I gain the cove with pushing prow
And quench its speed in the slushy sand.

Then a smile of warm sea-scented beach,
Three fields to cross till a farm appears ;
A tap at the pane, the quick sharp scratch

And blue spurt of a lighted match,
And a voice less loud through its joys and fears
Than the two hearts beating each to each.

2.

Round the cape of a sudden came the sea,
And the sun look'd over the mountain's rim :
And straight was a path of gold for him,
And the need of a world of men for me.

ROBERT NICOLL.

1814—1837.

BONNIE BESSIE LEE.

Bonnie Bessie Lee had a face fu' o' smiles,
An' mirth round her ripe lip was aye dancing slee ;
An' light was the footfa', an' winsome the wiles
O' the flower o' the parochin, our ain Bessie Lee.

Wi' the bairnies she would rin, and the school laddies paik,
And o'er the broomy braes like a fairy would flee,
Till auld hearts grew young again wi' love for her sake :
There was life in the blithe blink o' bonnie Bessie Lee.

She grat wi' the waefu' an' laugh'd wi' the glad ;
An' light as the wind 'mang the dancers was she ;
And a tongue that could jeer too the little limmer had,
Whilk keepit aye her ain side for bonnie Bessie Lee.

An' she whiles had a sweetheart, an' sometimes had twa,—
A limmer o' a lassie ! but, atween you and me,
Her warm wee bit heartie she ne'er threw awa,
Though monie a ane had sought it frae bonnie Bessie Lee,

But ten years had gane since I gazed on her last,
For ten years had parted my auld hame an' me ;
And I said to mysel' as her mither's door I pass'd—
" Will I ever get anither kiss frae bonnie Bessie Lee ?"

But Time changes a' things, the ill-natured loon !
Were it ever sae rightly, he'll no let it be :
But I rubbit o' my een, and I thought I would swoon,—
How the carle had come roun' about our ain Bessie Lee.

The wee laughing lassie was a gude-wife growing auld,
Twa weans at her apron and ane on her knee ;
She was douce too, an' wise-like,—an' wisdom's sae cauld :—
I would rather hae the ither ane than this Bessie Lee.

MENIE.

Fu' ripe, ripe, was her rosy lip ;
  An' gowden was her hair ;
An' white, white was her swan-like neek ;
  Her een like starnies were :
An' raven, raven was her hair ;
  So like the snaw her brow ;
An' the words that fell from her wee saft mouth
  Were happy words, I trow.

An' pure, pure was her maiden heart ;
  An' ne'er a thought o' sin
Durst venture there,—an angel dwelt
  Its borders a' within :
An' fair as was her sweet bodie,
  Yet fairer was her mind :—
Menie's the queen amang the flowers,
  The wale o' womankind.

THE GRAVE OF BURNS.

By a kirk-yard yett I stood, while many enter'd in :
Men bow'd wi' toil and age, wi' haffets auld an' thin,
And ithers in their prime wi' a bearin' proud an' hie,
An' maidens pure an' bonnie as the daisies o' the lea,
An' matrons wrinkled auld wi' lyart heads an' grey,
An' bairns like things owre fair for Death to wede away.

I stood beside the yett while onward still they went,
The laird frae out his ha' an' the shepherd frae the bent :
It seem'd a type o' man and o' the grave's domain,
But these were livin' a' an' could straight come forth again.
And o' the bedral auld wi' meikle courtesie
I speer'd what it might mean, an' he bade me look an' see.

On the trodden path that led to the house o' worshiping,
Or before its open doors, there stood nae livin' thing ;
But awa amang the tombs ilk comer quickly pass'd,
An' upon ae lowly grave ilk seekin' ee was cast :
There were sabbin' bosoms there, an' proud yet saften'd eyes,
And a whisper breathed around—" There the Loved and
    Honour'd lies ! "

There was nae a murmur there, the deep-drawn breath was
    hush'd ;
And o'er the maiden's cheek the tears o' feelin' gush'd ;
An' the bonnie infant's face was lifted as in prayer ;
An' manhood's brow was flush'd wi' the thoughts that movin'
    were :—
I stood beside the grave, and I gazed upon the stone :
And the name of Robert Burns was engraven thereupon.

THOMAS OSBORNE DAVIS.

1814—1845.

THE WELCOME.

Come in the evening, or come in the morning,—
Come when you're look'd for, or come without warning,—
Kisses and welcome you'll find here before you,
And the oftener you come here the more I'll adore you !
Light is my heart since the day we were plighted ;
Red is my cheek that they told me was blighted ;
The green of the trees looks far greener than ever ;
And the linnets are singing—True lovers don't sever !

I'll pull you sweet flowers to wear, if you choose 'em ;
Or, after you've kissed them, they'll lie on my bosom ;
I'll fetch from the mountain its breeze to inspire you ;
I'll fetch from my fancy a tale that won't tire you.
O ! your step's like the rain to the summer-vex'd farmer,
Or sabre and shield to a knight without armour !
I'll sing you sweet songs till the stars rise above me ;
Then wandering I'll wish you in silence to love me.

We'll look through the trees at the cliff and the eyrie ;
We'll tread round the rath on the track of the fairy ;
We'll look on the stars, and we'll list to the river,
Till you ask of your darling what gift you can give her.
O ! she'll whisper you—" Love, as unchangeably beaming,
And trust when in secret most tunefully streaming :
Till the star-light of heaven above us shall quiver,
As our souls flow in one down Eternity's river."

So come in the evening, or come in the morning,—
Come when you're look'd for, or come without warning,—
Kisses and welcome you'll find here before you ;
And the oftener you come here the more I'll adore you !
Light is my heart since the day we were plighted ;
Red is my cheek that they told me was blighted ;
The green of the trees looks far greener than ever ;
And the linnets are singing—True lovers don't sever !

WILLIAM BELL SCOTT.

1811—

THE NORNS WATERING YGGDRASILL.

Within the unchanging twilight
  Of the high land of the Gods
Between the murmuring fountain
  And the Ash-tree, tree of trees,
The Norns, the terrible Maidens,
  Forevermore come and go.

Yggdrasill, the populous Ash-tree
  Whose leaves embroider heaven,
Fills all the grey air with music :
  To Gods and to men sweet sounds,
But speech to the fine-ear'd Maidens
  Who evermore come and go.

That way to their domestead thrones
  The Æsir ride each day,
And every one bends to the saddle
  As they pass beneath the shade :
Even Odin, the strong All-Father,
Bends to the beautiful Maidens
  Who cease not to come and go.

The tempest crosses the high boughs,
  The great snakes heave below,
The wolf, the boar, and antler'd harts
  Delve at the life-giving roots ;
But all of them fear the wise Maidens,
The wise-hearted Water-bearers
  Who evermore come and go.

And men far away, in the night hours
  To the North-wind listening, hear,—
They hear the howl of the were-wolf,
  And know he hath felt the sting
Of the eyes of the potent Maidens
  Who sleeplessly come and go.

They hear on the wings of the North-wind
  A sound as of three that sing ;
And the skald, in the blae mist wandering
  High on the midland fell,
Heard the very words of the o'ersong
  Of the Norns, who come and go.

But alas for the ears of mortals
  Chance-hearing that fate-laden song !

The bones of the skald lie there still :
  For the speech of the leaves of the Tree
Is the song of the three Queen-Maidens
Who evermore come and go.

PARTING AND MEETING AGAIN.

Last time I parted from my Dear
The linnet sang from the briar-bush,
  The throstle from the dell ;
The stream too carol'd full and clear,
It was the spring-time of the year,
And both the linnet and the thrush
    I love them well
Since last I parted from my Dear.

But when he came again to me
The barley rustled high and low,
  Linnet and thrush were still ;
Yellow'd the apple on the tree,
'Twas autumn merry as it could be,
What time the white ships come and go
    Under the hill ;
They brought him back again to me,
Brought him safely o'er the sea.

PYGMALION.

" Mistress of Gods and men ! I have been thine
From boy to man, and many a myrtle rod
Have I made grow upon thy sacred sod,
Nor ever have I pass'd thy white shafts nine
Without some votive offering for the shrine,
Carved beryl or chased bloodstone ;—aid me now !
And I will live to fashion for thy brow
Heart-breaking priceless things : O, make her mine."
Venus inclined her ear, and through the Stone
Forthwith slid warmth like spring through sapling-stems,

And lo ! the eyelid stirr'd, beneath had grown
The tremulous light of life, and all the hems
Of her zoned peplos shook——Upon his breast
She sank, by two dread gifts at once oppress'd.

ROSE-LEAVES.

Once a rose ever a rose, we say :
One we loved and who loved us
Remains beloved though gone from day :
To human hearts it must be thus,
The past is sweetly laid away.

Sere and seal'd for a day and year,
Smell them, dear Christina ! pray :
So Nature treats its children dear,
So memory deals with yesterday :
The past is sweetly laid away.

WILLIAM JAMES LINTON.

1812—

BRIDAL SONG.

Blessed Hours ! approach her gently ;
Peace ! smile on her excellently ;
Midnight Stars ! attend her pleasure :
    Veil thy splendour, Night !
Not even Love's own eyes should measure
    Love's delight.

Touch life's chords with lightest finger ;
Echoes sweet ! around her linger ;
By the love makes marriage holy,
    Tame thy carriage, Fate !
Like a bridesmaid murmuring lowly—
    Yet we wait !

THE HAPPY LAND.

The Happy Land!
Studded with cheerful homesteads, fair to see,
With garden grace and household symmetry :
How grand the wide-brow'd peasant's lordly mien,
The matron's smile serene !
　　　　　O happy, happy land !

The happy land!
Half-hid in the dewy grass the mower blithe
Sings to the day-star as he whets his scythe ;
And to his babes at eventide again
Carols as blithe a strain.
　　　　　O happy, happy land !

The happy land!
Where in the golden sheen of autumn eves
The bright-hair'd children play among the sheaves ;
Or gather ripest apples all the day,
As ruddy-cheek'd as they.
　　　　　O happy, happy land !

O happy land!
The thin smoke curleth through the frosty air ;
The light smiles from the windows ; hearken there
To the white grandsire's tale of heroes old,
To flame-eyed listeners told !
　　　　　O happy, happy land !

O happy, happy land !
The tender-foliaged alders scarcely shade
Yon loitering lover and glad blushing maid :
O happy land ! the Spring that quickens thee
Is human liberty.
　　　　　O happy, happy land !

IPHIGENEIA AT AULIS.

I am Achilles.   Thou wast hither brought
  To be my wife, not for a sacrifice.
Greece and her kings may stand aside as nought
  To what Thou art in my expectant eyes.

Or kings or Gods : I too am heaven-born.
  I trample on their auguries and needs.
Where the foreboding dares to front my scorn
  Or break the promise from my heart proceeds?

But thou Belovèd! smilèst down my wrath
  So able to protect thee.   Who should harm
Achilles' Bride ?—Thou pointest to the path
  Of sacrifice, yet leaning on my arm.

There is no need of words ; from me reply
  As little requisite : Thy lightest hand
Guideth me, as the helm the ship ; Thine eye
  Doth more than all the Atridæ could command.

Thou givèst life and love for Greece and Right :
  I will stand by thee lest thou shouldst be weak—
Not weak of soul.—I will but hold in sight
  Thy marvelous beauty.—Here is She you seek !

AUBREY THOMAS DE VERE.
1814—

SONG.

Seek not the tree of silkiest bark
  And balmiest bud,
To carve her name while yet 'tis dark
  Upon the wood !
The world is full of noble tasks
  And wreaths hard won :

Each work demands strong hearts, strong hands,
          Till day is done.

Sing not that violet-veined skin,
          That cheek's pale roses,
The lily of that form wherein
          Her soul reposes !
Forth to the fight, true man ! true knight !
          The clash of arms
Shall more prevail than whisper'd tale,
          To win her charms.

The warrior for the True, the Right,
          Fights in Love's name ;
The love that lures thee from that fight
          Lures thee to shame :
That love which lifts the heart, yet leaves
          The spirit free,—
That love, or none, is fit for one
          Man-shaped like thee.

SORROW.

When I was young, I said to Sorrow
  "Come, and I will play with thee !"
      He is near me now all day,
      And at night returns to say
"I will come again to-morrow—
  I will come and stay with thee."

Through the woods we walk together,—
  His soft footsteps rustle by me :
      To shield an unregarded head
      He hath built a winter shed ;
And all night in rainy weather
  I hear his gentle breathings by me.

SONG.

Love laid down his golden head
    On his mother's knee :
" The world runs round so fast "—he said,
    " None has time for me."

Thought, a sage unhonor'd, turn'd
    From the on-rushing crew ;
Song her starry legend spurn'd ;
    Art her glass down threw.

Roll on, blind world ! upon thy track
    Until thy wheels catch fire :
For that is gone which comes not back
    To seller nor to buyer.

SONG.

Softly, O midnight Hours !
Move softly o'er the bowers
Where lies in happy sleep a Girl so fair :
For ye have power, men say,
Our hearts in sleep to sway
And cage cold fancies in a moonlight snare.
Round ivory neck and arm
Enclasp a separate charm :
Hang o'er her poised ; but breathe nor sigh nor prayer !
Silently ye may smile,
But hold your breath the while
And let the wind sweep back your cloudy hair !

Bend down your glittering urns
(Ere yet the dawn returns)
And star with dew the lawn her feet shall tread ;
Upon the air rain balm ;
Bid all the woods be calm ;

Ambrosial dreams with healthful slumbers wed !
That so the Maiden may
With smiles your care repay
When from her couch she lifts her golden head,
Waking with earliest birds
Ere yet the misty herds
Leave warm 'mid the grey grass their dusky bed.

NOTHING MORE.

A sigh in the morning grey,—
And a solitary tear,
Slow to gather, slow to fall,—
And a painful flush of shame
At the mention of thy name :
This is little, this is all,
False One ! that remains to say
That thy love of old was here,
That thy love hath pass'd away.

THOMAS BURBIDGE.

1816—

LOVE'S INSISTENCE.

If I desire with pleasant songs
To throw a merry hour away,
Comes Love unto me, and my wrongs
In careful tale he doth display ;
And asks me how I stand for singing
While I my helpless hands am wringing.

And then, another time, if I
A noon in shady bower would pass,
Comes he with stealthy gestures sly
And, flinging down upon the grass,

Quoth he to me—" My Master dear !
Think of this noontide such a year."

And if elsewhile I lay my head
  On pillow, with intent to sleep,
Lies Love beside me on the bed
  And gives me ancient words to keep :
Says he—" These looks, these tokens number !
May be they'll help you to a slumber."

So every time when I would yield
  An hour to quiet, comes he still,
And hunts up every sign conceal'd
  And every outward sign of ill ;
And gives me his sad face's pleasures
For Merriment's or Sleep's or Leisure's

CHARLES GEORGE ROSENBERG.
1815—1876.

THE WINGED HORSE.

Wake from your homes in tomb and shroud !
  Wake, Splendours of the Past !
  Joy divine, and Passion proud,
  Hope sublime, and Vision vast !
  Let our love your glories trace
  Eye to eye and face to face ;
  Let our arms your beauties bind :—
    Or are ye like the wind
To sight impalpable, too thin for our embrace ?

  Fire and water have we bound
  To the car and to the wheel
With harness and with trace of steel ;
A living speech and utterance found
  For the very lightning's speed :
    Every element compell'd

To our luxury or need;
And with a certain prophecy
Learn'd to count the courses held
By the chance-worlds that whirl on high,
The nightmares of a dreaming sky.

Surely it were an easy task
After this to bend and yoke
The mighty Thought of ages past,
The Horse our younger fathers broke :
The wondrous Steed
Whose wind-wing'd speed
Treads on the hill-top and the cloud,—
The glorious Horse
Whose sun-paved course
The young Greek and Roman bow'd,—
The Steed whose mane,
Like golden rain,
A glory round the Italian shed
On the great road through Hell and Heaven
His restless will alone might tread,—
The Horse with living music shod
To the one bard of England given,
By whom, as by a guiding God,
His tramp of melody was driven
Through every deep and hidden part
Of that strange thing the human heart.

And yet the Song is still,
And on the cloud and hill
Does the strong Steed unbitted stray ;
The wave and air we tame,
Harness the wind and flame,—
Uncurb'd and free his glories play.
None the Wing'd One's speed may yoke,—
Lost the bit, the bridle broke,—
Unknown the might, unseen the way.

He alone may mount the Steed
To whom the ancient spell is known ;
He its magic letters read
Who has the Will, and he alone :
And the Will our souls have sold
For the love of steel and gold,—
Sold the mighty for the mean,
Truck'd the priceless for the vile,
Barter'd for the foul the clean ;
And, instead of weeping, smile.

In the name of Truth alone
Might the ancient rider feel
The strength to curb the heavenly Steed :
A very child would scarcely need
Scourge in hand or spur on heel
If that little word were known ;
But giant brawn and Titan force—
Strength of muscle and of mind—
Human wit and might combined,
Were those letters five unread,
Ill upon the task were sped
To mount and curb the glorious Horse.

Earth is old, but then was young :
They were children, We are men :
Youth's great hymn of faith is sung :
Clay which counts could worship then.

Give us a God—a living God,
One to wake the sleeping soul,
One to cleanse the tainted blood
Whose pulses in our bosoms roll :
A vigorous faith's refreshing breath,
To make us hunger for the True,—
A faith to quicken and renew
The nightmare of our Life-in-Death !
II.—14

Come it how or whence it may,
That Faith divine, that earnest Will,—
This alone may teach the way
To curb and bit the Wing'd One still.
Truth and Faith are ever wed,—
Faith alone the cloud may tread
And look unblinded on the Sun.
This was the magic of the Dead :
They had a faith,—and we have none.

HENRY SEPTIMUS SUTTON.

1825—

THE BATTLE OF GOD.

So strive, so rule, Almighty Lord of All !
So greatly win thy planet-victory !
So gloriously what baffles bring in thrall !
So strongly work, Earth's final jubilee
With gladness and with singing to instal !

And man may work with the great God : yea, ours
This privilege,—all others how beyond !
To tend the great Man-root until it flowers ;
To scorn with godly laughter when Despond
Tamely before a hoary hindrance cowers ;

Effectually the planet to subdue,
And break old savagehood in claw and tusk ;
That noble end to trust in and pursue
Which under Nature's half-expressive husk
Lies ever from the base conceal'd from view ;

To draw our fellows up, as with a cord
Of love, unto their high-appointed place,
Till, from our state barbaric and abhorr'd,
We do arise unto a royal race :
To be the blest companions of The Lord.

CHARLES WELDON.

18— 1856 ?

_____

THE POEM OF THE UNIVERSE.

The Poem of the Universe
  Nor rhythm has nor rhyme ;
Some God recites the wondrous song
  A stanza at a time.

Great deeds is he foredoom'd to do—
  With Freedom's flag unfurl'd—
Who hears the echo of that song
  As it goes down the world.

Great words he is compell'd to speak
  Who understands the song :
He rises up like fifty men,
  Fifty good men and strong.

A stanza for each century :—
  Now heed it, all who can !
Who hears it, he, and only he,
  Is the elected man.

ARTHUR HUGH CLOUGH.

1819—1861.

_____

PESCHIERA.

What voice did on my spirit fall,
Peschiera ! when thy bridge I cross'd ?
" 'Tis better to have fought and lost
Than never to have fought at all ! "

The tricolour—a trampled rag
Lies, dirt and dust ; the lines I track
By sentry boxes, yellow-black,
Lead up to no Italian flag.

I see the Croat soldier stand
Upon the grass of your redoubts;
The eagle with his black wings flouts
The breadth and beauty of your land.

Yet not in vain, although in vain,
O men of Brescia! on the day
Of loss past hope I heard you say
Your welcome to the noble pain.

You said—" Since so it is, good-bye,
Sweet life! high hope! but whatsoe'er
May be, or must, no tongue shall dare
To tell—the Lombard fear'd to die."

You said (there shall be answer fit!)—
" And if our children must obey,
They must; but thinking on this day
'Twill less debase them to submit."

You said (O not in vain you said)—
" Haste, brothers! haste, while yet we may,
The hours ebb fast of this one day
When blood may yet be nobly shed."

Ah! not for idle hatred, not
For honour, fame, nor self-applause,
But for the glory of the Cause
You did what will not be forgot.

And though the stranger stand, 'tis true,—
By force and fortune's right he stands:
By fortune, which is in God's hands;
And strength, which yet shall spring in you.

This voice did on my spirit fall,
Peschiera! when thy bridge I cross'd:
'Tis better to have fought and lost
Than never to have fought at all.

NOT UNAVAILING.

Say not, the struggle nought availeth,
  The labour and the wounds are vain,
The enemy faints not, nor faileth,
  And as things have been they remain.

If hopes were dupes, fears may be liars;
  It may be, in yon smoke conceal'd,
Your comrades chase even now the fliers
  And, but for you, possess the field.

For while the tired waves, vainly breaking,
  Seem here no painful inch to gain,
Far back, through creeks and inlets making,
  Comes silent, flooding in, the main.

And not by Eastern windows only,
  When daylight comes, comes in the light;
In front the sun climbs slow, how slowly!
  But Westward, look! the land is bright.

JULIA WARD HOWE.

1819—

BATTLE HYMN OF THE REPUBLIC.

Mine eyes have seen the glory of the coming of the Lord :
He is trampling out the vintage where the grapes of wrath are
    stored ;
He hath loosed the fateful lightning of his terrible swift sword ;
His truth is marching on.
      Glory! glory! hallelujah! his truth is marching on.

I have seen Him in the watchfires of a hundred circling camps ;
They have builded Him an altar in the evening dews and
    damps ;

I can read his righteous sentence by the dim and flaring lamps ;
His day is marching on.
　　　　Glory ! glory ! hallelujah ! his day is marching on.

I have read a fiery gospel writ in burnish'd rows of steel :
As ye deal with my contemners, so with you my grace shall
　　　　deal :
Let the hero born of woman crush the serpent with his heel !
Since God is marching on.
　　　　Glory ! glory ! hallelujah ! since God is marching on.

He hath sounded forth the trumpet that shall never call re-
　　　　treat ;
He is sifting out the hearts of men before his judgment seat :
O, be swift, my soul ! to answer Him ; be jubilant, my feet !
Our God is marching on.
　　　　Glory ! glory ! hallelujah ! our God is marching on.

In the beauty of the lilies Christ was born, across the sea,
With a glory in his bosom that transfigures you and me :
As he died to make men holy, let us die to make men free !
While God is marching on.
　　　　Glory ! glory ! hallelujah ! while God is marching on.

WALT WHITMAN.

1819—

PIONEERS.

Come, my tan-faced children !
Follow well in order, get your weapons ready !
Have you your pistols ? have you your sharp-edged axes ?
　　　　Pioneers ! O pioneers !

For we can not tarry here ;
We must march, my darlings ! we must bear the brunt of
　　　　danger :

We, the youthful sinewy races,—all the rest on us depend,
        Pioneers ! O pioneers !

    O you youths, Western youths !
So impatient, full of action, full of manly pride and friendship :
Plain I see you, Western youths ! see you tramping with the
    foremost,
        Pioneers ! O pioneers !

    Have the elder races halted ?
Do they droop and end their lesson, wearied, over there be-
    yond the seas ;
We take up the task eternal, and the burden, and the lesson,
        Pioneers ! O pioneers !

    All the past we leave behind :
We debouch upon a newer, mightier world, varied world :
Fresh and strong the world we seize, world of labour and the
    march,
        Pioneers ! O pioneers !

    We detachments steady throwing,
Down the edges, through the passes, up the mountains steep,
Conquering, holding, daring, venturing, as we go the unknown
    ways,
        Pioneers ! O pioneers !

    We primeval forests felling,
We the rivers stemming, vexing we and piercing deep the
    mines within,
We the surface broad surveying, and the virgin soil upheaving,
        Pioneers ! O pioneers !

    Colorado men are we :
From the peaks gigantic, from the great sierras and the high
    plateaus,

From the mine and from the gully, from the hunting trail, we
    come,
                Pioneers! O pioneers!

      From Nebraska, from Arkansas,
Central inland race are we, from Missouri, with the continental
    blood intervein'd,
All the hands of comrades clasping, all the Southern, all the
    Northern,
                Pioneers! O pioneers!

      O resistless, restless race!
O belovèd race in all! O my breast aches with tender love for
    all!
O I mourn and yet exult—I am rapt with love for all,
                Pioneers! O pioneers!

      Raise the mighty Mother Mistress!
Waving high the delicate Mistress, over all, the starry Mis-
    tress!—bend your heads all!
Raise the fang'd and warlike Mistress, stern, impassive, wea-
    pon'd Mistress!
                Pioneers! O pioneers!

      See my children, resolute children!
By those swarms upon our rear, we must never yield or falter,
Ages back in ghostly millions frowning there behind us urging,
                Pioneers! O pioneers!

      On and on, the compact ranks,
With accessions ever waiting, with the places of the dead
    quickly fill'd,—
Through the battle, through defeat, moving yet and never stop-
    ping,
                Pioneers! O pioneers!

      O to die advancing on!
Are there some of us to droop and die? has the hour come?

Then upon the march we fittest die, soon and sure the gap is
    fill'd,
           Pioneers! pioneers!

    All the pulses of the world,
Falling in, they beat for us, with the Western movement beat,
Holding single or together, steady moving, to the front, all for us,
           Pioneers! O pioneers!

    Life's involved and varied pageants,
All the forms and shows, all the workmen at their work,
All the seamen and the landsmen, all the masters with their
    slaves,
           Pioneers! O pioneers!

    All the hapless silent lovers,
All the prisoners in the prisons, all the righteous, and the
    wicked,
All the joyous, all the sorrowing, all the living, all the dying,
           Pioneers! O pioneers!

    I too with my soul and body,
We a curious trio, picking, wandering on our way,
Through these shores, amid the shadows, with the apparitions
    pressing,
           Pioneers! O pioneers!

    Lo! the darting bowling orb,
Lo! the brother orbs around, all the clustering suns and
    planets,
All the dazzling days, all the mystic nights with dreams,
           Pioneers! O pioneers!

    These are of us, they are with us,
All for primal needed work, while the followers there in em-
    bryo wait behind,
We to-day's procession heading, we the route for travel clear-
    ing,
           Pioneers! O pioneers!

O you daughters of the West!
O you young and elder daughters! O you mothers and you
    wives!
Never must you be divided, in our ranks you move united,
                Pioneers! O pioneers!

Minstrels latent on the prairies!
(Shrouded bards of other lands! you may sleep—you have
    done your work)
Soon I hear you coming warbling, soon you rise and tramp
    amid us,
                Pioneers! O pioneers!

Not for delectations sweet,
Not the cushion and the slipper, not the peaceful and the
    studious,
Not the riches safe and palling, not for us the tame enjoyment,
                Pioneers! O pioneers!

Do the feasters gluttonous feast,
Do the corpulent sleepers sleep, have they lock'd and bolted
    doors,—
Still be ours the diet hard and the blanket on the ground!
                Pioneers! O pioneers!

Has the night descended?
Was the road of late so toilsome? did we stop, discouraged,
    nodding on our way?
Yet a passing hour I yield you, in your tracks to pause ob-
    livious,
                Pioneers! O pioneers!

Till with sound of trumpet,
Far, far off the day-break call! Hark! how loud and clear I
    hear it wind.
Swift! to the head of the army! swift! spring to your places!
                Pioneers! O pioneers!

THE SOLDIER'S LETTER.

1.

Come up from the fields, Father! here's a letter from our
    Pete ;
And come to the front door, Mother! here's a letter from thy
    dear son.

2.

Lo! tis Autumn :
Lo! where the trees, deeper green, yellower and redder,
Cool and sweeten Ohio's villages, with leaves fluttering in the
    moderate wind ;
Where apples ripe in the orchards hang, and grapes on the
    trellis'd vines !
(Smell you the smell of the grapes on the vines ?
Smell you the buckwheat, where the bees were lately buzzing ?)

Above all, lo! the sky, so calm, so transparent after the rain,
    and with wondrous clouds ;
Below too all calm, all vital and beautiful,—and the farm pros-
    pers well.

3.

Down in the fields all prospers well :
But now from the fields come, Father! come at the daughter's
    call ;
And come to the entry, Mother! to the front door come, right
    away.

Fast as she can she hurries—something ominous—her steps
    trembling ;
She does not tarry to smooth her hair, nor adjust her cap.

Open the envelope quickly !
O, this is not our son's writing, yet his name is sign'd ;

O, a strange hand writes for our dear son—O stricken Mother's
     soul !
All swims before her eyes—flashes with black—she catches the
     main words only ;
Sentences broken,—" gun-shot wound in the breast, cavalry
     skirmish, taken to the hospital,
At present low, but will soon be better."

4.

Ah ! now the single figure to me,
Amid all teeming and wealthy Ohio with all its cities and farms,
Sickly white in the face and dull in the head, very faint,
By the jamb of a door leans.

" Grieve not so, dear Mother ! "   The just grown daughter
     speaks through her sobs ;
The little sisters huddle around speechless and dismay'd :
" See, dearest Mother ! the letter says Pete will soon be
     better."

5.

Alas, poor boy ! he will never be better (nor may-be needs to
     be better, that brave and simple soul).
While they stand at home at the door, he is dead already.
The only son is dead.

But the Mother needs to be better,—
She, with thin form, presently dress'd in black ;
By day her meals untouch'd,—then at night fitfully sleeping,
     often waking,
In the midnight waking, weeping, longing with one deep long-
     ing—
O that she might withdraw unnoticed—silent from life escape
     and withdraw,
To follow, to seek, to be with her dear dead son !

THOMAS WILLIAM PARSONS.

1819—

DIRGE.

What shall we do now, Mary being dead,
Or say, or write, that shall express the half?
What can we do but pillow that fair head,
And let the Spring-time write her epitaph?

As it will soon, in snow-drop, violet,
Wind-flower, and columbine, and maiden's tear:
Each letter of that pretty alphabet
That spells in flowers the pageant of the year.

She was a maiden for a man to love,
She was a woman for a husband's life,
One that had learn'd to value far above
The name of Love the sacred name of Wife.

Her little life-dream, rounded so with sleep,
Had all there is of life—except grey hairs:
Hope, love, trust, passion, and devotion deep,
And that mysterious tie a Mother bears.

She hath fulfill'd her promise and hath pass'd.
Set her down gently at the iron door!
Eyes! look on that loved image for the last:
Now cover it in earth—her earth no more!

SAINT PERAY.

When to any saint I pray,
It shall be to Saint Peray.
He alone, of all the brood,
Ever did me any good:
Many I have tried that are
Humbugs in the calendar.

On the Atlantic, faint and sick,
Once I pray'd Saint Dominick :
He was holy (sure), and wise ;—
Was't not he that did devise
Auto-da-fès and rosaries ?
But for one in my condition
This good saint was no physician.

Next, in pleasant Normandie,
I made a prayer to Saint Denis,
In the great cathedral where
All the ancient kings repose ;
But how I was swindled there
At the " Golden Fleece,"—he knows !

In my wanderings vague and various
Reaching Naples,—as I lay
Watching Vesuvius from the bay,
I besought Saint Januarius.
But I was a fool to try him,—
Nought I said could liquefy him ;
And I swear he did me wrong,
Keeping me shut up so long
In that pest-house, with obscene
Jews and Greeks and things unclean :
What need had I of quarantine ?

In Sicily at least a score,
In Spain about as many more,
And in Rome almost as many
As the loves of Don Giovanni,
Did I pray to—sans reply :
Devil take the tribe ! said I.

Worn with travel, tired and lame,
To Assissi's walls I came :
Sad, and full of home-sick fancies,
I address'd me to Saint Francis ;

But the beggar never did
Anything as he was bid,
Never gave me aught—but fleas :
Plenty had I at Assisse.

But in Provence, near Vaucluse,
Hard by the Rhone, I found a Saint
Gifted with a wondrous juice
Potent for the worst complaint !
'Twas at Avignon that first,
In the witching time of thirst,
To my brain the knowledge came
Of this blessed Catholic's name,
Forty miles of dust that day
Made me welcome Saint Peray.

Though till then I had not heard
Aught about him, ere a third
Of a litre pass'd my lips,
All saints else were in eclipse :
For his gentle spirit glided
With such magic into mine
That methought such bliss as I did
Poet never drew from wine.

Rest he gave me, and refection,
Chasten'd hopes, calm retrospection,
Softened images of sorrow,
Bright forebodings for the morrow,
Charity for what is pass'd,
Faith in something good at last.

Now, why should any almanack
The name of this good creature lack ?
Or wherefore should the breviary
Omit a Saint so sage and merry ?
The Pope himself should grant a day

Especially to Saint Pcray.
But, since no day hath been appointed
On purpose by thc Lord's Anointed,
Let us not wait!   We'll do him right.
Send round your bottles, Hal! and set your night!

CHARLES KINGSLEY.

1819—1875.

TO THE NORTH-EAST WIND.

Welcome, wild North-Easter!
  Shame it is to see
Odes to every Zephyr,
  Ne'er a verse to thee.
Welcome, black North-Easter!
  O'er the German foam,
O'er the Danish moorlands,
  From thy frozen home.
Tired we are of Summer,
  Tired of gaudy glare,
Showers soft and steaming,
  Hot and breathless air ;
Tired of listless dreaming
  Through the lazy day :
Jovial Wind of Winter!
  Turn us out to play!
Sweep the golden reed-beds!
  Crisp the lazy dyke!
Hunger into madness
  Every plunging pike!
Fill the lake with wild fowl!
  Fill the marsh with snipe,
While on dreary moorlands
  Lonely curlew pipe!
Through the black fir-forest

Thunder harsh and dry,
Shattering down the snow-flakes
Off the curdled sky !
Hark ! the brave North-Easter !
Breast-high lies the scent :
On, by holt and headland,
Over heath and bent !
Chime, ye dappled darlings !
Through the sleet and snow :
Who can over-ride you ?
Let the horses go !
Chime, ye dappled darlings !
Down the roaring blast :
You shall see a fox die
Ere an hour be pass'd.
Go ! and rest to-morrow,
Hunting in your dreams,
While our skates are ringing
O'er the frozen streams.
Let the luscious South-Wind
Breathe in lover's sighs,
While the lazy gallants
Bask in ladies' eyes !
What does he but soften
Heart alike and pen ?
'Tis the hard grey weather
Breeds hard Englishmen.
What's the soft South-Wester ?
'Tis the ladies' breeze,
Bringing home their true loves
Out of all the seas.
But the black North-Easter,
Through the snow-storm hurl'd,
Drives our English hearts of oak
Seaward, round the world.
Come ! as came our fathers,
Heralded by thee,

II.—15

Conquering, from the East-ward,
  Lords by land and sea.
Come ! and strong within us
  Stir the Vikings' blood,
Bracing brain and sinew !
  Blow ! thou Wind of God !

THE SANDS OF DEE.

" O Mary ! go and call the cattle home,—
  And call the cattle home,
  And call the cattle home
  Across the sands of Dee ! "
The Western wind was wild and dank with foam,
  And all alone went she.

The creeping tide came up along the sand,
  And o'er and o'er the sand,
  And round and round the sand,
  As far as eye could see ;
The blinding mist came down and hid the land ;
  And never home came she.

" O, is it weed or fish or floating hair,
  A tress of golden hair,
  A drowned maiden's hair,
  Above the nets, at sea ?
Was never salmon yet that shone so fair
  Among the stakes on Dee."

They row'd her in across the rolling foam,
  The cruel crawling foam,
  The cruel hungry foam,
  To her grave beside the sea :
But still the boatmen hear her call the cattle home
  Across the sands of Dee.

A HOPE.

Twins stars, aloft in ether clear,
  Around each other roll alway,
Within one common atmosphere
  Of their own mutual light and day.

And myriad happy eyes are bent
  Upon their changeless love alway :
As, strengthen'd by their one intent,
  They pour the flood of life and day.

So we through this world's waning night
  May, hand in hand, pursue our way ;
Shed round us order, love, and light,
  And shine unto the perfect day.

MARY ANN EVANS LEWES.

"GEORGE ELIOT."

1819—1880.

THE DARK.

Should I long that dark were fair ?
  Say, O Song !
Lacks my Love aught that I should long ?

Dark the Night, with breath all flowers,
And tender broken voice that fills
With ravishment the listening hours,—
  Whisperings, wooings,
Liquid ripples, and soft ring-dove cooings
In low-toned rhythm that love's aching stills !
Dark the Night : yet is she bright,
For in her dark she brings the mystic star,
Trembling yet strong as is the voice of love,
  From some unknown afar.
O radiant Dark ! O darkly foster'd Ray !
Thou hast a joy too deep for shallow Day.

JAMES RUSSELL LOWELL.

1819—

HEBE.

I saw the twinkle of white feet,
I saw the flash of robes descending,—
Before her ran an influence fleet
That bow'd my heart, like barley bending.

As in bare fields the searching bees
Pilot to blooms beyond our finding,
It led me on,—by sweet degrees,
Joy's simple honey-cells unbinding.

Those Graces were that seem'd grim Fates;
With nearer love the sky lean'd o'er me;
The long-sought secret's golden gates
On musical hinges swung before me.

I saw the brimm'd bowl in her grasp,
Thrilling with godhood; like a lover,
I sprang the proffer'd life to clasp:
The beaker fell, the luck was over.

The earth has drunk the vintage up:
What boots it patch the goblet's splinters?
Can Summer fill the icy cup
Whose treacherous crystal is but Winter's?

O spendthrift Haste! Await the Gods!
Their nectar crowns the lips of Patience.
Haste scatters on unthankful sods
The immortal gift in vain libations.

Coy Hebe flies from those that woo,
And shuns the hands would seize upon her;
Follow thy life, and she will sue
To pour for thee the cup of honour!

THE COURTIN'.

God makes sech nights, all white an' still
  Fur'z you can look or listen,
Moonshine an' snow on field an' hill,
  All silence an' all glisten—

Zekle crep' up quite unbeknown
  An' peek'd in thru' the winder,
An' there sot Huldy all alone,
  'Ith no one nigh to hender.

A fire-place fill'd the room's one side
  With half a cord o' wood in,—
There warn't no stoves (tell comfort died)
  To bake ye to a puddin'.

The wa'nut logs shot sparkles out
  Towards the Pootiest, bless her !
An' leetle flames danced all about
  The chiny on the dresser.

Agin the chimbley crook-necks hung,
  An' in amongst 'em rusted,
The ole queen's-arm that gran'ther Young
  Fetch'd back from Concord busted.

The very room, coz she was in,
  Seem'd warm from floor to ceilin',
An' she look'd full ez rosy agin
  Ez the apples she was peelin'.

'Twas kin' o' kingdom-come to look
  On sech a blessed cretur :
A dog-rose blushin' to a brook
  Ain't modester nor sweeter.

He was six foot o' man, A 1,
  Clean grit an' human natur' ;
None couldn't quicker pitch a ton,
  Nor dror a furrer straighter.

He'd spark'd it with full twenty gals,
  He'd squired 'em, danced 'em, druv 'em,
Fust this one, an' then thet, by spells :
  All is, he couldn't love 'em.

But long o' her his veins 'ould run
  All crinkly, like curl'd maple ;
The side she bresh'd felt full o' sun
  Ez a South slope in A'pil.

She thought no v'ice hed such a swing
  Ez hisn in the choir ;
My ! when he made Old Hundred ring,
  She *know'd* the Lord was nigher.

An' she'd blush scarlit, right in prayer,
  When her new meetin'-bunnet
Felt somehow thru' its crown a pair
  O' blue eyes sot upon it.

That night, I tell ye, she look'd *some !*
  She seem'd to've gut a new soul,
For she felt sartin-sure he'd come,
  Down to her very shoe-sole.

She heer'd a foot, an' know'd it tu,
  A-raspin' on the scraper,—
All ways to once her feelins flew
  Like sparks in burnt-up paper.

He kin' o' l'iter'd on the mat,
  Some doubtfle o' the sekle ;
His heart kep' going pity-pat,
  But hern went pity Zekle.

An' yit she gin her cheer a jerk
  Ez though she wish'd him furder,
An' on her apples kep' to work,
  Parin' away like murder.

" You want to see my Pa, I s'pose ? "
　　" Wal——no——I come dasignin'—— "
" To see my Ma ?　She's sprinklin' clo'es
　　Agin to-morrer's i'nin'."

To say why gals act so or so,
　　Or don't, 'ould be presumin' ;
Mebbe to mean Yes an' say No
　　Comes nateral to women.

He stood a spell on one fut fust,
　　Then stood a spell on t'other ;
An' on which one he felt the wust
　　He couldn't ha' told ye nuther.

Says he—" I'd better call agin ; "
　　Says she—" Think likely, Mister ! "
That last word prick'd him like a pin,
　　An'——Wal, he up an' kist her.

When Ma bimeby upon 'em slips,
　　Huldy sot pale ez ashes,
All kin' o' smily roun' the lips
　　An' teary roun' the lashes.

For she was jes' the quiet kind
　　Whose naturs never vary,
Like streams that keep a summer mind
　　Snow-hid in Jenooary.

The blood clost roun' her heart felt glued
　　Too tight for all expressin',
Tell mother see how matters stood,
　　And gin em' both her blessin'.

Then her red come back like the tide
　　Down to the Bay o' Fundy.
An' all I know is they was cried
　　In meetin' come nex' Sunday.

THE FOUNTAIN.

Into the sunshine,
  Full of the light,
Leaping and flashing
  From morn till night,—

Into the moonlight,
  Whiter than snow,
Waving so flower-like
  When the winds blow,—

Into the starlight
  Rushing in spray,
Happy at midnight,
  Happy by day,—

Ever in motion,
  Blithesome and cheery,
Still climbing heavenward,
  Never aweary,—

Glad of all weathers
  Still seeming best,
Upward or downward,
  Motion thy rest,—

Full of a nature
  Nothing can tame,
Changed every moment,
  Ever the same,—

Ceaseless aspiring,
  Ceaseless content,
Darkness or sunshine
  Thy element,—

Glorious Fountain !
  Let my heart be
Fresh, changeful, constant,
  Upward, like thee !

SHE CAME AND WENT.

As a twig trembles which a bird
  Lights on to sing, then leaves unbent,
So is my memory thrill'd and stirr'd :
  I only know She came and went.

As clasps some lake, by gusts unriven,
  The blue dome's measureless content,
So my soul held that moment's heaven :
  I only know She came and went.

As at one bound our swift Spring heaps
  The orchards full of bloom and scent,
So clove her May my wintry sleeps :
  I only know She came and went.

An angel stood and met my gaze
  Through the low doorway of my tent,—
The tent is struck, the vision stays :
  I only know She came and went.

O, when the room grows slowly dim,
  And life's last oil is nearly spent,
One gush of light these eyes will brim,
  Only to think She came and went.

MARIA WHITE LOWELL.

1821—1853.

AN OPIUM FANTASY.

Soft hangs the opiate in the brain,
And lulling soothes the edge of pain,
Till harshest sound, far off or near,
Sings floating in its mellow sphere.

What wakes me from my heavy dream ?
  Or am I still asleep ?
Those long and soft vibrations seem
  A slumbrous charm to keep.

The graceful play, a·moment stopp'd,
  Distance again unrolls,
Like silver balls that, softly dropp'd,
  Ring into golden bowls.

I question of the poppies red,
  The fairy flaunting band,
While I, a weed with drooping head
  Within their phalanx stand :

" Some airy one, with scarlet cap !
  The name unfold to me
Of this new minstrel who can lap
  Sleep in his melody ! "

Bright grew their scarlet-kerchief'd heads,
  As freshening winds had blown,
And from their gently-swaying beds
  They sang in undertone :—

" O, he is but a little Owl,
  The smallest of his kin,
Who sits beneath the Midnight's cowl
  And makes this airy din."

" Deceitful tongues of fiery tints !
  Far more than this ye know :
That he is your Enchanted Prince
  Doom'd as an Owl to go.

" Now his fond play for years hath stopp'd ;
  But nightly he unrolls
His silver balls that, softly dropp'd,
  Ring into golden bowls."

WILLIAM ROSS WALLACE.

1820—1881.

EL AMIN—THE FAITHFUL.

Who is this that comes from Hara? not in kingly pomp and
    pride,
But a great free Son of Nature, lion-soul'd and eagle-eyed :

Who is this before whose presence idols tumble to the sod?
While he cries out—" Allah Akbar! and there is no god but
    God ! "

Wandering in the solemn desert, he has wonder'd, like a child
Not as yet too proud to wonder, at the sun and star and wild.

" O thou Moon ! who made thy brightness ?   Stars ! who hung
    ye there on high ?
Answer ! so my soul may worship : I must worship, or I die."

Then there fell the brooding silence that precedes the thun-
    der's roll ;
And the old Arabian Whirlwind call'd another Arab soul.

Who is this that comes from Hara? not in kingly pomp and
    pride,
But a great free Son of Nature, lion-soul'd and eagle-eyed.

He has stood and seen Mount Hara to the Awful Presence
    nod ;
He has heard from cloud and lightning—" Know there is no
    god but God ! "

Call ye this man an Impostor ?   He was call'd The Faithful,
    when
A boy he wander'd o'er the deserts, by the wild-eyed Arab men.

He was always call'd The Faithful. Truth, he knew, was
        Allah's breath ;
But the Lie went darkly gnashing through the corridors of
        Death.

He "was fierce !" Yes ! fierce at falsehood, fierce at hideous
        bits of wood
That the Koreish taught the people made the sun and solitude.

But his heart was also gentle ; and affection's graceful palm
Waving in his tropic spirit to the weary brought a balm.

" Precepts ? "—Have on each compassion ! Lead the stranger
        to your door !
In your dealings keep up justice !   Give a tenth unto the poor !

"Yet, ambitious !" Yes ! ambitious, while he heard the calm
        and sweet
Aidenn-voices sing, to trample conquer'd Hell beneath his
        feet.

" Islam ? "—Yes ! submit to heaven !—" Prophet ? "—To the
        East thou art.
What are prophets but the trumpets blown by God to stir the
        heart ?

And the great Heart of the Desert stirr'd unto that solemn
        strain
Rolling from the trump at Hara over Error's troubled main.

And a hundred dusky millions honour still El Amin's rod,
Daily chanting—" Allah Akbar ! know there is no god but
        God ! "

Call him then no more Impostor ! Mecca is the Choral Gate
Where, till Zion's noon shall take them, nations in the morning
        wait.

EBENEZER JONES.
1820—1860.

RAIN.

More than the wind, more than the snow,
  More than the sunshine, I love rain :
Whether it droppeth soft and low,
  Whether it rusheth amain.

Dark as the night it spreadeth its wings,
  Slow and silently, up on the hills ;
Then sweeps o'er the vale, like a steed that springs
  From the grasp of a thousand wills.

Swift sweeps under heaven the raven cloud's flight ;
  And the land and the lakes and the main
Lie belted beneath with steel-bright light,
  The light of the swift-rushing rain.

On evenings of summer, when sunlight is low,
  Soft the rain falls from opal-hued skies ;
And the flowers the most delicate summer can show
  Are not stirr'd by its gentle surprise.

It falls on the pools, and no wrinkling it makes,
  But touching melts in, like the smile
That sinks in the face of a dreamer, but breaks
  Not the calm of his dream's happy wile.

The grass rises up as it falls on the meads,
  The bird softlier sings in his bower,
And the circles of gnats circle on like wing'd seeds
  Through the soft sunny lines of the shower.

WHEN THE WORLD IS BURNING.

  When the world is burning,
  Fired within, yet turning
    Round with face unscathed ;

Ere fierce flames, uprushing,
O'er all lands leap, crushing,
  Till earth fall, fire-swathed,—
Up, amidst the meadows,
Gently through the shadows,
  Gentle flames will glide,
Small and blue and golden :
Though by bard beholden
When in calm dreams folden,
  Calm his dreams will bide.

Where the dance is sweeping,
Through the greensward peeping,
  Shall the soft lights start ;
Laughing maids, unstaying,
Deeming it trick-playing,
High their robes upswaying,
  O'er the lights shall dart ;
And the woodland haunter
Shall not cease to saunter
  When, far down some glade,
Of the great world's burning
One soft flame upturning
Seems, to his discerning,
  Crocus in the shade.

DENIS FLORENCE McCARTHY.

1820—1881.

SUMMER LONGINGS.

Ah ! my heart is weary waiting,
  Waiting for the May :
Waiting for the pleasant rambles
Where the fragrant hawthorn brambles,
With the woodbine alternating,
  Scent the dewy way :

Ah! my heart is weary, waiting,
　　Waiting, for the May.

Ah! my heart is sick with longing,
　　Longing for the May :
Longing to escape from study,
To the young face fair and ruddy,
And the thousand charms belonging
　　To the summer's day :
Ah! my heart is sick with longing,
　　Longing for the May.

Ah! my heart is sore with sighing,
　　Sighing for the May :
Sighing for their sure returning
When the summer beams are burning,—
Hopes and flowers that dead or dying
　　All the winter lay :
Ah! my heart is sore with sighing,
　　Sighing for the May.

Ah! my heart is pain'd with throbbing,
　　Throbbing for the May :
Throbbing for the seaside billows
Or the water-wooing willows
Where in laughing and in sobbing
　　Glide the streams away :
Ah! my heart, my heart is throbbing,
　　Throbbing for the May.

Waiting, sad, dejected, weary,—
　　Waiting for the May :
Spring goes by with wasted warnings,
Moonlit evenings, sun-bright mornings,—
Summer comes, yet, dark and dreary,
　　Life still ebbs away :
Man is ever weary, weary,
　　Waiting for the May.

FREDERICK LOCKER.

1821—

THE UNREALIZED IDEAL.

My only Love is always near,
  In country or in town :
I see her twinkling feet, I hear
  The whisper of her gown.

She foots it ever fair and young,
  Her locks are tied in haste,
And one is o'er her shoulder flung
  And hangs below her waist.

She ran before me in the meads,
  And down this world-worn track
She leads me on ; but while she leads
  She never gazes back.

And yet her voice is in my dreams,
  To witch me more and more :
That wooing voice ! Ah me, it seems
  Less near me than of yore.

Lightly I sped when hope was high
  And youth beguiled the chase,—
I follow, follow still : but I
  Shall never see her face.

ALICE CARY.

1820—1871.

OPEN SECRETS.

The truth lies round about us,
  All too closely to be sought :
So open to our vision that
  'Tis hidden to our thought.

We know not what the glories
  Of the grass, the flower, may be :
We needs must struggle for the sight
  Of what we always see. '

Waiting for storms and whirlwinds,
  And to have a sign appear,
We deem not God is speaking
  In the still small voice we hear.

In reasoning proud, blind leaders
  Of the blind through life we go ;
And do not know the things we see,
  Nor see the things we know.

Single and indivisible,
  We pass from change to change,
Familiar with the strangest things,
  And with familiar strange.

We make the light through which we see
  The light, and make the dark :
To hear the lark sing we must be
  At heaven's gate with the lark.

PHŒBE CARY.

1824—1871.

THE MAIDEN'S SONG.

Laugh out, O stream ! from your bed of green,
  Where you lie in the sun's embrace ;
And talk to the reeds that o'er you lean
  To touch your dimpled face.
But let your talk be sweet as it will,
  And your laughter be as gay,
You can not laugh as I laugh in my heart,—
  For my Lover will come to-day.

II.—16

Sing sweet, little bird ! sing out to your mate
  That hides in the leafy grove ;
Sing clear, and tell him for him you wait,
  And tell him of all your love.
But though you sing till you shake the buds
  And the tender leaves of May,
My spirit thrills with a sweeter song,—
  For my Lover must come to-day.

Come up, O winds ! come up from the South
  With eager hurrying feet,
And kiss your red rose on her mouth
  In the bower where she blushes sweet.
But you can not kiss your darling flower,
  Though you clasp her as you may,
As I kiss in my thought the Lover dear
  I shall hold in my arms to-day.

ALAS !

Since, if you stood by my side to-day,
  Only our hands could meet,
What matter if half the weary world
  Lies out between our feet ?

That I am here by the lonesome sea,
  You by the pleasant Rhine ?
Our hearts were just as far apart
  If I held your hand in mine.

Therefore, with never a backward glance,
  I leave the past behind ;
And standing here by the sea alone
  I give it to the wind.

I give it all to the cruel wind,
  And I have no word to say :
Yet, alas to be as we have been,
  And to be as we are to-day !

MATTHEW ARNOLD.

1822—

PHILOMELA.

Hark! ah, the Nightingale!
The tawny-throated!
Hark! from that moonlit cedar what a burst,
What triumph!—Hark! what pain!—
O wanderer from a Grecian shore!
Still after many years, in distant lands,
Still nourishing in thy bewilder'd brain
That wild, unquench'd, deep-sunken, old-world pain.
Say! will it never heal?
And can this fragrant lawn,
With its cool trees, and night,
And the sweet tranquil Thames,
And moonshine, and the dew,
To thy rack'd heart and brain
Afford no balm?
Dost thou to-night behold,
Here, through the moonlight, on this English grass,
The unfriendly palace in the Thracian wild?
Dost thou again peruse
With hot cheeks and sear'd eyes
The too clear web, and thy dumb sister's shame?
Dost thou once more essay
Thy flight, and feel come over thee,
Poor fugitive! the feathery change
Once more, and once more seem to make resound
With love and hate, triumph and agony,
Lone Daulis and the high Cephissian vale?—
    Listen, Eugenia!
How thick the bursts come crowding through the leaves!
    Again—thou hearest?
    Eternal passion!
    Eternal Pain!

GROWING OLD.

What is it to grow old?
Is it to lose the glory of the form,
The lustre of the eye?
Is it for Beauty to forego her wreath?
Yes! but not this alone.

Is it to feel our strength,
Not our bloom only, but our strength decay?
Is it to feel each limb
Grow stiffer, every function less exact,
Each nerve more weakly strung?

Yes! this: and more! but not,
Ah! 'tis not what in youth we dream'd 'twould be:
'Tis not to have our life
Mellow'd and soften'd as with sunset glow,
A golden day's decline.

'Tis not to see the world
As from a height, with rapt prophetic eyes
And heart profoundly stirr'd;
And weep, and feel the fulness of the past,
The years that are no more.

It is to spend long days
And not once feel that we were ever young;
It is to add, immured
In the hot prison of the present, month
To month with weary pain.

It is to suffer this,
And feel but half and feebly what we feel:
Deep in our hidden heart
Festers the dull remembrance of a change,
But no emotion,—none.

It is (last stage of all)
When we are frozen up within, and quite
The phantom of ourselves,
To hear the world applaud the hollow ghost,
Which blamed the living man.

WILLIAM (JOHNSON) CORY.

1823—

MIMNERMUS IN CHURCH.

You promise heavens free from strife,
    Pure truth, and perfect change of will ;
But sweet, sweet is this human life,
    So sweet I fain would breathe it still :
Your chilly stars I can forego ;
This warm kind world is all I know.

You say there is no substance here,
    One great reality above :
Back from that void I shrink in fear,
    And child-like hide myself in love.
Show me what angels feel ! till then
I cling, a mere weak man, to men.

You bid me lift my mean desires
    From faltering lips and fitful veins
To sexless souls, ideal choirs,
    Unwearied voices, wordless strains :
My mind with fonder welcome owns
One dear dead friend's remember'd tones.

Forsooth the present we must give
    To that which can not pass away ;
All beauteous things for which we live
    By laws of time and space decay :
But O, the very reason why
I clasp them is because they die.

A FRENCH SAILOR'S SCOTTISH SWEETHEART.

I can not forget my jo ;
  I bid him be mine in sleep :
But battle and woe have changed him so,
  There's nothing to do but weep.

My mother rebukes me yet,—
  And I never was meek before :
His jacket is wet, his lip cold set,—
  He'll trouble our home no more.

O, breaker of reeds that bend !
  O, quencher of tow that smokes !
I'd rather descend to my sailor friend
  Than prosper with lofty folks.

I'm lying beside the gowan,
  My jo in the English bay ;
I'm Annie Rowan, his Annie Rowan,—
  He call'd me his Bien-Aimée.

I'll hearken to all you quote,
  Though I'd rather be dead and free :
The little he wrote in the sinking boat
  Is Bible and charm to me.

SYDNEY THOMPSON DOBELL.
1824—1874.

A SLEEP SONG.

Sister Simplicitie !
Sing, sing a song to me,—
    Sing me to sleep !
Some legend low and long,
Slow as the summer song
    Of the dull Deep :

Some legend long and low,
Whose equal ebb and flow,

To and fro, creep
On the dim marge of grey,
'Tween the soul's night and day,
Washing " awake " away
        Into " asleep " :

Some legend low and long,
Never so weak or strong
        As to let go
While it can hold this heart
Withouten sigh or smart,
Or as to hold this heart
        When it sighs No :

Some long low-swaying song
As the sway'd shadow long
        Sways to and fro
Where, through the crowing cocks,
And by the swinging clocks,
Some weary mother rocks
        Some weary woe.

Sing up and down to me !
Like a dream-boat at sea,
        So, and still so,
Float through the " then " and " when,"
Rising from when to then,
Sinking from then to when,
        While the waves go !

Low and high, high and low,
Now and then, then and now,
        Now, now,—
And when the now is then and when the then is now,
And when the low is high and when the high is low,
        Low, low,—
    Let me float, let the boat
        Go, go !

Let me glide, let me slide,
　　Slow, slow!
Gliding boat, sliding boat,
　　Slow, slow,
Glide away, slide away!
　　So! so!

HOW'S MY BOY?

" Ho, sailor of the sea!
　How's my Boy, my Boy? "
" What's your boy's name? good wife!
　And in what good ship sail'd he? "

" My boy John!
　He that went to sea—
　What care I for the ship? sailor!
　My boy's my boy to me.

" You come back from sea,
　And not know my John?
　I might as well have ask'd some landsman
　Yonder down in the town.
　There's not an ass in all the parish,
　But he knows my John.

" How's my boy, my boy?
　And unless you let me know,
　I'll swear you are no sailor,
　Blue jacket or no,—
　Brass buttons or no, sailor!
　Anchor and crown or no.
　Sure his ship was the Jolly Briton! "
　—" Speak low, woman! speak low! "

" And why should I speak low, sailor!
　About my own boy John?
　If I was loud as I am proud,
　I'd sing him over the town :

Why should I speak low ? sailor !"
—" That good ship went down."

" How's my boy ? how's my boy ?
What care I for the ship ? sailor !
I was never aboard her :
Be she afloat or be she aground,
Sinking or swimming, I'll be bound
Her owners can afford her.
I say, how's my John ? "
—" Every man on board went down,—
Every man aboard her."

" How's my boy, my boy ?
What care I for the men ? sailor !
I'm not their mother.
How's my boy, my boy ?
Tell me of him, and no other !
How's my boy, my boy ? "

HENRY HOWARD BROWNELL.
1824—1872.

THE BURIAL OF THE DANE.

Blue gulf all around us,
  Blue sky overhead :
Muster all on the quarter !
  We must bury the dead.

It is but a Danish sailor,
  Rugged of front and form,—
A common son of the forecastle,
  Grizzled with sun and storm.

His name and the strand he hail'd from
  We know,—and there's nothing more :
But perhaps his mother is waiting
  In the lonely Island of Fohr.

Still as he lay there dying,
  Reason drifting, a wreck,
" 'Tis my watch ! " he would mutter,—
  " I must go upon deck ! "

Ay, on deck, by the foremast !—
  But watch and look-out are done :
The Union-Jack laid o'er him,
  How quiet he lies in the sun !

Slow the ponderous engine !
  Stay the hurrying shaft !
Let the roll of ocean
  Cradle our giant craft !
Gather around the grating,
  Carry your messmate aft !

Stand in order, and listen
  To the holiest page of prayer ;
Let every foot be quiet,
  Every head be bare !
The soft trade-wind is lifting
  A hundred locks of hair.

Our captain reads the service
  (A little spray on his cheeks),
The grand old words of burial,
  And the trust a true heart seeks—
" We therefore commit his body
  To the deep ! "—and as he speaks,

Launch'd from the weather-railing
  Swift as the eye can mark,
The ghastly shotted hammock
  Plunges, away from the shark,
Down, a thousand fathoms,
  Down into the dark !

A thousand summers and winters
  The stormy Gulf shall roll

High o'er his canvas coffin :—
  But, silence to doubt and dole !
There's a quiet harbour somewhere
  For the poor aweary soul.

Free the fetter'd engine !
  Speed the tireless shaft !
Loose to'gallant and topsail !
  The breeze is far abaft.

Blue sea all around us,
  Blue sky bright o'erhead :
Every man to his duty !
  We have buried our dead.

QU'IL MOURÛT!

Not a sob, not a tear he spent
  For those who fell at his side !
But a moan, and a long lament
  For him—who might have died !

Who might have lain, as Harold lay,
  A King, and in state enow,
Or slept with his peers, like Roland
  In the Straits of Roncesvaux.

GEORGE WILLIAM CURTIS.

1824—

SONG.

Rushes lean over the water,
  Shells lie on the shore,
And thou, the blue Ocean's daughter,
  Sleep'st soft in the song of its roar.

Clouds sail over the ocean,
  White gusts fleck its calm,

But never its wildest motion
   Thy beautiful rest should harm.

White feet on the edge of the billow
   Mock its smooth-seething cream ;
Hard ribs of beach-sand thy pillow,
   And a noble lover thy dream.

Like tangles of sea-weed streaming
   Over a perfect pearl,
Thy fair hair fringes thy dreaming,
   O sleeping Lido girl.

MAJOR AND MINOR.

A bird sang sweet and strong
   In the top of the highest tree :
He sang—" I pour out my soul in song
   For the Summer that soon shall be."

But deep in the shady wood
   Another bird sang—" I pour
My soul on the solemn solitude
   For the Springs that return no more."

THOMAS D'ARCY McGEE.
1825—1868.

THE PENITENT RAVEN.

The Raven's house is built with reeds,—
   Sing woe, and alas is me !
And the Raven's couch is spread with weeds,
   High on the hollow tree ;
And the Raven himself, telling his beads
In penance for his past misdeeds,
   Upon the top I see.

Telling his beads from night to morn,—
   Sing alas ! and woe is me !

In penance for stealing the Abbot's corn,
    High on the hollow tree.
Sin is a load upon the breast ;
And it nightly breaks the Raven's rest,
    High on the hollow tree.

The Raven pray'd the Winter through,—
    Sing woe, and alas is me !
The hail it fell, the winds they blew,
    High on the hollow tree,—
Until the Spring came forth again,
And the Abbot's men to sow their grain
    Around the hollow tree.

Alas ! alas for earthly vows,—
    Sing alas ! and woe is me !
Whether they're made by men or crows
    High on the hollow tree !
The Raven swoop'd upon the seed,
And met his death in the very deed,
    Beneath the hollow tree.

So beat we our breasts in shame of sin,—
    Alas ! and woe is me !
While all is hollowness within :
    Alas ! and woe is me !
And when the ancient Tempter smiles,
So yield we our souls up to his wiles :
    Alas ! and woe is me !

BAYARD TAYLOR.

1825—1878.

THE WISDOM OF ALI.

The Prophet once, sitting in calm debate,
Said—" I am Wisdom's fortress ; but the gate
Thereof is Ali." Wherefore some who heard
With unbelieving jealousy were stirr'd ;

And, that they might on him confusion bring,
Ten of the boldest join'd to prove the thing.
" Let us in turn to Ali go ! " they said,—
" And ask if Wisdom should be sought instead
Of earthly riches : then, if he reply
To each of us in thought accordantly,
And yet to none in speech or phrase the same,
His shall the honour be, and ours the shame."

Now, when the first his bold demand did make,
These were the words which Ali straightway spake :
" Wisdom is the inheritance of those
Whom Allah favours ; riches of his foes."

Unto the second he said—" Thy self must be
Guard to thy wealth ; but Wisdom guardeth thee."

Unto the third—" By Wisdom wealth is won ;
But riches purchased Wisdom yet for none."

Unto the fourth—" Thy goods the thief may take ;
But into Wisdom's house he can not break."

Unto the fifth—" Thy goods decrease the more
Thou givest ; but use enlarges Wisdom's store."

Unto the sixth—" Wealth tempts to evil ways ;
But the desire of Wisdom is God's praise."

Unto the seventh—" Divide thy wealth, each part
Becomes a pittance ; give with open heart
Thy Wisdom, and each separate gift shall be
All that thou hast, yet not impoverish thee."

Unto the eighth—" Wealth can not keep itself ;
But Wisdom is the steward even of pelf."

Unto the ninth—" The camels slowly bring
Thy goods ; but Wisdom has the swallow's wing."

And lastly, when the tenth did question make,
These were the ready words which Ali spake :

" Wealth is a darkness which the soul should fear ;
But Wisdom is the lamp that makes it clear."

Crimson with shame the questioners withdrew,
And they declared—" The Prophet's words were true :
The mouth of Ali is the golden door
Of Wisdom."   When his friends to Ali bore
These words, he smiled and said : " And should they ask
The same until my dying day, the task
Were easy,—for the stream from Wisdom's well,
Which God supplies, is inexhaustible."

BEDOUIN SONG.

From the Desert I come to thee,
  On a stallion shod with fire ;
And the winds are left behind
  In the speed of my desire !
Under thy window I stand,
  And the midnight hears my cry—
I love thee, I love but thee,
  With a love that shall not die
      Till the sun grows cold
      And the stars are old
And the leaves of the Judgment Book unfold.

Look from thy window, and see
  My passion and my pain !
I lie on the sands below,
  And I faint in thy disdain.
Let the night winds touch thy brow
  With the heat of my burning sigh,
And melt thee to hear the vow
  Of a love that shall not die
      Till the sun grows cold
      And the stars are old
And the leaves of the Judgment Book unfold.

My steps are nightly driven
  By the fever in my breast
To hear from thy lattice breathed
  The word that shall give me rest.
Open the door of thy heart!
  And open thy chamber door!
And my kisses shall teach thy lips
  The love that shall fade no more
        Till the sun grows cold
        And the stars are old
And the leaves of the Judgment Book unfold.

THE ARAB TO THE PALM.

Next to thee, O fair Gazelle!
O Beddowee Girl, beloved so well!

Next to the fearless Nedjidee,
Whose fleetness shall bear me again to thee,—

Next to ye both I love the Palm,
With his leaves of beauty, his fruit of balm :

Next to ye both I love the Tree
Whose fluttering shadow wraps us three
With love and silence and mystery.

Our tribe is many, our poets vie
With any under the Arab sky :
Yet none can sing of the Palm but I.

The marble minarets that begem
Cairo's citadel-diadem
Are not so light as his slender stem.

He lifts his leaves in the sunbeam's glance,
As the Almehs lift their arms in dance :

A slumbrous motion, a passionate sign,
That works in the cells of the blood like wine.

Full of passion and sorrow is he,
Dreaming where the Belovèd may be.

And when the warm South-Winds arise,
He breathes his longing in fervid sighs,

Quickening odours, kisses of balm,
That drop in the lap of his chosen Palm.

The sun may flame and the sands may stir,
But the breath of his passion reaches her.

O Tree of Love! by that love of thine,
Teach me how I shall soften mine!

Give me the secret of the Sun,
Whereby the woo'd is ever won!

If I were a king, O stately Tree!
A likeness, glorious as might be,
In the court of my palace I'd build for thee :

With a shaft of silver burnish'd bright,
And leaves of beryl and malachite,

With spikes of golden bloom ablaze,
And fruits of topaz and chrysoprase.

And there the poets in thy praise
Should night and morning frame new lays,—

New measures sung to tunes divine :
But none, O Palm! should equal mine.

RICHARD HENRY STODDARD.

1825—

BRAHMA'S ANSWER.

Once, when the days were ages,
    And the old Earth was young,
The high Gods and the sages
From Nature's golden pages
    Her open secrets wrung.

II.—17

Each question'd each to know
Whence came the Heavens above, and whence the Earth
　　below.

Indra, the endless giver
　　Of every gracious thing
The Gods to him deliver,
Whose bounty is the river
　　Of which they are the spring,—
Indra, with anxious heart,
Ventures with Vivochunu where Brahma is apart.

"Brahma!　Supremest Being!
　　By whom the worlds are made,—
Where we are blind, all-seeing,—
Stable, where we are fleeing,
　　Of Life and Death afraid,—
Instruct us, for mankind,
What is the body, Brahma?　O Brahma! what the mind?"

Hearing us though he heard not,
　　So perfect was his rest,
So vast the Soul that err'd not,
So wise the lips that stirr'd not,—
　　His hand upon his breast
He laid, whereat his face
Was mirror'd in the river that girt that holy place.

They question'd each the other
　　What Brahma's answer meant.
Said Vivochunu—"Brother!
Through Brahma the Great Mother
　　Hath spoken her intent :
Man ends as he began,—
The shadow on the water is all there is of Man."

" The Earth with woe is cumber'd,
　　And no man understands ;

They see their days are number'd
By One that never slumber'd
  Nor stay'd his dreadful hands.
I see with Brahma's eyes :
The body is the shadow that on the water lies."

Thus Indra, looking deeper,
  With Brahma's self possessed.
So dry thine eyes, thou weeper !
And rise again, thou sleeper !
    The hand on Brahma's breast
Is his divine assent
Covering the soul that dies not.   This is what Brahma meant.

A JAR OF WINE.

Day and night my thoughts incline
To the blandishments of wine :
Jars were made to drain, I think ;
Wine, I know, was made to drink.

When I die (the day be far !)
Should the potters make a jar
Out of this poor clay of mine,
Let the jar be fill'd with wine !

UNDER THE ROSE.

She wears a rose in her hair,
  At the twilight's dreamy close :
Her face is fair,—how fair
    Under the rose !

I steal like a shadow there,
  As she sits in rapt repose,
And whisper my loving prayer
    Under the rose.

She takes the rose from her hair,
  And her colour comes and goes,
And I,—a lover will dare
  Under the rose.

ELIZABETH DREW BARSTOW STODDARD.

1823—

MERCEDES.

Under a sultry yellow sky
On the yellow sand I lie :
The crinkled vapours smite my brain,
I smoulder in a fiery pain.

Above the crags the condor flies,—
He knows where the red gold lies,
He knows where the diamonds shine :
If I knew, would she be mine ?

Mercedes in her hammock swings,—
In her court a palm tree flings
Its slender shadow on the ground,
The fountain falls with silver sound.

Her lips are like this cactus-cup,—
With my hand I crush it up,
I tear its flaming leaves apart :
Would that I could tear her heart !

Last night a man was at her gate :
In the hedge I lay in wait :
I saw Mercedes meet him there,
By the fire-flies in her hair.

I waited till the break of day,
Then I rose and stole away ;
But left my dagger in her gate :
Now she knows her lover's fate.

ADELAIDE ANNE PROCTER.
1825—1864.

A WOMAN'S QUESTIONING.

Before I trust my fate to thee,
  Or place my hand in thine,
Before I let thy Future give
  Colour and form to mine,
Before I peril all for thee,
Question thy soul to-night for me!

I break all slighter bonds, nor feel
  A shadow of regret :
Is there one link within the Past
  That holds thy spirit yet?
Or is thy faith as clear and free
As that which I can pledge to thee?

Does there within thy dimmest dreams
  A possible future shine
Wherein thy life could henceforth breathe,
  Untouch'd, unshared by mine?
If so, at any pain or cóst,
O tell me, before all is lost!

Look deeper still !   If thou canst feel
  Within thy inmost soul
That thou hast kept a portion back,
  While I have staked the whole,
Let no false pity spare the blow,
But in true mercy tell me so !

Is there within thy heart a need
  That mine can not fulfil,
One cord that any other hand
  Could better wake, or still ?
Speak now, lest at some future day
My whole life wither and decay !

Lives there within thy nature hid
  The demon spirit—Change,
Shedding a passing glory still
  On all things new and strange ?
It may not be thy fault alone :
But shield my heart against thy own !

Couldst thou withdraw thy hand one day,
  And answer to my claim
That Fate, and that to-day's mistake,
  Not thou, had been to blame ?
Some soothe their conscience thus : but thou
Wilt surely warn and save me now.

Nay ! answer not !   I dare not hear :
  The words would come too late.
Yet I would spare thee all remorse :
  So comfort thee, my Fate !
Whatever on my heart may fall,
Remember—I would risk it all.

LUCY LARCOM.
1826—

SLEEP-SONG.

Hush the homeless baby's crying,
  Tender Sleep !
  Every folded violet
  May the outer storm forget :
Those wet lids with kisses drying,
  Through them creep !

Soothe the soul that lies thought-weary,
  Murmurous Sleep !
  Like a hidden brooklet's song,
  Rippling gorgeous woods among,
Tinkling down the mountains dreary,
  White and steep.

Breathe thy balm upon the lonely,
        Gentle Sleep !
    As the twilight breezes bless
    With sweet scents the wilderness,
Ah, let warm white dove-wings only
        Round them sweep !

O'er the agèd pour thy blessing,
        Holy Sleep !
    Like a soft and ripening rain
    Falling on the yellow grain,
For the glare of suns oppressing,
        Pitying weep !

O'er thy still seas met together,
        Charmed Sleep !
    Hear them swell a drowsy hymning,
    Swans to silvery music swimming,
Floating with unruffled feather
        O'er the deep !

MORTIMER COLLINS.
1827—1876.

SNOW AND SUN.

Fast falls the snow, O Lady mine !
Sprinkling the lawn with crystals fine :
But, by the Gods, we won't repine,
        While we're together ;
We'll chat and rhyme and kiss and dine.
        Defying weather.

So stir the fire, and pour the wine !
And let those sea-green eyes divine
Pour their love-madness into mine !
        I don't care whether
'Tis snow or sun or rain or shine,
        If we're together.

WILLIAM ALLINGHAM.
1828—

THE TOUCHSTONE.

A man there came, whence none could tell,
Bearing a Touchstone in his hand;
And tested all things in the land
    By its unerring spell.

Quick birth of transformation smote
The fair to foul, the foul to fair;
Purple nor ermine did he spare,
    Nor scorn the dusty coat.

Of heirloom jewels, prized so much,
Were many changed to chips and clods;
And even statues of the Gods
    Crumbled beneath its touch.

Then angrily the people cried—
" The loss outweighs the profit far :
Our goods suffice us as they are,—
    We will not have them tried."

And since they could not so avail
To check his unrelenting quest,
They seized him, saying—" Let him test
    How real is our jail ! "

But though they slew him with the sword,
And in a fire his Touchstone burn'd,
Its doings could not be o'erturn'd,
    Its undoings restored.

And when, to stop all future harm,
They strew'd its ashes on the breeze,
They little guess'd each grain of these
    Convey'd the perfect charm.

ARTHUR JOSEPH MUNBY.
1828—

VIOLET.

She stood where I had used to wait
  For her, beneath the gaunt old yew,
And near a column of the gate
  That open'd on the avenue.

The moss that capp'd its granite ball,
  The grey and yellow lichen stains,
The ivy on the old park wall,
  Were glossy with the morning rains.

She stood amid such tearful gloom ;
  But close behind her, out of reach,
Lay many a mound of orchard bloom,
  And trellis'd blossoms of the peach.

Those peaches blooming to the South,
  Those orchard blossoms, seem'd to me
Like kisses of her rosy mouth
  Revived on trellis and on tree :

Kisses that die not when the thrill
  Of joy that answer'd them is mute,
But such as turn to use and fill
  The summer of our days with fruit.

And she, impressing half the sole
  Of one small foot against the ground,
Stood resting on the yew-tree bole,
  A-tiptoe to each sylvan sound.

She, whom I thought so still and shy,
  Express'd in every subtle move
Of lifted hand and open eye
  The large expectancy of love.

Until, with all her dewy hair
   Dissolved into a golden flame
Of sunshine on the sunless air,
   She came to meet me as I came.

But in her face no sunshine shone;
   No sunlight, but the sad unrest
Of shade that sinks from zone to zone
   When twilight glimmers in the West.

What grief had touch'd her on the nerve?
   For grief alone it is that stirs
The full ineffable reserve
   Of quiet spirits such as hers.

'Twas this——that we had met to part;
   That I was going, and that she
Had nothing left but her true heart
   Made strong by memories of me.

What wonder then she quite forgot
   Her old repression and controul,
And loosed at once, and stinted not,
   The tender tumult of her soul?

What wonder that she droop'd and lay
   In silence, and at length in tears,
On that which should have been the stay
   And comfort of her matron years?

But from her bosom, as she lean'd,
   She took a nestled violet,
And gave it me: " because 'twas mean'd
   For those who never can forget."

This is the flower! 'tis dry—or wet
   With something I may call my own.
Why did I rouse this old regret?
   It irks me, now, to be alone.

Triumphs, indeed !   Why, after all,
    My life has but a leaden hue :
My heart grows like the heart of Saul,
    For hatred, and for madness too.

Why sits that smirking minstrel there ?
    I hate him and the songs he sings :
They only bring the fond despair
    Of inaccessible sweet things.

I will avoid him once for all,
    Or slay him in my righteous ire ;—
Alas ! my javelin hits the wall,
    And spares the minstrel and his lyre.

Yea ! and the crown upon my head,
    The crown of wealth for which I strove,
Shall fall away ere I be dead
    To yon slight boy who sings of love.

Why are we captive, such as I,
    Mature in age and strong in will,
To one who harps so plaintively ?
    I struck at him : why lives he still ?

Why lives he still ?   Because the ruth
    Of those pure days may never die.
He lives because his name is Youth,
    Because his harp is Memory.

MARY ANERLEY.

Little Mary Anerley, sitting on the stile !
Why do you blush so red, and why so strangely smile ?
Somebody has been with you : somebody, I know,
Left that sunset on your cheek, left you smiling so.

Gentle Mary Anerley, waiting by the wall,
Waiting in the chestnut walk where the snowy blossoms fall !

Somebody is coming there : somebody, I'm sure,
Knows your eyes are full of love, knows your heart is pure.

Happy Mary Anerley, looking O so fair !
There's a ring upon your hand, and there's myrtle in your hair.
Somebody is with you now : somebody, I see,
Looks into your trusting face very tenderly.

Quiet Mary Forester, sitting by the shore,
Rosy faces at your knee, roses round the door !
Somebody is coming home : somebody, I know,
Made you sorry when he sailed. Are you sorry now ?

DANTE GABRIEL ROSSETTI.

1828—1882.

THE CARD-DEALER.

Could you not drink her gaze like wine ?
 Yet, though its splendour swoon
Into the silence languidly
 As a tune into a tune,
Those eyes unravel the coil'd night
 And know the stars at noon.

The gold that's heap'd beside her hand
 In truth rich prize it were ;
And rich the dreams that wreathe her brows
 With magic stillness there ;
And he were rich who would unwind
 That woven golden hair.

Around her, where she sits, the dance
 Now breathes its eager heat;
And not more lightly or more true
 Fall there the dancers' feet
Than fall her cards on the bright board,
 As 'twere a heart that beat.

Her fingers let them softly through,
  Smooth polish'd silent things ;
And each one as it falls reflects
  In swift light-shadowings,
Blood-red and purple, green and blue,
  The great eyes of her rings.

Whom plays she with ?   With thee who lovest
  Those gems upon her hand ;
With me, who search her secret brows ;
  With all men, bless'd or bann'd.
We play together, she and we,
  Within a vain strange land.

A land without any order,—
  Day even as night (one saith),—
Where who lieth down ariseth not
  Nor the sleeper awakeneth ;
A land of darkness as darkness itself
  And of the shadow of death.

What be her cards ? you ask.   Even these :
  The heart, that doth but crave
More, having fed ; the diamond,
  Skill'd to make base seem brave ;
The club, for smiting in the dark ;
  The spade, to dig a grave.

And do you ask what game she plays ?
  With me 'tis lost or won ;
With thee it is playing still ; with him
  It is not well begun :
But 'tis a game she plays with all
  Beneath the sway o' the sun.

Thou seest the card that falls ;—she knows
  The card that followeth :

Her game in thy tongue is call'd Life,
    As ebbs thy daily breath :
When she shall speak, thou'lt learn her tongue,
    And know she calls it Death.

FIRST LOVE REMEMBERED.

Peace in her chamber ! whereso'er
    It be, a holy place :
The thought still brings my soul such grace
    As morning meadows wear.

Whether it still be small and light,
        A maid's, who dreams alone,
As from her orchard gate the moon
        Its ceiling show'd at night :

Or whether, in a shadow dense,
        As nuptial hymns invoke,
Innocent maidenhood awoke
        To married innocence :

There still the thanks unheard await
        The unconscious gift bequeath'd,—
For there my soul this hour has breathed
        An air inviolate.

LILITH.

Of Adam's first wife, Lilith, it is told
(The witch beloved before the gift of Eve)
That, ere the Snake's, her sweet tongue could deceive,
And her enchanted hair was the first gold.
And still she sits, young while the earth is old,
And, subtly of herself contemplative,
Draws men to watch the bright net she can weave,
Till heart and body and life are in its hold.

The rose and poppy are her flowers : for where
Is he not found, O Lilith ! whom shed scent

And soft-shed kisses and soft sleep shall snare?
Lo! as that youth's eyes burn'd at thine, so went
Thy spell through him, and left his straight neck bent,
And round his heart one strangling golden hair.

TRUE WOMAN.

To be a sweetness more desired than Spring;
A bodily beauty more acceptable
Than the wild rose-tree's arch that crowns the fell;
To be an essence more environing
Than wine's drain'd juice; a music ravishing
More than the passionate pulse of Philomel;—
To be all this 'neath one soft bosom's swell
That is the flower of life:—how strange a thing!
How strange a thing to be what man can know
But as a sacred secret! Heaven's own screen
Hides her soul's purest depth and loveliest glow,—
Closely withheld as all things most unseen:
The wave-bower'd pearl,—the heart-shape seal of green
That flecks the snowdrop underneath the snow.

LOST DAYS.

The lost days of my life until to-day,
What were they, could I see them on the street
Lie as they fell? Would they be ears of wheat
Sown once for food but trodden into clay?
Or golden coins squander'd and still to pay?
Or drops of blood dabbling the guilty feet?
Or such spill'd water as in dreams must cheat
The undying throats of Hell, athirst alway?
I do not see them here; but after death
God knows I know the faces I shall see,—
Each one a murder'd self, with low last breath:
" I am thyself,—what hast thou done to me?"
" And I—and I—thyself" (lo! each one saith)—
" And thou thyself to all eternity."

CHRISTINA GEORGINA ROSSETTI.

1830—

SONG.

When I am dead, my Dearest !
  Sing no sad songs for me ;
Plant thou no roses at my head,
  No shady cypress-tree !
Be the green grass above me,
  With showers and dew-drops wet ;
And, if thou wilt, remember !
  And, if thou wilt, forget !

I shall not see the shadows,
  I shall not feel the rain,
I shall not hear the nightingale
  Sing on as if in pain :
And dreaming through the twilight
  That doth not rise nor set,
Haply I may remember,—
  And haply may forget.

THE BOURNE.

Underneath the growing grass,
Underneath the living flowers,
Deeper than the sound of showers,
There we shall not count the hours
By the shadows as they pass.

Youth and health will be but vain,
Beauty reckon'd of no worth,—
There a very little girth
Can hold round what once the earth
Seem'd too narrow to contain.

JEAN INGELOW.
1830—

EXPECTING.

I lean'd out of window, I smell'd the white clover ;
Dark, dark was the garden, I saw not the gate :
Now, if there be footsteps, he comes, my one lover :—
Hush, nightingale ! hush ;   O sweet nightingale ! wait,
   Till I listen and hear
   If a step draweth near !
   For my Love he is late.

The skies in the darkness stoop nearer and nearer,
A cluster of stars hangs like fruit in the tree,
The fall of the water comes sweeter, comes clearer :
To what art thou listening, and what dost thou see ?
   Let the star-clusters glow,
   Let the sweet waters flow,
   And cross quickly to me !

You night-moths that hover where honey brims over
From sycamore blossoms, or settle, or sleep !
You glow-worms, shine out and the pathway discover
To him that comes darkling along the rough steep !
   Ah, my sailor ! make haste !
   For the time runs to waste
   And my love lieth deep.

Too deep for swift telling : and yet, my one lover !
I've conn'd thee an answer, it waits thee to-night.
By the sycamore pass'd he and through the white clover,—
Then all the sweet speech I had fashion'd took flight.
   But I'll love him more, more,
   Than e'er wife loved before,
   Be the days dark or bright.

II.—18

EDMUND CLARENCE STEDMAN.

1833—

THE DOORSTEP.

The conference meeting through at last,
  We boys around the vestry waited
To see the girls come tripping past,
  Like snow-birds willing to be mated.

Not braver he that leaps the wall
  By level musket-flashes bitten,
Than I, who stepp'd before them all
  Who long'd to see me get the mitten.

But no! she blush'd and took my arm :
  We let the old folks have the highway,
And started tow'rd the Maple Farm
  Along a kind of lover's by-way.

I can't remember what we said,—
  'Twas nothing worth a song or story ;
Yet that rude path by which we sped
  Seem'd all transform'd and in a glory.

The snow was crisp beneath our feet,
  The moon was full, the fields were gleaming ;
By hood and tippet shelter'd sweet,
  Her face with youth and health was beaming.

The little hand outside her muff
  (O sculptor! if you could but mould it)
So lightly touch'd my jacket-cuff,
  To keep it warm I had to hold it.

To have her there with me alone,—
  'Twas love and fear and triumph blended :
At last we reach'd the foot-worn stone
  ·Where that delicious journey ended.

The old folks too were almost home :
  Her dimpled hand the latches finger'd,
We heard the voices nearer come,
  Yet on the doorstep still we linger'd.

She shook her ringlets from her hood,
  And with a " Thank you, Ned!" dissembled ;
But yet I knew she understood
  With what a daring wish I trembled.

A cloud pass'd kindly overhead,
  The moon was slyly peeping through it,
Yet hid its face, as if it said—
  " Come, now or never do it ! do it !"

My lips till then had only known
  The kiss of mother and of sister,—
But somehow, full upon her own
  Sweet rosy darling mouth—I kiss'd her.

Perhaps 'twas boyish love : yet still,
  O listless woman ! weary lover !
To feel once more that fresh wild thrill
  I'd give——But who can live youth over ?

TOUJOURS AMOUR.

Prithee tell me, Dimple-Chin !
At what age does love begin ?
Your blue eyes have scarcely seen
Summers three, my fairy queen !
But a miracle of sweets,
Soft approaches, sly retreats,
Show the little archer there,
Hidden in your pretty hair :
When didst learn a heart to win ?
Prithee tell me, Dimple-Chin !

" O ! " the rosy lips reply,—
" I can't tell you if I try :
   'Tis so long I can't remember,—
   Ask some younger lass than I ! "

   Tell, O tell me, Grizzled-Face !
   Do your heart and head keep pace ?
   When does hoary love expire ?
   When do frosts put out the fire ?
   Can its embers burn below
   All that chill December snow ?
   Care you still soft hands to press,
   Bonny heads to smooth and bless ?
   When does Love give up the chase ?
   Tell, O tell me, Grizzled-Face !

" Ah ! " the wise old lips reply,—
" Youth may pass and strength may die,
   But of Love I can't foretoken
   Ask some older sage than I."

MINE.

Thou art mine, thou hast given thy word,
Close, close in my arms thou art clinging ;
Alone for my ear thou art singing
A song which no stranger hath heard :
But afar from me yet, like a bird,
Thy soul in some region unstirr'd
On its mystical circuit is winging.

Thou art mine, I have made thee mine own,—
Henceforth we are mingled for ever :
But in vain, all in vain I endeavour,
Though round thee my garlands are thrown
And thou yieldest thy lips and thy zone,
To master the spell that alone
My hold on thy being can sever.

Thou art mine, thou hast come unto me :
But thy soul, when I strive to be near it,
The innermost fold of thy spirit,
Is as far from my grasp, is as free,
As the stars from the mountain-tops be,
As the pearl in the depths of the sea
From the portionless king who would wear it.

GEORGE ARNOLD.

1834—1865.

GLORIA.

IN TIME OF WAR.

The laurels shine in the morning sun,
  The tall grass shakes its glittering spears,
And the webs the spiders last night spun
  Are threaded with pearly tears.

At peace with the world and all therein,
  I walk in the fields this summer morn :
What should I know of sorrow or sin
  Among the laurels and corn ?

But hark ! through the corn a murmur comes,—
  'Tis growing, 'tis swelling, it rises high :
The thunder of guns and the roll of drums,
  And an army marching by.

Away with the sloth of peace and ease !
  'Tis a nation's voice that seems to call :
Who cares for aught in times like these
  Save to win, or else to fall ?

Farewell, O shining laurels ! now,
  I go with the army marching by :
Your leaves, should I win, may deck my brow,—
  Or my bier, if I should die.

JOHN NICHOL.

1833—

___

IMPATIENCE.

Our life is spent in little things,
  In little cares our hearts are drown'd ;
We move, with heavy-laden wings,
  In the same narrow round.

We waste on wars and petty strife,
  And squander in a thousand ways,
The fire that should have been the life
  And power of after days.

We toil to make an outward show,
  And only now and then reveal
How far the under currents flow
  Of all we think and feel.

Mining in caves of ancient lore,
  Unweaving endless webs of thought,
We do what has been done of yore :
  And so we come to nought.

The Spirit longs for wider scope,
  And room to let its fountains play
Ere it has lost its love and hope,
  Tamed down or worn away.

I wander by the cloister walls,
  My fancy fretting to be free
As, through the twilight, voices call
  From mountain and from sea.

Forgive me if I feel oppress'd
  By Custom, lord of all and me !
My soul springs upward, seeking rest,
  And cries for liberty.

LEWIS MORRIS.

1833—

LOVE'S SUICIDE.

Alas for me that my love is dead !
Sunk fathom-deep, and may not rise again :
Self-murder'd, vanish'd, fled beyond recall :
          And this is all my pain.

'Tis not that She I loved is gone from me ;
She lives, and grows more lovely day by day :
Not Death could kill my love,—but, though She lives,
          My love has died away.

Nor was it that a form or face more fair
Forswore my troth, for so my love had proved
Eye-deep alone, not rooted in the soul :
          And 'twas not thus I loved.

Nor that, by too long dalliance with delight
And recompense of love, my love had grown
Surfeit with sweets, like some tired bee that flags
          'Mid roses overblown.

None of these slew my love ; but some cold wind,
Some chill of doubt, some shadowy dissidence,
Born out of too great concord, did o'ercloud
          Love's subtle inner sense.

So one sweet changeless chord too long sustain'd
Falls at its close into a lower tone ;
So the swift train, sped on the long straight way,
          Sways and is overthrown.

For difference is the soul of life and love,
And not the barren oneness weak souls prize :
Rest springs from strife, and dissonant chords beget
          Divinest harmonies.

HELEN FISKE JACKSON.
1833-5—

CORONATION.

At the king's gate the subtle Noon
  Wove filmy yellow nets of sun ;
Into the drowsy snare too soon
  The guards fell, one by one.

Through the king's gate unquestion'd then
  A beggar went, and laugh'd—" This brings
Me chance at last to see if men
  Fare better, being kings."

The king sat bow'd beneath his crown,
  Propping his face with listless hand,
Watching the hour-glass shifting down
  Too slow its shining sand.

" Poor man ! what wouldst thou have of me ? "
  The beggar turn'd and, pitying,
Replied, like one in dream—" Of thee
  Nothing : I want the king."

Uprose the king, and from his head
  Shook off the crown and threw it by :
" O man ! thou must have known," he said,
  " A greater king than I."

Through all the gates unquestion'd then
  Went king and beggar, hand in hand :
Whisper'd the king—" Shall I know when
  Before his throne I stand ? "

The beggar laugh'd (free winds in haste
  Were wiping from the king's hot brow
The crimson lines the crown had traced):
  " This is his presence now ! "

At the king's gate the crafty Noon
    Unwove its yellow nets of sun ;
Out of their sleep in terror soon
    The guards waked, one by one.

" Ho here ! ho there ! has no man seen
    The king ? " the cry ran to and fro :
Beggar and king they laugh'd, I ween,
    The laugh that free men know.

On the king's gate the moss grew grey ;
    The king came not.   They call'd him dead ;
And made his eldest son one day
    Slave in his father's stead.

WILLIAM MORRIS.
1834—

SONG.

Fair is the night, and fair the day,
Now April is forgot of May,
Now into June May falls away :
Fair day ! fair night !   O give me back
The tide that all fair things did lack
Except my Love, except my Sweet !

Blow back, O wind ! thou art not kind,
Though thou art sweet : thou hast no mind
Her hair about my Sweet to bind.
O flowery sward ! though thou art bright,
I praise thee not for thy delight,—
Thou hast not kiss'd her silver feet.

Thou know'st her not, O rustling tree !
What dost thou then to shadow me,
Whose shade her breast did never see ?
O flowers ! in vain ye bow adown :
Ye have not felt her odorous gown
Brush past your heads my lips to meet.

Flow on, great river! thou mayst deem
That far away, a summer stream,
Thou saw'st her limbs amidst the gleam,
And kiss'd her foot, and kiss'd her knee:
Yet get thee swift unto the sea!
With nought of true thou wilt me greet.

And Thou that men call by my name!
O helpless One! hast thou no shame
That thou must even look the same
As while agone, as while agone
When Thou and She were left alone,
And hands and lips and tears did meet?

Grow weak and pine, lie down to die,
O body! in thy misery,
Because short time and sweet goes by.
O foolish heart! how weak thou art:
Break, break, because thou needs must part
From thine own Love, from thine own Sweet!

BEFORE OUR LADY CAME.

Before our Lady came on earth
Little there was of joy or mirth:
About the borders of the sea
The sea-folk wander'd heavily;
About the wintry river side
The weary fishers would abide.

Alone, within the weaving-room,
The girls would sit before the loom,
And sing no song and play no play,—
Alone, from dawn to hot mid-day,
From mid-day unto evening,
The men a-field would work, nor sing
'Mid weary thoughts of man and God,—
Before thy feet the wet ways trod.

Unkiss'd the merchant bore his care,
Unkiss'd the knights went out to war,
Unkiss'd the mariner came home,
Unkiss'd the minstrel men did roam.

Or in the stream the maids would stare,
Nor know why they were made so fair :
Their yellow locks, their bosoms white,
Their limbs well-wrought for all delight,
Seem'd foolish things that waited death,—
As hopeless as the flowers beneath
The weariness of unkiss'd feet :
No life was bitter then, or sweet.

Therefore, O Venus ! well may we
Praise the green ridges of the sea
O'er which, upon a happy day,
Thou camest to take our shame away.
Well may we praise the curdling foam
Amidst the which thy feet did bloom—
Flowers of the Gods ; the yellow sand
They kiss'd atwixt the sea and land ;
The bee-beset ripe-seeded grass
Through which thy fine limbs first did pass ;
The purple-dusted butterfly
First blown against thy quivering thigh ;
The first red rose that touch'd thy side,
And overblown and fainting died ;
The flickering of the orange shade
Where first in sleep thy limbs were laid ;
The happy day's sweet life and death,
Whose air first caught thy balmy breath :—
Yea ! all these things well praised may be,
But with what words shall we praise Thee ?
O Venus ! O thou Love alive !
Born to give peace to souls that strive.

JOHN JAMES PIATT.
1835—

THE OLD MAN AND THE SPRING-LEAVES.

Underneath the beechen tree
All things fall in love with me !
Birds, that sing so sweetly, sung
Ne'er more sweet when I was young ;
Some sweet breeze, I *will* not see,
Steals to kiss me lovingly ;
All the leaves so blithe and bright,
Dancing, sing in Maying light
Over me—"At last, at last,
He has stolen from the Past."

Wherefore, leaves ! so gladly mad ?
I am rather sad than glad.

"He is the merry child that play'd
Underneath our beechen shade
Years ago, whom all things bright
Gladden'd, glad with his delight."

I am not the child that play'd
Underneath your beechen shade ;
I am not the boy ye sung
Songs to, in lost fairy tongue.
He read fairy dreams below,
Legends leaves and flowers must know ;
He dream'd fairy dreams, and ye
Changed to fairies, in your glee
Dancing, singing from the tree ;
And awaken'd fairy-land
Circled childhood's magic wand.
Joy swell'd his heart, joy kiss'd his brow :
I am following funerals now.
Fairy shores from Time depart ;

Lost horizons flush my heart :
I am not the child that play'd
Underneath your beechen shade.

" 'Tis the merry child that play'd
Underneath our beechen shade
Years ago, whom all things bright
Loved, made glad by his delight."

Ah! the bright leaves will not know
That an old man dreams below.
No! they will not hear nor see,
Clapping their hands at finding me,
Singing, dancing from their tree.
Ah! their happy voices steal
Time away : again I feel,
While they sing to me apart,
The lost child come in my heart :
In the enchantment of the Past
The old man is the child at last.

CELIA LEIGHTON THAXTER.

1835—

MEDRAKE AND OSPREY.

Medrake, waving wide wings low o'er the breeze-rippled
    bight !
Osprey, soaring superb overhead in the fathomless blue,
Graceful, and fearless, and strong ! do you thrill with the
    morning's delight
Even as I ?   Brings the sunshine a message of beauty for you ?

O the blithe breeze of the West, blowing sweet from the far
    away land,
Bowing the grass heavy-headed, thick-crowding, so slender
    and proud !

O the warm sea sparkling over with waves by the swift wind
    fann'd !
O the wide sky crystal clear, with bright islands of delicate
    cloud !

Feel you the waking of life in the world lock'd so long in the
    frost ?
Beautiful birds, with the light flashing bright from your ban-
    ner-like wings !
Osprey, soaring so high, in the depths of the sky half lost !
Medrake, hovering low where the sandpiper's sweet note
    rings !

Nothing am I to you, a blot perhaps on the day ;
Nought do I add to your joy, but precious you are in my
    sight ;
And you seem on your glad wings to lift me up into the ether
    away ;
And the morning divine is more radiant because of your glori-
    ous flight.

BYRON FORCEYTHE WILLSON.
1837—1867.

THE ESTRAY.

" Now tell me, my merry woodman !
    Why standest so aghast ? "—
" My lord ! 'twas a beautiful creature
    That hath but just gone past ! "—

" A creature,—what kind of a creature ? "—
    " Nay, now, but I do not know."—
" Humph ! what did it make you think of ? "—
    " The sunshine, or the snow."—

" I shall overtake my horse then."—
    The woodman open'd his eye :
The gold fell all around him ;
    And a rainbow spann'd the sky.

AUTUMN-SONG.

In Spring the poet is glad,
  And in Summer the poet is gay ;
But in Autumn the poet is sad,
  And has something sad to say :

For the wind moans in the wood,
  And the leaf drops from the tree,
And the cold rain falls on the graves of the good,
  And the mist comes up from the sea :

And the Autumn Songs of the poet's soul
  Are set to the passionate grief
Of winds that sough and bells that toll
  The dirge of the Falling Leaf.

WILLIAM WINTER.

1836—

LOVE'S QUEEN.

He loves not well whose love is bold :
  I would not have thee come too nigh.
The sun's gold would not seem pure gold
  Unless the sun were in the sky :
To take him thence and chain him near
Would make his beauty disappear.

He keeps his state : do thou keep thine,
  And shine upon me from afar !
So shall I bask in light divine
  That falls from Love's own guiding-star :
So shall thy eminence be high,
And so my passion shall not die.

But all my life shall reach its hands
  Of lofty longing tow'rd thy face,

And be as one who speechless stands
  In rapture at some perfect grace :
My love, my hope, my all shall be
To look to heaven and look to thee.

Thine eyes shall be the heavenly lights ;
  Thy voice shall be the summer breeze,
What time it sways, on moonlit nights,
  The murmuring tops of leafy trees ;
And I will touch thy beauteous form
In June's red roses rich and warm.

But thou—thyself—shalt not come down
  From that pure region far above ;
But keep thy throne and wear thy crown,
  Queen of my heart and queen of love :
A monarch in thy realm complete,
And I a monarch at thy feet !

AFTER ALL.

The apples are ripe in the orchard,
  The work of the reaper is done ;
And the golden woodlands redden
  In the blood of the dying sun.

At the cottage-door the grandsire
  Sits, pale, in his easy chair,
While a gentle wind of twilight
  Plays with his silver hair.

A woman is kneeling beside him ;
  A fair young head is press'd,
In the first wild passion of sorrow,
  Against his agèd breast.

And far from over the distance
  The faltering echoes come

Of the flying blast of trumpet
  And the rattling roll of drum.

Then the grandsire speaks in a whisper :
  " The end no man can see,—
But we give him to his Country,
  And we give our prayers to Thee ! "—

The violets star the meadows,
  The rose-buds fringe the door,
And over the grassy orchard
  The pink-white blossoms pour.

But the grandsire's chair is empty,
  The cottage is dark and still;
There's a nameless grave on the battle-field,
  And a new one under the hill.

And a pallid tearless woman
  By the cold hearth sits alone;
And the old clock in the corner
  Ticks on with a steady drone.

THE LAST SCENE.

Here she lieth, white and chill :
  Put your hand upon her brow !
Her sad heart is very still,
  And she does not know you now.

Ah ! the grave's a quiet bed :
  She will sleep a pleasant sleep,
And the tears that you may shed
  Will not wake her,—therefore weep !

Weep ! for you have wrought her woe ;
  Mourn ! she mourn'd and died for you :
Ah ! too late we come to know
  What is false and what is true.

II.—19

THOMAS BAILEY ALDRICH.
1836—

PALABRAS CARIÑOSAS.

Good-night! I have to say good-night
To such a host of peerless things !
Good-night unto that fragile hand
All queenly with its weight of rings,
Good-night to fond up-lifted eyes,
Good-night to chestnut braids of hair,
Good-night unto the perfect mouth
And all the sweetness nestled there !
    The snowy hand detains me,—then
    I'll have to say Good-night again.

But there will come a time, my Love !
When, if I read our stars aright,
I shall not linger by this porch
With my adieus. Till then, Good-night !
You wish the time were now ? And I.
You do not blush to wish it so ?
You would have blush'd yourself to death
To own so much a year ago.
    What ! both these snowy hands ? ah, then
    I'll have to say Good-night again.

TIGER-LILIES.

I like not lady-slippers,
Nor yet the sweet-pea blossoms,
Nor yet the flaky roses,
    Red, or white as snow ;
I like the chaliced lilies,
The heavy Eastern lilies,
The gorgeous tiger-lilies,
    That in our garden grow.

For they are tall and slender ;
Their mouths are dash'd with carmine ;

And, when the wind sweeps by them,
    On their emerald stalks
They bend so proud and graceful :
They are Circassian women,
The favourites of the Sultan,
    Adown our garden walks.

And when the rain is falling,
I sit beside the window
And watch them glow and glisten,—
    How they burn and glow !
O for the burning lilies,
The tender Eastern lilies,
The gorgeous tiger-lilies
    That in our garden grow !

RICHARD GARNETT.
1835—

VIOLETS.

Cold blows the wind against the hill,
  And cold upon the plain;
I sit me by the bank, until
  The violets come again.

Here sat we when the grass was set
  With violets shining through,
And leafing branches spread a net
  To hold a sky of blue.

The trumpet clamour'd from the plain,
  The cannon rent the sky ;
I cried—O Love ! come back again
  Before the violets die !

But they are dead upon the hill,
  And he upon the plain ;—
I sit me by the bank until
  My violets come again.

FADING LEAF AND FALLEN LEAF.

Said Fading-Leaf to Fallen-Leaf—
I toss alone on a forsaken tree,
It rocks and cracks with every gust that rocks
Its straining bulk : say! how is it with thee?

Said Fallen-Leaf to Fading-Leaf—
A heavy foot went by, an hour ago :
Crush'd into clay, I stain the way ;
The loud Wind calls me, and I can not go.

Said Fading-Leaf to Fallen-Leaf—
Death lessons Life, a ghost is ever wise :
Teach me a way to live till May
Laughs fair with fragrant lips and loving eyes!

Said Fallen-Leaf to Fading-Leaf—
Hast loved fair eyes and lips of gentle breath?
Fade then, and fall! thou hast had all
That Life can give ; ask somewhat now of Death!

THOMAS ASHE.

1836—

DALLYING.

Dear Love ! I have not ask'd you yet ;
  Nor heard you, murmuring low
As wood-doves by a rivulet,
  Say if it shall be so.

The colour in your cheek, which plays
  Like an imprison'd bliss,
In its unworded language says—
  " Speak, and I'll answer Yes ! "

See ! pluck this flower of wood-sorrel,
  And twine it in your hair !

Its woodland grace becomes you well,
　And makes my Rose more fair.

Oft you sit 'mid the daises here,
　And I lie at your feet;
Yet day by day goes by,—I fear
　To break a trance so sweet.

As some first Autumn tint looks strange,
　And wakes a strange regret,
Would your soft Yes our loving change ?—
Love ! I'll not ask you yet.

ALGERNON CHARLES SWINBURNE.
1837—

BEFORE THE MIRROR.

(*Written under a picture.*)

I

White rose in red rose garden
　Is not so white ;
Snowdrops, that plead for pardon
　And pine for fright
Because the hard East blows
Over their maiden rows,
Grow not as this face grows from pale to bright.

Behind the veil, forbidden,
　Shut up from sight,
Love ! is there sorrow hidden ?
　Is there delight ?
Is joy thy dower, or grief ?
White rose of weary leaf !
Late rose whose life is brief, whose loves are light !

Soft snows, that hard winds harden
　Till each flake bite,

Fill all the flowerless garden
　　Whose flowers took flight
Long since, when summer ceased,
　　And men rose up from feast,
And warm West wind grew East, and warm day night.

2

"Come snow, come wind, or thunder
　　High up in air,
I watch my face and wonder
　　At my bright hair:
Nought else exalts or grieves
The rose at heart, that heaves
With love of her own leaves and lips that pair.

"She knows not loves that kiss'd her
　　She knows not where:
Art thou the ghost? my sister!—
　　White sister there!
Am I the ghost?—who knows?
My hand, a fallen rose,
Lies snow-white on white snows, and takes no care.

"I can not see what pleasures
　　Or what pains were;
What pale new loves and treasures
　　New years will bear;
What beam will fall, what shower;
What grief or joy for dower:
But one thing knows the flower,—the flower is fair."

3

Glad, but not flush'd with gladness,
　　Since joys go by,—
Sad, but not bent with sadness,
　　Since sorrows die,—
Deep in the gleaming glass

She sees all past things pass,
And all sweet life that was lie down, and lie.

There glowing ghosts of flowers
    Draw down, draw nigh;
And wings of swift spent hours
    Take flight and fly;
She sees by formless gleams,
She hears across cold streams,
Dead mouths of many dreams that sing and sigh.

Face fallen and white throat lifted,
    With sleepless eye
She sees old loves that drifted,
    She knew not why;—
Old loves and faded fears
Float down a stream that hears
The flowing of all men's tears beneath the sky.

CHORUS.

When the hounds of Spring are on Winter's traces,
The Mother of Months in meadow or plain
Fills the shadows and windy places
With lisp of leaves and ripple of rain;
And the brown bright nightingale amorous
Is half assuaged for Itylus,
For the Thracian ships and the foreign faces,
The tongue-less vigil, and all the pain.

Come, with bows bent and with emptying of quivers,
Maiden most perfect! Lady of Light!
With a noise of winds and many rivers,
With a clamour of waters, and with might:
Bind on thy sandals, O Thou most fleet!
Over the splendour and speed of thy feet:
For the faint East quickens, the wan West shivers,
Round the feet of the Day and the feet of the Night.

Where shall we find her? how shall we sing to her,
Fold our hands round her knees, and cling?
O that man's heart were as fire and could spring to her,
Fire, or the strength of the streams that spring!
For the stars and the winds are unto her
As raiment, as songs of the harp-player:
For the risen stars and the fallen cling to her,
And the Southwest-wind and the West-wind sing.

For Winter's rains and ruins are over,
And all the season of snows and sins;
The days dividing lover and lover;
The light that loses, the night that wins;
And time remember'd is grief forgotten;
And frosts are slain, and flowers begotten;
And in green underwood and cover
Blossom by blossom the Spring begins.

The full streams feed on flower of rushes;
Ripe grasses trammel a traveling foot;
The faint fresh flame of the young year flushes
From leaf to flower and flower to fruit;
And fruit and leaf are as gold and fire;
And the oat is heard above the lyre;
And the hoofèd heel of a satyr crushes
The chestnut husk at the chestnut root.

And Pan by noon, and Bacchus by night,
Fleeter of foot than the fleet-foot kid,
Follows with dancing, and fills with delight
The Mænad and the Bassarid;
And, soft as lips that laugh and hide,
The laughing leaves of the trees divide,
And screen from seeing and leave in sight
The God pursuing, the Maiden hid.

The ivy falls with the Bacchanal's hair
Over her eyebrows, hiding her eyes;

The wild vine slipping down leaves bare
Her bright breast shortening into sighs;
The wild vine slips with the weight of its leaves,
But the berried ivy catches and cleaves
To the limbs that glitter, the feet that scare
The wolf that follows, the fawn that flies.

THE SUNDEW.

A little marsh-plant, yellow green,
And prick'd at lip with tender red!
Tread close, and either way you tread
Some faint black water jets between,
Lest you should bruise the curious head.

A live thing, may be : who shall know?
The Summer knows, and suffers it :
For the cool moss is thick and sweet
Each side, and saves the blossom so
That it lives out the long June heat.

The deep scent of the heather burns
About it; breathless though it be,
Bow down and worship! more than we
Is the least flower whose life returns,
Least weed renascent in the sea.

We are vex'd and cumber'd in Earth's sight
With wants, with many memories :
These see their Mother what she is,—
Glad-growing, till August leave more bright
The apple-colour'd cranberries.

Wind blows and bleaches the strong grass,
Blown all one way to shelter it
From trample of stray'd kine (with feet
Felt heavier than the moor-hen was),
Stray'd up past patches of wild wheat.

You call it Sundew : how it grows,
If with its colour it have breath,
If life taste sweet to it, if death
Pain its soft petal, no man knows :
Man has no sight nor sense that saith.

My Sundew ! grown of gentle days,
In these green miles the Spring begun
Thy growth ere April had half done
With the soft secret of her ways,
Or June made ready for the Sun.

O red-lipp'd mouth of marsh-flower !
I have a secret halved with thee :
The name that is love's name to me
Thou knowest, and the face of Her
Who is my festival to see.

The hard sun, as thy petals knew,
Colour'd the heavy moss-water :—
Thou wert not worth green midsummer
Nor fit to live to August blue,
O Sundew ! not remembering Her.

RONDEL.

These many years, since we began to be,
What have the Gods done with us ? what with me,
What with my love ?   They have shown me fates and fears,
Harsh springs, and fountains bitterer than the sea,
Grief a fix'd star, and joy a vane that veers,
          These many years.

With her, my Love,—with her have they done well ?
But who shall answer for her ? who shall tell
Sweet things or sad, such things as no man hears ?
May no tears fall, if no tears ever fell,
From eyes more dear to me than starriest spheres,
          These many years !

But if tears ever touch'd, for any grief,
Those eyelids folded like a white-rose leaf,
Deep double shells where through the eye-flower peers,
Let them weep once more only, sweet and brief,
Brief tears and bright, for One who gave her tears
     These many years !

JAMES THOMSON.

1834—1882.

THE THREE THAT SHALL BE ONE.

 Love, on the earth alit
 (Come to be Lord of it),
 Look'd round and laugh'd with glee :
 Noble my empery !
 Straight ere that laugh was done
 Sprang forth the royal sun,
 Pouring out golden shine
 Over the realm divine.

 Came then a lovely May,
 Dazzling the new-born day,
 Wreathing her golden hair
 With the red roses there,
 Laughing with sunny eyes
 Up to the sunny skies,
 Moving so light and free
 To her own minstrelsy.

 Love with swift rapture cried—
 Dear Life ! thou art my bride :
 Whereto with fearless pride—
 Dear Love ! indeed thy bride :
 All the earth's fruit and flowers,
 All the world's wealth, are ours ;

Sun, moon, and stars, gem
Our marriage diadem.

So they together fare,
Lovely and joyous pair!
So hand in hand they roam
All through their Eden home,
Each to the other's sight
An ever-new delight:
Blue heaven and blooming earth
Joy in their darlings' mirth.

Who comes to meet them now?
She with the pallid brow,
Wreathing her night-dark hair
With the red poppies there,
Pouring from solemn eyes
Gloom through the sunny skies,
Moving so silently
In her deep reverie.

Life paled as she drew near,
Love shook with doubt and fear.
Ah, then (she said) in truth
(Eyes full of yearning ruth)
Love! thou wouldst have this Life,
Fair May, to be thy wife?
Yet at an awful shrine
Wert thou not plighted mine?

Pale, paler poor Life grew;
Love murmur'd—It is true!
How could I thee forsake?
From the brief dream I wake.
Yet, O belovèd Death!
See how She suffereth:
Ere we from earth depart,
Soothe her, thou Tender-Heart!

Faint on the ground she lay :
Love kiss'd her swoon away ;
Death then bent over her,
Death the sweet comforter!
Whisper'd with tearful smile—
Wait but a little while !
Then I will come for thee :
We are one family.

WAITING.

O, what are you waiting for here ? young man !
What are you looking for over the bridge ?—
" A little straw hat with the streaming blue ribbons
Is soon to come dancing over the bridge.

" Her heart beats the measure that keeps her feet dancing,
Dancing along like a wave o' the sea ;
Her heart pours the sunshine with which her eyes glancing
Light up strange faces, in looking for me.

" The strange faces brighten in meeting her glances ;
The strangers all bless her, pure, lovely, and free ;
She fancies she walks, but her walk skips and dances,
Her heart makes such music in coming to me.

" O, thousands and thousands of happy young maidens
Are tripping this morning their sweethearts to see :
But none whose heart beats to a sweeter love-cadence
Than hers who will brighten the sunshine for me."

O what are you waiting for here ? young man !
What are you looking for over the bridge ?—
" A little straw hat with the streaming blue ribbons."
—And here it comes dancing over the bridge.

JOHN HAY.
1839—

A WOMAN'S LOVE.

A sentinel angel sitting high in glory
Heard this shrill wail ring out from Purgatory :—
" Have mercy, mighty angel ! hear my story.

" I loved,—and, blind with passionate love, I fell.
Love brought me down to death, and death to Hell :
For God is just, and death for sin is well.

" I do not rage against His high decree,
Nor for myself do ask that grace shall be ;
But for my Love on earth, who mourns for me.

" Great Spirit ! let me see my Love again,
And comfort him one hour, and I were fain
To pay a thousand years of fire and pain ! "

Then said the pitying angel—" Nay ! repent
That wild vow : look ! the dial-finger's bent
Down to the last hour of thy punishment."

But still she wail'd—" I pray thee let me go !
I can not rise to peace and leave him so :
O, let me soothe him in his bitter woe ! "

The brazen gates ground sullenly ajar,
And upward, joyous, like a rising star,
She rose and vanish'd in the ether far.

But soon adown the dying sunset sailing,
And like a wounded bird her pinions trailing,
She flutter'd back, with broken-hearted wailing.

She sobb'd—" I found him by the summer sea
Reclined, his head upon a maiden's knee,—
She curl'd his hair and kiss'd him.   Woe is me ! "

She wept : " Now let my punishment begin !
I have been fond and foolish.   Let me in
To expiate my sorrow and my sin ! "

The angel answer'd—" Nay, sad soul ! go higher !
To be deceived in your true heart's desire
Was bitterer than a thousand years of fire."

HENRY AUSTIN DOBSON.

1840—

BEFORE SEDAN.

Here in this leafy place
    Quiet he lies,
Cold, with his sightless face
    Turn'd to the skies :
'Tis but another dead :
All you can say is said.

Carry his body hence !
    Kings must have slaves :
Kings climb to eminence
    Over men's graves :
So this man's eye is dim ;—
Throw the earth over him !

What was the white you touch'd,
    There, at his side ?
Paper his hand had clutch'd
    Tight ere he died :
Message or wish, may be :
Smooth the folds out and see !

Hardly the worst of us
  Here could have smiled !
Only the tremulous
  Words of a child :
Prattle that has for stops
Just a few ruddy drops.

Look !—" She is sad to miss,
  Morning and night,
His (her dead father's) kiss ;
  Tries to be bright,
Good to Mamma, and sweet : "
(That is all)—" Marguerite."

Ah ! if beside the dead
  Slumber'd the pain :
Ah ! if the hearts that bled
  Slept with the slain :
If the grief died :—but no !
Death will not have it so.

ROBERT WILLIAMS BUCHANAN.

1841—

THE MODERN WARRIOR.

O Warrior for the Right !
Though thy shirt of mail be white
As the snows upon the breast of The Adored,
  Though the weapon thou mayst claim
  Hath been temper'd in the flame
Of the fire upon the Altar of the Lord,
  Ere the coming of the night
  Thy mail shall be less bright,
And the taint of sin may settle on the sword.

For the foemen thou must meet
Are the phantoms in the street,
And thine armour shall be foul'd in many a place,
And the shameful mire and mud
With a grosser stain than blood
Shall be scatter'd 'mid the fray upon thy face ;
And the helpless thou dost aid
Shall shrink from thee, dismay'd,
Till thou comèst to the knowledge of things base.

Ah, mortal ! with a brow
Like the gleam of sunshine, thou
Mayst wander from the pathway in thy turn ;
In the noontide of thy strength
Be stricken down at length,
And cry to God for aid, and live, and learn :
And when with many a stain
Thou arisest up again,
The lightning of thy look will be less stern.

Thou shalt see with humbler eye
The adulteress go by,
Nor shudder at the touch of her attire ;
Thou shalt only look with grief
On the liar and the thief ;
Thou shalt meet the very murtherer in the mire :
And to which wouldst thou accord,
O thou Warrior of the Lord !
The vengeance of the Sword and of the Fire ?

Nay ! batter'd in the fray,
Thou shalt quake in act to slay,
And remember *thy* transgression and be meek !
And the thief shall grasp thy hand,
And the liar blushing stand,
And the harlot if she list shall kiss thy cheek ;
And the murtherer, unafraid,

II.—20

Shall meet thee in the shade
And pray thee for the doom thou wilt not wreak.

Yet shalt thou help the frail
From the phantoms that assail,—
Yea ! the strong man in his anger shalt thou dare ;
Thy voice shall be a song
Against Wickedness and Wrong,
But the wicked and the wronger thou wilt spare.
And, while thou lead'st the van,
The ungrateful hand of man
Shall smite thee down and slay thee unaware.

With an agonizèd cry
Thou shalt shiver down, and die,
With stained shirt of mail and broken brand ;
And the voice of men shall call—
" He has fallen like us all,
Though the weapon of the Lord was in his hand : "
And thine epitaph shall be—
" He was wretched even as we ; "
And thy tomb may be unhonour'd in the land.

But the basest of the base
Shall bless thy pale dead face ;
And the thief shall steal a bloody lock of hair :
And over thee asleep
The adulteress shall weep
Such tears as she can never shed elsewhere,
Shall bless the broken brand
In thy chill and nerveless hand,
Shall kiss thy stained vesture, with a prayer.

Then, while in that chill place
Stand the basest of the base
Gather'd round thee in the silence of the dark,
A white Face shall look down
On the silence of the town

And see thee lying dead, with those to mark;
    And a Voice shall fill the air—
    " Bear my Warrior lying there
To his sleep upon my Breast!" and they shall hark.

    Lo! then those fallen things
    Shall perceive a rush of wings
Growing nearer down the azure gulf untrod ;
    And around them in the night
    There shall grow a wondrous light,
While they hide affrighted faces on the sod :
    But ere again 'tis dark
    They shall raise their eyes, and mark
White arms that waft the Warrior up to God.

ROBERT BRIDGES.

1844—

THE SEA-POPPY.

A Poppy grows upon the shore
Bursts her twin cup in summer late :
Her leaves are glaucous green and hoar,
Her petals yellow, delicate.

Oft to her cousins turns her thought,
In wonder if they care that she
Is fed with spray for dew, and caught
By every gale that sweeps the sea.

She has no lovers like the Red
That dances with the noble Corn :
Her blossoms on the waves are shed,
Where she sits shivering and forlorn.

EDMUND WILLIAM GOSSE.
1849—

THE SUPPLIANT.

Beneath the poplars o'er the sacred pool
The halcyons dart like rays of azure light :
Fair presage !   By the columns white and cool
        I'll watch to-night.

Perchance the Goddess, at the twilight's breath,
Will come with silver feet and braidless hair
And, all too startled to decree my death,
        Will hearken to my prayer.

So when at moon-rise by the farm I go,
The lovely girl who near the fig-tree stands
May turn no more on scornful feet and slow,
        But hold out both her hands.

THEOPHILE MARZIALS.
1850—

RONDEL.

To-day what is there in the air
That makes December seem sweet May ?
There are no swallows anywhere,
Nor crocuses to crown your hair
And hail you down my garden way.
Last night the full moon's frozen stare
Struck me, perhaps ; or did you say
Really—you'd come, sweet Friend and fair !
        To-day ?
To-day is here : come ! crown to-day
With Spring's delight or Spring's despair !
Love can not bide old Time's delay :—
Down my glad gardens light winds play,
And my whole soul shall bloom and bear
        To-day.

PAKENHAM THOMAS BEATTY.

1855—

IN MY DREAMS.

Come to me in my dreams, and say
Sweet words I never hear by day,
And murmur lovingly and low,
And take my hand and kiss my brow!

And I will whisper all night through
What I can only say to you :
My hopes I had, my life I plann'd,
That only you can understand.

Rest with me, Love! until the day ;
Then kiss me once, and pass away !
And let me waken, Dear ! to weep,
You can but kiss me in my sleep.

ANDREW LANG.

1844—

IN ITHACA.

'Tis thought Odysseus, when the strife was o'er
With all the waves and wars, a weary while,
Grew restless in his disenchanted isle,
And still would watch the sunset, from the shore,
Go down the waves of gold ; and evermore
His sad heart follow'd after, mile on mile,
Back to the Goddess of the magic wile—
Calypso, and the love that was of yore.
Thou too, thy haven gain'd, must turn thee yet
To look across the sad and stormy space,
Years of a youth as bitter as the sea,
Ah! with a heavy heart and eyelids wet :
Because within a fair forsaken place
The life that might have been is lost to thee.

WILLIAM DAVIES.

1829—

DOING AND BEING.

Think not alone to *do* right and fulfil
Life's due perfection by the simple worth
Of lawful actions call'd by justice forth,
And thus condone a world confused with ill!
But fix the high condition of thy will
To *be* right, that its good's spontaneous birth
May spread like flowers springing from the earth
On which the natural dews of heaven distil!
For these require no honours, take no care
For gratitude from men,—but more are bless'd
In the sweet ignorance that they are fair ;
And through their proper functions live and rest,
Breathing their fragrance on the joyous air,
Content with praise of bettering what is best.

NOTES.

WORDSWORTH. Born at Cockermouth, Cumberland. Wordsworth belongs to the close of the eighteenth century as well as to half of the nineteenth. His *Evening Walk* was written in 1793; his *Lyrical Ballads* were published in 1798. *Peter Bell* also was written in 1798, though not published till 1815. NATURE'S DARLING bears date of 1799; the ODE TO DUTY, 1805; the INVOCATION TO THE POWER OF SOUND and the TRIAD, 1828; the SONNET—"Methought I saw the footsteps of a throne," 1836. Of his two longest poems, the *Excursion* came out in 1814; the *Prelude*, begun in his early days, was not published till after his death.

In later editions of the ODE TO DUTY the last two lines of the second stanza read as follows:

> O, if through confidence misplaced
> They fail, thy saving arms, dread Power! around them cast!

COLERIDGE, "logician, metaphysician, and bard," as Lamb calls him, born at Ottery St. Mary, Devonshire, belongs almost wholly to the eighteenth century, little of his poetry being written later, except in 1814-16 the tragedy of *Zapolya*. *Christabel*, first printed in 1816, had been mainly written in 1797. So also *Remorse*, a tragedy, acted in 1813. The *Rime of the Ancient Mariner* was printed with Wordsworth's *Lyrical Ballads*, 1798; and in 1798-1800 he translated from Schiller's MSS., for simultaneous publication in Germany and England, the *Piccolomini* and *Death of Wallenstein*, which Carlyle praised as "the best translation from German then produced, except Sotheby's Oberon." GENEVIEVE may be taken as of his earliest, the poems at pp. 24, 25, as of his latest writing.

GENEVIEVE is only part of the poem as originally written for introduction to a longer poem never completed. Coleridge himself struck out some stanzas at the beginning and end, and published it as a complete poem, on *Love*, in its present form. One stanza, that beginning " And how he cross'd—" (p. 21), seems to have been inadvertently dropped, and is omitted from the usual copies.

SOUTHEY, born at Bristol, had also written before 1800: *Joan of Arc*, *Wat Tyler*, and many minor poems. *Thalaba the Destroyer* is dated 1800; *Madoc*, 1805. The *Curse of Kehama* was begun in 1801 and finished in 1809; and *Roderick, the last of the Goths*, begun in 1809 and finished in 1814. These are his principal works, *quasi* epics (except *Wat Tyler*): all of weight and considerable worth. The HOLLY TREE was written in 1798; the SCHOLAR in 1818.

TANNAHILL. A Scottish minor poet. The " Lake poets " have been kept together partly on account of their early work before the present century: so Tannahill may follow, his poems being chiefly of the same date. He was dead before Hogg, born two years earlier, had done anything of mark.

Gart is forced, compelled; *tine*—lose; *dowie*—doleful; *a' my lane*—all alone; *daffin*—joking; *short syne*—a short time ago; *aboon*—above; *wair'd*—spent; *coft*—bought; *fa'*—fall; *gowden*—golden; *gloaming*—twilight.

SCOTT (Sir Walter). Born at Edinburgh. The Poet preceded the Novelist. The *Minstrelsy of the Scottish Border* (with some ballads by himself) was published in 1802; the *Lay of the Last Minstrel*, 1805; *Marmion*, 1808; *Lady of the Lake*, 1810; *Vision of Don Roderick*, 1811; *Rokeby* and the *Bridal of Triermain*, 1813; *Lord of the Isles*, 1814. In 1814 appeared *Waverley*, the first of the novels.

The PIBROCH OF DONUIL DHU was written for Campbell's *Albyn Anthology* in 1816; JOCK O' HAZELDEAN also, except the first stanza, which " is ancient." LIGHT LOVE will be found in *Rokeby;* the DEATH-CHANT in *Guy Mannering;* and PROUD MAISIE in the *Heart of Mid-Lothian.*

Loot is let; *birn*—lightning.

MONTGOMERY. Another Scottish-born poet. His lengthier poems are the *Wanderer in Switzerland*, 1806; the *World before the Flood*, 1812; *Greenland*, 1819; the *Pelican Island*, 1828. He wrote also Songs and Hymns. As Editor of the *Sheffield Iris* he was in 1795 imprisoned for " seditious " writing.

HOGG. The " Ettrick Shepherd." Born at Ettrick in Selkirkshire, and in early life a shepherd and farmer laborer. Though so closely following Scott in order of birth, his poems are of later date. The first in time and importance is his *Queen's Wake*, 1813, not written till he was forty years of age. He wrote afterward the *Pilgrims of the Sun; Queen Hynde;* and numerous short pieces and songs; took part with Professor Wilson in the *Noctes Ambrosianæ* of Blackwood's Magazine; and in 1819 and 1821 edited a collection of " Jacobite Relics."

The *laverock* is the lark.

LAMB. Born in London. Besides the *Essays of Elia* and other prose works, he wrote a few poems: some printed with those of Coleridge in 1797; *John Woodvil*, a tragedy, 1802; the *Wife's Trial*, 1828; *Album Verses*, 1830.

LANDOR. Born at Ipsley House, Warwickshire. The magnificence of Landor's prose works has overshadowed the excellence of his poetry, ranging over nearly three-quarters of a century. Besides his most poetic prose,—the *Imaginary Conversations*, the *Citation and Examination of Shakespeare* (which Lamb said " only two men could have written "), *Pericles and Aspasia*, and the *Pentameron*,—he wrote an epic poem in seven books, *Gebir*, in 1797; a tragedy, *Count Julian*, in 1811; in later time *Hellenics, Heroic Idylls, Dramatic Scenes;* and short poems and epigrams down to the very close of life, in his ninetieth year.

Agen is a spelling insisted upon by him.

CAMPBELL. Born at Glasgow, but, like Montgomery, only for place of birth to be called a Scottish poet. The *Pleasures of Hope* appeared in 1798; *Gertrude of Wyoming* in 1809; *Theodoric* in 1824. The MARINERS OF ENGLAND was written in 1800; the BATTLE OF THE BALTIC commemorates the seizure in Copenhagen harbor, by Nelson, in 1807, of the Danish fleet, to prevent its being of service to Napoleon.

MOORE. Born in Dublin. *Odes of Anacreon*, 1800; *Irish Melodies* (and Songs to other national airs), from 1807 to 1834; *Lalla Rookh*, 1817; *Loves of the Angels*, 1823.

SMITH (Horace or Horatio). *Amarynthus, the Nympholept*, a pastoral drama, 1821; *Gaieties and Gravities*, 1825. He also had part with his brother James in *Rejected Addresses*, parodies of Wordsworth, Byron, and other contemporary poets.

ELLIOTT. Born near Rotherham in Yorkshire. Working at his father's foundry in early days, and afterward in business as an ironmonger in Sheffield. Chiefly known as the "Corn-law Rhymer," his rhymes having materially aided the popular movement in England for repeal of the bread-tax. His longer poems are the *Vernal Walk*, written in his seventeenth year, 1798 ; and the *Village Patriarch*, 1829.

LEIGH HUNT. Poet and Essayist. *Juvenilia* appeared in 1801 ; his most important poem, the *Story of Rimini*, in 1816. Besides many shorter poems, and translations, should be noted a very noble play, the *Legend of Florence*, written and acted in 1840. The SONG OF PEACE is from the *Descent of Liberty*, a masque, written in 1814 while in prison (imprisoned for two years) for ridiculing the Prince Regent, afterward George the Fourth. The *Grasshopper and Cricket* (p. 63) was composed in competition with and at the same time as that by Keats, p. 101.

CUNNINGHAM. In 1810 one Cromek published *Remains of Nithsdale and Galloway Song*, supposed to have been collected, but certainly much of it written, by Allan Cunningham, a Dumfries stone-mason. The song at page 65 Cromek gives as sent to him by a lady ; but Peter Cunningham claims it for his father, and the father printed it, with some variations, in his collected works. It is hard to know certainly what is really and entirely his, as he was in the habit (as Burns was) of adapting and completing ancient fragments : this song therefore may be taken as his, but doubtfully. He is chiefly known for his *Lives of British Painters*.

DARLEY. The *Errors of Ecstasie*, and other poems, 1822 ; *Sylvia, or the May-Queen*, a lyrical drama, 1827 ; *Ethelstan* and *Becket*, dramatic chronicles, 1840 and 1841.

PEACOCK. Novelist, satirist, and poet. His poetry consists of Songs in his novels (*Headlong Hall, Maid Marian, Gryll Grange*, etc.) ; *Palmyra*, 1806 ; the *Genius of the Thames*, 1810 ; *Rhododaphne*, a long, learned, fanciful poem, 1818 (the year of *Endymion*) ; the *Deceived*, a comedy, 1831 ; *Paper-money Lyrics*, 1837 ; and *Ælia Lælia Crispis*, 1862.

PROCTER. Play-wright as well as writer of Songs. Better known by his pseudonym, "Barry Cornwall." Born in London. He published *Dramatic Scenes* in 1819 ; *Marcian Colonna* and *Mirandola*, plays, in 1820 and 1821 ; the *Flood of Thessaly*, 1823 ; and *English Songs*, 1832, with additions in 1851.

DANA. Born at Cambridge, Massachusetts. *The Idle Man*, 1821; *The Buccanier and Other Poems*, 1827; *Poems and Prose Writings*, 1850.

BYRON. Born in London. *Hours of Idleness*, 1807; *English Bards and Scotch Reviewers*, 1809; the first two cantos of *Childe Harold*, 1812; the third and fourth, 1816-17; metrical romances,—the *Bride of Abydos*, *Corsair*, etc., *Beppo*, and *Manfred*, between 1813 and 1818; *Marino Faliero*, 1820; *Heaven and Earth*, *Sardanapalus*, the *Two Foscari*, and *Cain*, in 1821. *Don Juan*, his greatest work, was begun in 1818.

THE ISLES OF GREECE from *Don Juan;* AND THOU ART DEAD, one of several poems "to Thyrza," written in 1812; the SONG OF SAUL, the PATRIOT, and SHE WALKS IN BEAUTY, from *Hebrew Melodies*. Byron's LAST VERSE was written at Missolonghi on the 22d of January, 1824, within three months of his death.

SHELLEY. Born at Field Place, Sussex. *Queen Mab*, 1813; *Alastor*, 1816; *Laon and Cythna* (the *Revolt of Islam*), 1817; *Rosalind and Helen*, 1817-18; the *Cenci*, the *Masque of Anarchy*, and *Peter Bell the Third*, 1819; *Prometheus Unbound*, *Œdipus Tyrannus* (*Swell-foot the Tyrant*), and the *Witch of Atlas*, 1820; *Epipsychidion* and *Adonais*, 1821; *Charles the First* (a fragment), 1821-22; *Hellas*, 1822.

The different editions of Shelley (Forman's latest and best) have various readings of his poems, but not often so important as to justify departure from that issued by Mrs. Shelley. Allingham suggests *pine*, for *fail* (an evident misprint), in the second stanza of LINES TO AN INDIAN AIR; and surely *strain* should be taken instead of the usually printed *stain* in the WAIL at page 92. In the song TO-NIGHT all the authorities have *Day* both male and female, probably following Shelley's careless manuscript. Rossetti suggests *her* for *his* in the third stanza; but the alteration in the second stanza, in our text, seems preferable, Day being always male and Night female. In most, if not all, editions wrong punctuation destroys the poetic beauty and the sense of the first four lines of A BRIDAL SONG, p. 90.

KEATS. Born in London. His first verse appeared in 1817. In 1818 he published *Endymion* (in which are the ROUNDELAY and HYMN TO PAN, pp. 92, 94); and in the two following years *Lamia*, *Isabella*, the *Eve of St. Agnes*, his shorter poems, and the glorious fragment—*Hyperion*.

WOLFE. Born in Dublin. He owes his immortality to this one poem: besides which he wrote only a few songs of little importance.

Sir John Moore, in command of the British army in Spain, in the war against Napoleon, was slain at the battle of Corunna, in 1809, when covering the embarkation of his troops, in their retreat before Ney and Soult.   In the last stanza but one *sullenly* is generally misprinted for *suddenly*.   Wolfe's manuscript has *suddenly ;* and in the account in the *Edinburgh Annual Register* (which suggested the poem) we find it stated that the burial " was hastened, for about eight in the morning some firing was heard,"—a renewed attack feared.

HEMANS.   Felicia Dorothea Browne, afterward Mrs. Hemans, was born at Liverpool.   Between 1803 and 1835 she wrote numerous poems, graceful and musical, if not of high imagination or intellectuality : historic poems on Welsh, Greek, Spanish themes ; two dramas, the *Siege of Valencia* and the *Vespers of Palermo ; Scenes and Hymns of Life ; Songs of the Affections ;* translations from Horace ; etc., etc.

BRYANT.   Born at Cummington, Massachusetts.   *The Embargo,* 1809 ; *The Ages,* 1821 ; *Poems,* 1832 ; *The Fountain and Other Poems,* 1842 ; *The White-Footed Deer and Other Poems,* 1844 ; *Poems,* 1846 ; *Letters of a Traveller,* 1850 ; *Thirty Poems,* 1863 ; *Letters from the East,* 1859 ; *Translation of the Iliad,* 1870 ; *Translation of the Odyssey,* 1871–72.

CARLYLE.   Some few slight verses were written by the great historian and essayist.

REYNOLDS, Hood's brother-in-law.   The author of *Peter Bell the Second,* making fun of Wordsworth's *Lyrical Ballads,* in the same year as and seemingly suggestive of Shelley's *Peter Bell the Third,* a profounder and more elaborate criticism, serious though jocose.   He wrote also the *Garden of Florence,* with other poems, " by John Hamilton," 1821.

COLERIDGE (Hartley), eldest son of the Poet, wrote a number of minor poems, published in 1833.

MOTHERWELL.   Born at Glasgow.   *Poems,* lyrical and narrative, 1832–3.   In 1827 he edited *Ancient and Modern Minstrelsy* (a collection).
Beltane—May-day ; *Yule*—Christmas ; *blinks*—glances ; *ae laigh bink*— one low seat ; *leir ilk ither lear*—teach each other ; *loof*—palm ; *brent*— burn'd ; *weans*—children ; *cleek'd*—hook'd, clung ; *skailt*—dispersed ; *speel*—climb ; *hinnied*—honey'd ; *simmer*—summer ; *deavin'*—deafening ; *croon*—murmur ; *whusslit*—whistled ; *knowe*—knoll ; *abune* or *aboon*— above ; *grat*—wept ; *gin*—if ; *grit*—full.

HOOD. Born in London. Great not only as a humorist, but also as a serious poet, though not so recognized until the appearance of his *Song of the Shirt* in *Punch*, in 1843, barely two years before his death. The *Plea of the Midsummer Fairies* (with *Hero and Leander, Lycus the Centaur*, and other poems) was printed in 1827. *Tylney Hall*, a novel (in which our poem of CONSTANCY), came out in 1834 ; *Miss Kilmansegg and her Golden Leg*, a serio-comic poem, in 1840 ; the *Haunted House* and the *Bridge of Sighs* in 1844.

WELLS. The friend of Keats. Author of *Joseph and his Brethren*, a Scriptural drama, published with the pseudonym of " Howard," in 1824, republished in 1876. He wrote also poetical-prose *Stories after Nature*, in one of which is the SONG at page 124.

TAYLOR (Sir Henry). Dramatist. His principal work is *Philip Van Artevelde*, an historical play, published in 1834. His other plays are *Isaac Comnenus, Edwin the Fair, A Sicilian Summer* (called in the first edition the *Virgin Widow*), and *St. Clement's Eve.*

BARNES. The Rev. William Barnes, a Dorsetshire clergyman, is author of some three or four hundred, or more, poems of rural life, in the Dorset dialect, and others in common English.

NEWMAN. John Henry, Cardinal Newman. *Verses on several occasions*, 1868. THE ELEMENTS, p. 127, written in 1833 ; A VOICE FROM AFAR, 1829.

MARTINEAU. This single hymn and a song in one of her tales may entitle Harriet Martineau to a corner in our anthologies.

BEDDOES. The son of Dr. Beddoes (physician) and nephew of Maria Edgeworth. He published the *Improvisatore* in 1821 and the *Bride's Tragedy* in 1822. *Death's Jest Book, or the Fool's Tragedy*, the *Second Brother* and *Torrismond* (unfinished dramas), dramatic fragments and poems, were printed after his death.

HORNE. Poet, dramatist, and prose writer. He has published,—in 1835, the *Death of Marlowe*, a tragedy in one act ; in 1837, *Cosmo de' Medici*, a tragedy ; in 1840, *Gregory the Seventh*, a tragedy, and the *Death-Fetch ;* in 1843, *Orion*, an epic poem ; in 1846, *Ballad Romances ;* in 1864, *Prometheus the Fire-Bringer* (written in Australia); in 1880, *Laura Di-*

balzo, a tragedy ; and in 1881, *John the Baptist, Rahman* (Job's Wife), and *Judas Iscariot*—a miracle play.   He has also very extensively contributed to the magazines and other periodical publications.

EMERSON.   Born at Boston, Massachusetts.   *Nature*, 1836 ; *Essays and Lectures*, First Series, 1840 ; *Essays and Lectures*, Second Series, 1844 ; *Poems*, 1846 ; *Miscellanies*, 1849 ; *Representative Men*, 1850 ; *English Traits*, 1856 ; *The Conduct of Life*, 1860 ; *May Day and Other Poems*, 1867 ; *Solitude and Society*, 1870 ; *Prose Works*, 1870.

GRIFFIN.   One of the " Young Ireland" party of 1842–48, and contributor to the Irish *Nation* of those years.   Born at Limerick.   He wrote in his twentieth year his drama of *Gisippus*, put on the stage by Macready in 1842.   His poetical works were published in 1851.   He is more generally known as a novelist of merit.

MANGAN.   Another Irish poet of the Young Ireland time.   Born in Dublin.   Of genius similar to that of Poe.   His poems are free translations (rather new poetic renderings from prose translations) of early Irish ; translations from the German ; and original contributions to the *Nation* and the *United Irishman*.   His collected works, original and translated, were published in New York in 1859.

BLANCHARD.   A bright essayist and writer of society verses.   *Lyric Offerings*, 1828.

HAWKER, Vicar of Morwenstow in Cornwall, published *Tendrils of Reuben* (juvenile poems) in 1821 ; *Records of the Western Shore* in 1832 ; the *Quest of the San Graal* in 1864.
Isha Cherioth is the Cherioth woman, or maiden.

ADAMS.   Mrs. Adams, the daughter of Benjamin Flower, Editor of the *Cambridge Intelligencer* (one of the first liberal newspapers in England), and wife of William Bridges Adams, notable as a civil engineer and political writer.   She wrote *Vivia Perpetua*, a drama, 1841 ; anti-corn-law rhymes, contemporaneously with Elliott ; and *Hymns* (set to music by her sister, Eliza Flower) for the Unitarian religious services conducted by W. J. Fox at South Place, Finsbury, London.

HAMILTON.   Mathematician, and astronomer-royal for Ireland.   Born in Dublin.

WADE. Author of the *Jew of Arragon*, a tragedy brought out by Charles Kemble in 1830; *Woman's Love*, a comedy, 1828; *Mundi et Cordis Carmina* (Songs of the Universe and the Heart), 1835; the *Contention of Death and Love, Helena*, and the *Shadow-Seeker*, 1837; *Prothanasia*, 1839.

STERLING. Born in the Isle of Bute. *Minor Poems*, 1839; *The Election*, 1841; *Strafford*, a drama, 1843.
Dædalus is the type of inventive genius.

SIMMS. Born at Charleston, South Carolina. A voluminous writer of poems, plays, stories, romances, histories, biographies, and criticisms, his works numbering upward of sixty different titles. His poetical writings are: *Lyrical and Other Poems*, 1827; *Early Lays*, 1827; *The Vision of Cortes and other Poems*, 1829; *The Tri-Color, or Three Days of Blood*, 1830; *Atalantis, a Drama of the Sea*, 1832; *Southern Passages and Pictures*, 1839; *Donna Florida, a Tale*, 1843; *Grouped Thoughts and Scattered Fancies*, 1845; *Areytos; or, Songs of the South*, 1846; *Songs of the Palmetto*, 1848; *The Eye and the Wing*, 1848; *The City of the Silent*, 1850; *Poems*, 1854.

WILLIS. Born at Portland, Maine. One of the most accomplished and versatile of American authors, magazinists, and journalists. His principal poetical writings are: *Sketches*, 1827; *Fugitive Poetry*, 1829; *Melanie and Other Poems*, 1835; *Tortesa the Usurer*, 1839; *Bianca Visconti*, 1839; *The Lady Jane and Other Poems*, 1844.

LONGFELLOW. Born at Portland, Maine. The most popular writer of English verse in the nineteenth century. *Coplas de Manrique*, a translation from the Spanish, 1833; *Outre-Mer, a Pilgrimage beyond the Sea*, 1835; *Hyperion, a Romance*, 1839; *Voices of the Night*, 1839; *Ballads and Other Poems*, 1841; *Poems on Slavery*, 1842; *The Spanish Student*, 1843; *The Waif, a Collection of Poems*, 1845; *The Poets and Poetry of Europe*, 1845; *The Belfry of Bruges and Other Poems*, 1846; *The Estray, a Collection of Poems*, 1847; *Evangeline, a Tale of Acadie*, 1847; *Kavanagh, a Tale*, 1849; *The Seaside and the Fireside*, 1850; *The Golden Legend*, 1851; *The Song of Hiawatha*, 1855; *The Courtship of Miles Standish*, 1858; *Tales of a Wayside Inn*, 1863; *Flower-de-Luce*, 1867; *The New England Tragedies*, 1868; *Translation of Dante's Divine Comedy*, 1867-70; *The Divine Tragedy*, 1872; *Christus, a Mystery*, 1872; *Three Books of Song*, 1872; *Aftermath*, 1874; *The Masque of Pandora*, 1875; *Keramos and Other Poems*, 1878; *Ultima Thule*, 1880; *Michael Angelo, a Tragedy*, 1883.

WHITTIER. Born at Haverhill, Massachusetts. A grave and earnest thinker, whose inspiration is largely drawn from moral and political questions, and with whom poetry is a passion, not an art. The following are his principal works : *Legends of New England*, 1831 ; *Moll Pitcher*, 1831 ; *Mogg Megone*, 1836 ; *Lays of My Home, and Other Poems*, 1843 ; *The Bridal of Pennacook*, 1848 ; *Leaves from Margaret Smith's Journal*, 1849 ; *The Voices of Freedom*, 1849 ; *Songs of Labor and Other Poems*, 1850 ; *Old Portraits and Modern Sketches*, 1850 ; *The Chapel of the Hermits*, 1853 ; *The Panorama and Other Poems*, 1856 ; *Home Ballads and Other Poems*, 1860 ; *In War Time and Other Poems*, 1863 ; *Snow-Bound, a Winter Idyl*, 1866 ; *The Tent on the Beach and Other Poems*, 1867 ; *Among the Hills and Other Poems*, 1868 ; *Miriam and Other Poems*, 1870 ; *The Pennsylvania Pilgrim and Other Poems*, 1872 ; *The Vision of Echard and Other Poems*, 1878 ; *The King's Missive and Other Poems*, 1881 ; *The Bay of Seven Islands and Other Poems*, 1883.

TRENCH. Archbishop of Dublin. *Justin Martyr* and other poems, 1835 ; *Honor Neale*, 1838 ; *Genoveva*, 1842 ; *Sacred Poems*, 1846 ; *Alma* and other poems, 1855.

POE. Born in Boston, Massachusetts, the son of strolling players, he was lavishly, if not wisely, indulged by his adoptive father. A reckless student and a cashiered cadet, he wrote melodious verses and ghastly stories : edited the *Southern Literary Messenger* and *Graham's Magazine*, made enemies by writing captious criticisms about his brother authors, and was himself his own worst enemy. " The rest is silence." *Tamarlane and Other Poems*, 1827 ; *Al Araaf, Tamarlane and Minor Poems*, 1829 ; *Poems*, 1831 ; *The Narrative of Arthur Gordon Pym*, 1838 ; *Tales of the Grotesque and Arabesque*, 1839 ; *Poems*, 1845 ; *Eureka*, 1848.

HOLMES. Born at Cambridge, Massachusetts. A witty and ingenuous writer in verse and prose, he was educated as a physician, and filled for thirty-five years the chair of Anatomy and Physiology in the Medical School attached to Harvard College. His non-professional writings are *Poems*, 1836 ; *Urania, a Rhymed Lesson*, 1842 ; *Astrea, The Balance of Illusions*, 1850 ; *The Autocrat of the Breakfast-Table*, 1858 ; *The Professor at the Breakfast-Table*, 1859 ; *Elsie Venner, A Romance of Destiny*, 1861 ; *Songs in Many Keys*, 1861 ; *The Guardian Angel*, 1867 ; *The Poet at the Breakfast-Table*, 1873 ; *Songs of Many Seasons*, 1874 ; *The Iron Gate and other Poems*, 1880.

TENNYSON. His first verse in *Poems by two Brothers* (Alfred and Charles). *Poems chiefly lyrical,* 2 vols., 1830; with additions in 1832, and again in 1840 to 1846; the *Princess,* 1847; with the Songs, 1850; *In Memoriam,* 1850; *Maud,* 1855; *Idylls of the King,* part published in 1859, completed in 1872; *Enoch Arden,* 1864; *Lucretius,* 1868; *Queen Mary,* 1875; *Harold,* 1877.

MILNES. *Historical Poems,* 1835; *Poems of Many Years,* 1838; *Poetry for the People,* 1840.

THACKERAY. The *Chronicle of the Drum;* the Great Cossack Epic (the Legend of St. Sophia of Kioff); the *Poems of the Molony of Kilbally-molony;* the *Ballads of Policeman X;* etc.

DOYLE. The *Return of the Guards* and other poems, 1866.
Moyse was a private in the regiment of the " Kentish Buffs." Taken prisoner, along with some Sikh soldiers, by the Chinese, he was ordered to perform *Kotoo.* Looking on it as a degradation, the Englishman refused.

DOMETT. *Flotsam and Jetsam,* Rhymes old and new, 1834 to 1875. *Venice,* 1839. *Ranolf and Amohia,* 1877.

BROWNING (Mrs.). *Prometheus Bound,* from Æschylus, translated before she was twenty, published with other poems in 1833. *The Seraphim,* 1838; *A Drama of Exile* and other poems, 1844; *Casa Guidi Windows,* 1851; *Aurora Leigh,* 1856; *Poems before Congress,* 1860. Her *Sonnets* "from the Portuguese" (a modest mask of her own identity), are the fullest expression of womanly love ever written, as Sidney's may be taken for the manly correspondence.

BROWNING (Robert). *Paracelsus,* 1835; *Strafford,* 1837; *Sordello,* 1840; *Bells and Pomegranates,* 1841 to 1846 (containing the *Return of the Druses, A Blot in the 'Scutcheon, Colombe's Birthday, Luria,* and other poems); *Christmas Eve and Easter Day,* 1850; *Men and Women,* 1855; *The Ring and the Book,* 1868; *Prince Hohenstiel-Schwangan—Saviour of Society,* 1871; *Fifine at the Fair,* 1872; *Balaustion's Adventure,* 1871,— The *Last Adventure,* 1875; *Red Cotton Night-cap Country,* 1873; the *Inn Album,* 1875; *Pacchiarotto,* 1876; *La Saisiaz, the Two Poets of Croisic,* 1878; *Dramatic Idylls,* 1879; *Jocoseria,* 1882.
There are at least three versions, apparently by Browning himself, of the second stanza of the *Lost Leader.* Our text seems to be the latest.

NICOLL. Born at Auchtergaven, Perthshire. *Poems and Lyrics*, 1835.
A second edition, with additions, in 1842, after his death.

Slee—sly; *parochin*—parish; *paik*—tease; *grat*—wept; *limmer*—villain; *weans*—children; *douce*—sedate; *starnies*—stars; *wale*—choicest; *yett*—gate; *haffets*—the temples; *lyart*—grizzled; *bent*—the rough grass on the hill-side.

DAVIS. Born at Mallow, Cork County. Another of the Irish patriotic singers of 1842-48. Most and the best of his songs treat of historical subjects.

SCOTT (William Bell). Born at Edinburgh. A painter and engraver of eminence, and writer upon Art. As a poet only known to the " fit audience though few." He has published *Hades or the Transit*, 1838; *The Year of the World*, a philosophical poem, 1846; *Poems by a Painter*, 1854; *Poems*, 1875; and a *Poet's Harvest Home*, 1882.

LINTON. Engraver and political writer. In poetry *Bob Thin*, a poor-law tale, 1845; the *Plaint of Freedom*, 1852; *Poems*, 1865; and verses in the Irish *Nation* and elsewhere.

DE VERE. Irish-born, but descended from one of Cromwell's officers, named Hunt, who had a grant of lands in Ireland and settled there. His works, dating from 1842, are numerous, generally inspired by pious Catholic and patriotic Irish feeling. The *Waldenses*, or the *Fall of Rora;* the *Infant Bridal;* the *Search after Proserpine;* *May Carols* (poems to the Virgin Mary); the *Sisters; Inisfail; Legends of St. Patrick; Legends of Saxon Saints; Alexander the Great;* etc.

BURBIDGE. College companion and friend of Clough, with whom in 1848 he brought out a book of poems, *Ambarvalia*. He wrote also the *Bridal of Ravenna* (with other juvenile poems), 1838; and *Hymns and Days*, 1851. He is now British chaplain at Palermo.

ROSENBERG. Born at Bath, but emigrated to America. Author of *Tiberius* and other unpublished plays, but only known as a miscellaneous writer in American newspapers and magazines.

SUTTON. *Clifton Grove;* and some verses in *Quinquenergia*, an essay toward a new religion, 1854.

WELDON, an Englishman (the name perhaps only a pseudonym), wrote some short poems over the signature O. O. in the New York *Tribune*, between 1850 and 1856.

CLOUGH. One very notable poem, the *Bothic of Tober-na-Vuolich*, a long-vacation pastoral, 1848; Poetical Remains, 1869.
After Charles Albert's defeat at Novara, the inhabitants at Brescia nevertheless rose against the Austrian garrison, on the 21st of March, 1849.

HOWE. Mrs. Howe was born in New York City. *Passion Flowers*, 1854; *Words for the Hour*, 1856; *The World's Own*, 1857; *Hippolytus, a Tragedy*, 1858; *A Trip to Cuba*, 1859; *Later Lyrics*, 1866; *From the Oak to the Olive*, 1868.

WHITMAN. Born at West Hills, New York. *Leaves of Grass*, 1855; *Drum Taps*, 1865; *Specimen Days, and a Collect*, 1883.

PARSONS. Born at Boston, Massachusetts. *Translation of the First Ten Cantos of the Inferno of Dante*, 1843; *Poems*, 1854; *The Magnolia*, 1866; *The First Canticle (Inferno) of the Divine Comedy*, 1867.

KINGSLEY. Born in Devonshire; Vicar of Eversley in Hampshire. Novelist, and poet if only for the songs in his novels. But he also wrote the *Saint's Tragedy*, a drama of mediæval time, 1848; and *Andromeda*, a sustained poem, 1858. His collected poems were published in 1872.

LEWES. Mary Ann Evans (Mrs. Lewes). The *Spanish Gypsy*, 1868; the *Legend of Jubal* and other poems, 1874.

LOWELL (James Russell). Born at Cambridge, Massachusetts. *A Year's Life*, 1841; *Poems*, 1844; *Conversations on some of the Old Poets*, 1845; *Poems*, 1848; *The Vision of Sir Launfal*, 1848; *A Fable for Critics*, 1848; *The Biglow Papers*, First Series, 1848; *Fireside Travels*, 1864; *Biglow Papers*, Second Series, 1867; *Under the Willows and Other Poems*, 1868; *The Cathedral*, 1869; *Among My Books*, 1870; *My Study Windows*, 1870.

LOWELL (Maria White). Born at Watertown, Massachusetts. The first wife of J. R. Lowell.

WALLACE. Born at Lexington, Kentucky. *Alban, a Poetical Romance,* 1848; *Meditations in America and Other Poems,* 1851.

JONES. A single volume of poems, *Studies of Sensation and Event,* 1843; republished in 1879.

MCCARTHY. Another poet of the Irish *Nation.* Born in Dublin. *Poems and Ballads,* translated and original, 1850; *Under-glimpses* and other poems, and the *Bell-Founder,* 1857; translations from Calderon.

LOCKER. *London Lyrics,* 1862; *Lyra Elegantiarum,* 1867; *Patchwork* (prose and verse), 1879.

CARY (Alice). Born near Cincinnati, Ohio. *Clovernook Papers,* First Series, 1851; *Hagar, a Story of To-Day,* 1852; *Clovernook Papers,* Second Series, 1853; *Lyra and Other Poems,* 1853; *Clovernook Children,* 1854; *Married, not Mated,* 1856; *Pictures of Country Life,* 1859; *Lyrics and Hymns,* 1866; *The Bishop's Son,* 1867; *The Lover's Diary,* 1867; *Snow Berries,* 1869.

CARY (Phœbe). Sister of Alice, and born at the same place. *Poems and Parodies,* 1854; *Poems of Faith, Hope, and Love,* 1868.

ARNOLD (Matthew). Poet, essayist, critic. His chief poems are *Sohrab and Rustam; Tristan and Iseult; Balder dead; the Scholar Gypsy; Thyrsis; Empedocles on Ætna;* and *Merope,* a tragedy.

CORY. William Johnson, a master at Eton, changed his name to Cory. He published a small collection of poems, *Ionica,* in 1858; and printed privately a few more in 1877. Mimnermus was a Greek elegiac and amatory poet of the time of Solon.

DOBELL. *The Roman,* 1850; *Balder,* 1853; *Poems* collected after his death.

BROWNELL. Born in New York City. *Poems,* 1849; *Lyrics of a Day,* 1864; *War Lyrics and Other Poems,* 1866.

CURTIS. Born at Providence, Rhode Island. *Nile Notes of a Howadji,* 1851; *The Howadji in Syria,* 1852; *Lotus Eating,* 1852; *Potiphar Papers,* 1853; *Prue and I,* 1856; *Trumps,* 1861.

McGee. Born at Carlingford, Ireland. Was associate editor with Charles Gavan Duffy of the Irish *Nation;* and poetical contributor to its columns. He emigrated to America, settling finally in Canada, where he was assassinated on account of his opposition to Fenianism. His collected poems were published in New York, in 1869.

Taylor (Bayard). Born in Pennsylvania. *Zimena,* 1844; *Views a-Foot,* 1846; *Rhymes of Travel,* 1848; *El Dorado,* 1850; *The American Legend,* 1850; *Book of Romances, Lyrics, and Songs,* 1851; *A Journey to Central Africa,* 1854; *Poems and Ballads,* 1854; *The Lands of the Saracen,* 1854; *A Visit to India, China, and Japan,* 1855; *Poems of the Orient,* 1855; *Poems of Home and Travel,* 1855; *Northern Travel,* 1857; *Travels in Greece and Russia,* 1859; *At Home and Abroad,* First Series, 1859; *At Home and Abroad,* Second Series, 1862; *The Poet's Journal,* 1862; *Hannah Thurston,* 1863; *John Godfrey's Fortunes,* 1864; *The Story of Kennett,* 1866; *The Picture of St. John,* 1866; *Byways of Europe,* 1869; *The Ballad of Abraham Lincoln,* 1869; *Joseph and His Friend,* 1870; *Translation of Goethe's Faust* (both parts), 1871; *Beauty and the Beast,* 1872; *The Masque of the Gods,* 1872; *Lars,* 1873; *The Prophet, a Tragedy,* 1874; *Home Pastorals, Ballads, and Lyrics,* 1875; *Prince Deucalion,* 1878.

Stoddard (R. H.). Born at Hingham, Massachusetts. *Footprints,* 1849; *Poems,* 1852; *Adventures in Fairy Land,* 1853; *Songs of Summer,* 1857; *The King's Bell,* 1862; *The Story of Little Red Riding Hood,* 1863; *The Children in the Wood,* 1864; *Abraham Lincoln, an Horatian Ode,* 1865; *Putnam the Brave,* 1869; *The Book of the East,* 1871; *Poems,* 1880.

Stoddard (E. D. B.). Born at Mattapoisett, Massachusetts. *The Morgesons,* 1862; *Two Men,* 1865; *Temple House,* 1867; *Lolly Dinks' Doings,* 1874.

Procter (Adelaide). Daughter of B. W. Procter ("Barry Cornwall"). Poems in Dickens' *Household Words,* the first by "Miss Berwick" in 1853; *Legends and Lyrics,* two series, 1858 and 1861; *A Chaplet of Verses,* 1862.

Larcom. Miss Larcom was born in Massachusetts. *An Idyl of Work,* 1875; *Poems,* 1878; *Wild Roses of Cape Ann and Other Poems,* 1881; *Childhood's Songs,* 1883.

Collins. *Idylls and Rhymes,* 1855; *Summer Songs,* 1860; the *Inn of Strange Meetings* and other poems, 1871.

ALLINGHAM.   Born at Ballyshannon, Ireland.   *Poems*, 1850 ; *Day and Night Songs*, 1854 ; *Lawrence Bloomfield in Ireland*, a descriptive poem characteristic of Irish life, 1869 ; *Songs and Ballads*, 1877.

MUNBY.   *Benoni*, 1852 ; *Elegiacs*, 1859; *Verses New and Old*, 1865 ; *Dorothy*, a country story, 1880.

ROSSETTI (Dante Gabriel).   Painter and Poet.   Notable as the founder of the pre-Raffaelite school of painting in England.   His poetical works are *Ballads and Songs ;* the *House of Life*, a series of sonnets ; and Translations from the early Italian poets, and of the *Vita Nuova* of Dante.

ROSSETTI (Christina).   The sister of Dante Gabriel.   *Goblin Market ;* the *Prince's Progress ;* and miscellaneous poems, 1862–1881.

INGELOW.   *Poems*, 1863 ; *A Story of Doom*, 1867.

STEDMAN.   Born at Hartford, Connecticut.   *Poems Lyrical and Idyllic*, 1860 ; *Alice of Monmouth and Other Poems*, 1864 ; *The Blameless Prince and Other Poems*, 1869 ; *Poetical Works*, 1873 ; *The Victorian Poets*, 1875 ; *Hawthorne and Other Poems*, 1877.

ARNOLD (George).   Born in New York City.   *Drift and Other Poems*, 1866 ; *Poems Grave and Gay*, 1867.

NICHOL.   Born at Montrose.   *Hannibal*, an historical drama ; the *Death of Themistocles*, and other poems, 1881.

MORRIS (Lewis).   *Songs of Two Worlds*, 1871 ; *The Epic of Hades*, 1877 ; *Gwen*, 1879 ; *The Ode of Life*, 1880.

JACKSON.   Mrs. Jackson (her earlier poems " by H. H.," Mrs. Hunt) was born at Amherst, Massachusetts.   *Verses*, 1870.

MORRIS (William).   The *Defence of Guinevere* and other poems, 1858 ; the *Life and Death of Jason*, 1867 ; the *Earthly Paradise*, 1868–70 ; *Love is enough*, 1873 ; the *Story of Sigurd*, 1876.

PIATT.   Born at Jackson, Indiana.   *Nests at Washington and Other Poems*, 1864 ; *Poems in Sunshine and Firelight*, 1866 ; *Western Windows and Other Poems*, 1869 ; *Landmarks and Other Poems*, 1871.

THAXTER. Mrs. Thaxter. Born at Portsmouth, New Hampshire. *Poems*, 1874.

WILLSON. *The Old Sargeant and Other Poems*, 1867.

WINTER. Born at Gloucester, Massachusetts. *My Witness, a Book of Verse*, 1871.

ALDRICH. Born at Portsmouth, New Hampshire. *The Bells*, 1854; *Daisy's Necklace, and What Came of it*, 1856; *The Ballad of Babie Bell and Other Poems*, 1858; *The Course of True Love never did Run Smoothly*, 1858; *Pampinea and Other Poems*, 1861; *Out of His Head*, 1862; *Poems*, 1863; *The Story of a Bad Boy*, 1869; *Marjorie Daw and Other People*, 1873; *Cloth of Gold*, 1873; *Prudence Palfrey*, 1874; *Flower and Thorn*, 1877; *The Queen of Sheba*, 1877; *The Stillwater Tragedy*, 1880; *Poems*, 1882; *From Poukapog to Pesth*, 1883.

GARNETT. *Primula*, 1858; *Io in Egypt* and other poems, 1859; Translations from the German, 1862; *Idylls and Epigrams*, from the Greek Anthology, 1869. Since 1875 Mr. Garnett has been Superintendent of the Reading Room at the British Museum.

ASHE. The Rev. Thomas Ashe has written *Poems*, 1859; *Sorrows of Hypsipyle*, a drama, 1866; *Edith*, 1873; *Songs Now and Then*, 1876.

SWINBURNE. The *Queen Mother* and *Rosamond*, 1861; *Chastelard*; *Atalanta in Calydon*, 1864; *Poems and Ballads*, 1866; *A Song of Italy*, 1867; *Songs before Sunrise*, 1871; *Bothwell*, 1874; *Songs of Two Nations*, 1875; *Erechtheus*, 1876; *Poems and Ballads* (second series), 1878; *Songs of the Spring-tides*, 1880; *Mary Stuart*, 1881; *Tristram of Lyonesse*, 1882.

THOMSON. Born at Port Glasgow. The *Doom of a City; Bertram to the Lady Geraldine;* the *Lord of the Castle of Indolence; Vane's Story; Sunday at Hampstead; Sunday up the River;* the *City of Dreadful Night* (written between 1870 and 1874, and published in 1880); and other poems.

HAY. Born at Salem, Indiana. *Pike County Ballads and other Pieces*, 1871; *Castilian Days*, 1872.

DOBSON. *Vignettes in Rhyme*, 1874; *Proverbs in Porcelain*, 1877; *Latter-day Lyrics*, 1878.

BUCHANAN. The collected edition of his poetical works (he is also well known as a novelist), comprises *Ballads and Poems of Life ; London Lyrics*, 1866 ; *Sonnets ; Political Mystics ;* and a long Ossianic poem, the *Book of Orm.*

BRIDGES. *Poems*, 1873.

GOSSE. *Madrigals, Songs, and Sonnets*, 1870 ; *On Viol and Flute*, 1873 ; *King Erik*, a drama, 1876 ; *New Poems*, 1879.

MARZIALS. *The Gallery of Pigeons*, 1873.

BEATTY. *To my Lady*, 1878 ; *Three Women of the People*, 1881 ; *Marcia*, a tragedy.

LANG. *Ballads and Lyrics of Old France*, 1872 ; the *Prince of Omur, and other poems*, 1880 ; XXII *Ballades in Blue China*, 1880 ; XXII *and* X, 1881 ; *Helen of Troy*, 1882.

DAVIES. *Songs of a Wayfarer*, 1869 ; the *Shepherd's Garden*, 1873.

INDEX OF FIRST LINES.